ACCLAIM FOR  N

"Move over Twilight! Here comes Aaron Patterson!"

—*Joshua Graham, bestselling author of Beyond Justice and Darkroom*

"I was surprised by how much I really, really liked this book. I have not jumped on the whole "fallen angel" bandwagon, just as I didn't jump on all of the vampire stories that came out after Twilight. This is not your typical fallen angel story. It is one that has left me breathlessly waiting for the next one in the series. Hurry up please!!!"

—*Sandra Stiles*

"It takes rare talent for a man to write a novel from a male POV and have it published to great critical and commercial acclaim. But it takes a miracle for that same male, or in this case males, to write a novel from the POV of a teenage girl and have it turn out as incredibly as did the new StoneHouse YA by Aaron Patterson and Chris White, Airel. From the first sentence, I felt compelled to dive into this young woman's story and just as importantly, I felt like I personally knew her, which means I laughed, stressed and cried right along with her. A beautifully written and crafted fiction about teenage innocence, faith, loss and love. A must read for teens and adults alike."

—*Vincent Zandri, International Bestselling Author of The Remains, The Innocent, and Concrete Pearl.*

I am happy to say that this novel is one of my favorites of its kind. I never thought I could read a novel like this and be so swept away! I am always willing to try new books, but I usually steer clear of this kind of novel. Not anymore! Not when I can be so engrossed into the character's story, like I was with the beautiful Airel, that before I know, it's over. I kept turning the pages, wanting to, no-NEEDING, to know what was going to happen next.

—*Molly Edwards, Willow Spring, NC*

"I just finished reading Airel. One of the best book I've ever read, if not the best. Of all the books I read, I related to Airel the most. I mean she's just so REAL. I'm blown away that two guys could write a girl's character so perfectly, so right. Better than a lot of female writers. I loved this book. It's so versatile, I was never bored. The story is told from various points of view. Normal girl, check. Epic warrior angel, check. Psycho killer, check. The manifestation of all evil 'the seer,' check. Even Kim and Michael had their share. And it's so great to see how everyone thinks and what really goes on in their mind and how it goes on there. Also, it had different times and places and that was very cool. I mean when I first started reading the part in Stuttgart, Germany, 1897 I was intrigued. I was a little disappointed that it was too short until I got into Airel's mind. Then out of nowhere visions of 1250 B.C. Arabia, I was blown away. The characters were beautifully written, I related to each of them in a way but Airel is just out of this world! She's me! Minus the half human, half angel thing lol. And the end was something else."

—*E.M. Book Review*

SWEET DREAMS

"Sweet Dreams was a book I read in 2 days. I truly enjoyed the read. It kept me wanting to know more. I'm looking forward to Part 2 of the WJA Trilogy!"

—*Sharon Adams, Novi, MI*

"Suspense, thriller with a perfect ending, leaving me wanting more. An on the edge of your seat, all night read. I most certainly will be reading "Dream On.""

—*Sheri Wilkinson, Sandwich, IL*

"New authors come and go every day. Very few come on the scene with the ability to weave a tale that will make you sad to reach the end, longing for more. At a time when the world needs a real hero, Patterson delivers big with the WJA's Mark Appleton—an unlikely hero for the 21st century."

—*The Joe Show*

"Aaron Patterson spins a good tale and does it well."

—*W.P.*

"*SWEET DREAMS* is packed with action, suspense, romance, betrayal, death, and mystery."

—*Drew Maples, author of "28 Yards from Safety"*

DREAM ON

"Once again, Aaron Patterson has made a home run! 'Dream On' is a wonderful read from cover to cover! I am now anxiously awaiting his next book 'In Your Dreams.' I originally purchased his first book by mistake, and was pleasantly surprised at how much I enjoyed it... so now I'm hooked! Aaron has got to start writing faster!!! Although his books are definitely worth the wait! Bet'cha can't read just one! This guy has real talent for writing and keeping the suspense growing... the worst part about the book is the last page... I hated it to stop!"

—*Ruth P. Charlotte, NC*

"After reading Patterson's first novel, 'Sweet Dreams,' I was really looking forward to reading 'Dream On.' This book was amazing. I couldn't put it down. If you're looking for an exciting read, read this book."

—*Paul Carson, Boise, ID*

"I read the first book by Aaron Patterson (Sweet Dreams) and was very anxious for this sequel. I was not disappointed. This book kept me guessing with every page turn. It's very well written and I really enjoyed the technology employed, which makes it just a bit futuristic without being overdone. This was a fantastic suspenseful thriller that kept me guessing throughout the entire book. Mr. Patterson has become my favorite fiction writer."

—*Donna H. Boise, ID*

"This is the second book of Aaron's I have read and I have to say he is a very talented writer!!! I read this book in under 12 hrs; it was so good I couldn't put it down. He managed to surprise me with a twist that I did not expect! It is filled with suspense and keeps you guessing throughout. I will be suggesting this book to everyone I know…"

—*Amanda Garner, Oklahoma*

ACCLAIM FOR CHRIS WHITE

THE MARSBURG DIARY

"Yikes! This is one well written and very strange book which will pique your interest from beginning to end. The author does a masterful job of moving you between centuries as you read two different point of view stories about one very unusual book. The telling of the tale, as found in the father's diary from the 1800's, is very well portrayed and the writer has you believing you are actually back in that time period. Stepping forward to today, you experience the son's horror as he reads both his father's diary, and the unusual book, and discovers it is currently driving him into the same mindset it created in his father… near insanity. This is one roller coaster of a read and is sure to delight fans of the occult, supernatural occurrences and mystery. A solid 4 1/2 star read."

—*POIA, top Amazon reviewer*

"A story that conjures mystery, suspense, and dark evils, *THE MARSBURG DIARY* is a page turner. White calls on the spirit of Steven King, Jules Verne, and Edgar Allen Poe to create a contemporary story that is as compelling as it is enduring. Marsburg learns of his father's past through a diary, a past filled with horror and mystery. But history doesn't stay in the past, and visits Marsburg, sending him into his own thrilling adventures. *THE MARSBURG DIARY* is to AIREL what Torchwood is to Doctor Who: a grownup, stay- up- late, dark theme on a masterful series."

—Peter Leavell, Meridian, ID

"I really love Chris White's writing. He's extremely talented and he is quickly becoming a favorite of mine."

—Michelle Vasquez, Life in Review

K: [PHANTASMAGORIA]

"Chris White has the talent of long ago writers interlaced with his own unique voice. Anything this man writes keeps me up. I literally have to schedule time to read his work because I know when I start I'll not eat, sleep, or bathe until I've finished it. *K: [PHANTASMAGORIA]* is nothing short of his signature work. In fact this might be his best novel to date. K is a character that you can't even begin to summarize. His experiences are all too familiar on so many levels. His relationship with others and God is eerily too close to home for not only myself but so many I know. You simply have to read this book."

—Bri Clark, Meridian, ID

Also by Aaron Patterson

Sweet Dreams (Book 1)
Dream On (Book 2)
In your Dreams (Book 3)
Airel (Book 1)
Michael (Book 2)
Uriel (Book 3 Coming Soon)
19 (Digital Short)
The Craigslist Killer (Digital Short)
Breaking Steele (Coming Soon)

Also by Chris White

Airel (Book 1)
Michael (Book 2)
Uriel (Book 3 Coming Soon)
The Marsburg Diary (Book 1, A Novella)
The Wagner Diary (Book 2, A Novella, Coming Soon)
The Great Jammy Adventure of the Flying Cowboy
(A Children's Book)
K: [phantasmagoria] (Book 1)
Strongbox (Digital Short)
Yes Dear (Digital Short)
Amethyst (Digital Short)

MICHAEL

Aaron Patterson

Chris White

StoneHouse Ink 2012
StoneHouse Ink
Boise, ID 83713
http://www.stonehouseink.net

First eBook Edition: 2012
First Paperback Edition 2012

ISBN: 978-0615568614

Michael: a novel/by Aaron Patterson & Chris White
Cover design by © Claudia McKinney - phatpuppyart.com
Layout design by Ross Burck
Model/Jake Rafus

Published in the United States of America
StoneHouse Ink

PART FIVE

THE CURSE

From the Book of the Brotherhood, Volume 3:

Introduction
Dear esteemed Host, you know by now, from previous
volumes, what great struggles we endure for the Master,
the Leader of our righteous rebellion. The Brothers
have taken you into the fold of the horde. The Seer has
bestowed upon you the Leader's imprimatur. Ye stand
now ready to do battle against the Sons and Daughters of
El, cursed be the name. Be it now known the Four Great
Principles of our Dominion under the sun:

1. *The Dominion belongs to the Brothers. It was given to*
   the Master Lucifer by the first created man at Eden.
   The Master has delegated to the Brothers various
   Principalities…

CHAPTER I

Sawtooth mountains of Idaho, present day

ALL I COULD FEEL was speed. Everything was racing along under me and my body was like an arrow shot at the speed of sound, only there was no sound. I could feel the turn of the earth as if I was about to step off—or be pushed off.

Thoughts—I guess you could call them thoughts—were whizzing through me even faster. I was an observer of my own life, and everything came back in random flickers.

I saw Kim making a silly face. We were—where were we? At the mall? She looked younger. But we were shopping all right. She must have dragged me along again.

I saw the valley. The big tree where I first read the Book of Kreios. My spot was still there.

I smelled apricots. I was in the kitchen, and I must have been young, because I was looking up at my mom, my head at about countertop height, and she was canning. The sun was low and warm in the room, and everything glowed like gold. Apricots. She smiled at me.

I felt the stress knotting my center as I relived that moment in

the movie theater restroom… when I first saw Kreios. I thought I
was going to die.

And then I did.

I saw Michael Alexander's smile. We were at school. That was
the Great Day of the Coffee Disaster, and I *so* wanted to be Mrs.
Napkins.

My heart fluttered.

I could feel it. But it was broken. Pierced.

Echoes from outside, somewhere else.

"…sorry…"

"…sorry…"

"…sorry…"

The Alexander residence. I was carrying Kim, busting through
the garage door like Kung Fu master through paper. I tripped and
tumbled. Kung Fu beginner.

The face of evil was a sidewalk chalk sketch and it came up at
me off the driveway, and Kim was gone. It was black and it grew
arms and reached for me, enfolded me, then became smoke and
disappeared.

I smelled death.

Then I smelled Abercrombie Fierce.

Weird.

Again, the walls of my hurtling bullet-arrow rattled with the
refrain: *"…sorry…"*

I wanted to cry.

Why?

I was floating over the lake looking at the cliff. That's when
I realized there was someone with me. But I couldn't tell who.
Michael? Then the cliff-top scene appeared and played out in front
of me as I floated there.

Michael was crawling there. There was a trail of blood behind him.

The lake below boiled, the massive disturbance of an angel of El exploding out of it. Kreios hunched over my body there on the top of the cliff, and it struck me as odd: I had been husked. My dead shell remained and he was trying desperately to save it. I looked to my side, trying to see whoever was with me. I still couldn't tell.

Michael was there on the dirt, sobbing uncontrollably, lying beside my body. Then Kreios brought the Bloodstone near to him.

What in the world...?

Michael howled furiously.

And then everything changed.

Michael was carrying me and I was in his arms.

There was a streak in the sky and I knew Kreios was gone. *Where?*

Then I was on my bed again. Not my bed at home, no. It was the bed I had slept in as a captive of my grandfather. *My grandfather!* And everything was cold. So cold.

Echoes: *stabbingpain, lifedeath, fury, angercold, watergrave, AIREL,* a scratching noise like pen on paper and, *"...sorry... sorry... sorry..."*

Icefire. That's what it was. My heart was consumed with burning cold, and I could feel it. I hovered over myself; something was hovering over me.

Then my ears popped.

And I could hear it:

"Airel, I'm so sorry... please forgive me. I love you!"

CHOICES.

Choices that we make lead us to make other choices, and those choices can sometimes bust us in half and dump us in a blind alley with no way out.

Michael Alexander sat on the edge of Airel's deathbed, his mind tearing. He could physically feel his heart rip inside his chest, crushed under the weight of his decisions. And he thought about the paradox—the utter craziness—that he was both lover and traitor to the most beautiful girl in the world.

He wanted to rip into himself. *Yeah. Starting with this new scar right here.* He felt the mark on his abdomen; the mark of a coward. *Add that one to the list.*

But what choice did he have?

The words echoed back to him from downstairs in the library:

"But she lived."

He had watched the page crinkle under his tears as they dropped to the parchment, smudging the ink. This was not what he wanted. She was just another mission, just another cursed threat that needed to be cleansed from the earth. She was a job like so many others. But Airel somehow got in, snuck past all his defenses and took hold of his heart. He had never known love, never really cared about it. She broke the rules as if they'd never even existed.

Then he had run back to her room, hoping what he had dared to do would work, that the pen on the page would be powerful, that she would indeed live. But all he could do upon entering was stare at her lifeless body.

Airel. Her corpse was pallid and blue. It broke him afresh; tears stung his eyes. He could not help but mutter a curse against himself. He ran a nervous hand through his hair, grasping at it, wanting to tear it out.

After all I've done!

He thought of his wicked father, Stanley Alexander. The lies. *Who can honor something like that?* Yet he tried.

He had allowed James…he turned his head and let his body crumple down and down, withering. *I can't think about James and what he did.*

But he continued to list off his many sins.

He had been all-in for the excitement of finding one of the immortals, the Nephilim descendants. Using his training, tracking her, finding her, observing her, standing right in front of his prey while she was totally oblivious, allowing her to take the bait, and then to spite her and all she stood for— the immortals, creation, El—he had delivered her up to the destroyer.

The Seer.

Tengu. And Tengu's host, Stanley Alexander.

All that remained from it was total and empty desolation.

Michael stood up and violently stalked around the room, shouting, screaming at God, at El, at the whole world. He could take them on, right here, right now. His rage was a tower of all-consuming fire.

But it cooled quickly in a dousing sea of desperation. Most of his rage was directed inwardly.

At himself.

That rage quickly changed to passionate sobs of grief. He found himself on his knees at her bedside, smothering his face in her wet hair and whispering again, again and again, "I'm so sorry, so sorry."

Michael's heart shattered. His world was a ruin. He had become what he had only just learned to hate, and a moment too late: evil.

CHAPTER II

I WAS UNDERWATER AGAIN. Dragged kicking and screaming.
Soaked. Stuck deep. Everything hurt. My heart was frantic in my
chest like it was lapping my ribcage and going for a new track
record. My limbs were numb and cold. My hair tangled around my
face. I couldn't breathe.

And then it happened: it was like getting my back popped at
the chiropractor; everything felt electric, like somebody flicked
a switch. I burst to the surface, my arms and legs flailing in one
spastic twitch, my fingers and toes tingling with nervous energy, my
lungs gasping, grabbing for air by the shovelful.

My muscles contracted and I shot up to a sitting position,
eyes wide and blinking, spending my first precious breath on a
bloodcurdling shriek that could wake the dead—me. I could feel the
memory of the speedy place, wherever I had been, being vigorously
wiped away like a picture on a whiteboard. It quickly became blank
like a vanishing dream.

Panic set in. *Where is he?*

There he was, kneeling. Well, more like he had been knocked
over onto his butt from a kneeling position. He looked so shocked.

"Michael!"

He jumped up to his feet, confusion and disbelief flashing across his face. Then he collapsed to his knees again sobbing uncontrollably, his arms around my waist, his head in my lap. All I could hear were little snippets through his tears.

"I'm so sorry! Please forgive me!"

My own eyes dampened in response to him. For a long time all I could do was pet his shoulder and run my fingers through his hair. *Was this all just a dream?*

Then *She* came to the forefront of my mind, loud and clear, with an emphatic *"No."* And I understood. "Oh. Oh, my God."

Michael was starting to regain his composure. His body was racking itself with those little jerky ticks that come after a massive sobbing fit. He rocked back on his knees, his eyes puffy and bloodshot, and looked at me. He should have looked like a train wreck. But he was a gorgeous sight to me, and I felt that resound deep within. Deep within both of us. "Hey, mister."

He whispered my name. "Airel."

We sat still as statues for a long moment, just staring at each other.

He took the lead. "There are… no words to begin to tell you how sorry I am…" His eyes said the rest, and there was the quietest, most desperate plea for forgiveness embedded within them.

I had to look down, away. *How on earth do I begin to understand this? She* gave me some ideas. Some of them were quite violent and vengeful.

"Michael…what happened?"

He took a moment to breathe, but his eyes stayed locked on mine. Something was different. Besides the obvious, I mean. Something was very different, and I couldn't tell what it was. "You were dead."

I took a moment to process. *Like, what? That's totally impossible.*

He saw my skepticism. "I brought you back."

"What?"

He issued a retraction immediately, as if he was about to be struck by lightning. "No! I mean, I carried you up here. And then I..."

"Ask him how long that took," She said. I could tell my conscience was decidedly hostile to Michael—Michael, who had led me to the brink of death and then allowed his demon friend to push me over, quite literally. But I was of the opposite persuasion. I had forgiven him while I was drowning. Why would I take that back now, especially when, however impossible for anyone to understand, I had been given a second chance?

I found myself saying it. "How long was I... um..."

"Dead?"

"Uh. Yeah. Dead."

"It was forever."

I could practically hear *She* doing the facepalm thing and making barf noises. I rolled my eyes a little, but that was for *She,* not Michael, and I hoped he didn't see me. I wasn't quite sure just how it might look if *She* and I came to blows, but we were getting there quickly.

Lay off him, I thought, trying to silence her.

"Michael. How long was I dead?" The question echoed absurdly back at me. *But that speedy place...that was so real. I was flying.* Somewhere, somehow. I was in between that and this; nothing was real, and at the same time, everything was *too* real.

I was stuck right in between. A *me* sandwich.

I didn't know what to do or think. My eyes filled with tears and the flood started.

Michael simply held me for what felt like hours, and I let him. I had far too many questions to even begin to articulate them. I was outraged. I wanted to shout at him, strike his face, curse at him and ask him why he let the Brotherhood *kill* me, for crying out loud. I wanted to ask him over and over again *why, why, why*. But all I could do was sob in his arms.

I felt pathetic and used up, unstable.

I started to shiver. I was still soaked to the bone, and I realized as my sanity came back around for a little visit that there were some practical concerns needing my immediate attention. *Like the crazy idea that, however this had happened and whatever explanation there was for it, I might completely ruin my resurrection by succumbing to hypothermia.*

"You need to get out of those clothes, lady," Michael said, my shivers racking even his body.

"Y-you better w-watch it, mis-s-ster. You can't talk like that to me. It's-s indecent."

For the first time, a smile dawned on his face. "You're beautiful," he said, "And it's good to have you back."

His smile was glorious and new, even if it was mingling with the tears streaming down his face. It lit something in me that warmed me to my toes.

"What I mean is," he said, correcting his former indiscretion, "*you've* got work to do."

"Like w-what?"

He looked at me funny. "How do I say this? You smell like lake trout. And death."

"Oh."

"You need a nice hot bath. And dry clothes."

I blushed. It felt good, but it too was just slightly off kilter.

"I'll leave you to it?"

I nodded.

He stood and I feared something again for the first time. I feared being alone. He turned to go, walking for the door and the long hall in the impossibly enormous house.

"But don't go too far!" I shouted.

He gave me a confused look. "I won't. I need to go find Kim, though."

"Okay."

"K. Be safe. No more drowning."

This time I let him see me roll my eyes. "Hey. You too." I gave him a little "I've got my eye on you" gesture and then he left.

I was alone.

CHAPTER III

MICHAEL WALKED OUT OF her bedroom questioning his sanity. *Am I losing it? Airel's back and I'm off on some Good Samaritan mission five minutes later?* He didn't want to let her out of his sight.

His feet nevertheless kept going, away, out, taking him farther and farther away from the one person he felt now—and strongly—he couldn't live without.

The real kicker was that what he was about to do was right inside his wheelhouse: tracking. Because of the job he used to have with James, every demonic memory, every kill, every tactic, every savage act—all of it—was there for the showing and telling in his mind. He had to admit, it had made his "training" in the Brotherhood easy and swift; almost a joke. These things had become second nature, and quickly; maybe because of the fact that Stanley was the Seer, maybe not.

But Airel was like ice that had taken up lodging in the stone of his heart. Love was the spark that would cause that potentially life-giving moisture to warm and expand and shatter all of him. She could wreck him with a glance. He knew it because he felt it.

It was bizarre: being only eighteen, yet having instant access to time immemorial through the daguerreotype of James's thoughts. It was a demonic and evil perspective of things. He knew that he would have to turn and face what he had done. The demonic pathways in his mind caused him to possess a kind of twisted life experience that made certain things quite clear.

Airel.

She had changed everything. He never saw her coming. One day he was just tracking, shadowing like he was shadowing Kim even now, and then he was falling for one of those whom he had been taught were nothing but a plague to be eradicated.

Even with all that, his instincts were telling him there wasn't much chance for the two of them. *There's not much chance for anything, really. How can I ever go back?* He couldn't. There were some things that couldn't be undone.

Except death? That was still totally crazy, and he wondered what it was that had made it work. *Was it the book? The pen?* He took more steps, consciously avoiding the next thought building in the back of his conscience. *El? Sworn enemy.*

"Crap," he said, walking out of the enormous house onto the porch. It seemed like only minutes ago, he had been having breakfast with her. And Kreios…. But that was a different world.

So where did Kreios go?

More questions, and lots of them.

He walked on with them for a time, down the steps.

"Where's Kim?" He looked around.

He was on the floor of the great valley again. Only moments ago he had carried the lifeless body of his true love…right across these very steps. *True love? Do I know what that is?*

He shook his head, trying to clear up his thinking. "All right. Where is she?" He looked around for signs in the grass, on the path, skillfully processing divots and pebbles and skids and filing them against the database of his demonically shared memories. "Come on, Kim. Where are you?" He kept walking.

Down the path he went, following thousands of years of inherited instinct and looking for something more solid. A bent blade of grass…a broken twig…even a partial footprint. But there was nothing that said *Kim*.

At length he found himself breaking out into the clear area at the top of the cliff. If he was looking for signs of activity, here there were plenty. He could sense it all, and it was like walking into the overpowering stench of a field of dead. He could see with his mind's eye innumerable historical instances of this very type of thing, and it swept over him and drove him to his knees. He couldn't help gagging; it was so real.

All the decisions he'd made—whether with good intentions or bad—were tallied up before his eyes and it was like that old Hebrew legend: *Mene. Mene. Tekel. Upharsin.* And he could hear what it meant; that he had been weighed in the scales and found wanting. And perhaps a lesser person— *what am I, a man or a boy?*—would have crumbled into tears, but Michael Alexander didn't. He simply stood to his feet, numb. Overwhelmed. He looked out on the lake below, the mountains in the distance. He stood now just past the boulders near the edge of the cliff.

"Michael?" The voice was right behind him.

He spun, instinct driving him instantly into his fighting stance, fists up in the guard.

"What are you doing here?" It was Kim.

He let out a breath and relaxed, forcing his arms down to his sides. "Looking for you."

Kim's face showed flashes of unbridled rage. "Murderer," she breathed, her eyes flashing.

Michael's eyes widened in comprehension. "No…no, that's not

true—"

"How can you say that?" her eyes filled with tears, her fists clenched at her side.

"Kim, I mean—"

"Shut up! Just shut your mouth!" She wiped at her eyes. "You killed my best friend!"

"Kim—"

"Traitor! Bastard! Murderer!"

Michael grimaced. *I guess this is where it starts.*

She stalked closer to him and looked up at his face. "I want to kill you!" She was pointing her finger at his chest. "I should push you off this cliff. You don't deserve to live. You are a…" She stuttered—face flushed.

"Kim, listen to me. Airel is alive."

Her jaw dropped. Then she stepped back from him, shock spreading across her face. "Liar!" she hissed. "I don't believe you!"

"Kim, trust me. I am all those things you said I am. I have to live the rest of my life knowing what I did to her. But I'm telling you the truth—she's alive."

Kim looked like she was dizzy, and her eyes darted around as if a torrent of different emotions were pouring through her.

"Kim. Can I take you to her? Let me take you to her."

She eyed him warily. "Why should I trust you?"

He shrugged, harrumphing. "I've got no reason for you to trust me, Kim. None at all. Like I said, you were right. I am a traitor and a murderer. And I am a…a bastard. You don't know how right you are about that. Are you going to follow me back to the house or not?"

"How 'bout not," she said, crossing her arms and cupping her elbows with her hands.

I can see how this is going. "Tell you what. Why don't you head back, now that we've found each other, and see for yourself. I'll wait here for a bit and let you two have some time. You probably need it. I'll probably see you in the kitchen by the time I get back. I bet she'll need something to eat anyway."

She sniffed at him. "Whatever."

"That's our Kim." *She's probably going to make me regret saying that.*

Kim turned and sprinted into the woods like a cat.

"It'll be dark soon," he called after her. "Better hurry." He had decided to take his time getting back, coming dark or no. Maybe try to see if *El* would answer a question or two…

BEFORE MICHAEL COULD ARTICULATE a single question in his mind, watching Kim scurry off, he felt something new within him, a kind of draw to light and warmth. It was magnetic, and as he opened his heart and mind to it, he was surprised at how the light seared his mind, how the warmth burned him, it felt good to be truly honest about all that he was.

But what he was was ugly.

Then he could see what was happening. It was El. *He's here, somehow, right now,* he thought panicking, and, completely opposite to everything he had ever known or been taught, without really choosing to, he fell to his knees right there in the dirt.

It felt then to Michael that everything made sense: that he really had more in common with dirt than he had ever dreamt. He felt low, and his decisions paraded before him, accusing him in a strangely familiar voice: *"Manipulator. You manipulated Airel."*

Is that me? he wondered.

"You got close and lied to her, charmed her, fully intending to

kill…and then you stood by and did nothing until it was too late…
and then, dear boy, what did you do? Something very, very selfish…
and very, very risky indeed, did you not? Yes, you did. And you know
why you wrote in the Book, don't you? Yes, you do…. You didn't do
it for Airel; don't kid yourself. You did it for YOU."

Michael collapsed, his face in the dirt, weeping, trying with all
his heart to argue, "No! I did it for her; I love her! I love her with all
my heart! More than my own life!"

"Nevertheless, you stood by and watched her die…"

Truth was hard to come by. He didn't really know up from
down. "But it wasn't too late! I made it right!"

"Did you?"

Michael was silent.

"…or have you made it worse? Some things cannot be
undone."

He felt like he was going crazy, talking to voices inside his own
head, begging El like a dog. That one fact, that he felt like begging
his sworn enemy for relief, filled him with shame and regret. All
he could do was hope that what he had done would work out in the
end…that she could forgive him when she saw who he really was.

CHAPTER IV

STEAM.

Ah, that feels really, really good. I stood under the shower of near-scalding water, washing the cold and grime from my body, my eyes closed.

All kinds of things were running through my head. Given a little distance from Michael, I felt like I could think more clearly. As the smell of lake trout and death rinsed away and fell from my body, the fog in my mind also dispelled, leaving a pristine clean. One thing was pretty clear already.

Michael and I had unfinished business. A lot to talk through, I mean. What had happened between us was life and death. It wasn't just some stupid interpersonal friend drama resulting from someone flapping their gums about a rumor overheard in the girls' locker room. I guessed the best way to say it was that I needed answers. Like yesterday.

She expressed it perfectly. *"Caution."*

And *She* was right, I had to admit. This girl wouldn't be making any rash decisions in the future. Especially about Michael. I also had to admit things had gone too far too fast. *Well, probably.* It was pretty obvious, anyway, that I didn't really know him or what he was capable of, in just about every direction. For the first time I could see that I had acted like a love-struck teenager, letting all my rationale go out the window when it came to Michael. Anyway, I needed more time, so I resolved to be unresolved about things until I had more information.

What if that confuses him? "So what?" I asked the shower tile, scrubbing shampoo into my scalp for the third time.

It was weird. I was thinking of new slogans for the shampoo I was using. *It's the kind that gets out the worst smells! Even death!* I was still a little punchy. I sighed heavily and rinsed.

It had been about an hour. *He might be back by now,* I thought, and that made me more nervous about him than when he picked me up on our first date. Why? Because now I knew him better. There was danger and desire roundabout him, and that did weird and conflicting things inside me. It pushed and pulled at the same time.

I turned the water off, turned to grab for my towel and then realized the bathroom door was cracked open. I had left it closed.

"Ohmygawd!"

I gasped and covered myself with the towel, looking toward the sound of the voice. Could it be? I saw an unkempt mop of red hair. "Kim!"

"Airel…"

I could tell she was going to cry. I wanted to run to her but that would have been a little awkward. "What are you doing here? Are you all right?"

"Am *I* all right? How about you? Are you really alive?" she said.

I found myself blushing. "Stop looking at me."

"I'm sorry, I just can't believe it." Kim rushed forward and hugged me hard.

"Kim!" I held her for a long moment, starting to cry again. My head hurt from all the crying. I had to get ahold of myself.

"Knock knock!" It was Michael, his voice coming from out in the bedroom.

"Oh my gosh! Stay out there!" I shouted, a hint of irritation in my voice. "Kim!" I said, turning back to her.

She got the message. Best friends are good at reading in between the lines. She winked at me and ran out, saying, "We *are* gonna talk later."

I heard her verbally abusing him out there and I smiled. In a minute she shouted back at me through the door, announcing that they would meet me down in the kitchen whenever I was ready. I said, "Okay," and breathed a sigh of relief.

After Michael and Kim left me in peace, I felt the pulling again. Part of me was still broken and I wasn't sure what would fix it. Or if Michael would even be involved in that healing.

Anyway, why should *I* be the one to feel bad? *"Exactly,"* She said. I wasn't the one who had declared war. They had.

I toweled off and began to wring and brush out my hair. Horrible dark jokes clattered in the back of my mind. How could I be so beautiful? I was dead an hour ago. I shrugged it off and kept brushing.

Remembering who I was made me think of Kreios. Where was he? When I reached out in my mind for him, all I got back was silence. Blackness. Was he even alive? Why was I alone? Why had he been taken from me when I needed him most?

And who was Michael? *Yeah, really.* It was there nagging me in the back of my mind, but if I opened that door, what if I didn't like what I found there? Did I have to go there? He had lied to me about his past and who his dad was. What else had he lied about? Had he really planned to kill me?

How can a girl know and be sure about love when she's not sure who, precisely, she loves? Everything I thought I knew about him—that he was gentle, strong, beautiful and flawed, funny and serious, perfect and broken—how much of it was true? And considering what he had lived with... what he had to do to be the son of Stanley Alexander...I couldn't begin to make sense of it.

In the end all of it made me want to be in his corner. There was something unexplainable about my attraction to him. Sure, it was physical. That was the attention-getter for everyone, right? But there was also a deep mystery to him; something both compelling and unknowable. That was the hook in my jaws, and it had been there since that fateful day I had spilled my coffee.

I tried to shrug off the deep thoughts and dressed in cargo pants, hiking boots and a dark blue tank top. I would be ready to hike out to the cliff later. Hopefully. I had to find Kreios.

I also figured my life, my school, my friends outside of Kim and Michael were all gone now. Everything was different now.

I had been shoved violently out of the nest, just like that baby eagle I had dreamt about. I sighed. So much about life was just impossible and huge. Would I learn to fly before I hit bottom?

Would I ever see my parents again? Would it be safe? For them? Was it better if they thought I was dead?

My head ached.

My chest ached too, but I refused to look at the scar in the mirror or touch it. I knew it was there and it made sure I did. It throbbed endlessly, pulsing with my cleaved and restarted heart.

But now I was ready for my day.

"Ready for anything?" She asked.

Sure. I've already cheated death today. Who else wants a piece?

CHAPTER V

Portland, Oregon, Pearl District, present day

KREIOS COULD REMEMBER THE battles he had fought. He knew the look of each man that had died under the edge of his sword. Through it all he was the master of his temper, his anger, his rage. Time and conscience had taught him to hold it in check, to act and not let emotions rule.

But he could also remember the few times that he had lost his temper. Time and conscience had also taught him that everything was personal. The difference between angel and animal was self-control, keeping instinct and impulse in check. This was one of those times when he was more animal, operating on instinct.

Wide open and out of control.

The howling inferno of his righteous anger—his prickling sense of justice—filled him, and he allowed it to consume him to the core of his being.

There were three women he had ever dared to love. The manifestation of that love to each one was different but no less complete. And now his loss was complete. Filled up for each of them. He knew about price. And he knew he was nothing more than a fallen angel, in the final analysis. He deserved all of it. All of the futility. All of the pain.

He thought it especially ironic that the Seer's Bloodstone was red—his anger was hatefully red as well. It pulsed through him in a fire that only the red of guilty blood could quench.

"Look," the woman said, "I don't know who you are or what you want, but I'm not the one you're looking for!" She sounded confident, but it was a thin shell. In the same way, she was rough and untended, the slightest hint of femininity beneath it all.

"I am not surprised anymore," said Kreios, half to himself, half to the jeans-clad woman with wild red hair. "But this will be messy; an embarrassment." They stood in the back parking lot of the Riverside Bar facing one another.

She bent her knees slightly as Kreios advanced toward her. "What do you want?" She lowered her shoulder, hand on hip. The front of her shirt, its buttons undone just a bit too far, fell slightly open, revealing a leather string that held something around her neck.

Kreios continued to move closer, towering over her by a foot or more.

"Hey," she said, looking alarmed, "I've taken down bigger guys than you..." She widened her stance and dropped her hands to her sides.

"Woman, you are of the Brotherhood. Admit it and stand to fight." He came off a little bored. Kreios did not want to argue with the demon, he just wanted to kill it and be on to the next. There were so many to kill, so many on which he could spread around the load of pain and suffering.

"Brotherhood? What are you talking about? She tossed her wiry hair in the jaundiced street lighting. The lot was empty other than a few lingering cars. It was past closing time.

Trina Wilson was her given name. She managed and tended the

bar. She usually took home over $500 in tips, too, though she wasn't beautiful. Whatever men saw in her was simply what happened when an excess of alcohol fogged the mind. She was good at working what she had, and it served her well.

More importantly, the demon for whom she played willing host was the Infernal—the leader— of a pod of the Brotherhood in the city of Portland, principality of Oregon. This Infernal had once answered to the Seer—Stanley Alexander's overthrown master, Tengu.

"As I said," Kreios continued, "I know who you are." He stood weighing just shy of three hundred pounds and almost seven feet in height, wearing jeans, athletic shoes and a hoodie, blending into— sort of—the background of Pacific Northwest street scenery. He was massive.

"Dude," she pleaded. "I just run the bar. I mind my own business. C'mon…you're gonna pick on a woman?"

Kreios looked around. He didn't want to have to kill any witnesses tonight. It was better to go in and out clean. "Demon, I am going to kill you, woman or not." He began to tell his version of a joke: "After all, I believe in equal pay for equal work. If you give me usable information on your… associates…and their whereabouts, I will make your end quick. If not, you will suffer. There is no difference to me."

She crouched and bared her teeth, hissing. Trina Wilson shook violently and then doubled over. Black wings emerged from her back as her Infernal master exited its place of refuge. The demon's tail whipped around, clipping an old dented green dumpster and sending it across the parking lot. It careened off the brick wall of the building and smashed into a rusted-out Chevy truck behind Kreios.

He smiled and bent at the knees. "Ah, good," he said.

"Kreiosssss!"

The host Trina staggered away as the winged creature leapt
fully free of her body. It was insect-like, its segmented body over
ten feet tall, its midsection thick. The wings draped outward by ten
feet on each side. The double barbed tail slithered and cracked like
a whip.

Trina gathered herself together. Hunched down, she pulled a
SIG P-225 from its ankle holster and fired three shots at the angel.
The 9mm Parabellum projectiles grazed him but mostly spun out
wild.

It stung, and he blinked at her. "You annoy me, woman." In a
single motion he lunged backward to the dumpster and tossed the
heavy green steel trash box at her like a wad of paper.

It hit her full in the chest and she went down hard, the upside
down dumpster finally pinning her between the asphalt and its
grimy metal edge. She shrieked in pain, blood running down her
forehead into her eyes from a large gash.

Kreios turned his full attention again toward the demon, but the
lot was empty. He looked around, knowing that the demented thing
would not run. It would fight.

He looked up just as it fell upon him from above.

A thunderous roar. Black drool flew from the maw of the demon
as it waggled its head in apparent victory. It filled its lungs and
screeched.

Kreios burst up and out in massive strength, throwing the huge
black insect-like mass off him. He grabbed the tail as the demon
tumbled end over end and yanked it back toward him, cracking the
whip in reverse. The demon yowled in pain.

It flew, pivoting by tail held in the vise of angel hand, up over
Kreios's head in an arc. It landed on its back, raising a cloud of dust
around them.

Kreios still held fast to the double-barbed tail. He braced

himself to rip it from the beast, but the demon righted itself and rushed him.

The angel took up the challenge with a shout, tail in hand, rushing the creature with double the speed. With a deft spin in mid-stride Kreios twisted the tail, stiffening it, wielding it like a massive pike. He drove it deep into the creature at the joint between thorax and abdomen, severing it completely in half, following through in one motion, cracking the whip again.

The demon's voice was a wretched gurgle; pathetic. Thick and juicy innards were thrown out into the arena of combat, burning like phosphorus on contact wherever they landed.

Kreios looked down at what his hands had wrought. The demon's exoskeleton began to break apart, turning into wisps of black smoke that rose up briefly and then fell back to the tarmac, boiling there for a moment before being sucked up by the pavement like a sponge, disappearing.

"Now for the other one." Kreios walked to the side of the dumpster and looked down at the pinned and bleeding woman.

"And you…?" asked Kreios.

Trina coughed. Blood poured from her mouth.

Kreios knew her lungs were filling up. "Oh. That is…sad for you."

He leaned down and took hold of the object that hung from her neck and ripped it from the leather thong. He held it up to the lights of the parking lot. It was an amulet, the figure of a chameleon rendered in pure white jade. It changed colors even as he looked at it. His face became grim; he knew precisely what it meant.

The woman spoke. "Please! Don't kill me…I…"

"I will not kill you, Trina Wilson." Kreios pocketed the object. "I will leave you here to die slowly. Your body will bleed out soon. It will hurt then more than it does now. Much more. Your legs will swell when you begin to burn. Your eyes will melt in their sockets. And when that happens...you will see where you are bound. Wait until the veil is lifted. Then you will see in truth. Your remains will disintegrate in the fire that I have come to set. There will be nothing left."

Kreios stood, looking to the sky. "I will find every one of your clan...The Nri?" He looked at her; he wasn't asking, he was taunting.

She hissed at him again, angered at the mention of the truth.

"I will burn all of them as well. They will wish for a quick death, but they too...will not taste it." He felt the anger surging within him again and he clenched his fists in order to contain it.

He knelt down, his face inches from hers. "Blood for blood," he said. And then he was gone.

Soon the Riverside Bar was a blazing inferno. And Trina Wilson was burning.

Arabia, 1244 B.C.

THERE SHE WAS. AT play in the grass with one of the kittens, surrounded by wildflowers and ancient trees. He was there in the grass too, relaxing, smoking his pipe, blowing smoke rings. He looked through them to the mountains beyond and closed his eyes.

It was summer. Beautiful. He lived alone with Eriel, the battle to defend Ke'elei six years behind them. It had made her safe, had bound his people together and scattered the rest of the Brotherhood. He and Yamanu had hunted them for another year after the great battle. If any were left, they were deep underground.

Eriel laughed and teased the tiny bundle of fur with a ball on a string. "Kitty," Eriel called him, pawed and jumped at the ball, arching his back and hissing. This made her laugh even harder and Kreios smiled in spite of himself.

"Look, Daddy, Kitty is trying to be a big boy. See how he hisses?" She tossed back her black hair and yanked the ball and string away, making Kitty hiss even more.

"You should be nice to that kitten," he laughed. "One day it will be a big cat. You do not want him to be mean." They both laughed and Eriel continued her little game.

Like ripples in a pond, the laughter smoothed its own way out of him, and all too soon. Kreios didn't know what to think of the quiet; didn't know what to do with it. He was accustomed to war and its particulars, hiding and trying to blend in. The quiet, the solitude, the peace…though it was still at alien to him, it made all the difference.

He saw a few friends—Yamanu for instance—on occasion. For the most part this new life was safely off the beaten path. Out here in the wild he could be himself. Eriel could grow and learn without being looked at with suspicion and fear. He knew one day it wouldn't be enough for her. Eriel would need people, need to engage life, perhaps even start a family of her own. Then he would need to let go.

But that time would be far off, wouldn't it?

Kreios stood and stretched his legs. The cabin he had built for them was simple. One room. But it was cozy. He picked a low open valley and built the cabin just beyond the tree line. It nestled at the base of massive Sawtooth Mountains and looked out over a perfect meadow of grass and wildflowers, a misty waterfall nearby that cast rainbows out into the air.

"When can we go back to Ke'elei? I miss everyone. I want to see Mary. I want to see uncle Yam."

"Soon, my lovely."

"Why can't we live there?" Eriel stood. Kitty took the ball and string, running a few feet off in the grass with his spoils.

"We've talked about this. It is better out here. Quiet." Kreios hated the politics of life in the big city. The Council also did not look kindly on him after all that had happened. Yet he could not help his six-year-old daughter understand any of this.

"I know..." Eriel said with a pout. She hung her head and looked up at Kreios with big eyes.

His smile broke wide. "You know I cannot resist those eyes. Come here."

She came to him.

He lifted her into his arms and took to the sky, twisting and twirling with her wrapped tightly to his chest. She giggled, pulling him tighter with her little arms. She loved to fly with him and would beg and chip away at him for hours if he let too much time go by without "a sky adventure."

"I love you, Eriel," he said, kissing her cheek.

"I love you too, daddy." Her eyes bright, she looked out over the world without any fear.

CHAPTER VI

Sawtooth mountains of Idaho, present day

LARGE QUESTIONS LOOMED OVER all of us. It had been a few hours. Now all of us were showered and changed and we had finished up in the kitchen, having feasted on whatever we could find in the house.

We were now sitting comfortably in the library.

"Okay, I'm ready to talk about the elephant in the room," Kim said. We had to clear the air. I was really glad at least one of us finally broke the ice.

The fire was roaring nicely, casting the three of us in a warm light. It was just past midnight. Kim and I were sitting on the antique loveseat and Michael was seated on an armchair, leaning forward toward the fire, elbows on knees, staring into the flames.

Kim went on. "First of all, Michael—are you going to be okay?"

Michael looked like he had been caught doing something naughty. "Yeah, I just…this is…"

"I get it, you're a jerk, a loser, and you don't deserve her." Kim pointed to me.

My heart felt stabbed.

"But she likes you. She loves you—I think—"

"Hey," I said, trying to deflect the direction of the conversation. "How about you, Kim? Are you okay? You look pretty rough…"

Kim said, "Yeah, I'm fine. Just a little bruised up. It's like that when you're duct taped to a chair for a day or so."

Again my heart felt wounded. *This is all my fault.* But the look on Michael's face said otherwise.

She turned back to him. "Anyway, Michael, you'd better make it up to her."

"I'm sitting right here, Kim," I said. "I can handle my problems."

She ignored me, laying into him again in attack mode, and I couldn't interject. "What are you? Who was your dad? And James…I don't even know where to begin."

He sighed. I had never seen him like this. He looked older than eighteen. There was even a shadow of stubble on his face in spite of the fact that he—that all of us—had had a chance to wash the blood from our hands, our bodies.

"I know. Who am I really other than a backstabbing demon?" He looked her dead in the eyes.

Again, something I found arresting. There was some strength about him. It was way beyond the look he had given me on our first and only date. Before we were kidnapped.

"Right?" she said. It was a total Kim thing to say; ditzy, childish, playful. It seemed like she was back. Maybe.

Michael went on, "For once in my life, I wonder what's going to happen to me. To us, I mean. I'm not used to this feeling. I'm used to having a plan; *the* plan. Stanley…always made sure of that."

I found it very telling that he called his father Stanley instead of Dad. I wanted to interject something but I couldn't think of anything to add.

"Stanley trained me to kill. To blend in. To win people over with charm, make friends, find out about their friends' friends, and sniff out any that had angelic blood running in their veins. Like you." He looked at me, eyes cutting into me for the briefest of moments before looking away.

It got quiet. Kim and I traded a glance.

"About that…" I said.

"I'm so sorry," he said, tears filling his eyes in the firelight.

I spoke, and as I did, I choked up too. "I know. I know you're sorry. I believe you. You don't have to keep saying it." I was a little frustrated.

"I know; I'm sorry…"

Kim slapped her palm to her forehead and we all laughed.

"But seriously," I said. And then I softly blurted it out: "I love you, Michael." It was as if a bomb went off. And it was crazy; like both of us knew it but neither of us wanted to be the one to actually say it.

The answer came even softer. "I love you too."

It was very still in the room, like being in a deep forest right before a storm breaks; there was a buzz in the air, anticipation.

And then Kim popped the balloon. "Okay, you two totally need to kiss now."

My jaw dropped.

Michael said precisely what I was thinking: "Awkwarrrrd…"

I laughed.

"How about a raincheck, mister."

"Totes," he said smilingly in Kim's vernacular. He relaxed for the first time that day.

Kim rolled her eyes before speaking. "Okay, whatever. But I still have questions. Like, Michael, what freaking *happened* out there?"

He nodded, again looking older than he was. "It's hard to know where to begin." He sat back, crossing an ankle over one knee, his fingers interlaced over his stomach. "If you want explanations...I guess I could start at the beginning. My first...assignment."

He breathed in and out. "Her name was Sally Potts. She was twelve, the youngest by far to change. I was thirteen. It was at a little school in West Texas; a one-room schoolhouse, just like in *Little House on the Prairie.*"

"Okay, creepy," Kim said. "We're not looking for a full-on confession here, dude. So save it. I just want to know how in the world we got here. How did we get *here* from whatever happened out *there* on the cliff?"

"Sorry."

"Don't worry, Michael. I think you're a good enough guy. You did save her in the end," she said, looking at me. "...even if it took you long enough. But can you, *pretty please,* fill me in on what I missed out there?"

"Okay, it's simple: Stanley killed Airel."

"I know. I saw that much," she shivered.

"So did I," I said.

"Then I killed Stanley," Michael said. "And that's when everything went wrong. Really wrong. James—my demon—tried to finish the...the...job? No, no. That's not the right word."

"You can say it," I said. "I was just a job."

Michael looked like I had stabbed him. "At first. But that changed..." He was beginning to defend himself, but he let his words fade and stared back into the fire.

I looked at him. There was something different about him now. Something good. And bad. It was as if he was under a burden or in restraint. It made him seem...like a man and not a boy.

"Airel, you have completely wrecked me," he said, his eyes bright and piercing. "I wish…I mean, I never wanted any of this to happen. I found my courage too late to help you. And I was desperate. That's why I wrote you back to life."

I was shocked. "Wait. What?"

He just pointed to the mantelpiece, the rough wooden shelf above the fire, the inkwell and quill pen…those old books. Call me crazy or stupid, but it had only just then occurred to me that I was alive and kicking for a definitive reason. I hadn't put two and two together yet. I was normally really observant, smart as a whip, but somehow this one had come at me from my blind side.

"Michael, what are you talking about?"

"This," he said, standing. He walked to the shelf slowly, quietly, with reverence. When his finger brushed one of the books, I heard a shout go out and echo back to me from the deepest recesses of my heart and mind: *Michael*.

He took my Book—I knew it was *my* Book—and gently delivered it to me.

I opened it and saw what he had done. I saw the three words he had written there:

"But she lived."

The page was warped from his tears. I was stunned. Shocked. "How could you…" I felt violated. "How could you write in my book?" I didn't even know I *had* a book. I thought only full angels had them.

"Airel, I—"

I was overcome. "I can't believe it," I stammered. What I meant to say was something along the lines of this: *I can't believe you're that bold, that amazingly desperate…for me.* The bigger picture started to come into focus. I reached for *She*. But there was nothing there. I felt completely alone…I felt like my childhood was over and, ready or not, I was now an adult. Far from what I had always thought, it wasn't glorious. It wasn't liberating. Nope. It scared the crap out of me.

I was beginning to hyperventilate. "Michael!"

He knelt in front of me, naked anxiety on his face. "Breathe."

I held my book open on my lap, dumbfounded. "I have a book!" Everything about my life, if it was bigger than the universe before, was now totally impossible. "I can't believe you did that…"

"I'm…sorry?"

Oh, no. He was taking it wrong. So was I. "No. *I'm* sorry."

He took my hands inside his own, wrapping them up in warmth and strength.

"I just can't believe you *did* that! It was incredibly brave. How did you even know? How did you figure it out? How did you find this, and—how could it have even *worked?"*

Michael flashed me his trademark smile, the crooked smirk that could melt me in a second. "It wasn't me. It was *El."*

I was really confused. "It was—?"

He nodded. "It was *El*. I asked Him and He told me. I had a…a conversation with Him. After I found Kim."

We looked at her.

She gave Michael a look. "You are so weird."

"All I remember is being tackled…falling off the cliff, splashing into the lake. I saw you…" I looked at him. "I saw you!" It was all coming back in a flood. I couldn't say that I thought I had lost him too. I wiped my eyes.

"And I remember: I forgave you." I looked at him, grabbed his face with my hands and locked my eyes on his. "I still choose that, and you." I collapsed on his shoulder, weeping, wrestling with my rash words in juxtaposition to my doubtful and damaged heart. It was all true, sure. But the trouble was that it was all true.

He simply held me. When I finally recovered, Kim was gone. I figured she felt like a third wheel. Or that she had gotten the answers she wanted, at least in part.

Michael and I rested against each other, our heads touching. I could feel the heat of his breath on my cheek, smell the rugged clean sweetness of his scent. It was Abercrombie Fierce. *Oh.* "Oh!" Memories, impossible ones, came back to me. I caught my breath, my heart in a frenzy beneath the scar on my chest. I pulled back from him; it felt dangerous.

Hey, speaking of wounds... "How come I never healed completely? Why the scar..." I asked no one. There was no answer. "And how did you heal?" I looked up at him from my Book. "Can you heal too?"

He looked straight into my eyes, and I saw how deep the pain in him went. I couldn't see the end of it. "Something like that." He stood and walked back to the fire. He leaned against the mantelpiece, half turned back toward me. "I guess Kim took off, huh?"

"Yeah," I said.

He nodded.

I could tell the conversation had moved on, but I didn't know how he felt about that. I wished I could hear what he was thinking. "So...Stanley is dead. James is dead...? Or something. And Kreios is gone."

"I don't know—I guess so. I haven't seen him since...since I was carrying you back. He looked really, really pissed."

I wasn't getting it, but I could tell he was trying to tell me something.

"I'm pretty sure he still thinks you're dead."

I didn't get it at first, but then it hit me like a city bus.

The implications were enormous. *What would a five-thousand-year-old supernaturally powerful angel be doing if he had just lost his granddaughter to…yeah…this is not good.*

IN THE SPIRITUAL DARK that surrounded the Master, three iniquitous shapes cowered, bent under the burden of his countenance. There was no exchange. No information changed hands on the air. When orders were given, they were understood and that was all. Everything was disconnected.

There were more like them, these three, but they were an ancient kind and rarely beheld. In the earliest days under the sun, when the Master—the great Leader—had procured the Dominion, these three had a different appearance. They were once tall, strong, robust, even beautiful. Now they, as well as all the others of their kind, were shriveled, encrusted with a growth of filth and fungus. Open pustules spewed forth clouds of black spores from their once beautiful skin, now threatening contagion wherever they went. Milky pus glided across the deep crevices of their hides, and they moved as if they were diseased, as if they were puppets on strings, jerking and spastic and shaky.

But they were fast. Dangerous. Deceptive. And as they stood before the Master, the Leader, they understood what mission he had conceived for them. As always, there would be at least two objectives: one that was disclosed…in a fashion…and another that the Leader kept to himself. In a kingdom populated by usurpers, command was executed ruthlessly, because it was true that a kingdom divided against itself could not stand. None dared to contradict what was understood in this room: the seat of all deception; the antithrone of Self.

The room was a clean space. Pure white. But it was all mockery; it was empty and plunged at all times in deepest hollow blackness. For that was the essence of clean: blankness. Up was down, right was wrong. And hatred was righteousness.

The three now stood taller, having imbibed the desires of the Leader. They knew. The thought-language was pre-Babylonic, very clean, direct. In one unarticulated thought they understood numberless ideas about the girl, the Immortal, the one who had wielded the Sword…and the one who had betrayed the Seer. They understood death. And how to use it.

They were gone.

CHAPTER VII

MICHAEL FOUND KIM ALONE near sunrise in the massive ballroom. She was looking out of the ornate windows under the waterfall. The moon hung in the sky obscured by haze, giving it a halo. Angels were on his mind.

"Kim," he called out from a good distance away. Still, she jumped—even though he had tried to give her fair warning. "Sorry."

"You say that a lot."

"Hmm," he said. "Sorry."

She rolled her eyes.

"How are you? Bruises healing up all right?" he asked.

"Yeah. I guess so. And look who's Mr. Dad all of a sudden."

Michael considered asking himself what he did to deserve this. And then he thought better of it. "You look like you're deep in thought."

"Yeah. Go figure. The ditz has a brain."

"We missed you earlier. In the library."

"No you didn't."

"Okay," He actually blushed.

It was quiet for a moment, and Michael looked out the window to the valley below. It was beautiful. The grasses were black, but the mind made them green somehow, a mixing of nerve impulses and memory; a sense of what was right and orderly in the world.

"I grew up being taught that the Sons of God were to be banished from the earth," he said. "El gave the earth to the Brotherhood, not the Sons of God. The reason was never important. It was just how it worked."

"Where'd you find that verse? First Book of Crap, chapter one? Hello—Michael: God didn't give the earth to anyone but Mankind. Then Adam and Eve chose to give it away in the Garden, and all of us got to inherit that. It's Sunday School 101, dude."

He couldn't help but be shocked. "Wow, Kim."

"Yeah, I know," she said, turning back to the scene below. "You weren't expecting me to be smart, right?"

"Kim. Is it just an act?"

"Don't start on me, dude. I am who I have to be in order to fit in. But I have a brain. I can figure things out." She looked down, regret written on her face. "I just can't believe I never figured you and James out." She took a breath. "Airel is more delicate than you know. You need to be careful with her. She overthinks everything. I know her. I know her a lot better than you do."

"Okay, truce." He held up his hands.

She smirked. "So. Be careful with my friend, dude." Her eyes took on a sparkle. "And try not to get her killed again, okay?"

Michael shook his head. "Only if everyone will stop cracking death jokes."

"Deal."

"Deal."

"All right, Mr. Recovering Satan-oholic. If that's what you call yourself. Tell me more about where we're at and where we're going. I'll get behind you if you have a good enough plan. Otherwise I'm taking Airel out of here whenever she wakes up, and we're going back to her parents. End of story."

"All right, what do you want to know?"

"You can start by explaining to me just how everything freaking worked, dude. Why Airel? Why James? Why all this death and crap? If the Devil's in the details, then show me the cards he's trying to play."

He sighed. "Okay. My bloodline is connected to the Bloodstone; all of it interacts with them— with her kind. It activates them, makes them change into immortals, but only in their teen years. During adolescence. Otherwise we miss our chance. And it's weird, because the Brotherhood, which is like—I don't know, a secret society—is going around activating the Sons of El, helping them find and access their power, which could destroy us. I mean them. But they do that for one reason only: to destroy El's agents on earth. Does that make sense?"

"Yeah, sure."

"The Brotherhood exists to hunt them down and kill them, period. When they think they've found one they send out pairs, like investigative teams. I was a team with 'James,' who was an Infernal. It was my Brother."

"'It?'"

"Well. I wouldn't call a demon a he or a she. It's a beast. A spiritual manifestation."

"Oh…"

"Kasdeja," he said. "That was the Infernal's actual name."

She looked at him blankly.

"Stanley was paired with the Seer, Stanley was his host. He was like a general. Or a commander in chief. It's complicated. But the Infernals are a little further down the ranks; they're like captains."

"Whatever."

"Hey, you asked." Michael wanted to apologize again, but he figured he'd been doing enough of that to irritate everyone including himself. "Anyway, what would happen is, I would drop in, try to get close and let Stanley's stone do its work. Once I was sure a change was going on we would initiate the job."

Kim had a horrified look on her face.

"I know, but this was normal for me."

"Normal? These are people, and that is twisted. I mean, you killed people. Really killed them. People!"

"Yes, I did. But to me…back then…they were *things*. Not people." *This is not going to end well.*

"I see," she said, then became very quiet. She crossed her arms and locked her gaze on the graying view through the window. The sun was beginning to lighten the night sky and a low mist began to creep out over the grasses of the meadow. "So what's your plan?"

"The plan." He breathed in and out. "I think we need to find Kreios. And I think we need to get out of here."

CHAPTER VIII

MICHAEL WALKED ALONE UNDER the rising sun along the path to the little training shack.

He did not choose this life. At least he didn't know what he was choosing when he made the choice. It was a choice made in ignorance. *Is that fair to say?* Everything he had ever been taught was an opposite. True was actually false. Up was actually down. He really did believe that the Sons of God needed to be exterminated. Once. But now everything had changed.

The day he had left Airel here now haunted his memory.

He remembered what Stanley—his father?—had said to him after he had hitched all the way back, when he had walked in the door of their—home?—in Eagle. "You're late," and that was all. No "Where have you been all this time?" No "I was worried"; nothing. Just an accusation that made no sense. *At least it made sense until I found out that I had really only been gone for about a day... not weeks.* Michael wondered what was so different about this place. *What did Kreios build here... and how? Time ran different, faster—or slower—somehow.*

He remembered his training.

We desire the primal. We take the world by force back and back, back to the Chthonic, back to the pre-created darkness of the underworld and the things that spring forth from it. We then shall be Master. Creator. And it shall be a clean nothingness.

If he had one wish now, it was to unsee what he had seen, to undo what he had done. To unhear the voices that still whispered to him out of the folds of his mind.

What had he done to be so viciously thrust into this Hell? It was real enough; painfully so. Did he dare reach out to El again? Would God hear him again? El whispered truth and wisdom to him once, but twice was too much to ask for. After all he had done…. How could he make atonement for all that?

Where did I go wrong?

It was so simple. All he had done was fall in love with one of the Fallen, one of the Immortals. He messed up, blew his mission, killed the Seer and loosed the Bloodstone from its vessel—and for that every horde clan would be tracking him down ruthlessly in a week's time. Or less.

He groaned.

He touched the scar where Kreios healed him with it—the Bloodstone. He could feel the evil there as it leached into his skin. In the shower earlier he had seen tiny fingers of red branching out from the center of the wound.

"Just finish her and be done with it! Every Brother is going to be after you for saving her and for killing one of your own."

"Shut up!" Michael yelled into the air. The sound echoed through the valley and bounced back to him in waves. He sounded to himself like his father. *Stanley. Not my father.* "Am I…that?"

"Writing in the book is going to get you killed. The Sons of God will stop at nothing. They will hunt you down—and her. It was her destiny to die!"

"Kasdeja, shut up." He named his old friend and Infernal Brother, his newest adversary.

"Traitor." It was a vile whisper.

His gut wrenched. He could feel the Bloodstone as if it were inside him. "I should have never…"

"AIREL, WE'VE GOTTA TALK."

Kim woke me up early. The sun was just peeking up over the horizon. "Whu? Who…"

"Airel, wake up. I need to talk to you." Her voice was urgent.

"Kim," I croaked. "Is that you?" I looked up from my drool-soaked pillow. *Oh, that's nice.* Kim looked a little excited, even for her.

"Are you awake?"

"Yeah. Yeah. Thank God I didn't die again."

"Okay, that's not funny. Especially after the conversation I just had with your beau, Mr. Perfect."

"He's Mr. Napkins, Kim," I said, as if everybody knew that. Clearly I was still half asleep.

"Airel, what are you talking about? *Wake up!"*

"Fine, whoa…okay. What's going on? What are *you* talking about?" The cobwebs of a truncated sleep were still clearing away. I felt stiff and sore all over but I shoved the covers down and sat up. "I think I've got rigor mortis."

"That's not funny!"

"Okay," I chuckled, "I'm sorry, Kimmie. What's up?" I sat up a bit on my elbows and looked at her.

"I'm talking about Michael. I'm worried."

I could see her expression through slitted eyes. "That much is obvious."

"I mean, do you know who he is? What he's capable of?"

"Hey—easy, what's wrong?"

"What's wrong? I'll tell you what's wrong! Michael, your boyfriend, the love of your life, is a creep! A liar." Kim was twisting her hair with a finger. "Do you realize how he thinks about you? I mean, he just told me to my face that you were a 'job to do'; that he was planning on killing you all along. And that's not the only thing. He said…he was talking like we're in some kind of danger here, like we need to get out as quick as possible—"

"Kim, stop. You're acting totally crazy. Besides, I seem to recall I was the one who used that word on myself, first. By the fire? Remember?"

She ignored that. "Crazy?! Forget you, Airel! I'm your best friend! I was kidnapped and almost beaten to death for you! And all you can do is crack death jokes! I thought you were *actually* dead, and now you're back but you're not the same and I'm worried about you because of Michael freaking me out and—" she took a breath "—and *I'm* crazy! Nice. Glad you think so highly of me!"

"Kim! Caaallllllllmness. Pleeeeeeeease." I gave her an example by breathing in deeply and then letting it out slowly.

"Ew," she said. "Brush your teeth before you breathe on me."

"What," I *hoshed* a breath into my cupped hands to check, "do I smell like death or something?"

"Airel!" she growled.

"Well, I'm sorry, Kim! I can tell you're upset; you're doing that talk-a-mile-a-minute thing you do when you're mad. Just breathe," I said. "Talk to me." I could see her try to regain control.

She inhaled long and deep, let it out, and then started in just as fast as before. "He's a killer. He was sent to our school to find you, to become your friend and kill you! He's part of some secret society called the Brotherhood and he has killed other people before! Other girls…and you're next. He thinks 'your kind,' his words—not mine—are just animals or something." She stopped to breathe, looking at me with wide-open eyes.

"Kim, were you not there when we talked about this downstairs? What is wrong with you? Look, I know why he came here, okay, honey? I know what he is and what he was planning. But the key word here is *was.* You forget he tried to save me. He stabbed himself trying to kill the thing that was James." I didn't know that for sure, but it was plausible. "That has to count for something. Don't you think this is just as confusing for him as it is for you and me?"

I breathed. "We're all in a mess, Kim. This whole thing is a mess. We need to stick together; it's the only way we're going to find out what's true. Look. He's still here with us; he hasn't run off or tried to kill us. We're alive. That's all I can think about right now. I'm so tired my brain hurts."

Kim looked at me. "I just love you. That's all. I'm a little scared. I feel like we're all out here alone, lost." She started to cry.

I took her hand. "Hey. Stop that. I love you too, Kim. You're my total BFF, and we'll get through this together. Just let me talk to him and don't get in the middle of it."

"But I am in the middle of it. Whether you like it or not, I am smack dab in the middle of all of this."

"Good point."

"So now what?"

Another good point. I didn't know what to do really. I felt like Kreios was the only being on earth who could answer that question. "I wish Kreios was here. He would know."

"Are we in danger?" She was looking at me like a frightened little girl.

I considered my response. "My heart tells me yes."

"So he's right. We need to jet. Like ASAP."

"Yup," I said.

"Sounds like a plan to me."

"Just one thing: Can you keep yourself from killing Michael for now?"

"I'll be watching him. You can bet on that." Her eyes were dark.

CHAPTER IX

Springdale School, Oregon, present day

STILLNESS.

The building had been a school at one point, the kind found in small towns. The gym also served as the cafeteria and the concert hall; it had a stage on one side. There was a baseball field out back too, maybe four buildings including the maintenance shed.

This one…like a judge he had made determinations, ruling out possibilities until he made his ruling on…this one.

The mostly abandoned buildings had been commandeered as a staging ground for the Portland pod of the Brotherhood. The leader, Trina, had foolishly kept studious records, images on her computer at the bar, and even more good information at her apartment. She wasn't the first woman to find her way into the Brotherhood. The Celts of old had started it. Their women were fierce in battle; plus it was a clever tactical decision.

This clan boasted one thousand three hundred twenty-one members, not counting stragglers and recruits. It was simple to do, really; an emergency meeting called by the Infernal—through Trina's easily hijacked Facebook account—and the pod members gathered like dumb little sheep.

The deputy Infernal called the meeting to order. The hosts of the demon horde sat on folding metal chairs like obedient Nazi party members, ready to salute. They all awaited the Infernal, the master propagandist. Soon she would come out from the shadows, stride to the dais and begin the exhortation.

Kreios could feel his power draining with each second. He would need to make this quick. "This should be quick and easy," Kreios said softly as he quietly bolted the door and drew his sword. He couldn't think about the questions surrounding the disappearance of the Sword of Light. He could think of no reason why it should be lost—he was the last of his bloodline—again, and he should be carrying it. Why was he not? Only El knew. He had simply placed a lid on those questions, purchased a massive hand-made Irish hand-and-a-half sword from Fred Harmon's smith shop in Portland, and got on with it. He was just a workman who needed a tool.

His battle plan was elegantly simple. Kreios threw the breakers, killing all the lights. He stepped in, took to flight in a circle around the room, and cut down each putrid crust of flesh as he moved inward, tightening the noose. By the time those in the middle perceived him it was too late for them.

They had sown the wind.

They would reap the whirlwind—Kreios.

And then it was still.

Dark.

Kreios was soaked in it.

The familiar smell of blood, urine, and bile filled his nostrils; it was strong, pungent. He took in the enshrouded scene in the dark. He cracked a smile, an indulgence. It was the sort of smirk one might suffer to admit upon the countenance after stealing something, getting away with a crime.

Bodies. The detritus was littered everywhere. It was difficult to get a count, but the carnage was nothing if not complete. Kreios stepped over a head and made his way to the door. There was moaning and whimpering. The room hummed with it. Most were in the throes of death and missing limbs, bleeding out. They were soft, untrained. Compared to what Kreios could muster they were but children in the arts of war.

A voice stopped him in his tracks. "You will pay for what you've done. Our Infernal will not stand for this!"

He opened the door, allowing a shaft of orange-yellow brightness from the security light outside to penetrate into the meat grinder of the gym, illuminating a man. "Shame. I missed you," Kreios said.

The man stood twenty feet away holding an H&K Granatpistole; a compact 40mm grenade launcher. It was in his only hand. His other arm was gone. His voice trembled. "Our Infernal will—"

"Your Infernal is already dead. Trina Wilson, the host? She burned to death not long ago."

The man tried to keep a bead on the angel, but the weapon was heavy and his hand shook too much; he was going into shock. Evil laughter. "Why should I believe anything you say, Kreios Son of God—" his mouth clamped shut involuntarily; it was asymmetrical, out of order.

Kreios brought the massive Irish sword around to guard again, point to the ceiling, both hands on the grips. "Your Brother still lives, I see. Turn your weapon on yourself now or I shall finish you myself." He bent at the knees, ready to spring.

"We know of Airel! We will kill her!"

"Filthy Infernal! I should remove your mouth from your face for speaking those words!" Kreios felt his world collapse in on itself a little more at the mention of her name. "She's already dead, fool! One of this clan killed her!" Rage exploded within him once again, but he stalled for more information, circling his prey.

"Maggot, it was *you* and *your kind* that started this; it has *always* been that way. *Your* kind declared war. And now…this last thing you have done…you have unbridled me. *You* have backed me into a cave, provoking me. *I* am now about the business of finishing." Kreios leaned into him. "I will erase—*unmake* all of you." Before he could go further, the ripping sound of a demonic separation broke through the room.

"KREIOS!" a booming guttural voice tore from the jaws of a skinny one-armed beast as it broke free of the man. Both fell to the floor and the winged creature rolled and slipped in the greasiness of rent bodies and limbs.

The man came to his feet, bringing the grenade launcher around, pulling the stock into the crook of his remaining arm. The deputy Infernal was struggling to rise up with only one arm, saying, "We know of The Alexander, Kreios! We know what he has wrought!" Kreios ignored it, focusing instead on the man. Kreios feinted left as the man took his shot.

The grenade launched with a little pop as Kreios spun right. It sailed across the gym and exploded in the opposite corner, shattering brick and tile, sending chunks of flesh into the rancid air and setting fire to a large banner. "Thank you," Kreios said as he closed and took the man in the midsection, thrusting his sword into his abdomen.

Man and beast screamed at the same time. Quickly he brought the sword around and decapitated the man.

The Infernal fell to the ground writhing in pain. The wounds shared between demon and host were only in the mind, but the mind was a powerful thing. Kreios took full advantage of the demon's temporary insanity and hacked its head off. The demon burst into thousands of shards and scattered across the floor. In seconds each piece evaporated into the air leaving nothing but a memory.

Kreios wasn't even breathing hard. He stood and scanned the area. The fire was spreading to the ceiling. From there it would find the hundred-year-old rafters, dry as a tinderbox.

They knew his name. They knew of Airel and the boy Michael, that he had betrayed both the Seer and the Brotherhood. Kreios knew what it all meant but he did not care. *Let him die. He deserved it after all, did he not?*

The blackness of his wounded and grieving heart suited him as he sheathed his sword into its scabbard on his back.

He then burned them. "Just a taste of what is to come." He lit a single match and dropped it onto the hideous floor. Human remains spontaneously combusted, filling the air with burning sulfur and phosphorous. He watched the unholy fire wound the evening sky with red haze.

Airel. And the boy, Michael.

It is a lie. He tried to convince himself that the falseness that had been spoken into the air did not matter, that it was meaningless. But it mattered. He remembered Airel. And Kreios wept as his eyes reflected the light of the consuming blaze.

CHAPTER X

Sawtooth mountains of Idaho, present day

"HEY," I SAID, WALKING toward Michael along the path to the little training shed. He was sitting there on the ground staring into space, the graying clouds of a potential thunderstorm looming over the mountains beyond.

He looked up at me when I spoke. "Hey yourself," he smiled.

I sat down next to him, looking out at the view along with him. "So now we're fake smiling at each other? We've come a long way in no time at all."

"I've got a lot on my mind, that's all." He seemed agitated. "Look, I hate to ruin the mood, but we need to get out of here and quick. The Brotherhood is probably already headed in this direction. They will want to finish the job."

"The job, huh. I know. That's what Kim said you called me."

He sighed. "That was the wrong thing to say."

"Why? Seems like it was honest. What's wrong with that?"

He let out a heavy sigh. "Nothing; I—"

I could tell I was irritating him. Not what I wanted. But I couldn't help myself. "You know what…you have a lot of explaining to do." *How can I defend him to Kim and then stab him in person? Arrgh!*

His eyes took on a deeper look. This time he did not sigh. "I know." He was looking right at me—into me. "I know." He looked back out into the mountains, the forest, the meadow, all of it on parade in front of us, a total gift. "If anyone knows where they stand, it's me. I have a lot of work to do. But it has to start with getting us—you and Kim and me—out of here. Like now."

"Michael, I—"

He grasped my arm and raised his voice a little. "Stop it. Trust me, I know. I know, okay? But you have no idea what kind of danger we're in. If you've ever trusted me, you have to trust me now. You have to let me lead. This is the only time I will ask for your permission in this. I know I don't have much to go on; you don't have much reason—any reason, really—to open yourself to me again. Not after what I did. I know it; I know it; I know it. I don't need you to freaking harp on me about it in order to know it."

"Whoa, dude. Just stop right there."

"Airel, we don't have time for this! Don't you understand that we're in danger right now? Every second we waste talking about this touchy-feely bullcrap is a second taken away from our lives! I'm just concerned about our safety—"

"Oh, *heck* no. Michael, you are crossing a line. I'm not trying to attack you here." But I was, in a way.

He stood and began to pace. He talked with his arms, pleading with me. "Airel, please. I understand already that you're upset with me for what—for everything that I've done. I don't need to talk about it—"

"Well, maybe I do! Did you ever think of that? Huh, traitor?"

Oh, no.

My words cut him deep. I could tell that I would regret them for the rest of my life; it was one of those things I would never forget: how he looked at me then.

"Please…"

Who's the traitor now. I reached out to *She,* but all I could sense was glib satisfaction coming from her. *She* didn't care much for him from the beginning, evidently. *Great. Just great. I can tell how this is going to end.* "I'm sorry, but there is a difference between forgiveness and trust." I was really desperate and confused.

He continued to look at me with those ice blue eyes. If it is true that the eyes are the window to the soul, I had seen his. It was honest, clean, rough and dangerous, and I wanted every bit of it. Regret for my rash words was already heaping itself on my head: hot coals.

"We really don't have *time* for this, okay? I want to leave this place *with* you. At my side. I want to protect you from what is already coming for us. But you have to trust me."

I looked at him, tears already clouding my vision. I shouted at him, "Do you have any idea how difficult that is going to be?! For me?!" I wanted to punch something.

He came closer.

"Keep your distance. I will hurt you." I remembered Kreios's teaching in the little training hut behind us, that mixing my abilities with raw and undiluted emotion, anything other than love, was very dangerous and almost impossible to control.

He simply said, "Go on. I deserve it."

"No! Stay back. Please."

He walked closer, his arms out, ready to enfold me in his embrace, I wanted to feel those arms wrap me up nice and tight, good and strong, smell his skin, feel the soft spikes of his hair as my hands and fingers interwove themselves in it. I wanted to surrender to all of the nameless feelings and potentials that cavorted within

my written-back-together heart. But I felt the danger. It was coming
at me from inside, deep. It was coming at me from outside, near, far.

He came still closer, within an arm's reach.

"Michael!"

His face was inches from my own and I could smell the
masculine cleanness of his breath on my lips.

I did what any girl might have done. I collapsed into a sobbing
mess in the arms of my lover. He was flawed but strong enough.
Filled to the brim with courage, and all of it for me. I let myself go,
let myself cry for a good long time.

The gray clouds overhead then burst, drenching us both to the
bone.

I thought of how horrible the world was to have given a place
for people like Stanley Alexander to live and exist. I thought of
how painfully dear to me my parents were. *Would I ever see them
again?* I thought about Kreios and wondered why he would have
abandoned me, even if he did think I was dead. *Wouldn't he at least
have wanted to bury my body?* Maybe he just couldn't deal with it.
I thought about Kim and how much I loved her, how sorry I was for
how she had been caught up in all this nonsense with me and my
drama. And I thought about Michael.

That's when the storm within started to finally clear up.

We were soaked, our clothes clinging to our bodies.

I pulled back from him. I felt bad; his shirt was covered with
rain, with my tears, slobber, and snot. I wiped my nose with my
shirt front, revealing part of my stomach as I dabbed at my eyes
with it.

He pulled me in close to him again, but not all the way—his
eyes were locked on mine, the puffs of our breathing intermingling
in the misty aftermath of the storm.

He leaned in, but off to one side, brushing the softest, gentlest kiss against my cheek and then pulling back. "Airel," he said, his voice a husky whisper.

CHAPTER XI

THE MORNING SUN AND fresh after-rain smell of the woods
turned to heavy sticky humidity as we walked back to the house. We
had to get going, we had agreed. I looked up through the trees and
saw dark clouds moving in quickly as they do at high elevations. It
could be sunny one moment and snowing the next.

I was still shaking a little from the moment before, but the rain
starting and just shutting off like that, like a faucet, pulled us into
awkwardness. He had pulled away then. I wondered what it was that
held him back from me. Was he scared that I would judge him; that
he was not good enough or something?

"I think we need to cut each other some serious slack," I said.
Michael stepped over a fallen log and I followed.

"Word up, homie."

I laughed. "Who *are* you?"

"Gangsta, girl."

"That's actually kind of true…" I thought of his late antisocial
associations.

"Take it easy," he said. "Remember: slaaaaack."

"Yeah, yeah," I said, giving him a little shove in the back.

He laughed.

How could we go from rain-soaked dream moment to adorkable in two seconds? I shook my head but realized that I liked his dorky side.

We walked on for a bit and I came alongside him as the trail widened.

"So, do you really think we can find Kreios?"

"Sure. Besides, that's what I'm good at. I've tracked guys like him my whole life. Kind of what I do."

"And how are you going to do that?"

"Google," he said. "Get me a network connection and I can find just about anybody pretty quick." He pulled a smartphone from his pocket.

"That thing survived the rain?"

"Oh, yeah. Are you kidding me? I don't mess around with my tools. You could drop this into a bucket of water and it would be fine. I have people."

"Yeah, I don't wanna hear about your people."

"But seriously. This is a mil-spec case around it." He pointed to his phone.

"So you have a 4G pocket protector. You're a nerd."

He just looked at me. "This is serious stuff."

"I can tell, mister. But what are you gonna search for?" I wondered if he knew something that he was not telling me about where Kreios went.

"Murder. Crime. And in big numbers."

I raised my eyebrows.

"Kreios was beyond angry when he left. There was something uncontrolled about him. He wouldn't even look at me." He looked down as he walked. "Personally, I think he's going after the Brotherhood clans, maybe one by one. He'll go down the rank and file until he gets what he wants."

"Which is?" I asked.

"Revenge. I'm betting he'll leave a wake of bodies. We find the bodies, we find him."

"Or at least a trail that might lead to him," I added.

"Yep. I just need to get somewhere that has more bars than…" he checked his phone display, "than zero."

We laughed.

"The Brotherhood has been waiting on word from Stanley, but they won't wait for long. When they don't get it they'll know something's up, maybe even by now, and start moving."

"Hey, I agree. You made your point, okay?" I looked around as we walked, up through the trees and into the troubled sky. It looked like it had a stomachache; it was all churny. "Well…we *should* get going…I'm a little weirded out by this place anyway. With Kreios not here it seems kind of out of sync and wild…or is that just me?"

Michael looked at me. "I know what you mean. It does seem off somehow, as if time is different here."

"Yeah, and have you even once seen a plane fly overhead?"

"Those are called contrails. Those little white trails they leave."

"Nerd alert," I said, pointing to his pocket where he stashed the phone.

He sighed at me. "Are you done?"

"Why? Want me to be?"

"Desperately."

"Then no," I said playfully.

"Okay. If I'm a nerd, then you're a dork." He nudged me with his arm.

It sent tingles through me. *Just like always.* I felt relieved by that, but all my words were stolen as a result.

He went on. "The seasons change by the hour…the weather has

moods."

Thank God he's kept things going. "I feel like it's based on *my* mood. When I get emotional it gets stormy. If I'm, like, normal, it's all sunny. I don't mean to sound self-important, but I've been watching it for a while now."

Michael looked at me. "You need to cheer up. Dork." He smiled at me, just a little too broadly, and I laughed at him and shook my head.

We finally arrived at the house, panting and grinning, still soaked to the bone but at least not dripping wet.

"Kim!" I called out as we walked in.

"She's probably upstairs," Michael said.

"Or in the kitchen," I said.

"Try the kitchen!" Came a voice. It was Kim. We walked toward it and her. We turned the corner to find her standing at the counter by a plate of sandwiches. A duffel bag was at her feet. She turned to us. "'Bout time you two lovebirds showed up," she said. "Kiss yet?"

I blushed.

"Ooooo," she cooed, coming closer to me, "do tell!"

"Stuff it," I said.

"How 'bout *you* stuff it," she said, motioning to the sandwiches. "I made us some lunch. And I'm packed. I've just gotta go powder my nose. You guys try to keep up, okay?" She scampered out, headed upstairs.

MICHAEL WATCHED KIM AS she hurried off. "She's an odd duck," he said. The scar under his shirt burned, and he felt something call to him, back in a hidden place in his mind. It sat there, waiting: *"Come to me—find me and be whole."*

He blinked and looked at Airel, his mind flitting over her Book, over the other books on that shelf. Anxiety filled him.

The Bloodstone.

He wanted Stanley's stone. But, no, he didn't. Why should he? He didn't know what he would do with it. But he had to have it back. No, he didn't. *Where is it? Does Kreios have it? He might have kept it as a sort of talisman.*

The Bloodstone that had owned Stanley Alexander was more powerful than anything Michael had ever known, and it was calling to *him.* He clenched his jaw. He picked up a sandwich.

"SHE *IS* AN ODD duck," I said, "But I love her." I had to confess though, Kim wasn't who was on my mind. It was *She,* and *She* was not helping—it was hard enough without her input, especially when it was so negative. *"He almost died, sure…almost killed you too. Did you ever think he might have planned it all? Made sure he didn't die, made it look like he was saving you, that he cared?"*

I blinked. *Why? Just so he can kill me again?*

"Believe what you want, Airel. Maybe he wants you alive…"

We grabbed a quick bite and then packed up to leave…perhaps forever? I wasn't sure.

MICHAEL LEFT AIREL AFTER lunch so she could go pack.

He ducked into the library, resolved to check on her Book. He told himself that it was out of a desire to protect her, that he wanted to be sure he did all within his power to keep her safe, do whatever it took. But her Book was gone. All that was left was the old quill pen, the inkwell, a few old trinkets standing there on the mantelpiece.

Oh. She already grabbed it. "Impressive," he said to himself, and turned to pack up what little he anticipated he would need for their trip.

I WATCHED MICHAEL TWIRL a set of keys on his finger. He had found them in the kitchen. I thought that was just far too normal to be possible, but I guessed they were for Kale's—Kreios's—black SUV. The kidnapmobile.

We found Kim, and then all three of us walked the massive spaces of the house one last time. The enormous ballroom with the waterfall windows, the midday sun glittering through into the space like God's own disco ball, the impossible kitchen, down the long and dark hallway that Michael and I had been carried, one at a time, when we were first-date-first-time prisoners—only this time back out.

Michael went first, climbing the stairs to the weird door that lay on the forest floor, opening it upward. He let it down slowly, wide open on the pine needle floor of the clearing. Above us yawned a dark portal to the Milky Way, door-shaped, massive ponderosa pines leaning in and up, and stairs leading right up to the edge of it.

It was otherworldly.

"How can it be nighttime?" Kim asked what we were all thinking.

"No clue," I said.

"Let's go," Michael said, gesturing us up the stairs. For a while, we just stood at the threshold of the door in amazement at the night sky turning above us, millions of stars placed precisely in the indigo tapestry.

For me, it was all too familiar. It felt like the very night I had first been taken. I almost wondered aloud if it was. But that would have been too crazy, even for me, after all I had been through. "Let's get going," I said.

"Couldn't have said it better," Michael replied, shutting the door back on itself. It looked like a discarded random wooden door in the dirt, left by some random prospector, utterly forgotten.

The black SUV sat right where it should have been.

Had it ever moved? "That's just weird," I said.

Michael hit the unlock button and began loading our bags in the back.

"What's that one?" I asked, pointing to a long hard case. It looked professional, like it was designed to hold guns or sound equipment.

He looked over at me and his eyes sparkled. "Oh, just some protection. I figured we might need them."

"Them?"

He turned the complicated latches and opened the case. The gleaming blades of three different swords winked at the three of us.

"Holy crap!" Kim said.

The warrior in me smiled at the killer in him as he closed it again, shoving the case farther inside and packing my bag on top.

"Good call, mister." Things felt a little dangerous, a little grown up, and I liked that.

"I guess we'll find out," he said. He loaded Kim's bags and closed the doors.

"Does anybody else just feel weird?" she asked. "I mean, here we are basically stealing this dude's stuff—even his car—I guess because we need it…I just don't know."

"Kim," Michael said, "I guess this is as good a time as any to break it to you."

"Break what?" she and I said in unison.

"That Airel and I are taking you straight home," he said matter-of-factly.

Kim came out of her skin. "What?!"

"I just think it's best—"

"I don't give two eyelashes what you say," she said. "Who do you think you are?"

"Really, Michael," I tried to be the voice of reason.

"No, stop, Airel," Kim said. "This is between me and him. Listen up, Mr. Dad, you've got a lot of nerve talking to me like that. How dare you! You're gonna try to tell me how it's gonna be all of a sudden?"

"Kim, it's just not safe—"

"How 'bout shut up, Michael!" Her red hair swirled in a frenzy around her animated face. "If you think for one second that you have the right to tell me what to do, you're freakin' crazy!"

"Kim," I tried interjecting, "he kinda has a point here…"

"What?!" she was furious. "Airel, how could you? Don't you see what's going on here? He's trying to separate us. I'm trying to guard your back."

"What?" I was shocked. "What for?"

"Seriously? You're joking, right?"

"Aw, Kim! I thought we'd been through this already…"

"Ladies, please…"

"Shut up, Michael!" Kim said. "After all you've done!"

"Enough!" I said. "Kim, you're crossing the line." I glared at her.

She glared back. "Oh, so that's how it's gonna be." She turned to get into the kidnapmobile. Over her shoulder she said, "But guess what, lovebirds! You're stuck with little miss third wheel! Kimmy ain't goin' nowhere but wherever you two are. End of story." She climbed in and slammed the door.

"Michael…" I began.

"I just think she's really scared," he said.

"Uhm," was all I could manage.

"No big," he said, grabbing my hands. "I should know better than to try to control Kim, but it was worth a shot." He opened the passenger side door and he helped me up and in. "I've got you now."

Massive waves of déjà vu swept over me, and I couldn't help but be transported back to our first date, that night, how he looked at me, how we had made such innocent plans, and how they had been so cleanly blasted away. Perhaps this was the perfect opportunity to start over, forget the past, move forward? *He had compared me to Audrey Hepburn…!* A smile crept into my heart and spread across my face as I came back from that moment. "Well, mister…are we going or not?"

He smiled and nodded. Mr. Smooth was here. As he closed my door and walked around to the driver's seat, I couldn't help but imagine all kinds of delicious and fantastic things were destined to happen between us. But maybe that was just the irrational little girl speaking.

CHAPTER XII

Boise, Idaho, present day

"REID HERE," GRETCHEN SAID as she picked up the phone. The voice on the other end belonged to an overworked Boise PD detective, and it didn't take much to be able to tell. Gretchen Reid had been around the block long enough. She listened as the fatigued voice told her about a case he was handing off to her; BPD was basically asking the FBI field office for help. "This is a first," she said.

And it was a first. They usually saw her as a threat; they didn't like to share, much less volunteer brand new cases. She told herself they hated her because she was young, feminine and attractive; that she headed up the local FBI field office. Part of her just loved rattling the local authorities any chance she got. Jurisdictional pissing contests, nine times out of ten, were won by the FBI.

"Okay, secure fax me the docs and I'll have a look. Meanwhile, I'm going to need the case file number at least, via email, so I can start my own file." Gretchen nudged her new assistant and kept talking. "Okay, thanks, Detective Vukovic. Good day." She hung up. Turning, she said, "All right, Harry. BPD is faxing us a new one."

"What is it?"

"Missing persons."

"Cold case?"

"No way. This one hasn't even had time to get lukewarm."

"Really?"

"Yep," she said, bustling through the empty office toward the mailroom. She wore a gray pantsuit and short heels that hit the floor in little staccato cluck-clocks that struck terror into the hearts of every admin drone ever to have the misfortune to do a tour in the Boise Field Office: Special Agent Gretchen Reid's domain and undisputed kingdom.

"Must be important," Harry said, tailing her like a pet. He was the new guy, just learning the ropes.

She didn't respond. "Okay, Harry, when this is done coming in, you make copies for yourself and get the originals straight to my desk. Understand?"

"Yes, ma'am."

"Good, Harry. You'll do well here. Just keep doing as you're told." She looked at him. "It's not too late for you, is it? You didn't have plans for tonight, did you?"

"No, ma'am."

"Good, because I *can* replace you; it's just inconvenient for me right now. I don't want to have to wake up agent-next-in-line and wait for him to drag himself back to the office."

"It's fine, ma'am."

"Good, Harry. I like the way you think; not bad for a rookie. I want to get on this ASAP, like right now." Gretchen moved to take her leave, noting that it was after midnight but deducing that the parents of the missing girl would probably be up fretting anyway, so no worries.

"After that—"

"Get to work on whatever they're giving us via email. Compile. Collate. Fix their screw-ups. Research. And call me if you find any leads," she waggled her phone at him. "I'm going to interview the parents right now."

"Victim's name?"

Gretchen stopped and thought for a moment, looking up and left. "Actually, two. Both Borah High students. Amy? Ariel the mermaid? Something like that. Missing for about 24 hours. Suspect is male, about the same age, driving a late model white 4x4 pickup. I need to talk to the parents; apparently they know about both of these girls."

Harry nodded and turned back to the fax machine and watched as page after page came in.

There was more than the usual swarming of discordant thoughts in Gretchen Reid's head as she walked to her plain brown wrapper government Ford sedan. She had been on the phone with Timothy Darden in Portland about a couple of unusual blips that had come up on the wire. That was the reason she and Harry were working late in the first place.

Both incidents were in the region: one in Portland's Pearl district, a bar fire; the other way out in the sticks somewhere. But that was a fire as well, and both sites were looking like arson; unknown chemical accelerants. And anytime there were ways to link events together, she indulged herself for a while, working like mad to try to prove herself wrong. In the end, if she couldn't do that, she knew she was onto something.

And she was onto something here. It was more than Detective Vukovic's exhausted voice over the phone. It was more than what he had told her; that the dad was just about homicidal himself. All of that was possibly understandable, if all was as it seemed. But she had a feeling…a gut reaction… there was something different about this one. She had to find out, dig deeper, see the root cause with her own eyes.

CHAPTER XIII

Sawtooth mountains of Idaho, present day

"LOOKS LIKE KIM'S OUT cold," I said.

Michael looked over his shoulder. "No kidding," he replied. "Maybe you should get her a drool cup." He smiled wickedly in the dark.

I rolled my eyes. "That's my Kim."

"You think she'll ever forgive me?"

I raised my eyebrows. "Yeah. In time. But she'll fight it, make you think she's still mad at you. Just how she is."

"Good to know." He paused. "What about you?" He cringed as he asked.

"Huh," I said, "Michael, my forgiveness for you was total before I...before I drowned in the water."

"What?" He looked genuinely surprised.

"It wasn't hard to do. I was just looking up at you and saw you for who you are. It's never hard when you can see things— see people for who they actually are." I touched his shoulder. "You're...I mean..." I was stumbling for words. "You're amazing— but I'm a girl, and sometimes what I really believe and what I feel may not be the same. I know. It sounds crazy even to me, but it is what it is."

Michael nodded as if he understood what I was saying. "About all this, the fight, the killing, and you…I want to fix it, to make it better."

I wasn't sure about any of that. Part of him honestly repulsed me when he acted like that. It was like when he just kept apologizing over and over. I just wanted him to get over it. "All right, dude," I said, trying to change the mood a little bit. "Tell me something."

"Uh-oh."

"When did you know?"

"Know what?"

"That I was different; one of the—what do you call them?"

"Them? The Immortals." He paused for a moment, eyes on the spray of light made by the headlights as we drove along the twisty two-lane road. "I was suspicious when you fainted at football practice. On our date, I put it together. The kidnapping too…pretty much gave you away." He smiled.

I kept on. "And when did you decide to not kill me? To betray your father?"

Michael sighed. "I thought I would be able to clear my head when I left. You know, when I disappeared?"

"When Kreios let you go, you mean?"

"Sure. Stanley was furious, though. He got me to tell him where you were…but when he left to go after you…I knew that I couldn't allow him to do what he wanted to do anymore. I had to resist him. On some level I knew that it would require force…I knew that there would be consequences. I just never knew how deep all of it would go."

It was hard to hear him talk about it, but I needed to process.

"Well, I'm…I'm sorry you had to kill him…"

"He was dead already, really." Michael's eyes were narrow, piercing the darkness as it came at us over the hood, smacking the windshield, rushing around the doors and swirling into and through the wheels as we sped on through it. "The Bloodstone took over his mind. It will eat you from the inside out. It's just too much. Too much power."

I reached out and found his hand. He interlaced his fingers with mine and everything felt right again. I could feel my pulse quicken with his heartbeat through his hand, as if we had the same heart.

I thought about asking how many people he had killed before me. But I didn't. I wasn't ready for what he might say, I decided. I didn't know if I would ever be ready to hear that. "This is all so much. I don't understand even what I am. I mean, I have pieces of the puzzle. But so much is dark. Hidden somewhere. I don't know where to look."

"Maybe it's not important right now. I wish I had the answers. But I'm looking for my own answers too." He was quiet for a moment. "Just remember that you're special." He squeezed my hand.

"It's funny. I always wanted that, looking back. Though I never would have admitted it. I would have said to anyone who asked me that I only wanted to be real, normal, find my own way to fit into the world. And now that I *am* special…different…there's no going back. And that's *real* clear. It feels like all I want is whatever I can't have. I just feel so unsafe."

"I know exactly what you mean."

"Really?"

"Totally," he said.

"I guess I can see that. I mean, see how you could. You've been through a lot. We both have. You probably more than me."

He was silent for a moment. "I know sometimes life makes you break your word. No one can say what they will or won't do. Not with any guarantees." He was silent again for a moment. "If I know anything, I know that most of the crap we've been fed is a total lie. You know, like you were talking about."

"Like what? I bet you really want to tell me." I smiled at him. I could tell he was getting riled up, that side of his personality I had seen so briefly on our first date.

"Well…okay, I know you well enough to know that you'll appreciate this. Let's just look at our cultural obsession with fame. That whole *American Idol* thing. I mean, the minute anyone shows the slightest talent for singing, and this is just a little for-instance here, but people always just assume if they have talent that automatically means they should be rich and famous. But that's stupid. There's all this pressure to do the impossible. I mean, whatever happened to singing a song just because you want to express a feeling, tell a story, enjoy doing something well?" He took a breath. "People just don't think. They don't realize what they give up to chase after stupid stuff."

"How about you sing me a song right now, then?"

Michael grimaced.

"No?" I was enjoying making him squirm.

"Um…nope. I just love you. Do you believe me?" He looked at me with those eyes and I melted a little.

"I believe you. I do." I was overwhelmed by my feelings again. "I mean, I tried so hard to turn my back to you, force myself to stop caring about you, but I just can't! And I don't care if…"

"If what?" he asked.

"What is it about you?" I said.

"Airel…"

"Okay, here it is. I don't care if…if in the end it doesn't work out like we planned."

We were both quiet then.

"I mean, I just want to be with you, get to know you more. And if we end up one big fat mess, at least the ride will be fun. You gave up everything you ever knew for me. I mean…that's true love, isn't it?" I asked.

"Sure sounds like it to me." He looked at me and squeezed my hand. He brought it to his lips and softly kissed me there, making me crazy. "Well," he said, "Here's to today."

"And living in the now. Right now. Right?"

"Right," he said.

"Deal. Sun Valley up ahead. Wanna stop?"

"Sure," I said, looking at the clock on the radio and trying to breathe. "Almost midnight."

"I guess we should get a midnight snack or something…but what's open?"

"Maybe a convenience store?"

Michael pulled into a gas station and parked under the lights, shutting the engine off. "Man, that's nice and quiet," he said. He looked at me, mischief suddenly in his eyes. He turned back to Kim and shouted at the top of his lungs, "HEY, KIM!"

She jumped out of her seat, screaming, "Bogo! It's Bogo! Bo…. Wh—where?"

Michael just laughed, slapping his thigh as he got out of the car and stretched.

I shook my head at him. "That's real funny, funny man." I turned to Kim. "Sorry, Kim. You can kill him later."

She wiped the drool from her mouth and got out, mumbling.

AIREL'S HAND FELT GOOD. Michael could feel her heartbeat thrumming away through her fingers. He looked over at her as they browsed for plastic-encased foodstuffs—doughnuts, chips, chocolate, trail mix. Her skin was perfect. Smooth and beautiful. She was talking and the way her mouth moved made him want to stare at her and nothing else.

He looked back to the shelves of junk food.

The dark voice inside whispered again. He couldn't tell what it said but it scared him enough just knowing it was there.

His scar throbbed. He wondered if it would ever heal. Was this his curse? Was he to carry the voice and the scar with him as a payment for his betrayals? He bent his head to stretch his neck, flexing, trying to make the knot between his shoulders go away.

"You wrote in her Book. They will come for you. This will not go unnoticed."

"What are you thinking, Michael?" Airel said.

The sound of her voice made him melt. How did she have this power over him? He didn't know exactly what to do with it, but a part of him desperately craved being wanted, needed, loved. He had never been loved before. "I guess I'm trying to figure out whether I want powdered or chocolate. You know, end-of-the-world-type decisions."

"Hmm," Airel said, "I'd say neither."

"Neither?"

"Yeah, moron," Kim said, walking up to them from the restroom. "Everybody knows she likes the cinnamon ones. Sheesh." And with that she breezed on by, walking outside.

"She gets grouchy when she doesn't sleep," Airel said.

Michael was trying to figure the ins and outs of Airel's friendship with Kim. But all he could do was shake his head and look back at the donut rack. "Well, I like the powdered ones." He grabbed a little pack of pure white doughnuts. "And I guess we'll just *have* to get a packet of cinnamon ones too." He smiled at her. "But what's Kim's fave?"

"Hmm. Going for brownie points, huh?" Airel said. "Actually, she likes the cinnamon ones too."

"Really?"

"Yep. It's actually all that holds our friendship together." She turned to head toward the register. She turned back slightly and said, "I could tell you wanted to know that."

Michael dutifully grabbed another one and followed her to the front of the store. He sighed and felt that dark feeling again; the one that made the pit of his stomach ache and throb. It was the call of the demonic. The scar running through his midsection wanted him, wanted him to do horrible things.

"I love you, Airel," he said in a whisper half to himself as he joined her at the cash register.

"I love you too, Michael, and I like saying it." She took his hand and held it.

Michael blushed a little. "Me too." *Okay, Michael, get ahold of yourself. You need to figure out how to find Kreios. And you'd better have a plan for how you're going to survive him once you find him.*

Shortly all three were back in the black SUV and headed south. To I-84 west. And Boise.

CHAPTER XIV

A HUM.

A low pulse reverberated through my body.

It went in, faded out near to completeness, and then came back stronger and stronger until it felt like it was going to explode me, rattle me to pieces from the inside out.

I opened my eyes and saw it. A monster standing over a sea of blood.

My wrists were broken—both of them. I lifted my hands to inspect the damage but they hung limply from the ends of my arms. Sharp pain shot up my arm and into my heart. What was this? A dream? I could remember something familiar about this place. The jagged black earth, pointed and clustered like shark teeth. Barren woodlands, gaping mountains ringing the valley where I stood. And a smashed cage all around me.

The robed creature was motionless save for one hand, which was lifted up against me; pointing at me.

I stepped forward. The sea of blood flowed in waves and was about to cover my feet. But it wasn't blood—it was thousands, millions of small red stones. Each one pulsing, each one moving in hideous orgiastic rhythm to one another.

Bloodstones.

I could hear them as they moved. They grew in number, sounding like shards of glass clinking together. The red color was striking against the black landscape, vivid. The sky was a gray smudge, crowded with clouds.

Take it, Airel. You are the end.

I heard a familiar voice in my head, but it wasn't *She*. It was another.

Something about the whole scene was different this time. The robed figure was smaller. I walked closer to it, the Bloodstones breaking under my feet like the bodies of enormous insects. "What do you want? Why am I here?"

It continued to stand with hand outstretched.

I walked closer still. With each step of my hiking boot, the wet crunching sound made me want to scream in disgust. It sounded horrible. "There are so many…"

You are the key, Airel. You died and yet live. Now another must die.

I was close now. Its head was down, the hood covering all. I couldn't see what—or who—it was. "Who are you? Key to what?" My hands throbbed with pain, otherwise I would have reached out and pulled back the hood.

The Bloodstone tide was rising; they hummed and pulsed through me louder and louder, rising up to my knees. I couldn't breathe.

The hand came down.

The head was lifted up. Inside was total blackness. No eyes, no face. Just nothing.

"The key!" It said. No. Not *it*; I *knew* this voice. It couldn't be.

Now the pulsing grew exponentially. Bloodstones boiled out

from under the robe of the creature. The tide rose up to my chest. I tried to get free but my hands screamed in protest each time I reached down to push up from the billowing pile.

I looked over my shoulder. The huge valley was filling up with them. Red as blood. Boiling in from everywhere. The sound was deafening. "No. NO!"

It reached up with long white fingers and pulled back the hood. Red hair billowed out. Kim smiled at me with flaming eyes. She grabbed my arm.

"No—*No*—NO!"

I jolted awake.

The seatbelt yanked me back, giving me whiplash. I growled in confusion and rubbed my shoulder where the belt had dug in.

"You okay?" Kim was leaning over me, looking up from the back seat. She had her hand on my arm but I pulled it away, hugging myself.

"Geez! Fine, I was just trying to be nice." She sat back in her seat, folded her arms and pouted. "I'll just sit here in the super comfy plastic straitjacket chair, don't mind me."

"No, no, sorry. I just had a nightmare…" I reached back and took her hand, pulling her forward. "I'm sorry, Kim. I was just scared from the…er, dream."

Michael glanced over at me while driving. I gathered he had been watching the whole thing. "You were saying something about a key in your sleep." He eyed me suspiciously.

"I can't remember," I lied.

"Well, it was freaky. You were mumbling incoherently and then just screamed. Loud."

"Yeah, I just about peed my pants." Kim said with a snort. "Where are we? I think I dozed off too."

My stomach tightened into a little ball. *I wonder if she had the same dream. Nah, she would have told me…unless she can't remember.* I settled back into my seat and pretended to stare out the window.

WE STOPPED AT A truck stop in Mountain Home to eat breakfast. I excused myself for a moment and took a little walk through the chrome section. *Truckers…only a truck stop has a chrome section.* I looked around at all the accessories that could be bought and plastered onto those enormous freight trucks. It was crazy. There were those ubiquitous chromed mudflap girls, a totally skanky silhouette of a woman. I had to move on; I was *so* out of place; it creeped me out.

I walked outside and watched the traffic coming and going on the freeway; the eighteen-wheelers pulling in to gas up. *That's a life lived on the run. I wonder if that's all I have left.* After a few moments to myself and some fresh air, I had begun to feel a little worse.

*What am I doing? This is not the best plan…*letting myself fall even more in love with Michael. *If anything, I should be pulling away, watching, thinking it through, waiting to see if we ever could make it. I should be smart about all this…but I can't help myself.* It was like the undertow at the Oregon coast on those summer vacations when I was just a girl, a dangerous sweeping pull that I couldn't help or control.

Kim found me. "Hey girl."

"Hey. You feeling any better?"

"Yeah," she said. "I'm not homicidal anymore. Sorry about all that."

"Oh, no worries," I said, rolling my eyes. "As long as we have cinnamon mini doughnuts."

She didn't get it. Joke fail. D'oh. D'oh-nut. *Wow, Airel, get a grip.*

"Let's find Michael," we said simultaneously, and then giggled like the best friends we used to be. *That's how it feels. Like it used to be.* I was going to be overwhelmed again soon if things didn't start looking up. I shivered and was getting mad at myself for getting so worked up over a dream. My mood was in the tank now, when only an hour ago I was just enjoying being and talking with Michael.

We walked back to the kidnapmobile and found Michael horking down a huge egg and bacon breakfast sandwich. "Look at this," he said with his mouth full.

"Ew," Kim said.

"Holy Captain Chipmunk Cheeks," I said. "Hungry?"

He swallowed, washing it all down with an enormous swig of soda. "Seriously, look at this," he pointed to his superduperphone.

"Holy Bucket, Batman! How many ounces is that thing?" I asked, pointing at his drink. Kim spat and snorted, a burst of mean-spirited laughter. I leaned over to see the screen of his phone. It was an article about a mass murder in Oregon.

My mood got serious. "You think it's him."

"Yeah," he said.

Kim regained her composure too, and looked on.

"It was a group publicly called *The Brotherhood of the Chameleon*, a secret society. It looks like they had their own campus and everything. The only reason anyone knows anything about them now is because they're all dead. I guess the investigators were looking for some way to connect all of them. Look at that," he said, pointing to a picture of the blackened remains of a big building.

"What's that?" Kim asked.

"Looks like it might have been an old school or something," I said.

"Yep. The whole school was burned to the ground. This says over a hundred people died in the fire."

"Dang; he's not messing around," I said under my breath.

"How do they know it was murder and not just a fire?" Kim asked.

Michael handed out the rest of the contents of the bag of fast food to Kim and me. I unwrapped my own massive breakfast sandwich and scanned the rest of the article as I took a bite. "The burned bodies were in pieces—all over." I smacked my jaws together; I was hungrier than I thought I was.

Kim whistled. "So that's Kreios? Angel gone bad. Man, remind me never to piss him off."

"Well, it *could* be," Michael said.

"So we're heading to Oregon. When do we leave?" I asked. I wanted to find my grandfather as fast as we could. I needed to know what I was supposed to do now, where I was supposed to go; I was lost without Kreios.

"As soon as we gas up. We need to get a few things and buy a couple of Tracphones so you guys can try to call home."

"Where is all this money coming from?" I asked.

"Are you kidding? Kreios has been alive for thousands of years…and I know where to look. I found a stash of cash at the house."

"Now you tell us," Kim broke in. "If I would have known that I would have made you take me to the mall!"

"HELLO?"

When I heard my mom's voice I wanted to feel her arms around me so bad that I thought I would die of sheer anxiety. But all I could do was sigh into the phone and say, "Hey, Mom. It's me."

"Airel?! Airel, is that you?"

"Yeah, mom, it's me."

After a good ten minutes of excited screaming and crying and pleading, Mom and Dad finally calmed down and quit talking over each other. I missed them *so* much. I couldn't remember the last time I had seen them.

I could tell that Mom was just really glad that I was okay and unhurt. But Dad...that was another story. I had never in my life heard his voice sound that way. I guessed he was beyond angry. Maybe a little of it was directed at me, which was only human, but most of it was directed at the nameless and faceless kidnapper. *Well, he was nameless and faceless for now.* I didn't want to see how that particular confrontation would go down.

"Mom, I know. It sounds insane, but really it was all just a misunderstanding."

"Just tell us where you are. We will come and get you."

Then the phone changed hands. "Airel, this is Special Agent Gretchen Reid, FBI. We have geolocated your position and we're on our way to rescue you. Stay put, stay safe, and stay quiet. If your attacker comes back be sure to hide the phone you're using as long as possible. If he tries to move you, just dial 911 until you get a connection—"

"No! No, that's—you don't understand," I tried to explain. "It was just a misunderstanding and I know I've been gone for probably months, but I'm fine. Really, and—"

The phone was quiet. Then the FBI agent said, "Airel, you've only been missing for 36 hours. Are you sure you're okay?"

"Wh—"

"We'll be there in an hour. Maybe sooner if we can get a helo.

Stay put."

I heard some chatter in the background about mental instability. *Oh, no! Oh my gosh!* I hit the cancel button and ended the call; partly out of reflex and partly out of fear. *Oh, NO! Now what have I done?*

"What's wrong?" Michael asked, a look of concern on his face.

I tried to control my breathing. I looked back at Kim, who was passed out again. "Did she make her call yet?"

"No. What's wrong?"

"Dude, just please keep driving. Get us out of here."

I didn't know which way was up. All I knew was my fear. My parents had called the cops on me! *And what was all that about 36 hours? How was that even possible?* I felt massively unsafe; even more so now that my parents were wrapped up in all my problems. *Everything I touch turns to dust,* I thought. How could I even begin to explain this to them? I felt so powerless. *There really is no going back. If I try to get to my parents I would risk their safety. I could never do that to them...*

"Airel, seriously. What is going on?"

"It's nothing," I said, eyes locked dead ahead on the road. "It's just that the cops are after us now."

CHAPTER XV

Arabia, 1233 B.C.

"I AM NOT A child, father!" Eriel was furious. "I hate this place. I want to go to the city of Ke'elei and live my own life."

"Daughter, please be reasonable."

"You talk about reasonable? Talk! Mere talk! You are scared to live your life, father!" Eriel flipped her jet-black hair over her shoulder and huffed at him. "…And I do not want to miss mine because of you."

Kreios winced, saying nothing. Eriel's mind and heart were hard; as yet untested. She viewed the world through the eyes of a girl who had never known real danger or pain.

"Are you going to say something? Anything?"

Kreios sighed and turned a little away from her, dropping his chin. How could he tell her that she reminded him so very much of her mother? His wife…. That fire in the eyes. The beauty she had inherited from her. It hurt him deeply to think about his loss.

"I can see that your mind is made up. You condemn me already. For disobedience."

"Eriel, no—"

"No! I will not burden you further."

"I know you want to make your own life, but, daughter, you are not yet ready."

"I know, father, the Brotherhood will come, they will find us. I have heard it all before, ten thousand times."

"You must not try to find your abilities out in the open or you will—"

"I do not believe it, father! You have a naïve faith in children's stories. Have they ever come? No. They are not real!"

Kreios could feel the anger rise within him. "Daughter, they are real. And they are dangerous. What, do you now reject *all* the teachings of El? Why do you resist the truth?"

"*What* truth?! Yours? You live under the cloud of superstitious fear like a scared human. You are the most powerful angel on earth; yet you cower here in this little hut in isolation! Never going out, never seeing the others, never joining the family at Ke'elei!"

Kreios thundered: "I have very good reasons for staying away from the city."

"You're scared of the Council."

"I fear *NO ONE!*" The walls shook with his fury.

Eriel stepped back partially, momentarily shocked, but she quickly recovered. "And I do not fear *you*. No longer." She turned to go, and then turned back to him. "Why do you bury your power in the ground? El has blessed you with much, but you refuse to use it." She shook her head, stepping back. "I would rather you *were* a member of this Brotherhood of which you always speak. Perhaps then your power would not go unused. You are a waste." She walked out the door, slamming it behind her.

Kreios spoke a curse, grabbing the large wooden table by the edge and throwing it across the room. It splintered, dashing into tiny pieces against the stone wall.

Eriel whipped the door open again, poking her head back inside. "There. See father? You do have some life in you." She grabbed her pack from the hook by the door and left quietly, closing the door softly.

Kreios groaned in pain. He walked to the window to watch his only daughter leave him. Forever. Eriel made her way down the path leading away from their little hut and everything she had ever known. She was fearless. But she lacked wisdom. "She does not yet know the evil that lurks in the world. My God—El, I beg You—protect her."

He knew this was ultimately his fault; it was true. He had sheltered her from everything he could as she grew up. Like any well-intentioned father, he had smothered her. Now he—now both of them—had to pay for his overprotective nature.

Tears filled his eyes. He could not bear to lose the only woman in his life yet again. This time was far different. Far more intense. Far worse. He took his own pack from the hook, filling it with rations. He would fly to the city ahead of her.

Thankful at least that she had never been activated, that she had never made contact with the Brotherhood, that she was almost fully grown into womanhood, nearly untouchable, he thought about what he would do once he reached Ke'elei. What could he do for her now? He thought about it, continuing to pack.

He decided. He would find Yamanu at the city and talk with him about her arrival. She *could*... naturally…seek out her uncle. Kreios would pray fervently for that to happen.

CHAPTER XVI

Springdale School, Oregon, present day

SIDEWAYS RAIN. AGENT RAWLINGS loved it. A desk was a ball and chain; a Ford Crown Vic was a license to freedom, and he loved being in the field. Rain or not, he preferred that his office have wheels.

The wipers were off; he was parked at the curb near Springdale School—what was left of it, anyway. He had memorized the interoffice memo on it; he could recite the summary: "Site of case #RG71****** blah blah blah, unknown accelerants used in suspected arson at Springdale School, Oregon 97019…" He was following a hunch, FBI protocols notwithstanding.

It wasn't procedurally kosher to attempt to anticipate the next move of a person of interest— suspect, that is. He was supposed to tail the black SUV, make reports, coordinate with other agents, and that was all. But Agent Tom Rawlins had an itch to scratch, and her name was Gretchen Reid. He would do anything to beat her to the punch, especially on a case like this, when she was on the warpath. And, boy, could he tell. He could read her like a book. This one wasn't saving all the good parts for the end, either. It was spilling its guts. Her next early promotion was riding all over this one, but if he could bag the perp before her, well…

MICHAEL PULLED INTO THE parking lot of the place he had found on Google Maps using his phone. It was deserted except for a few cars scattered curbside on the street. He drove us up closer to the wreckage so we could have a look.

He shifted into park and we all got out. It was raining sideways, but only lightly; it was more of a mist. It was Springdale, Oregon. Portland wasn't far off, and neither was the Columbia River.

The wind was ripping through the place, making the yellow police tape gyrate wildly all around the burned out buildings. There wasn't much left but portions of some of the walls. The place was giving me the creeps.

"Wow. He really knows how to party," Kim said. She came alongside and together we ducked under the police WARNING tape. Two black birds, ravens I guessed, sat on the jagged top of one wall. They looked down at us as if we were the most interesting prey they had ever seen.

Michael had turned and walked off the other way, saying something to us about splitting up. I watched him walk toward the ruins of a different building.

"Okay," I said. "We'll have a look over here." I felt largely at his mercy, him being the professional. All I could go on were my feelings, whatever I sensed coming at me that had the feel and character of my grandfather. *What little I know of him, anyway.*

I turned and walked ahead. I was struck that we had managed to evade the cops—or the FBI or who knew what other agency—all the way to Oregon. I was thankful that Michael had it all together;

it was easy to follow his lead when he was sure enough for both of us. I wondered what gave him such easy confidence. Was it all that cash? The security that was lining his pockets? What would happen when that ran out? What was his plan then? Did he have a plan B? I didn't know. I shook my head and walked on.

Most of the ruin was wide open to the hanging and smudged sky. What used to be the floor was now a quarry for brick remnants—and, given who had destroyed the place, human remnants turned to ash and blown off—and I hobbled over the roughness of it in my lightweight hikers. It was cold. Off to one side, a solitary doorway led into a dark space. I saw the look on Kim's face as I looked back and forth between it and her. She grunted, shoving her hands into her pockets.

"Hey, at least it'll be shelter from the wind and rain." I pulled the hood of my sweater over my head.

"Go on with your bad self, then. I'll be right here if you need me. This place is way creepy."

I nodded and stepped through the rubble toward the doorway. I could make out little details, but not much. *"Be careful."* She said. I kept picking my way over the rubble.

"So what, Kim's intuition is right?" I asked under my breath. Nothing.

I stopped and closed my eyes, focusing. Better not to take chances, especially given how quiet *She* had been lately. I hoped that if Kreios was still close I could reach out and find him with my mind, possibly break loose and let him know I was here—I was alive. I waited for something but nothing happened. I felt really foolish, like an amateur in a pro world. "Come on. No use being all quiet now," I said quietly. "You're the one that might be able to help me right here, right now. Please."

I stood motionless. Finally *She* stirred again. I plugged my ears, drowning out the sound of the wind and rain. *"One is coming who will guide you on your path. Only be careful."* Classic *She;* I got nothing more.

"You know what, you are impossible." I opened my eyes and walked on, toward the black doorway. "This is stupid. What do we think we're gonna find? A love note, telling us where he's going next? To go kill and destroy?"

Just as I reached the frame of the door, a chill feeling crept into me. I turned back to Kim but she was in the zone, looking off to the horizon, in her own world. I shrugged the feeling off and turned back toward the doorway. I picked my way through crumbled brick and splintered ash. It was dark, and I had to pause to let my eyes adjust. I looked down and around on the floor inside the huge room. It was pitch black; I couldn't see anything beyond the first few feet inside the room.

A flash of bright light, and I was spun around. Something—someone—grabbed and yanked me from the side and I went down hard. I rolled over quickly and managed to get to one knee. Immediately my senses kicked in full force.

Thanks for the warning. Clearly *She* was laying down on the job.

I looked up to see a woman—a girl about my age—standing over me with a short curved sword.

I sprang to my feet. I reacted out of shock, grabbing her outstretched wrist, yanking her off balance. She pitched forward. I forced her to foul her blade against the ground, safely away from my body, and hit her hard as she came into me. I smacked her in the forehead with the heel of my hand, right between the eyes. The girl's head snapped backward, and she twisted back and around and away.

I scrambled to my feet. I knew my opponent would waste no

time in renewing her attack and I wanted to be ready.

"Stop!" The voice was so loud that it reverberated through my body. It was Michael.

The girl was on her feet again, but she stole a glance in his direction. I took the opportunity. I punched her across the jaw and followed that up with my elbow. The sword clanged to the ground and she dropped to her knees.

I snatched it up and stood over her at the ready.

"Stop!" Michael shouted.

I took a step back.

The girl was seething, staring daggers into me.

"Don't move or you will never move again." I growled through my teeth at her. I would not lose my advantage. She would not touch me again.

Kim came running around the corner, sliding to a clumsy stop on a low pile of debris. "Airel, where did you get a sword— ?" She stopped when she saw me standing over the girl. "What—"

"Airel," Michael said, "just calm down. I've got this."

I dared to glance at him for the first time, quickly bringing my eyes right back to my foe. It took a few seconds to register in my mind. *He has a gun. Where did he get a gun?* It was aimed squarely at the girl.

"I've got her. She's not going anywhere. Just step back slowly and—"

"Shut up! Both of you!" The girl spoke with an accent; it sounded Australian, but not quite. "Just listen to me," she said as she slowly came to her feet. "This is a mistake. I'm here to help. Not to kill."

"MY NAME IS ELLIE." She brought one hand to her lip, which was bleeding from where I had split it open. Piercing eyes regarded me from under the hood of her sweater.

I rolled my eyes. "And my name is Airhead Cindy. And all I want is world peace."

She scowled at me.

"You're here to help? Then what *was* all that? Your version of 'hello'?"

Kim moved closer and stood next to Michael. I looked at her a little annoyed, like *whatever happened to 'BFF's got your back, girl?'* But she seemed dazed. *The peanut gallery has no comment. Miracles will never cease.*

Ellie's hand came away from her lip and the blood was gone. "You've got a mean cross. You seem to be able to handle yourself." She pulled her hood back, exposing a bright blue explosion of spiky hair. "Sorry 'bout that. I thought you were someone else." She extended her hand to me.

As if I was going to shake it! I didn't move. I just stared at her and her look-at-me hair.

"Wow!" Kim said. "Great hair; it looks so cool."

"Thanks. Did it myself," Ellie replied, withdrawing her hand.

I sensed in that gesture the vague whiff of missed opportunity, but I stuffed it down inside. "Who are you? What are you doing here?" I was getting angry all over again.

Michael had relaxed his aim, allowing the gun to point downward at the ground. Other than that, he stood motionless, watching the proceedings like a wise man.

"Well?" I said the sword still up and ready to slice.

"As I said before, I'm Ellie. I'm an angel. I've been looking for Kreios. It's obvious that you all know exactly who that is." She eyed me in particular. "I don't have to tell you he's out of control. I'm here to find him and put a leash on him."

I gaped.

"How do you know who we are?" Michael said. He slid the gun into the small of his back and visibly relaxed. I lowered my sword but I was still tense.

"I keep my ear to the ground. I heard about the activation of one of the half-breeds—no offense," Ellie glanced at me with a fake smile, "And the way she fights I'm guessing she…is you. Airel, right?"

"Yeah, she's me," I said, blowing a wisp of hair out of my face.

"And who did you say sent you again?" Michael said.

"El," she said, her tone pat.

"And who did you think we were?" I asked. "I'm still a little confused about that."

"That's okay, dearie. I'll explain it for you," she replied. "It's simple. I thought you were the baddies."

Kim snickered.

"Laugh it up, red," I said to her. "Thanks for getting my back."

"Shut up, Airel," Kim said. "You knew it was stupid to walk in there. I didn't have to tell you that for you to know it."

"Just whatever," I said. *Great. Now I'm the peanut gallery.*

"Look, you guys," Ellie said. "Your little family quarrel is out of hand now. It's not just your problem anymore. We—the Fallen—would like to avoid all-out war." She looked at Michael, then glanced to Kim. "You're Michael?" she asked him, looking back.

"Yes."

"Well, aren't you guys just the motley crew. A half-breed Immortal, an exiled member of the Brotherhood, and…" she turned to Kim. "…and I'm not quite sure what you are. Or why you're here."

Kim looked like a cornered three year old. "You know a lot

about us…" Her face was white and drenched with fear.

"How about you leave her alone," I said, bringing the tip of the blade up again.

"How about you make me," Ellie responded, whipping out a dagger from under her baggy hoodie and turning back to me.

"Ladies, please," Michael said. "We don't have time for this nonsense. Can we just stop insulting each other and try to get on the same page here? Please? If you really want to avoid the fight Kreios is out there trying to pick, we have got to get past this little scuffle quickly."

Ellie's face was beautifully sinister, and I believe if she could have, she would have growled at me.

I scowled back at her, then looked down at her sword in my hand. "Think fast," I said, twirling the grips of the sword around in my hand. I flipped it down and around and tossed it end over end, right at her head.

She caught it directly in front of her face, one-handed by the grips, and smiled at me.

"I've got my own in the car, so don't mess with me," I said.

"You, young lady, need to get over yourself," she said.

"Precisely," She said, and I rolled my eyes and turned away from Ellie, but only slightly. I wasn't sure I could trust her yet.

Michael caught my eye and I knew he felt for me. "We're all looking for Kreios. We should work together." His gaze on me intensified. "Just like Ellie was trying to say."

"It's true," she added, heaping hot coals on me.

"I'm sorry, okay? It takes me a while to make friends." I kicked a brick, making it plop over. "Especially after I get attacked for no reason."

"Airel, please accept my apology. As I said, I didn't know it was you."

I looked Ellie in the eyes. I decided to trust her. *For now.* But she didn't need to know that.

"Ellie," Michael said, "we were hoping to find some clue as to where he's headed."

She laughed. "What! You think he was going to leave you a note or something?"

Kim giggled but turned serious when she looked at me.

"No," Michael said. "I'm a tracker. I don't need much. Just thought maybe you'd found something."

"Not yet. I'm still looking for clues myself. I'm still too far behind, unfortunately, to make much of what I have. I've been going round to suspicious looking sites and taking notes. What happened, how many were killed, stuff like that. Intel."

"Can't God see what's going on and just stop it?" Kim asked.

"Sure. But El has his ways and I don't question. I just do as I'm told." Ellie looked away off to the distance, her eyes illuminating a depth of experience that I knew I lacked. It made me jealous. "I really need to be on my way..."

"The cops are after us," I blurted out.

"Are you bragging?" she asked.

"No. Just...it's probably a good idea for you to clear on out," I said.

The wind was still gusting, but it was drier because the rain wasn't coming down with it.

Michael shook his head. "No. We should work together. We'll be better equipped to find him, and more quickly, if we go after him together."

"You want me to take orders from you, demon boy?" Ellie said.

"No," Michael said, "I just want you to be reasonable."

"That's pretty funny, coming from you. Oh, yes. I know all about your situation. Word gets around. And you talk about being reasonable?"

I wondered how much she *could* know, though. If I were a betting kind of girl, which I am not, but if I were, my money would be on fatal shock whenever she found out about Michael writing in my Book. She just couldn't know about any of that.

"Believe it or not, yeah. I *am* talking about being reasonable," Michael said. "I'm not going to get into all the reasons for or against right now, but it's pretty obvious—even to little demon boy— that this is a time for…I guess you might call it 'consolidation of force.' Even if the truce between us is uneasy."

Ellie spat on the ground and it sizzled in the dust of brick and mortar. Was she convinced? I couldn't tell.

"We need you," Michael continued. "Come on. You can't tell me that you're not at least a little suspicious that this is El, and not a chance meeting." He paused. "Airel needs you too," he said, looking at me, and I wanted to kill him where he stood. "She'll never admit it, but she needs anyone and everyone who can help her find her grandfather."

I gave him the stink eye.

"Yeah, I know exactly what you're talking about," Ellie said. "You can't hear him anymore, can you?" she asked me. "He's a brick wall for me too." She looked around at us with her piercingly beautiful blue eyes. I couldn't help noticing that she was beautiful, *darn it*. Why was I being so competitive, though? Michael wasn't just some fair weather boyfriend. I shoved my hood down off my head onto my shoulders and ran my fingers through my hair, redoing my ponytail.

"What do you say?" Michael asked her.

"Don't try to close the sale too hard," she said.

I looked at her again. There was something about her that drew me in. Part of me wanted to pull her aside and grill her with questions I couldn't even begin to know how to put into words. I wasn't sure if it was her or if it was what she represented. I was so hungry for truth. If she was a conduit to the end of at least some of the mystery in my life, I wanted to grab onto her and not let go. "Okay," I said. "Truce."

I held out my hand to her. "Let's start over. I'm Airel."

Her eyebrows arched in surprise. She walked to me and promptly took my hand and shook it— firmly. "Yeah. You can call me Ellie."

"Nice to meet you."

"Pleasure." She smiled wryly.

I wondered if Ellie was the one *She* had been trying to tell me about.

"Have you been to the other site yet? The one in Portland?" Ellie asked us as she sheathed her sword in the scabbard that was strapped to her back under her hoodie.

"No," Michael said.

"Yeah, well, don't bother. That's why I'm here. There wasn't much there to go on."

Ellie and Michael started trading information, syncing up their brains. I stole a look at Kim as they talked. I caught her eye, but she looked away from me. I would have to talk with her later. Make things right. *Should we have just sent her home?* Maybe Michael had been right about that. I didn't know for sure. I just needed Kreios so badly! *Why are you not here?!*

Ellie and Michael suddenly stopped talking and jerked their heads toward me. "What," I said.

They looked at each other. "We should get going," Michael volunteered. "Talk in the car."

"Agreed," Ellie said.

I couldn't help but feel like I was being taken on some kind of ride that I couldn't get off of. Not at least until it was all over.

The four of us began walking back toward Kreios's SUV. I looked at Michael. "Hey, and just where did you get a gun?"

All he did was give me his trademark crooked smile.

PART SIX
THE PATH

From the Book of the Brotherhood, Volume 3:

...

2. *The Brotherhood seeks above all else to undo El's cursed work. Brothers and Hosts, when you deceive or destroy a Son or Daughter of El, you engage in the pure and right; you restore the Chthonic to all that is; you unmake what has been made...*

CHAPTER I

U.S. Highway 97, Oregon, present day

RAIN. IT PELTED DOWN on the windshield loudly in the darkness, the wiper blades pushing at it in swipes, but the downpour was relentless, making it hard to see the road.

Headlights came and went behind us on the road. Someone else was caught out in this weather too.

I didn't know how Michael could see through this endless rain. I felt like my life was just like that. It was never going to end, and no matter what I did I couldn't see what was coming for me until I was right on top of it: pain and troubles…and they would just keep on coming.

I twisted in my seat and glanced at Ellie and Kim. Kim was right behind me in the very seat that at one time had held me captive. Ellie sat behind Michael, fully absorbed with her phone. *Should I try to start up some kind of conversation? Oh, what to talk about. How does it feel to be a full-blood angel?* I had angelic blood, but I was like one sixteenth or one thirty-second…I wondered if she had more abilities, if she was stronger than I was.

There was an awkward silence pressing down on us and I could feel the tension it produced. Michael looked like he was a little preoccupied with speed, but I tried not to worry about that. Kim was uncharacteristically quiet. The only one who seemed not to notice any of it—or not to care—was Ellie.

I looked at her with interest, studying her. Her skin was smooth, much like mine. There were no blemishes; it had this kind of cleanness to it. Her hair was crazy bright blue, it was even bright in the dark. It was like a neon sign made of cotton candy.

Ellie looked up from her phone to catch me staring at her. I turned back to the front, blushing. *Dang! What are we doing, anyway? What—we trust her just because she's an angel? Or says she is?*

Michael broke in, "So, Ellie…have you been here in the Portland area long?" He sounded like my Dad. *Just yikes.* Dad had that same exact tone when he wanted to break the silence and get me to talk when I didn't feel like it.

Ellie shifted in her seat a little and chuckled. "Yeah, mate. I lived there back when it was just a wide spot in the river. Y'know, a one-horse town that ain't big enough for the two of us."

He laughed quietly, shaking his head.

"But you're not really trying to start a conversation with me, are you?" Ellie was smarter than I gave her credit for, and direct.

"No, I—"

"It's just really awkward…" I tried to interject.

Then Kim blurted out, "All I want to know is where we're going!"

I turned and smiled at her. "Yeah, do we have a plan? A lead—anything?" I looked at Ellie. I had a weird gut feeling about her. *What is it? Jealousy? Would she try something with Michael? She's a pretty hardcore chick…. A threat, though?*

Ellie opened her mouth to say something when Michael cursed

loudly and swerved to the right, jerking the wheel, stomping the brakes. There was a bang and a thud on the driver's side. Then everything came back to the left and I went right, slamming against the door, grunting as my lungs flattened and the seatbelt tensed against me.

"Hold on!" Michael cranked to the right, trying to steer into the skid. The SUV felt like it was going to turn over. I reached out and grabbed the handle on the dash. Kim screamed. I couldn't turn around to see if she was okay. My body went rigid. I could see things flashing by the window in the darkness. The road was coming at us through my side window for a moment as Michael fought for control. The engine roared loudly at full throttle, scaring me. The wheels fought for traction and I could hear bits of gravel ricocheting off the wheel wells as the SUV fishtailed left and right, the back end dipping down low on the shoulder. Then we were back on the road, rocking side to side, coasting, stopping—I hoped.

I realized I was holding my breath and then I let out a deep sigh. "What the— ?" I was both confused and alert.

Michael slowly brought us to a full stop, looking out the windshield wide-eyed.

The car that had been following us was gone, the darkness growing more intense all around us.

One of our headlights remained, dim, casting a cockeyed eerie light through the rain across the double yellow lines on the road in front of us.

"We hit something! Big too, I think—" Michael was panting, trying to talk, his hands shaking, turning around in his seat and looking back through the rear windows, trying to see what it was.

The rain just hammered away at us. I could see steam rising from the engine in the single crooked beam of light. I flashed back to a horror movie, one where some hooded man with a hook stalked dumb blondes and hacked away at the car trying to get in. I shivered and felt my heart pound in my chest.

I looked out my side window and saw movement. I did a double take. *What's out there?* Then I saw it again: something big, all right. Big and dark. I gasped.

Before I could say anything about it, the whole inside of the car lit up from behind. A car? It was on our back bumper—right on top of us. *How...?*

A loudspeaker came on: "THIS IS THE FBI. EXIT THE VEHICLE WITH YOUR HANDS ON YOUR HEAD."

"Go!" Ellie yelled, grabbing Michael by the shoulders and forcing him to face front. "Go Michael, NOW!"

MICHAEL STOMPED THE GAS pedal to the floor. The engine roared like a beast, the tires howled, and the SUV launched forward.

"Those are the cops!" I said.

"The FBI will take care of itself," Ellie said. "DRIVE!"

I could feel it. It was in the space around me, reaching into me and drawing me down, consuming me. And I knew: "The Brotherhood. They're here."

"Oh, God," Kim said in a small voice. She gripped the back of my seat.

Kreios's bashed-up SUV howled into action, rocketing us into the darkness. As I glanced at the speedo, I saw the needle moving briskly past 80 and carrying on from there into the hundreds. I didn't know how Michael could see. The rain.... "Michael?"

He turned toward me. "It's okay..."

I turned back to see the headlights, the FBI. Now red and blue strobes flashed above them. My heart sank as I thought of my parents. *Are they okay?* The FBI had been tailing us the whole time. *The whole time! For how long?* And they weren't stopping now. They were right on our tail.

The SUV shifted into top gear, pushing me back into the seat again. I couldn't bear to look.

CHAPTER II

WHATEVER THAT WAS, IT was pretty big. Did I even see what I think I saw? Rawlins wondered to himself.

Hammer down. Triple digits in the rain.

He wished he had time to call in the pursuit. But he was gonna bag this little teenaged miscreant in just a few, and then he'd call it in. They wouldn't be able to get very far with a damaged vehicle.

He reached over and switched on the lights. There was something magical about those flashing lights. *What a rush.*

MICHAEL WANTED TO EASE Airel's mind a little, but deep down he knew that this might very well be their end, on this road, tonight.

It was wet, water stood on the road in the ruts. He put one set of tires on the double yellow, the high ground, as the speedo swept well past 120. *What did Kreios install under the hood of this thing?*

A train snaked along in the night not far away; he could see its lights stabbing steady through the night in his rearview mirror. It was a peaceful counterpoint to the thrashed chaos in which he felt immersed.

There were no other cars on the road except their relentless tail. It had been hours since he'd seen anything but that stupid pair of headlights. He knew he was right to be suspicious of that car. But he could never have guessed what would happen. *Why hadn't he done something? But what?*

It was hard to see through the windshield, especially with the broken headlight on his side.

"What did we hit?" Kim sounded worried. "Are you sure it wasn't just a deer or something?"

Michael didn't answer her. He didn't want to.

Airel turned and gave Kim a look that said it all anyway. It was a look that said, *we're in big fat trouble, girl.*

Just ahead, the road peaked in a gentle rise that Michael thought could pose problems at this speed if they caught too much air. Plus there was a spray of light blooming up from beyond it: oncoming traffic. He backed off the accelerator and coasted a bit, moving back into his lane.

It got brighter, closer.

He slowed still more, easing the brakes, down to 80.

It was a truck. A big one. Michael could see the orange clearance lights on its roof break just on the other side of the rise, and he braced for the brightness of the headlights that would follow.

Then a massive black shape, as big as a house, fell from the sky on the crest of the hill right in the middle of the road. It hit with such force that the asphalt split and cracked asunder. Shards of rubble ejected from the impact, flying in every direction.

They were too close to avoid it, he could see that; and for the briefest of moments, the strategy of the enemy impressed him.

Brilliant.

The oncoming truck could do even less than Michael could do.

It slammed hard into the massive demonic blackness and shredded itself, smashed from radiator grille to mud flaps. Jackknifed.

Its cargo, coming around and revealed now in the single pitiful headlight—three enormous old growth redwood logs—began to tip and disengage.

There was no time. "Airel, brace!"

There was nowhere to go.

Michael stood on the brakes, but they were carrying too much speed and closing on the wreck too fast.

Weirdly lit by the feeble headlight, large wings opened out and up, then swept powerfully down, launching the demon into the air, leaving them to collide with the four-foot-thick logs now skidding across the road on the remains of the trailer.

Compounding everything, the FBI vehicle—a Crown Victoria—crashed into the back of the SUV. It nosed up under the back bumper, pushing it up and forward.

The SUV, nose down, crashed into the logs head on, crumpling the front. The inertia of the car under and behind pushed the back of the SUV up and over, flipping it, catapulting it over most of the wreckage. The SUV went flying end over end as the FBI car smashed into the logs, which had far more mass and force than the car. They rolled over the entire thing, crushing the car like a pop can.

Michael could see Airel's face as they became airborne. It was the strangest look of determination intermingled with utter peace— as if she saw the situation for what it was, as if she knew all possible outcomes.

But how could that be?

She moved toward him and took him by the arm, ripping his seatbelt off him with her free hand. The vehicle rotated in the air around them, back to front, as she pulled him to her and enwrapped him within her embrace, holding his head tight to her chest as a mother would hold a child, the strength of her arms like a vise, irresistible. Michael returned the gesture, drawing his legs in tight under her, wrapping his arms around her, trying to curl them into a ball.

The power of the crash, the centrifugal forces involved, flung whatever was loose inside the SUV out through the back and front windows. Luggage and debris flew out the back. And as they came around, Michael could feel the force of the rotation pulling him toward the broken windshield.

WHAT AM I DOING, I couldn't help thinking. I knew the front of the SUV's roof structure was going to collapse in on us and kill us when we landed. There was no time to think, no time to wonder if Kim or Ellie would live. There was just Michael. I tore free of my seat belt, pushed out of it, and grabbed Michael, wrapping him up.

His seat belt was like paper in my hands as I ripped it off him. I could feel a new surge of energy pulse through my body as we slammed through the glass of the windshield. It gave way with a loud pop, shattering. There was nothing but open space, water, and glass raining down, up, sideways.

We were flying for a moment as the force of the vehicle propelled us through the air, but it was short lived.

My back made contact with the shoulder of the road, gravel ripping my clothes to ribbons. I could feel immense pressure, hear the shivering noise of massive logs splintering in the distance, the sounds of flying metal, dirt, rocks.

Fire.

Then everything went black.

CHAPTER III

"AIREL—AIREL, GET UP!"

My eyes flickered. I felt massive pain. I was still holding Michael. He was groaning, coming to, trying to get free. Rain was still pelting us in heavy sheets. I raised my head and looked around.

Ellie stood over me with her sword in her hand. Kim sat calmly in the middle of the road. Her knees were drawn up to her chest. She was in shock.

"You need to get up and help me," Ellie said. "We've got a problem." She was covered with scratches, her blue hair emanating its neon glow in the reflected light of the fire.

I released Michael and he rolled off me onto his back, gasping for air.

"Oh my God…ow," He just laid there in the rain at the side of the road, wheezing and groaning. I gave him a quick once-over to see if any of his injuries were serious. I knew I would heal, but him?

"He's fine; get on your feet and get ready." Ellie said with a hint of irritation.

I rolled my eyes but I did as she said. I brushed the rubble from my shirt and arms. My back began to itch like nobody's business, but I figured I was healing and it was a good thing. I turned to Ellie. "Hey," I said, "how much shirt do I have left?" I showed her my back.

"It's sexy. He'll love it. Now, let's go." She turned outward to the darkness, glancing in every direction, looking like a cornered animal.

"Jeez, keep your shirt on. I was just asking," I said.

"You're stronger than I thought you'd be. I thought you would have died after all that."

I shrugged.

She gave me a half-cocked smile. "Get your sword. We have some demons to kill."

"Um? I don't know where the swords went."

"What?"

"They probably got thrown in the wreck. They're in a big case, though…"

She spat on the ground and shook her head. "Great. Just try to stay out of my way and not get yourself done in."

If I was getting anything, it was mad. She was acting like I was a weakling. "You're confusing small with helpless. I'll be fine."

As if in response to my boast, and right out of the fiery wreckage, a large and evil thing approached us. "Okay. That one'll be yours, then," she said.

It used its raven-like wings to shield its appearance from us, probably to protect itself from the flames. Those wings were arrayed with thousands of darkly pearlescent scales that overlapped in patterns, trailing off at their edges to paper thinness, catching in the bursting updrafts of the fire. It stood well over ten feet above my head and its body was as wide as one full lane of road. Its wingspan had to be thirty feet or more.

It came closer still, folding its wings back slightly. I could see long, powerful arms and short, fat legs that were doubled up like those of a frog. Beneath eyes that burned deep red were crooked jagged teeth that dripped nasty blackness. It spoke in voices that fought each other in timing and pitch, like an overdubbed recording, a doubled-up vocal track.

"You will die. Give us the boy immediately and we might… graciously…make it quick and painless."

I felt movement nearer to me and discovered that Michael was limping to my side, joining Ellie and me. I shot him a look of warning. "Stay back," I whispered.

"You," the demon continued its threats, "are right to fear—we can kill you easily."

I wasn't convinced. I took a step toward the huge beast and it actually leaned back a little. *Is it scared of me? Or us? And why?*

Ellie touched my arm.

I looked toward where she motioned. There were three large men slinking out of the darkness. They were brandishing what looked like military hardware; big guns that shot lots of bullets. I looked back to Ellie.

"This is gonna be fun. Mind how you go, girl. They mean business." She left us, stepping toward the three men with her sword raised.

"Ellie…" I knew we were missing one host and three demon Brothers. "We don't know where all of them are yet…"

Ellie turned and glared at me for a split second, then motioned to the massive beast with a nod of her head. "Mind how you go!"

I guessed that meant to be careful killing the sucker. *No time like the present,* I figured, and charged, launching myself at its head.

It was quicker than I thought it would be. One of its wings swept around and clipped me in midair. I bounced off and landed awkwardly, deflected. I stood, clenched my fists and tried to puff my hair out of my face, except it was soaked and stuck to my cheeks.

I looked to Ellie. She was busy with the three men already, stepping into them, her sword swinging around. I watched as she effortlessly took one of their heads off. He went down like a dropped sack of flour and she did a little pirouette move toward her next victim.

I had my own problems, though. I faced my foe and tried to remember my training, such that it was. *Darn you, Kreios, where are you when I need you?* I looked toward Michael. He had found a blunt object for a weapon and had returned to Kim's side. He stood ready, with his feet apart. *Good. He'll keep her safe.*

There was nothing left for me but the mountain of nastiness that was waiting for me. I turned back to my enemy, sizing him—*it*—up. I remembered how Kreios had taught me about using hate or love to fuel and augment my abilities.

Then *She* spoke up. *"Believe in what can be, not only in what is."*

"Ooooooo-kay," I said, completely baffled. But something instinctual was rumbling within me, and before I knew it I had taken off running, directly at the monster.

The thing crouched into a battle stance.

"Feint," She said.

I knew what that was. It was pretending to do one thing while intending to do another in battle. It was a good idea, and might buy me time. I needed to sell it well.

When I was close enough, within a couple of strides of my enemy, I crouched in midstride as if I was going to leap up at the creature's head once more. Instead, I intended to slide beneath and try to get behind it.

It worked.

The thing rose up slightly and cocked one arm as if to backhand me. I dove into the opening this created, sliding right between its legs on wet pavement. I scrambled to my feet, stomping on and grabbing at one of its wings, trying to climb up, maybe get to the head, find a weak spot, a way to wound it. Clearly I needed a weapon. Something besides my bare hands. *Maybe I can poke it in the eye or something.*

I could feel my energy, my will to fight being sapped as the evil of the Brotherhood drained my power, feeding on it. *"Make it short and sweet," She* said.

The demon twisted and turned, shaking its back, trying to throw me off. I had it with one hand by the leading edge of its wing with one hand. My other hand flailed around for a moment, then came to rest on one of the strange flexible iridescent scales that were like feathers. I yanked on the scale as hard as I could, ripping it out, causing the demon to shriek with rage. It gyrated horribly then, and it was all I could do to hold on. Thankfully, no matter what the thing did, it couldn't reach me on its back. I felt stupid though, because all I was doing was just pissing it off.

"Take up the Sword."

A picture flashed into my mind. It was the cliff top. The place I had died. Ellie's words from a few moments ago came sweeping back to me: "Get your sword…" Ellie couldn't have known, but *She* certainly did.

The Sword. *Can I make it appear at will? Is that how it happened on the cliff's edge? Or is there something I'm missing…*

I didn't have time to deliberate. While I was forming a committee to vote on the issue in my head, the demon was working its own solutions to its problem: me.

"Hey!" I heard a voice in the distance.

Michael. I searched for him as the mountain of corrupt flesh heaved beneath me. Michael was trying to get its attention, running toward it with his piece of jagged street-brawl weaponry at the ready. I then realized what was happening: the beast was backing toward the fire. *It's going to try to burn me off! Crap.*

Michael was closer now, running faster. "Hey, reject! Yeah, you!" he swung his weapon as a warning. "I got somethin' for ya. Come get it."

The demon paused.

"Now!"

With as much strength and speed as I could muster, I vaulted up onto the demon's shoulders and clawed as hard as I could, digging deep into the monster's left eyeball, squeezing, wrenching, pulling. Something burst like a water balloon and a jelly-goo gushed in between my fingers.

Ewwwww!

The demon dropped to a crouch and doubled over, howling with pain and rage. I used its motion to get the heck off the ride and run for Michael.

"Michael, get back!" I ran at him gesturing for him to get back, to move away. "This thing's gonna be really angry now!"

The look on his face was priceless. *He's impressed,* was all I could think.

"Come on," I said, "stay back there with Kim! She needs you!" I wheeled back around to face my foe; I didn't have time to see if Michael was going to go for it or not. I was running on something higher than instinct now and I couldn't stop it if I wanted to: the energy drain had stopped for some reason.

I clasped my hands together as if holding the grips of a sword. It could have been a gesture of prayer too, and I was okay with that as well. I closed my eyes and tried to imagine in my mind's eye the Sword of Light, about which I had read so much in my grandfather's book. Listening intently, I kept all my other senses on the alert for my enemy. Ene*mies,* possibly. I exhaled, trying to relax a little, then opened my eyes and looked down.

"Aaaaaaaaand… nothing." *Darn it.* No Sword, not even just a regular sword. Hands still clasped, I eyeballed my monstrous foe as it howled in furious pain and slowly regained its footing.

Then I heard something absolutely crazy. It was *She. "Just pretend."* A flood of images from my childhood flashed into my mind. Playing house with little Kim when we were younger. We were princesses. We dressed up and pretended to be somebody we weren't. But it was real enough for us as kids. It was actually more real to us in our childhood than reality. I saw what *She* might have meant by that.

"Okay," I nodded and held my clasped hands up at the ready, feeling like a moron.

The demon was up again, sitting atop its frog-haunches, shaking its head in pain. It leaned forward onto its fists like a gorilla, roaring at me savagely, whipping its wings and stirring up dirty diesel smoke from the burning wreck.

Then I got a crazy idea of my own. I knelt down on the soaked road in the rain, right in the middle of the destruction, right there with a demon as big as a house in front of me, and began to pray to El. "Just keep Michael away while I do this," I whispered. I paused, willing myself to be still, to be quiet.

And then I asked for it: "Get that stupid ugly thing mad enough to attack me, and I'll split it from neck to loins with the Sword."

Neck to loins? When have I ever said anything like that?

Remaining on my knees, I snapped my eyes open and looked right at the enormous thing I wanted to kill. It was as if I had sounded a battle trumpet; its one good eye instantly locked onto mine, widened in momentary fear and then narrowed into distilled hate.

So it is me you fear.

It roared once more and launched itself right at me.

I stood my ground, on my knees in the rain, my gaze drilling holes in the center of my enemy, my hands clasped around the imaginary grips of my grandfather's Sword, ready to kill.

"This one's for Kreios," I said aloud, summoning as much love for him as I could muster given how very little I really knew about everything.

Exploding out in ribbons of light, appearing with great power in my hands, the Sword lit up the night. It caused the falling rain to bow outward around me, encapsulating me in a globe of stillness, light and energy.

I still didn't know if I was imagining it or if I had actually called up the Sword. *No need to pretend now.*

I looked up. The beast was almost on top of me. The dull bare hatred of its face was now raked aside in the light of the Sword.

I rose to one knee and jabbed upward as forcefully as I could, into the belly of the beast. Its momentum did the rest, the Sword gliding easily, deeply through demonic tissue, gutting it from neck to loins as I stood there, just as I had prayed. Unspeakable amounts of stench filled the air; I was sure I had killed it instantly.

It crashed on the other side of me, skidding to a dead stop right about where Michael and Kim had been. I stood up quickly, standing on tiptoes, looking over the split carcass, searching for them, trying to see if they were safe. "Michael! Kim!"

Their heads popped up just on the other side of the whale-sized beast. "Airel!" Michael said.

"Ohmygosh, are you guys okay?"

Michael laughed. "Du-huuude, wow!"

I blushed. "Where's Ellie?"

She answered for herself, off to one side where I had left her.

"Right here." She came walking up to me. "That's no toy, girl. Just where did you get *that?*" She was pointing to the Sword.

I looked down at it just in time to see it fade and disappear. I didn't look back up at her until after I had spoken, "It belonged to my grandfather." When I did look at her, the expression on her face was indescribable.

The huge demon crackled as the rain soaked into its skin, rendering the thing into little bursts of ash with each impacting raindrop. We just stared.

CHAPTER IV

I WAS ABOUT TO relax—*silly me.*

A trio of smaller demons fell to the earth—zippy little things. They looked like they might have once been children, at least in their faces. Apart from their classically cherubic countenances, though, they bore on every other surface of their bodies what I could only imagine was part of the penalty for their original rebellion in paradise. Sickly looking growths of fungus covered their bodies. Some of the growths were like little tubes, others had caps like mushrooms, others secreted ooze or bursts of black spore clouds.

I gagged. They moved in twitchy jerks; they were fast. They would be dangerous.

I quickly tried to assess the situation from a martial point of view. We stood in three separate units; Michael and Kim together on one side of the road, me on the opposite, Ellie off to one side. Michael was armed only with his street-brawl weapon, what looked like a piece of pipe. Kim, too, looked determined, brandishing a pistol. It could only be the gun Michael had flashed when we first met Ellie at the burned-out school.

As for Ellie, she stood off on one side of the road, forming the point of our little triangle. She was armed with her sword, but she also had slung the shoulder strap of some massive firearm over her shoulder. She had no doubt commandeered it from one of the three men she had just killed. The three fungus demons stood twitching like squirrels in front of her on the opposite side of the road.

Whether it was *She* or the Sword's power still ebbing through me, I knew that the way we were positioned was better than trying to get into one big defensive circle and face outward—at least this way, in order to totally take us out, these three evil little things would have to split up.

But as I scanned the scene, I saw movement in the darkness. "Ellie, behind you!" I shouted.

She wheeled, sword at the ready.

A huge man, over seven feet tall, strode out of the darkness.

Ellie backed off as he approached, joining Michael and Kim, which pissed me off. I couldn't understand why, one, she didn't stand her ground; two, why once again she basically sold me down the river and left me on my own with the strongest enemy; and three, why she had to be close to Michael, *darn that woman, I'm going to hurt her, and frickin' soon.*

"You dat one we come fo'," said the giant man, addressing me with his thick accent and wide, insane-looking eyes. He sounded native African or Caribbean, and his arms were like trees, the massive stubby branches of them his hands and fingers. His skin shone like the blackest bronze in the light of the burning wreckage behind me, which was starting to die out in the unrelenting downpour.

I looked him over, searching for chinks in his armor. A thick red vertical line had soaked through the fabric of his t-shirt, from his clavicle to the buckle of his belt. I figured I had just killed his Brother. I was happy to provide that service. He held a short sword loosely in one hand, a big gun in the other. *"It's H&K and you don't want to taste that medicine,"* **She** said, and I made a note for trivia night, saying a little prayer that I would live to see happy times again. *Will this not end?*

"Don' preten' you don' know what we talkin' 'bout," he said.

"Okay, fine. I'm not pretending," I said, baring my teeth in irritation. "I actually genuinely have no idea why you want to kill me or my friends. But I can promise you this: I can handle your stupid Brother; I can handle you too. So bring it!" I clasped my hands together and took my fighting stance.

For a split second, he looked scared. But then his brows furrowed and he bared his disgusting dirty teeth, yellow protrusions sharpened into points, and growled at me.

I heard a *pop*. A single gunshot. The man winced. *What just happened?* I looked around wildly. *Kim.* She had taken a shot! I looked quickly back to the giant man; he was grasping his left shoulder, applying pressure to his wound, and blood was flowing out in between his fingers. He looked at me, and I wondered if he knew who had just shot him.

Don't go after my Kimmie! I had to distract him.

I gave him my own crazy wide-eyed stare and called him on as if I had been the one that shot him. "That's right! You want more, big fella?" I said. Confusion worked as well as any other weapon, and it seemed to be working on this guy quite well. I advanced on him, hoping the Sword would show up on time again.

MICHAEL LOOKED AT KIM as if she had just slapped her own mom in the face. "Kim, not yet!" he hissed at her in a whisper.

She huffed at him. She looked at Ellie and returned her

disapproving glare.

He gently lowered Kim's hands, pointing the weapon away and down, hiding it from view. He looked past her to the trio of demons.

These were the worst. Very slippery and very fast. They were difficult to defeat because of that, but it wasn't impossible. He just had to outsmart them somehow, get them to walk into a trap. For now, it looked like they were waiting for something, perhaps a signal, from the giant man or something else.

He didn't much care about anything though, as long as Airel was safe. It was murder watching her stand up against and fight these evil things; almost unbearable. But she was obviously tougher than he gave her credit for. She was impressive, for sure. He couldn't help but smirk in admiration and satisfaction as he watched her.

"YOU CANNOT MAKE US die de death," the giant man continued on. "Da Bruddahood is beega dan you. Da Bruddahood can nevah die de death! Wen you kill one, you see, two or tree mo take de place of dat one; we beega dan you! You on ow-ah propahtee! Dis ow-ah place! We de originah rebels, not you!"

He was wagging a finger at me, as if he was going to sit me in a corner to punish me. "Would you just shut up and—" I raised my clasped hands above my head and swung them down together hard at the ground, "—BRING IT!" I was so sick of his stupid monologue.

The Sword became real once again, cutting through asphalt and rock like pie crust, opening up a huge gash in the road, melting the edges of the clean cut like a cauterized wound.

I brought the blade up between me and my enemy, who

outweighed me easily by a factor of three or four. I looked quickly up at him from my crouch, my eyes signaling as much danger as I could bring to bear on him in the awesome light of the Sword.

Just like his counterpart had done, the depths of his eyes betrayed foundations of fear within him.

"Fear is like castles of sand on the shore," She said.

What a stupid way to build a kingdom, I answered.

"Exactly. El is like the sea..."

I nodded and launched myself at my enemy.

MICHAEL WATCHED IN HONEST awe as Airel the warrior woman opened the earth with her Sword. *Sure,* he thought, *maybe that was Kreios's Sword...but she owns it now.* She was shouting at the giant and rushing forward.

As a matter of fact, he thought, *it sure as heck feels like we're being stalled out here.* For what reason, he couldn't figure, though.

Peeling his eyes away from Airel, he stole a glance at the trio of dangerous Anti-Cherubim. They were still waiting, watching; their wings, like those of a swallow, twitching nervously around them.

He looked back to Airel. She was launching herself at the man Sword-first. That's when Ellie poked him in the ribs and pointed back to the demons. He looked back just in time to see them take to flight, fleeing the scene.

Gone.

IT WAS TOO SIMPLE, too quick and too easy with the Sword. Almost unfair. I must have been moving very fast, because the whole world stood still around me as I moved in for the kill.

I didn't make any crafty zig-zaggy moves. I didn't feint, didn't do anything clever. I just went for him like a bullet, the blade of the Sword held parallel to the ground on my right side.

"Mandritto tondo," She said, and I understood her perfectly: forehand strike from right to left, *mandritto;* horizontal strike at the target's three o'clock, *tondo;* and just like that I was the picture of elegance in battle.

The Sword cut clean and easy at the man's undefended waist, and I could feel the *debole* of the blade pierce his skin, gliding through his innards. I could sense in detail when the Sword impacted and sliced cleanly through the bone and cartilage and nerve tissue of his spine; as it finished, exiting out the back of his body. I had cut him in half at the waist in a single fluid motion.

I finished on one knee, both hands grasping the Sword across my body and down to the left. The giant man collapsed in a heap of two great pieces at my right side in bloody spasms. I did not hear him speak another intelligible word.

As quickly as I could, I turned around, looking for the next objective. But all was quiet.

I found Michael as the Sword began to fade and disappear again. His face was marked with worry.

"The other three are gone," he said.

I felt my legs grow weak.

CHAPTER V

IT WAS STILL RAINING.

"Well, that sucked!" It was Kim.

"Hey, are you okay?" I asked. "Sharpshooter?"

She huffed at me, but that was all I got. I decided to let it go for now. I knew we needed to talk, and soon, but it was difficult with all the drama. She probably needed to decompress, being the only one of us who really had no business being entangled with all the supernatural stuff we were dealing with. *Michael was right. We should have taken her home....*

"How about you," Michael asked me, "are you okay?"

"Yeah," I said, looking at him, suddenly aware of my clothing hanging in tatters off my back. I quickly assessed the situation; it wasn't too bad. Lucky I was wearing jeans and a t-shirt under a thick hoodie. The jeans were mostly good. "My hoodie is thrashed, though," I said aloud.

"Let's find the luggage and get you some fresh clothes," he said. "But after that we gotta get outta here." He looked to Ellie. "Can you chill with Kim for a sec while we look for our stuff?"

Ellie nodded.

Then Kim interrupted. "The luggage is mostly right over there," she said, pointing off a little ways into a roadside ditch.

Michael and I froze, looking at her. "How did you know that?" I asked.

"You passed out after you were thrown," she said.

"I did?" Something wasn't right. "Ellie," I said, turning to her, "are you okay?" I was thinking of the minimal injuries she had sustained. I was trying to worm my way into the truth somehow, hoping somebody would let something slip. For sure there was some kind of cover-up going on here, and I wanted to know what was up. "I mean," I exhaled, "you and Kim were still in the truck when it hit. You seem to have fared all right."

"That's what happens when you use your belts," she said, making a buckle-up gesture. She shrugged.

I scowled. *I don't like this. Or you.* And I could have sworn I heard a snarky response from her, but I had no proof. Just nasty echoes in my head. Maybe it was just the look on her face. Then I jumped a little; there was something poking me in the rib.

It was Michael elbowing me. "Let's just get to the luggage and get you dressed."

"Fine," I said. "Lead on, fearless one." I didn't want him behind me, ogling my bra strap or something. But I could tell I had hurt him; he took it wrong. He looked for a second like a whipped dog. *He still feels like a traitor,* I guessed. It was pretty obvious, though he quickly changed his expression to the one we all wear: the mask.

As he walked by me, I tried to lighten the mood. "Too bad it's not raining soap too, cuz you need a shower, my friend."

"It's just smoke," he laughed.

"Dude. Then what's burning?" I made a gagging sound.

Actually, it was the semi truck burning in the middle of the road.

He laughed again and we walked toward the random exploded collection of bags. The sword case was there, which filled me with bittersweetness. I wanted to need what was inside that case. Clearly, however, I did not need to be lugging around a sword, not when I had the Sword of Light in my possession. However that was possible. Unless…unless I was *its* possession.

Is this what it means to grow up? Bitter mixed with sweet all the time? Part of me was indeed the warrior woman, but she was new and strange, unknown. The other part of me was still a scared little girl. Both of them had their bitter elements, their sweetnesses. It was a new way to taste life. I was glad to have Michael at my side. I made a decision right there to show him that I both loved and trusted him completely.

MICHAEL COULDN'T HELP ALLOWING his heart to flutter in her presence. Airel was the pinnacle of the art of the feminine to him. She was graceful, delicate, endowed with rare beauty. That, and she could handle herself admirably. She had this "don't mess with me" quality about her. She was an impossible coexistence of so many conflicting qualities; it boggled his mind. He hoped sincerely to deserve her at some point.

"This is it," he said as they approached the edge of the road above their scattered bags. "Not all of them, but…do you see yours?"

"Yeah," she said, skidding down the loose sandy soil of the embankment. "I see it."

He watched as she unzipped a duffel and started going through it. She pulled out a t-shirt and a wet weather parka.

"Turn around, stud. A lady has got to have some kind of

privacy, even out here in the wild."

Reluctantly and a little heartsick, Michael smiled and turned his back. "Fine. Have it your way. *Be* all proper and junk."

"You know you want it."

"You're making me crazy."

"The *propriety*," she said, teasing.

"Yeah," Michael said, breathing hard. *I gotta walk away.* "Hey. Will you grab me my parka, too?"

"Did I say something?"

"No. It's not your fault I'm completely head over heels for you. That's something I have to deal with."

She said nothing, but he heard her sigh from behind him.

"I'm gonna go check on Kim and Ellie, okay?"

Nothing.

"Airel?" Michael asked, ready to turn around but not actually doing it, fearing for her suddenly nevertheless.

"Michael," There was a long pause. "I love you."

He slumped his shoulders in the rain and sighed, stress visibly melting off. "Airel…"

"Michael, I'm sorry. I'm sorry about what I said earlier. I didn't mean—"

"Airel—"

"— what I said. I mean, I didn't mean for it to come out that way. I mean—"

"Airel!"

She gasped. "What?"

"Can I turn around now?"

"Oh! Well, yeah."

He turned and beheld her: soaked, miserable, tired, dirty, his one and only love. He slid down the incline to her. He wrapped his arms tight around her and pressed her to him, kissing her neck just below her ear. She shuddered, trembling in his arms.

She whispered, "Now you're making *me* crazy."

"Good," he said. He could feel her warm breath on his skin.

She did not push him away. Her lips were very close to his own.

All the buried feelings, all the little recurring deferments of their passions then flared to the surface and broke out into the open, running free. He gently let his hand glide up her back, tangling his fingers in her wet hair. He pulled her slowly closer.

She breathed haltingly; he could tell she held her desire mixed with the fear of the unknown. He drew her still closer, watching as she gave in, as she stood on tiptoes and closed her eyes in anticipation. Her breath came in hot bursts and he drank it in hungrily, savoring the essence of her, all of her, every bit of her.

The rain came down, straight down.

He closed his eyes and pressed his lips to hers. Every nerve ending ignited in the fulfillment of his dearest held passion for Airel, lighting his heart on fire. It made him dizzy. Her lips were so soft, their kiss so warm and tender, this moment so unexpected...

She responded to him, pulling him tighter to her.

Their kiss intensified.

She glided her hands up his arms, caressing his face with her fingertips, sending chills throughout his body as she returned his love, his kiss.

His mind raced, everything crashing to a stop all at once. He had to pull away; it was just overwhelming, too much. Eyes snapping open, he released her. Her gaze pierced him and held him entranced. He didn't want to move. Or even breathe. "Sorry," he finally said.

She blushed, whispering, "I can't say I don't enjoy it." Her eyes flashed at him. "But come on," she said, gasping.

"I know," he said grinning widely with a dash of evil. "I know.

Propriety."

"How dare you," she laughed, punching him lightly in the sternum.

He staggered back, clutching his chest as if she had dealt him a deathblow.

"Very funny," she said, rolling her eyes.

"Come on," he said, offering his hand. "Let's head back, love."

She blushed. After they had regained the road's surface and had walked on a little, she said, "I like that."

Michael felt like his heart was going to cave in. So much ecstasy, so much elation…he was completely hooked. Finally kissing her, his Airel, had been more amazing than he had ever imagined it would be. He was standing on the summit of Everest.

But something was off; something was being held back in reserve. He didn't know what it was or why.

AS THEY APPROACHED, MICHAEL could see from Kim and Ellie's body language that a dispute was in progress.

"How did they find us, anyway?" Kim was glaring at Ellie.

Ellie pointed a finger. "That's the question now, isn't it? How did they find us and how did they find us so fast?"

"I don't know! How about you tell me!" Kim shouted.

"Wow, Kim," Airel said, "you're not acting like your normal fun-loving self."

Kim's head jerked toward Airel. "Well, I'm not in the best of frickin' moods here!"

"Duh."

Kim crouched down and grabbed fistfuls of her own hair and screamed as loud as she could at the ground. It was repellent, like a temper tantrum; the others all leaned back and stared at her in disbelief.

"Kim!" Airel shouted. "Chill!"

Kim looked up at her with bitter tears streaming down her face. "I'm sorry, Airel," she sniffed; her eyes were wild, darting all around. "I just don't know how much more of this I can take…" She collapsed to her knees, sobbing.

Airel knelt at her side and began speaking to her in soothing tones, rubbing her back gently. Kim just leaned into her and sobbed harder.

Ellie looked at Michael. "She needed a good cry, that girl," she said softly, trying to keep Kim from hearing her.

He nodded.

Airel looked up at Michael and then to Ellie, as if trying to read them. She turned back to Kim and kept on rubbing her back.

"We need to get out of Dodge," Michael said quietly to Ellie. They stood slightly apart from Airel and Kim. His arms were crossed and he was looking down.

"You're preaching to the converted, choir boy," she said. "Just as soon as the weak link gets it together," she said lowly, engaging him in what amounted to a tactical conversation.

Michael did nothing, simply waiting on Kim. "You know what all this was about, don't you?"

"What, the tears?" Ellie said.

"No." He looked at her. "No. The chase. The ambush. The fight."

Ellie looked momentarily scared, but she narrowed her eyes. "What? They attacked and we prevailed. What more could there be, besides the bigger question of how they found us, and so quickly?"

"No, that's not it. Besides, it was mostly Airel who did the 'prevailing.'" He paused, looking at her accusatively. "You've never seen that kind before, I take it? The three?"

Ellie was motionless. She stared directly at him, right at his eyes and said nothing.

"The ones with the fungus. The quick ones. They're a different kind. They're like a specialized weapons system. You've heard of Special Forces? Navy SEALS? Marine Force Recon?"

"Sure."

"They're like those, only…" he sighed. "Only pure evil, Ellie. Those kind don't come from just anywhere; and they don't go just anywhere. So I'll ask you again: do you know what it means?"

"More than I can say," she said, looking away.

"It means we've graduated, let's say," he said. "From being in trouble to OMG we're in big fat trouble. Get it?"

"I get a lot more than you think, guv."

"I'm sure you do," he responded harshly, trying to corner her.

"So then," she dodged him, "where are we headed?"

"You play much chess?" he asked.

"What?" she looked back to him.

Michael hadn't stopped looking at her, his arms still crossed across his substantial chest. "I said, do you play much chess." His tone was flat and ominous.

She chuckled. "Can't say that I do."

"The only real defense, one-on-one, against an enemy knight is to close the gap. Get in close. Bring the fight to the enemy. Same thing as in a fist fight. Get in close and you minimize your opponent's power."

"All right, then…" her eyebrows were arched expectantly.

"Like I said. And we have to get the heck outta here." He looked off into the distance, where the train had passed earlier. *If we're lucky, another train will come along soon…*

"You said those fungus-types—"

"Anti-Cherubim."

"Very well; Anti-Cherubim. You said they only come from one place?"

"I said they don't come from just anywhere."

"Right, and we're taking the fight to them because it's safer to do so, I gather."

"Correct."

So where's 'there'?"

"South Africa. For starters. Because they're an Original Kind, very old…and if we don't find them there, we might have to go all the way back to the Tigris and Euphrates, the 'Cradle of Civilization,' in order to find and confront—"

Kim interrupted them. "I need to pee." She was standing up, holding her elbows, looking horrible and miserable. Airel stood by her with a look of concern on her face. Everybody looked at each other as awkward silence fell. "I'll be right back," she said, walking off toward the wreckage.

Most of the fire had burned out or burned down, and the rain had ebbed, the storm system moving on to drench other places. The massive logs remained, however, intact and strewn across the road. Kim rounded the end of one of them and disappeared behind it.

"Be careful!" Airel called after her.

"Yeah, yeah," came the dull reply. "I'll scream if I see a roach or something."

Airel turned back to Michael and Ellie. "Have you two figured out what to do next?"

Ellie wore an undisguised look of surprise on her face. "You're agreeable suddenly."

"Yeah, well, this sucks. I want to get warm and dry." Airel looked directly at Ellie. "I figure you two Type A's would have some orders to bark, that's all."

Michael just shook his head and smiled. "Actually…I was hoping to hop a train." He pointed to the tracks in the distance. "Just gotta make our way across that open range. Maybe a couple of miles across…"

"So we're going for a walk," Airel said.

"Yep," he said.

"Do we all have everything we necd?" Ellie asked. "Because we're not coming back."

In the direction from where Kim had gone came an exclamation of surprise. It sounded like she was in trouble.

Airel looked suddenly very worried. "Kim!" She bolted for her and the other two followed. "Kim! I'm coming, honey!"

Airel skidded around the end of the log to find Kim standing upright, holding a duffel. "Kim! Are you okay?"

"Yeah!" Kim said. "Look! I found my bag."

"Oh, for—" Ellie cursed.

"Kim! You scared me," Airel said. "I thought you were in trouble."

"Nope!" Kim said. "No roaches. But I got my stuff!" she patted the loosely packed duffel now strapped across her shoulder.

"Good," said Michael. "All is right with the world."

Michael glanced at the smashed FBI car. He sighed. "Well, I guess we'd better get moving. We've got more than one kind of pursuer after us."

CHAPTER VI

THE FOUR WALKED BACK up the road, right up the double-yellow, back the way they had come when he was driving. Michael wanted to leave as little obvious sign of their continued existence as possible. After about half a mile, at a curve in the road and a sign marked U.S. 97, they got off and took to the wilderness.

There were no fences. Just wide open high desert. The Cascades skimmed the moisture out of everything that came in off the Pacific, leaving their eastern side barren and dry, save for the fingers of green that crowded the draws—mountain streams and rivers that ran east, counter to the mighty Columbia.

That's where they were headed: the Columbia River. A massive body of water, irresistible in its rush to the sea, wide, deep, cold, fast, dangerous. Right along the river, freight trains more than two hundred cars long snaked along, headed upriver and inland, probably every couple of hours as far as Michael knew. Once again, he had to rely on gut instinct to get by. He tried as hard as he could not to let his training affect him too much—all the demonic files of experience that now, he was thankful, could be turned inward against themselves, against all their past masters, in self-destruction.

He caught himself more and more crying out in his heart and mind to El. It was crazy. But somehow crazy made good sense, in a way unexplainable with words.

Michael walked close to Airel. He wanted to be near her, to see her face in the darkness, to feel her presence.

Ellie broke the silence. "You all should know…I was able to get my phone up and running. I texted a friend back there. He can get us a plane, but he's at least a day away and we can't meet him near any big cities."

Kim looked confused. "Plane?"

"Yeah. You've packed your passports, I hope? My bloke can get us in but we'll need a safe place to land; we've gotta figure that out on the fly. He'll meet us in Arlington and we can take off from the Muni there."

Kim laughed aloud but then choked it off, wide eyed. "I don't have a passport." She looked to Michael with a panicked look on her face.

"All the more reason to meet him away from an international airport, then. If we're to hop a jet to South Africa, we'll need to fly under the radar. Quite literally, maybe."

"I don't have a passport," Kim said again.

"Michael," Airel said. "What's all this about South Africa?"

"Yeah, I meant to tell you." He took a moment to try to explain to them why they had to go, why they had to take the fight to the enemy. "It may be safest for everyone involved." He looked at Airel with a pained expression, hoping he wouldn't have to say out loud that he was concerned for her family back home. Among a great many other things.

"I don't want to go," Kim said, trudging along. "I don't want to go to Africa. Why Africa anyway?"

"Kim, I hate to say this…but you're going to have to just trust me." Michael said.

She huffed at him and stopped, forcing the rest of the group to stop as well. She crossed her arms.

"Kim..." Michael said.

"No. Just shut up! I'm sick of this. I'm sick of running, sick of walking, sick of crashing and freaking burning. I'm cold and wet. I need sleep and food—"

"Kim," he interrupted, "we all feel the same. Trust me, I know what you need; we all need it. That's why we're headed this way. To the next train." He gestured to the river, the freeway, the train tracks in the distance. "Things could be worse."

Kim gawked at him. "How?!"

"You could be dead, for one. Kim, this is our last remaining option. And it's a good one, considering where it'll lead us. And you know what, you're alive and you're with friends." He pointed to her bag. "And you found your stuff."

"Are you serious? We're hopping a train like a bunch of hobos?"

"Yep," he smiled at her and then looked up at a clear sky, the Milky Way easily visible in the dark firmament from horizon to horizon. "Plus, it's not raining, Kim. Come on." He turned and began to walk. "We need to keep moving."

Ellie followed him. Ariel stayed, her body half turned to go, half turned to Kim, a look of concern on her face. "I know it's hard, Kim, but you've gotta keep going. I promise," Airel said, touching her arm, "soon we'll grab a hotel or something and try to rest. But for now we've got to keep going if we don't want to..."

"What, die?" Kim asked.

Airel paused. "I guess so."

Kim looked at her, the expression on her face complicated. "This sucks."

Airel nodded and gently pulled on her to get her moving. They trailed along behind the other two.

Michael called back to them, "It's not far now. Maybe another fifteen minutes of walking."

"Oh, yeah. Well, I'm timing you, dude," Kim said.

THEY SAT UNDER A bridge in the darkness, waiting near the tracks for the next train.

Ariel hugged herself and asked, "How far is—what, Arlington—from here?"

Ellie said, "Probably no more than fifty miles."

"Yeah, and we're jumping a freight train to get there?" Airel continued.

"Don't worry," Michael said, "they move pretty slowly on this slog of the railroad; it's a long climb and they're really heavy."

Kim sat looking dazed, her hands playing in the dirt. The eastern horizon was threatening the sunrise.

"It had better hurry up and get here quick," Airel said, "if we're going to get away with jumping on board without being seen."

Michael exhaled, releasing stress.

"Michael, are we safe now?" Airel asked.

He looked at her, considering things. "Yes."

She studied his eyes. "You're lying."

"Airel—"

"No, I get it. It's sweet. But you don't need to protect me. I can take care of myself. If I haven't proven that yet, I don't know what I have to do."

He wagged his head a little in acquiescence. "True. I guess

you're right." He looked back at her. "Sorry. I'm not trying to keep anything from you. I want you to know that. I'm just thinking about lots of stuff, trying to process it all. I feel responsible for you. All of you."

"Rubbish," Ellie said. "You're not responsible for me, demon boy."

"Stop calling him that," Airel said. "Don't call him that ever again."

"Have we got a problem, girlie?" Ellie said, bristling.

"You bet your pointy blue hair we do," Airel said calmly, "if you keep insulting Michael like that."

Ellie rolled her eyes and had a mocking expression that said, *Wow, you're ridiculous.*

Airel moved very quickly, getting past Michael, who was seated between them, in an instant. There was a little plume of dust. In a crouch, she grabbed Ellie's shirt front and pulled her face to within inches of her own. "Look," Airel said, "I have had it with you, angel girl. Cut it out. You know what I mean, too." Airel held her there for a moment.

Ellie turned her head away slowly, looking down and smirking. "Relax, doll. I don't want your man-boy. Though he is pretty cute."

Airel jerked her around. "Shut up."

"No, really," Ellie said, looking back up, meeting Airel's threatening gaze. "I don't. I'll give you your little show of force this time round, girlie. But don't do it again, 'kay?" Ellie placed an index finger on Airel's forehead. "Or you'll regret it." She pushed her lightly away.

Airel stood fully to her feet, releasing her. "Whatever." She looked down the tracks and saw a faint light. "Hey…"

Michael stood up and joined her, looking down the tracks to the west. "Looks like our ride's finally here." His arm rested comfortably at her hip. He pulled her to him as they waited in the darkness under the bridge.

CHAPTER VII

"HERE IT COMES!" MICHAEL shouted.

My pulse was racing, but I tried to control myself, tamp the energy down a bit. The sunrise was on the way, but it was still dark enough for us to get away with what we were about to do.

The only one I worried about was Kim. I worried more and more about her, actually. *What is going on with her? Poor thing. She just needs some rest.* I hoped she'd be able to hop the train. Though it was only moving by us at about fifteen miles per hour, given how bad Kim was looking I didn't give her much chance to actually make the jump when it came time.

And the time had come.

"This is it!" Michael shouted at us. "Get ready! Look for a handhold or a step or something!" Everyone tensed, bent at the knees beside the rumbling tracks as the train went by. We were all dialed in on the boxcar, "bird-dogging it," as my dad would have said. *I miss him,* I thought, but immediately pushed the thought from my mind.

As it approached we all started jogging, pacing it.

To my shock, Kim took off first. At a dead sprint, she leapt up to the train car with ease, duffel and all. Standing on a foothold, she wrapped one arm through a handle and extended her free arm toward a small door, unlatching it, sliding it open and then jumping inside.

She poked her head back out. "Come on, guys! Let's go!"

I guessed she was motivated for that hotel room I had promised.

Ellie was next. She moved gracefully, like an athlete. Before I knew it she was up and inside with Kim. Michael, running along beside me, said, "Ladies first."

"Oh, you would," I grumbled. I dashed for it and quickly made it inside as well. It was easier than I thought. I forced my way back to the door, nudging Ellie and Kim to one side, away, looking for Michael.

He was already up on the step and swinging in. He met me full force, crashing into me, wrapping me up and knocking me back inside the boxcar. "Oops," he said, kissing me lightly on the lips. "Glad to see you here," he said.

I blushed in spite of myself, and I could feel the heat crawl up my neck and spread across my cheeks. *How can he do that to me, every time?* I thought back to when we kissed on the side of the road and my skin prickled. *He was so...so yummy.*

"Hey! Where'd everybody go?" I called out to Kim and Ellie.

IT MADE ME NERVOUS to think of waiting around in some small town knowing that the Brotherhood would be looking for us—and their missing Brothers—with bloodlust crazing their every action. Plus the FBI would be on high alert after the crash.

The train car was filled with large crates and boxes. We had to squeeze around some of them as we moved through it, looking for a place where we could all spread out a little, maybe even rest. The best we could find was a little nook created by the irregular shapes of different crates all shoved together.

A little patch of rough wood plank floor was ours, perhaps four feet by four feet. It was dry and we were all alive and well. I figured we would stay reasonably warm by staying close, using body heat. That it was dry made the most difference. Four of us crammed into the space, each one taking a corner. Michael sat at a right angle to me, our legs entwined together, his strong arm pressed firmly against my shoulder.

Ellie and Kim sat as far from us and each other as the small space would allow. It struck me then that Ellie was a misfit in our little bunch. I wondered why she stuck with us…or allowed us to stick with her…besides the obvious, anyway; that we were all looking for Kreios to some degree or another. She was definitely a square peg in a round hole. She didn't like any of us; that much was true. I did have to wonder, though, how far I could go with her; how much I could trust her.

She seemed bothered, I thought, whenever she talked to Kim. And since Kim was my best friend, I was a little put out. I wanted to say, *Hey, jerk face. Watch your mouth around my friend.*

"So," Michael began, "I'm still trying to wrap my head around how the Brotherhood nailed us." The crate he leaned against was all marked up with stenciled Chinese lettering. "I thought it was just… odd, you know…how they could find us with such accuracy. And speed."

"And that was only one small group, too," Ellie said. "El forbid we should have run into many more, much less an entire clan."

"Yeah," I said. I had wanted to get to the bottom of that question from the moment the Brotherhood had shown up. "How did they find us?" I looked at the faces of my companions. Nobody knew anything as far as I could tell.

"Did anyone else think their strategy was a little off?" Michael asked.

"Like how?" Kim asked.

"I mean, they didn't…they didn't…" Michael dug around for words. "They weren't shoot-to-kill types. Does that make sense? I mean, it's almost like they were just there to waste our time, to harass us."

"Yeah, but why would they do that?" I asked.

It was dead quiet for a second.

"It's almost like they were there to see what we were made of," Michael said. "I know if I wanted to size up my enemy…I mean, if it was my call, and I was up against an enemy force that was, say, an unknown quantity…that I would send scouts. Or a strongman, like they did. Throw something serious at the situation and see what happens."

"Well, we saw what happened," I said.

"Yeah," Kim said, "Airel kicked butt."

"Yeah," Michael said. "And I'm just wondering if we won back there. Really. Or not."

"I don't get it," Kim said.

"I do," I said. "I guess what you're asking is, 'what did we gain back there'—right?"

"Yeah," Michael said. "I mean, I know what it appears to be on the surface. We won, they lost. We took them out." He paused. "But I'm unsettled about it…when it's all said and done."

"What do you mean?" I asked.

Michael looked into my eyes. "I don't like that those three Anti-Cherubs showed up." He gestured to Ellie. "I talked about that with her. Those kind only show up when there's something really big going on." He paused again. "I have a few ideas…but I don't like what I'm thinking."

Ellie's eyes flashed and she shook her head. "Don't look at me."

Michael sighed. "We're a walking target. Somehow." He looked at me. "They could have been tracking us using your phone."

"How about your phone, captain connected?" I was annoyed. "Or even the ice queen here," I said, motioning to Ellie's vivid blue spikes.

"It doesn't matter how they found us," Michael said, "because in the end they found us and saw what we can do." He looked at me again. "They saw that you have the Sword—"

Ellie burst in, "How do you know— ?"

He stopped. All was quiet, save for the swaying, creaking motion of the train, the clack of the trucks as they rolled over the gaps in the rails. "— And they saw," he continued, his gaze moving from Ellie back to me, "that you know how to use it. That you can call it up at will."

He looked at Ellie and Kim. "What other reason would they have to allow us to do away with one of their strongmen and his Brother? Those two were enormous; very strong. And then, what did the Anti-Cherubs do? They just took off!"

I looked down, the seriousness of the situation becoming clearer.

"And you can bet that intelligence has already been shared with the powers that be," he said. "Fact is, we were played back there."

"What for?" Ellie said. "That is the question you should be asking."

"What do you mean?" I asked, growing irritated again.

"You're asking how they found us so quickly, right? How they found us, how they managed to draw us into all-out battle? And then how those three managed to get away from us, all the while making us believe we should be happy about it?"

"Dude," I said, "we kicked butt. The end."

Ellie rolled her eyes at me, waving me off.

"What!" I asked. "And by the way, Ellie, thanks so much for all your help back there. Thanks for taking the easy targets and leaving the strongman to me," I said. "I really appreciate your faith in my skill as a warrior."

She glowered at me.

"If I didn't know better," I said, "I'd think you had your own agenda."

"Careful," Ellie said.

"Maybe it's you," I said. "Maybe you led them right to us. Maybe you led them to us and then shoved me to the front of the battle lines so that I would be forced to reveal that I carry the Sword. Or maybe you just wanted to see me killed!"

She just looked at me.

"Hey, relax," Michael said. "It doesn't matter. All we can do now is stay off the phones and keep out of sight."

"Ha," I said, "That's pretty lame." A thought crept into my mind: *Is he the one who tipped them off? Is he still working with the Brotherhood, and I'm too blind to see it?* Before I said it, I wished I could retract it, unsay it, but I couldn't stop myself: "Maybe it was you. After all, you used to be one of them."

I stung him. Bad. *Airel, you stupid, stupid girl!*

I looked away from him, and my eyes landed on Ellie's face. I detected the faintest smirk of satisfaction. I was shocked at that, at her, at myself. *Who's the betrayer now?* I looked to Kim, but she wouldn't look at me. She just stared down at the planks in awkward embarrassment. *Great. I'm such a fool.* I couldn't look at him; I was too ashamed of myself.

"I don't like this," Kim said. "We *were* careful. We've been using cash and stuff. They just came out of nowhere, as if they knew the exact road we were taking and what we were driving. Plus, there was that cop."

It was uncomfortably quiet.

All our questions remained unanswered. All I had done was add more confusion to the pot and stirred it in real good.

"Maybe it's you," Michael's voice broke in. I looked up, feeling wild and dizzy suddenly. He was looking at Ellie. "I mean, we don't know you at all. We don't know if you are who you say you are." His jaw was set, his eyes narrowed. He would not look at me. "Do we?"

"Listen, you," she said to him, "I'm not the one who stood by idling with a stick in my hand back there. I was busy cutting demon-possessed flesh to ribbons."

"I was looking after Kim!" he said.

"So you say! But who called it on, eh? What brought them to us, *right* to us?"

"HEY," I said, placing a hand on each of them, "Cut it out, you guys."

Out of the corner of my eye, I saw Michael shoot me a glare. I clamped my mouth shut and my gut balled up into a knot.

Kim stood up abruptly. "I can't take this anymore," she said, whimpering. "You guys are too much for me." She struggled, wriggling into and through the small space between the crates and the wall of the car. "I'm gonna go find my own spot now." She was gone before any of us could say a word.

Ellie stood. "Me too. You two lovebirds enjoy." She was gone too, following in Kim's wake.

I assumed they would each find their own little patch of boxcar paradise, quite apart from each other, given all the love I felt bouncing off the walls. The problem was, Michael and I were finally alone. And I couldn't bring myself to look at him.

KIM FOUND A DARK little hole in the crates and crawled inside it, drawing her knees to her chest and wrapping her arms around her legs. She could feel something in her head nagging her mind. It felt like an inner ear itch but deeper, something she could never hope to get to, something from which she could never even hope to find relief.

She rubbed her temples.

She reached into her sweater pocket and touched the Bloodstone. It was warm; it calmed her mind to know that it was there; it scratched the itch a little. Who would have thought such a pretty little thing could mean so much? Who would have thought that moment on the cliff, when she lay in the dirt, afraid, angels and demons having finished their scuffling death-contest all around her, that she could find such a salve for her ragged mind?

It was a drug. Really. One she now needed. One she would guard like a jealous lover.

"She knows. You need to keep it from her; she wants to use it against you..." The whisper in her head grew louder as the itch vanished.

Am I losing my mind? she thought. She didn't think so, but this...the voices, the needs, the hunger to know...it had to stop. It was overpowering.

"It's not you, Kim, but her..."

Who? Airel?

"No. Ellie. Or maybe...maybe it's Michael and Ellie together..."

Yes...Michael. He was the real enemy. He had bewitched everyone with his handsome face and charm.

"Just what is he trying to do?"

"I don't know," Kim heard her own voice sounding off from far away, muffled, wrapped in heavy cloth. *What's going on here?* She wanted to run, to leap from the train, run as fast as she could, away. Just away. Away from this train, away from this mess, away from them, away from life.

Kim hugged herself. *It's cold in here, and it smells funny.*

What were they even doing anymore? Kim didn't know. Maybe she didn't want to know.

MICHAEL REACHED OUT GENTLY and brushed her cheek with his fingertips. "Airel." She looked up at him, the pain in her eyes completely naked. "Thank you for looking at me again."

"I'm so sorry…"

"No need," he said, smiling compassionately. "You can never push me away."

"But—"

"Shh," he said. "Just stop. I know you didn't mean it. I know." He pulled her closer and kissed her cheek, perilously close to her lips, igniting their passions again. "Love," he said.

"Oh, Michael." A tear escaped.

He caught it with his lips, kissing it away. "You can never do anything that will make me turn away from you."

There were more tears as she began to break. She reached out and pulled him to her, and they locked in embrace, holding each other fiercely, she weeping, he stroking her hair.

"I *am* sorry," she said.

"Shh."

She pulled away and looked deep into his eyes, searching

them. He could see understanding in her eyes, as if she really knew him and loved him for who he was. Twisting around with her back to his chest, she pulled his arms around her and leaned into him, laying her head against his shoulder. He cradled her with his body, wrapping his arms tight around her small frame. After a while, the smooth rocking motion of the train lulled them to sleep.

CHAPTER VIII

I OPENED MY EYES.

I was not on the train.

It was bright; the sun was high, its heat making my skin tingle.

I stood with the Sword of Light blazing like a star in my right hand.

To my left: Ellie, sword drawn, clothed in form-fitting robes. Across part of her neck and face there glowed a design that was reminiscent of a tattoo, only like nothing the world had ever seen. I bristled at her presence. *Who does she think she is, anyway?*

On my right stood Kreios. I turned to him and he smiled at me. *Grandfather.* My heart nearly burst with the release: all my nagging questions had found their end; it was like the final resolving chord of a symphony. I wanted to throw myself at him as those lovely tones echoed through the deepest crevices of my mind, wrap my arms around his massive frame and cry—I had found him!

Or had I?

His face, the expression he wore, told me there was something else happening. Something I had not yet seen.

We three stood on a low rise before a wide grassy meadow.

Beyond it were broken buildings, the ruins of a once great city. These ruins were roundabout; hemming us in. The jagged and wrecked skyline loomed over the meadow on all sides. It reminded me of a place I had only ever seen in pictures. *Is that where we are? Central Park? Is this—or was it—New York City?*

I hate nightmares. I thought I had moved past them. It seemed like they were just getting worse now.

Then *She* showed up, but instead of bursting into my consciousness and pelting me with words, *She* just painted picture after picture, flooding my mind with images, provoking memories, thoughts, emotions. I saw my life. I saw it for what it was: a mix of illness and emotion, danger and decision. Now everything I had ever known—or thought I believed in—was on its head. I saw a scared little girl in a dress and ribbons hiding behind a curtain, pulling the strings of a marionette below her. When I looked down I saw who the marionette was. It was me. And it was clear I was playing with something I didn't know how to operate.

What am I supposed to do with my newly long life?

"Will it be a gift to you, or a curse?" *She* asked.

That depends, I answered my pet voice-in-the-head, considering everything for a long while. Finally I thought, *How are Michael and I going to be together when I will outlive him? What about a normal life…a family, one day…kids…and a dumb barking dog?*

She posited something then, as if I was a student in her class. I saw a picture of the word NORMAL with a gigantic question mark superimposed on it, and the more I looked at the question mark the harder it was to see the word beneath it.

Oh, I get it. What's normal even mean?

She smiled. It was something felt rather than seen; it was weird.

I looked around me at the wreckage of the city. From time to time, pieces of rotten skyscrapers finally succumbed and fell from immense heights to the overgrown streets below, raising huge clouds of dust, the crashing more shocking because of the eerie silence in which it sounded. *Am I supposed to be some sort of hero…saving people from burning buildings?*

I turned to Kreios and looked at him, realizing he was only a figment of my own dream. "Will we ever find you?" I asked him. "And if we do…will you have the answers?"

"So much doubt and worry," She said, scolding me.

My mind would not stop working. Even in my own dreams, I could have no rest. *It's all just so complicated!*

"How do you really feel about Michael?" She asked.

I love him…

"Do tigers change their stripes?"

Cryptic. And freaking typical. *Will I ever get past what he was; that's what you're asking me. Might he do it again? How can I know? I understand why he told the lie.*

"Still…it was a lie."

My stomach ached. I hugged myself and became aware of Michael's arms around me. We were on the train and he was behind, holding me with strong, warm arms. *Isn't this enough?*

"Is it?"

In so many ways, it was not. *This is my demon…my curse.*

"Find the answer on your own. It's the only way you can really know the truth. And let her guide you."

She was gone. I was back in the city, on the little hillock again. Ellie was to my left, only she didn't appear to be sinister anymore. I wondered about her, but she didn't regard me. Kreios was to my right again, staring directly ahead as well.

"Be ready, Airel." Kreios whispered.

I snapped my eyes back to the front.

There was something in the meadow besides grass and

wildflowers. Something dark, something that flowed like a spill. Some noxious fume. I could just pick out details as the tentacles of the thing flowed into the open field and slowly took it over and choked the life out of it, like a gnarled hand grasping to kill.

Anti-Cherubs. Infernals. Brothers. Demons. Still others; an approaching army. The Horde was a single organism that breathed from the same cursed lungs, moving as onc.

At their front, in the midst of their leading edge, stood a figure cloaked in red, the pure white of its robe peeking out in the breeze that lifted and teased the cloak. A long black staff was in its hand. The Seer had miraculously returned from his overthrow. *Or perhaps a new one has been found.*

Three angelic warriors stood against the very essence of evil; all that could be mustered. I pretended to be calm but fear rose up inside me. I tried to count but then realized there were far too many thousands for me to continue.

A stone's throw away, the leader—the Seer—stopped, holding up a pasty white hand in signification to the Horde. They then halted in their many hundreds of thousands, perhaps millions. It was a sick greeting, like the kiss of Judas. The hand reached to the hem of the hood and pulled it back.

It was Michael.

I wasn't surprised. I was saddened instead.

His eyes were ablaze, darker and redder than his cloak. Set in the unfailing beauty of his face, it gave him such a striking appearance of beauty intermingled with hateful ugliness that I desperately wanted to look away; it was more than I could bear. His face was a mockery of beauty, a thin shell only just masking truly baleful intent.

Michael…what have you done? Where have you gone? What's become of you?

He stepped forward.

I met him stride for stride.

In a conference of commanders before the battle, we met alone on the field. The Bloodstone hung profanely on a tether around his neck. His pasty skin seeped black gooey beads of sweat. His voice was not his own, it was hideous and spastic. "What do you want from me?"

"Nothing, Michael. Nothing."

He spat prodigiously on the ground and wiped his mouth with the back of his hand. "You never believed in me, did you? You doubted. You worried. Well…" his eyes wandered over my body, giving me the creeps. "Now you have what you've always wanted. You were right. It was self-fulfilling prophecy. Besides…" his expression was wicked, "I am The Alexander…"

My heart was frantic; I didn't know what that meant. *Did I make him this way?* Was he forced back to the Brotherhood because I couldn't get past my own fears? Because I had never trusted him?

"Maybe if you would have been able to use more self-control…" His tone was mocking.

A flicker of movement. Ellie stepped forward. To my horror, she began advancing toward Michael.

"Ellie… Ellie, no!"

She looked back over her shoulder and I saw her smirk, but she kept going. Michael held out his hand to her and she took it. At his side, she turned to face me. Her eyes were deep red as well.

I was crying now, searching for Kreios, but he was gone. He had abandoned me again. They had all left me; I was here alone with all this evil. Why was I always the one who got discarded, the forgotten one, the one who never quite fit in?

I wanted to throw up.

Instead I threw down the Sword and fell to my knees. "Michael!

I will not fight you...I love you!" I choked on my own sobs as Ellie threw her head back and laughed.

Michael's face was then stripped, stark fear running rampant across his features. "Stand up, Airel, pick up your Sword!" His voice was harsh.

But I couldn't. The whole earth had stopped. It was the end of all things, and nothing mattered anymore. The sky began to tear like a veil, rolling back like a scroll...

CHAPTER IX

Arabia, 1233 B.C.

"I AM NO LONGER a little girl, father!" Eriel stood with fists clenched, eyes on fire.

Kreios stood before her, his heart burdened with worry and doubt. He was not in a mood to argue after having flown to the city in pursuit of his daughter. He feared another explosion of conflict between his people and the Brotherhood; he wondered what his beloved daughter might do, how she might instigate something deadly—intentional or not.

He gestured to her, palms out, a sign of peace. "Calm yourself, daughter. Please."

She growled at him in exasperation and then looked to her uncle Yam.

Yamanu's body language implied he wanted no part of the argument. He sat in a low chair smoking his pipe with a benevolent amused look on his face.

Kreios hated that calm-in-the-storm demeanor, especially when Yamanu wore it so smugly.

"Daughter—"

Eriel spoke through clenched teeth. "Can you not see that I will be free of you, one way or another?"

"You are my daughter and you will obey me. Still."

"Father!"

"We leave in the morning." Kreios turned to go.

She cursed at him, stopping him. "I am not going with you. You can do nothing to force my will any longer."

Kreios could feel his control slipping, anger and desperation rising. "Daughter, Eriel, I warn you…"

"Uriel, not Eriel! I am not asking, father. This is my decision and it is done. It is only one letter, but it is my letter."

Kreios sighed. It was no use trying to get her to see reason. No matter what she called herself, she would always be his little Eriel.

"And let me tell you how it will be from now on, father. I will stay with Uncle. He will keep me safe. Is not that what you want above all else? For me to be safe? Or do you *really* wish to control my every decision until the day I die?"

Kreios looked to Yamanu for some sign of assistance. Yamanu simply nodded, exhaling a luxurious ring of smoke. It drifted downward to the stone floor and dissipated outward, like ripples on a still pond.

That is what it was like to have a daughter, he decided. She dropped into the stillness of his life like a stone, disturbing everything. And now the ripples were beginning to fade; she was pulling away. He had to confess to himself that he mourned for the situation, for himself. He had not prepared. He was not ready. "Daughter, please…"

She ignored his feeble and late attempt at tenderness. "I will speak of it no more."

He looked up from the floor to behold her beautiful strong-willed face. Her eyes pierced him. There were echoes of her mother in there. It all came crashing back on him—the great Decision that could never be unmade, to dwell under the sun in the land of the fallen. He had sown the wind, truly. And now he would continue to reap what he had sown.

"Goodbye, father." She turned and left.

And he let her go, finally. He sighed in defeat and resignation. She had all the answers she now wanted. She would need more though, he knew.

"All in due time," Yamanu said. "That is the way of it here. Under the sun."

Kreios nodded. She was just as stubborn as her mother had been. He smiled in spite of the grief that was crashing down upon him. He loved her for that stubbornness, and so much more. He didn't want to let her go yet.

He breathed these words in her wake: "I love you, Eriel. Never forget who you are."

CHAPTER X

Banes, Cuba, present day

A COOL LIGHT BREEZE wafted across the dirt road, bringing with it the smell of salt water and wet grass. Kreios stood still, waiting. It was just past two in the morning and the moon hung full and fat, casting its shimmering light on the sea, long shadows over the landscape.

Beyond the single lane dirt road, a cemetery was stamped into the earth, bordered by a stone wall in disrepair. From the shaggy grass fed by ancient corpses jutted sun-bleached marble crosses, stone angels with broken wings outspread over raised tombs, mausoleums, overgrown paupers' markers. A huge Ceiba tree, its roots climbing like smooth gray buttresses to the massive trunk, stood in the midst of the graves. Its leaves were like six-fingered hands drooping low, shading the dead from the moonlight.

A scuffling noise.

Kreios turned eyes and ears to the lone tree, watching, waiting.

A man stole in amongst the graves in the darkness past a large Spanish stone cross. He looked around him suspiciously as he moved toward a mausoleum, a house for the dead.

Kreios prayed the information he had gained from the dying lips of his last kill was solid; that he would find what he sought and that this foolish idiot would lead him directly to it beneath the graveyard.

Kreios ran swiftly to within a few yards of the man, crouching behind a white stone plinth, moving without sound.

The man heaved his weight against a massive bronze placard on the side of the tomb. Silently it sunk in and back, swinging in to one side, revealing a secret passageway. The man ducked inside and began to turn around and close the heavy door.

Kreios leaped to the entrance so fast that the man didn't have time to react. Kreios withdrew his fist from the man's smashed face, grabbed him by the shirt collar, and roughly pulled him outside, dashing his brains against the foot of a statue of Gabriel.

He was dead.

Kreios quickly regarded the statue's likeness. "Not bad," he whispered under his breath. "…though Gabe is not that feminine." He drew his sword and ducked inside the doorway. Rough-hewn timber steps led down into the wormy darkness.

He felt at once the drain of energy that sounded the general alarm, making his presence known to the demons and men below.

Kreios prayed there was no escape route and charged down the stairs.

Ripping and tearing filled his ears as he descended: the Brotherhood were splitting, separating into demons and men. No two-for-one deal tonight.

He reached the bottom of the stairs and turned to the right, meeting a female directly. He blithely lifted an elbow, knocked her to the ground and then severed her head from her body.

"Kreios!" Something called out his name.

Kreios did not care for conversation, however. He hacked his way deeper into the torch-lit underground chamber, dodging fists and sword thrusts and stepping over freshly made corpses. Black stench hung chokingly in the air as demon after demon expired, leaving behind heavy wet ash.

Kreios gritted his teeth through it, suddenly taking a blindside strike across the jaw from a clawed hand. He recovered quickly, vengeance fueling angelic adrenaline, sword held vertically to one side with two hands, point up.

A thin and wiry creature stood before him sneering. "You have no idea what you have started! This is just the begi—"

Kreios's blade stabbed quickly up through the soft tissue of the thing's throat, piercing deep into its rotted brain.

"Shut it," Kreios said.

The eyes rolled dead in their sockets, arms twitching as Kreios withdrew his blade and pushed the body aside.

"Who is next!"

CHAPTER XI

By the Columbia River, present day

MICHAEL TRIED TO SLEEP.

But the act of holding Airel in his arms kept his mind racing, his heart slamming in his chest. He pulled her closer and felt her shiver as she warmed to the heat of his body. Soon she was in deep sleep, her breathing coming in soft rhythmic waves.

He closed his eyes at last, the gentle rocking of the train making his eyes heavy.

Ancient memories—none of them his own—twisted into his thoughts. It was a curse, the Brotherhood, and its influence could never be undone. When a man bonded with his Brother, especially in Michael's case, and mostly because of his father, an impartation took place. The burdens were his to bear the rest of his life. He could smell the blood-soaked earth of each battle, feel each wound as the host of the Bloodstone died and was reborn. His link to the line of demons that had gone before came with memories that did not end.

Michael was yet very young, but in his heart and mind he was ancient and full of regret. This he had never wanted, and it had never, of course, been disclosed to him. It wasn't in the brochure. But it was truer than truth itself. It was tearing him apart.

The train rocked back and forth like a boat on choppy seas. It was both soothing and uncomfortable to him. He could relate though. It was like the train wanted to go somewhere on its own, but was trapped on the tracks. With every lurch it tried to jump the rails. His life was on rails, too, he felt. He thought of El, considered praying to Him again, maybe asking Him for answers.

"Sacrilege."

He opened his eyes.

Ellie was there, standing over them, staring at him. Watching. He stifled a spasm; she had scared him.

"We need to talk." It was her voice, but inside his head. Her lips weren't moving.

"Are you reading my mind?" he whispered.

She rolled her eyes. *"No, you plonker. Come on."* Ellie gestured for him to come along with her.

"Oh," Michael whispered. "Just a sec." He felt like he had been caught with his hand in the cookie jar or something, like a kid on his way to the principal's office. As deftly as he could manage, he wriggled out from his interwoven reclined position with Airel. She stirred a little and then rolled away, nuzzling into the crook of her arm and settling in, snoring softly.

"Well?" Ellie was already headed somewhere, moving through the maze of crates and beckoning him to follow. *"We've got things to discuss, just you and me."*

Michael dutifully followed, though as he began to wake up and become more aware, more present, he began to ask more questions of himself. He wondered if perhaps he might have been smarter to have grabbed at least one sword back there at the site of the crash. He felt capricious for having trusted Kim with his late father's old

1911 Colt .45—the pistol he usually carried concealed but had failed to retrieve from her after the scuffle and the chaos back there at the scene of their stupendous wreck. After she had shot that big dude. He had to admit, it was possible that he was walking himself right to the gates of the slaughterhouse, with Ellie the butcher.

Ellie had climbed an ascending stack of crates like stairs, crawled along the tops for a bit and then lithely dropped down inside what Michael assumed was an empty space in the midst of them. He followed.

When he got to the edge of the crate tops, he looked down to see Ellie, hands on hips, looking up at him. "Come on down, demon boy. I won't bite. Hard."

Michael athletically dropped down inside a squared-off area that had been created by the irregular stacking of randomly shaped and sized crates, the "floor" an uneven surface of the tops of crates and boxes below.

"It's sharing time, Michael." Ellie's eyes flashed. It was clear she meant business. "If we're to work as one, be players on the same team…you've got to tell me a few more juicy bits." She ran one hand through her hair, gathering it away from her eyes.

Her skin was flawless, smooth, glowing and radiating light. She was beautiful and he couldn't help but acknowledge that to himself. "Okay…"

"I promise to reciprocate, don't worry."

Her eyes were the bluest he had ever seen. "What do you want to know? Can't you just read my mind or something?"

"No. I can project when I want. I don't have the gift of reading."

Michael sighed and sat down, resting his back against a corner. "I really should be sleeping." He looked up at her. She still stood over him. "And so should you, Ellie."

"No rest for the wicked," she said.

"Oh, for crying out loud, would you sit? You don't have to act like that."

"Like what?" She stayed put.

"Like you're running the whole show here." He looked up at her, his eyes widening a little in mockery.

"What—and you are?"

He sighed again, exasperated.

"You're doing a bang-up job, mate. Really, you are. Allowing the police to track us, starting a high speed chase that nearly killed all of us, being too stupid to know how and why the Brotherhood know where and when we're doing just what and how often. Yeah. Brilliant grasp of command in the field."

He was shocked. All he could say was, "What? You told me to outrun the cops! What would you have done?"

"Do you do *everything* you're told?" Her tone was mocking, but he noticed a hit of teasing in it.

"Would you sit," he spat, gesturing to the opposite corner of their little conference room.

"Fine," she said, and sat.

He couldn't help but think she was quite graceful. Beauty graced her movements; it was simply obvious.

She gave him a look. "Talk, then!"

He sighed a third time. "All right, where do I start?"

She removed her dagger from its concealed sheath and began polishing it with the hem of her sweater. "At the top. Tell me what you know of the Brotherhood; anything that might help us with the royal mess we are about to get into."

He was irritated at the implied threat of the drawn weapon, intentional or not. "Okay, then. My name is Michael Alexander—"

She cursed and jumped to her feet, dagger at the ready. "Say that again," she hissed at him.

"What?"

"Your name, captain courageous."

"Alexander."

Another curse. "Son of Stanley Alexander?"

"Yeah, why?"

She cursed again and sheathed the dagger, sitting down, pressing her palms to her temples. She muttered under her breath. "This is worse than I thought it was."

Michael eyed her warily.

"Mate...you're not just any demon boy. You're the son of the Seer."

He shrugged and smirked at her as if to say, *Duh.* "Um, I know?"

"You're *The Alexander.*"

"Yes. Michael Alexander."

Suddenly fierce again, she said, "Tell me more."

He told her as much as he could, wanting to get to the bottom of things with her. He told her how things worked in the Brotherhood, the rank structures, the way the training became manifest in the bond between man and Brother, the way he was a walking demonic encyclopedia. Something within him pulled at his heart, telling him to share as much as possible with her. He thought she would share as well in turn, and he needed to know what she knew if they were to have any hope for any kind of future that did not involve fighting for their lives at every turn.

But it's not just that, he thought as he went over the account of the cliff-top fight involving James, his Brother; how he had murdered his own father. It was more than that. They had become entangled in something for which there were *permanent* consequences. Decisions made now, he knew deep in his soul, would reverberate throughout eternity. And he wanted more than anything to make the right ones from now on.

"Wait," she said. "You killed your own father?"

"Yes," he said, "I did."

"How did you—how did you come to such a decision?"

Michael exhaled quickly, a brief laugh. "He was going to kill Airel. I killed him first."

She looked genuinely shocked. "I hadn't heard that part."

"That's what you get for trusting the rumor mill," he said, not really wanting to know how those machinations worked. Plus, truth be told, he had gone as far as he was willing to go until she gave him something in return for what he had let spill. He was genuinely fearful of telling anyone about how he had written Airel back to life. He wasn't sure yet just how that story was going to end, what it would mean for her, for him.

"Still though," she said, searching for something to say. "I suppose…I suppose I should say I'm sorry."

"Ellie, I'm done. Completely finished with the Brotherhood. My motivations have turned one-eighty and I'm trying to start over."

"What drew you in? If I may ask?"

"What, into the Brotherhood?"

She nodded.

"I dunno. How much choice does the son of the Seer really have?"

She nodded again.

"I mostly inherited everything, I guess. I never wanted that life. Not really, if I had truly known. It was just all I ever knew. I grew up into it blind. But Airel…changed it all." His eyes began to fill and he wiped at them with his palms. "She means so much to me. I would do anything for her. I hope I've proven that by now—even if it means giving myself up."

"To the Brotherhood? No." Ellie's eyes flashed. "You cannot do that, Michael. That means eternal…the Second Death."

Thoughts of fire and water flitted through his head, the symbology of the ages running roughshod over his ragged and tortured mind. *"Water is the first death. All flesh is required to pass through it one way or another. Fire is the second death. All spirit will be refined by it now or be tortured in it for eternity after the end of this age. "* He shook his head, trying to clear the echoes from his mind.

"Do you ever hear voices in your head?" he asked her.

"Depends," she said.

"Yeah, well, I get 'em. Trouble is, it's hard to know in my case just who's talking to me."

"Right. Who to trust," she said. "Well, demon—I mean… Michael, you can trust me."

"I hope to God you're right," he said.

"I think you're actually telling the truth. I can tell you've been searching Him out. Talking to Him."

He blushed.

"Nothing to be ashamed of, mate. Not at all. It's hard, at first, to know how to listen back, though. No worries. You'll figure it out. That's what life is."

"I will not let them get to her. Not again."

She nodded in understanding.

"So," he said, "you're here on orders? Why don't you know all this stuff? You're an angel; haven't you been fighting the Brotherhood forever?"

She sighed. "I know enough." Ellie's face became blank, lost in thought. "I've got to tell you…I think the best, most effective thing we can do is take the fight to them."

"You know I'm on the same page. We keep running; we'll be on the run forever."

"Yeah, but it's more than that. We're in their territory. Everywhere under the sun, it's theirs. At least until the end of all things. Until then we have to carefully pick our battles."

He knew all that, he had heard the shouts of rage in his mind, the radical violence of the blindly self-centered whining for revolution, for glory, for the subjugation of all things right and good, and he knew what it was all about. It was utter emptiness. "I'm listening," he said.

"I don't quite know how to say this…"

He looked at her carefully. "Go ahead."

She appeared to have a sudden change of mind. "Okay. I'm here for Airel."

He thought back to the battle, how Ellie had pulled back from Airel, even how he had done the same, though he still wasn't sure why. "You're here for her? What, to…take her?" He allowed his face to show total confusion. *What's she not saying?*

"No. I mean I'm not just here to protect her or to keep her alive. Guardian angel stuff."

"Okay, so what then?"

"I'm to guide her in the path she must take. And on some level, she should know that already. But she's still pretty hostile to me…"

Michael's expression became enlightened. "So that's what that was all about back there."

"I was throwing her out of the nest. She dislikes me for that."

"I might be able to persuade her for you." He paused for a moment, the warm trace of a smile on his lips as he thought of her. "So…" the smile faded, "you knew about the Sword, then?"

"No! I was simply trusting El's word to me. I knew nothing about what might happen. I was just as surprised as…as, well…as the baddies were."

He laughed.

"And, oh! Don't think it was me who called them on. It wasn't me. I'm so not the dirty girl."

"I never said that—"

"I'll just tell you this: we've gotta be careful. Very careful."

"What do you mean?"

"I mean that the most dangerous enemy is the one you don't see coming. The one that's on the inside." She stood, moved closer, and crouched before him, grasping his shoulders. "Michael, be on your guard. Always vigilant."

"Ellie, just say what you mean."

She looked at him, sizing him up. "I mean...everyone's got an axe to grind, mate. Not everyone will be totally straightforward with you at all times."

"And?"

"Look, I know something's cockeyed here and I've got half an idea. That just means I'd better not go sharing it and polluting the pool. But I will say...that you, Mr. Alexander...need to be very careful. With everyone."

A torrent of evil thoughts ran through Michael's head, but he would not give voice to them. Not until he had more information. And if there was anything from which the ancient part of his mind benefitted, it was perspective.

CHAPTER XII

ELLIE'S PHONE SOUNDED OFF: *In one mile, turn right on Route 19. Your destination will be on your right.* She looked at its GPS display and said, "We'd better get ready. This train won't stop for us."

Michael looked at her and the phone quizzically.

"All the phones I use go through testing before I trust them," she said. "They're re-routed so many times they're untraceable."

"I've been trying to stay off mine. There's probably nothing more dangerous to a wanted man than a smartphone."

"True. Good thing, then. Cuz I'm not a man." She smiled at him.

He would have considered it flirtatious if he didn't know better. "You get Kim. I'll wake Airel."

They parted ways. Michael scrambled down from the tops of the crates to where he had left Airel, assuming Ellie would be careful waking Kim. She might prove to be like a cornered cat; a real handful. He hoped her attitude would improve with some time spent in a hot shower and a real bed. He knew that's what he needed most, too, and he felt bad for her. For all of them, really.

He squeezed through the narrow space between the wall of the boxcar and the last row of crates, expecting to find Airel.

But she wasn't there. *Where did she go?*

Then from the opposite end of the boxcar, he heard a sound that made his heart sink. A whimper. Some kind of exclamation. A thud or a slam.

As fast as he could, he made his way through the maze of crates toward the scuffle, fearing the worst. He could hear words, though they were hard to make out.

Give it? Was that it? Or was it "give it up?" He couldn't tell. He did hear someone say, "No," but he wasn't sure who. *Great, I get to referee three cranky ladies. As if I didn't have my own problems.* He felt the anger rising and he didn't stop it.

He closed the distance, balling up his fists as he walked, turning his shoulders to the side as he slid through a narrow gap. In the back of his mind it occurred to him that there might be a reason for him to feel so angry suddenly…a reason beyond his fatigue…but it didn't surface. He wanted to taste the rage and let it out, anyway; he had had it with this whole operation, these little hens pecking away at petty nonsense.

As he rounded the final corner, he beheld them: three girls fighting over a bag. Kim's duffel. They were all pulling a different strap in a different direction. He roared at them, "HEY," slamming his fist into a crate. "CUT IT OUT!"

All three jumped in surprise, looking momentarily afraid. It stopped the bickering, at least, and it tasted good to him.

"This is our stop," he tried to explain, his eyes dark. "And if we miss it, we'll be walking for a long, long time." He began to get the shakes as adrenaline flooded his veins. "Anyone up for that?"

No response.

"I didn't think so. Kim," he addressed her directly, "get your bag and let's get going, already."

They stood like deer in the headlights for a moment.

"NOW!" he shouted at them, surprising even himself at the measure of his anger.

They all moved quickly, following him toward the side of the boxcar and the door.

"I don't know and I don't want to know right now," he tried to explain to them as he opened the sliding door, letting in the cool fresh air of a late afternoon day. It swirled around them, refreshing everything. He looked at the three girls as they assembled in a line near the edge of the opening. Airel's arms were crossed at her chest and she glared at him. "We don't get a second chance for this," he said, mostly to her, trying to get her to understand how serious things were.

He turned to Ellie, but she had already stuck her blue-crowned head out the opening and started to spy the way ahead, looking for a soft landing area. "Grass ahead," she said to them.

It was clear that this would be it.

Michael looked to Kim. She stood with her chin drooping a little, hands in the pocket of her dirty red hoodie. She had her bag, at least. She looked really quite unwell; pale and disheveled. *You need a shower,* he thought, a little repulsed. *And a good long sleep.* She looked out the door at the rapidly passing scene.

Michael shook his head. He was going to have a look in that bag, one way or another. *The group can't continue on like this, and my curiosity must be satisfied. Especially if I have any kind of authority or position of leadership, or even responsibility, for this cackling walking train wreck.* He shook his head and blinked. *Whoa. Where did that come from?*

But he knew. The fear that he might be right caused him to embrace his doubts about it. Doubt was a safe haven at times.

Ellie, head still poking out the door, reached back behind her. "Here it is!" She hooked arms with Airel, who was very surprised, and jumped out, taking them both for a tumble.

Michael was more than a little shocked, but there was no time to think about it. He gave Kim a violent shove in the back, sending her out of the car with a screaming yelp; the bag too, strapped across her shoulder. She landed awkwardly. He hoped she didn't break anything.

Nothing left for him, he too jumped. The landing hurt. Even though he tried to roll with it, take some of the edge off, he realized that their little Kreios-hunting party might not have come out of this little misadventure unscathed. Jumping from a moving train was a really stupid thing to do, and nothing like the movies.

He finally came to a skidding rolling stop in the high grass along the embankment of the railroad. He sat up. "Ow," he groaned, holding his forearms, which had borne the brunt of the impact. "That's worse than football," he decided.

He saw Airel and Ellie. They had already popped up, and Airel was giving her some words. "Uh-oh," He chuckled. He had to admire her. Mostly he was just glad to see she was okay. "Where's Kim?" he wondered aloud. He saw a little flash of red bobbing in the grass. "There she is."

"Kim!" he called out. He got to his feet, his body complaining. "Did you live?" As he stood, he could see that she was on her hands and knees in the high grass.

She didn't respond.

"Lose something?" He walked back up the line toward her as the train passed them by, on its way somewhere without them.

As he walked farther up the way, he could tell Ellie and Airel might possibly have more than words for each other, and pretty quick. He just shook his head. What was he supposed to do, anyway? If they wanted to fight it out—with swords, even—in broad daylight, so be it. He was tired. It might be a blessing to totally blow their cover, end it all right here. *No way,* he thought. *What am I thinking?* "Worst idea ever," he said.

"No kidding, dude!" Kim said as she rose up into a crouch. "Thanks for the warning," she cussed at him, adding all kinds of choice words her mother would be shocked to hear.

Or maybe not so shocked, he thought.

Kim stood there trying to dust herself off, pulling her ridden up hoodie back down, adjusting the strap of her bag as she stood, stuffing her hands back in the big pocket of the sweater.

He couldn't help but laugh at her. "Looks like you're no worse for the wear," he said. "Did you find what you were looking for?"

She stepped back ever so slightly. "Maybe. What's it to you?"

He laughed, a little too lightly. He sounded like a politician to himself, paper thin. "Nothing, Kim. Accept my apologies?" He extended a hand to her.

She slapped it away in contempt. "Shut your face, jerk. I'm not talking to you."

He rolled his eyes at her, letting her see the gesture. "Okay, whatever. You're ridiculous. I'm going to go pull these other two off each other; you coming?"

She looked him in the eyes. "Not with you."

He smirked and shook his head. "Well, then…follow along behind." He made his fingers walk through the air at her.

She spit at him as he left.

"Hey," Michael called to Ellie and Airel, "is the catfight over yet, or are there still tickets available?"

IF I WAS EVER ready to kill, this was the time. I actually scared myself a little, because I felt perilously close to how I had felt in Kreios's little training hut when he was explaining how to use my emotions.

"Now, listen—" Ellie started to say.

I was about to overflow with hatred and I had to get ahold of myself. The first thing I had to do was get out of Ellie's face, walk away.

I turned, breathing deep and slow, and put my hands on my knees like an outfielder. "Breathe," I commanded myself, trying to avoid the idea nestled in the back of my mind that said Ellie was going to personally assault me without warning again.

"You're quits, then," she chided from behind me.

I ignored her. "Breathe," I said again, and took a deep one. *Or someone will die,* I added. I could hear Michael cracking off smart somewhere behind me. I breathed again. *Okay, something is seriously not right here. One minute we're at each other's throats, the next...we're all buddy buddy?*

I felt in over my head again. Unlike most people, I knew precisely what that was. I knew precisely what it felt like to die. To drown in death itself; to fly free. Or was that really what it was to be free? *Because when I died, something wasn't quite right then, too, wasn't there? Yes.* Something like unfinished business. I knew what that made me: a ghost. At least it did if I failed whatever test still lay before me.

This was like the Whack-A-Mole game. Smack one test down and up pops another one somewhere else; it was maddening. It was like trying to hide smoke. It just seeped through any tiny crack, leaving me smelling like a stale campfire.

I kept thinking of what *She* had told me right before I first met Ellie. Something about "One to guide me." *Do I ever need that.* I was overwhelmed. Life? Death? I didn't know much about whatever happened to us when we moved past what we could see and feel here…but instinctually there was a point, I knew, where truth became absolute. And there were no more arguments.

"No more arguments," I said, thinking, *boy, wouldn't that be nice.*

"All right, then," I heard Ellie say, her voice much softer toward me than I thought I deserved.

I stood erect. "Deal," I said, without turning. I looked off to the horizon, the line of mountains lumping itself along from one side to the other in my field of view, making me think of the scissors-like shoulder blades of a dog as it walked.

"Hey," Michael said from behind me, "You guys okay?"

Michael. On my mind a lot, that's what he was. Not that I could help it much; when it was love…*Love. Betrayal*…I didn't even want to think of those words. But they were there, just under the oil slick, just under the surface, and they wouldn't go away. I could wrap my mind around why he had done what he had done, rationally, but my heart still hurt about it. *What if things had happened differently? What if his father had never stepped in? Would I have been his next kill?*

Gravel crunched under my feet as I shuffle-paced in circles, wrestling with Things Bigger Than I.

Ellie was talking on her phone now. I figured she was calling about hotel rooms. I *prayed* she was calling about hotel rooms. She caught my stare and raised an eyebrow at me. *What's she thinking?* I thought about trying to read her thoughts, but fear got the best of me and I didn't. Would she get into my head and read *me* like a book?

My gut ached with stress as more questions poured into me. *Just how did the Brotherhood find us?* I trusted Kim to be cool. If anyone was innocent, it was her. But what about Ellie? And what about Michael? *Have I been foolish to trust him so soon? Is he still in contact with them? No.* I wouldn't even consider it. If I was going to trust him I needed to do it and stop doubting him like this.

Michael was talking with Ellie. She put her hand on his arm and laughed at something. In the distance I saw Kim dusting herself off, standing all alone. She looked miserable, *poor thing.* I felt so bad for her. All Ellie could do was flirt casually—or tease—Michael, ignoring my poor, miserable best friend. And me, for that matter. The ache in my stomach left, replaced by frigid anger.

Fine.

I stalked over to Kim. I wanted to shove Michael into the dirt as I passed by him. *Bullies.* That's all they were.

I was so confused. I didn't know what was going on with me; why I was getting so angry so fast. It took only seconds to set me off. *But really…after all I've shared with Michael…all he's done for me! How can I not trust him?*

As I approached Kim, Michael said something from behind me that made Ellie laugh again. This time he laughed, too. *Come on, Airel, you're just being paranoid. Reading into something when nothing's there.* I wanted to believe that. I wanted to think that this girl, this angel, this perfect beautiful killer, wasn't trying to steal my boyfriend from me. But what did I know about her? What did any of us really know about her?

Something wasn't adding up. Maybe it was just my jealous heart talking too loudly.

CHAPTER XIII

Boise, Idaho, present day

"RAWLINS MISSED HIS CHECK-IN with his local," Harry said.

"Figures," FBI Special Agent Gretchen Reid mumbled into her coffee cup. "That guy's career was over before it started."

"Well, I don't know him."

"Consider it your lucky day then."

"Regional command said they're just passing the word along to us out of courtesy—"

"It's not courtesy, Harry, and nothing's ever optional. We need to get on this. What was his last known position?"

"I already pulled that up, ma'am. Here," he pointed to the display. "U.S. 97. Looks like it's right around milepost 25."

Reid sipped lustily at her coffee, looking at the map on the screen.

"I cross referenced it with local 9-1-1 dispatch. The only thing that's local out there is whatever traffic gets diverted to the Staties Dispatch—Oregon State Patrol—"

"Yes, Harry. Dear God, you are straight out of training, aren't you?"

He absorbed the slight. "And it turns out there was a call not more than an hour ago. I guess there's spotty cellular service out there…"

Reid sat bolt upright and seized the desk phone as he rambled on.

"…and whatever's happened is old, maybe a few hours old, even…"

She dialed a number from memory.

"…because whoever saw it had to get to a land line…possibly in, what is it…Grass Valley?" Harry finally silenced himself.

"Harry, get your stuff," Reid said, eyes still locked on the screen. Then she brightened a shade. An answer on the other end. "It's Reid here. I need the helo."

Harry dismissed himself to the restroom. It was going to be a long day.

Again.

Arlington, Oregon, present day

"KIMMIE…ARE YOU GOING TO be okay?" I asked. "You look like you've been to Hell and back, girl."

"Shut up, Airel. You don't look so hot yourself," Kim said.

I knew she was lying, just trying to keep up with me. Though I didn't have a mirror, I knew I probably looked a lot better than she did. She didn't have angel blood; I did. I wasn't bragging; it was just a fact.

I couldn't help but overhear Ellie as she conversed with Michael: "…he's an old friend. The best pilot I've ever known. Don't worry, he's been with me for many years. I trust him."

"And he gets here tomorrow?" Michael said to her.

"Yeah."

We were walking toward the little town of Arlington. To the left, the tracks continued on across a bridge. To our right, there was a nice little park. We veered that way and walked through it.

I turned back to Kim, who had been talking to me for a while already. "…I just really need a shower," she was saying. "And some real food. Do you think they have a hotel in this podunk town?"

"Yeah," I said to her as Michael and Ellie's conversation went on. I relayed to Kim the information that I gleaned from before, that I had overheard Ellie earlier on her phone, making us a reservation somewhere.

"Oh, good! I COULD EAT THE BACK END OUT OF A DEAD RHINOCEROS," she shouted with all her Kim-like drama.

"Ew," I said, acting repulsed by her crassness. But then we laughed, and sharing that moment with my Kimmie took me back to movie nights at my house, popcorn fights and talk about boys. It made my smile fade all too quickly. Those days might never return, I realized.

There was a picturesque little marina nearby on the other side of the railroad bridge, with I-84 roaring along above us as well. I looked up and stopped. Beech Street. And off in the distance, like a beacon of hope: A hotel. "Oh, thank GOD!"

"Do you think there's a restaurant?" Kim seemed to be perking up.

"Yeah, and I bet they even serve DEAD RHINOCEROS," I said, mimicking her raucous tone from earlier. We laughed until we nearly peed our pants and fell over in the grass, and then I decided what the heck: I tackled her. We rolled around giggling and wrestling, letting all the tension go at last, sending her bag flying. We rolled into Michael and Ellie, who stood there looking down at us, bemused. But we weren't done yet; there was more pent-up tension to release. We rolled around a bit more, wrestling each other.

When we were through, trying to recover, I pulled myself onto my elbows and looked up. Ellie had gone, presumably to get us some rooms, and Michael was sitting at a picnic table, his chin in his hand, looking out at the river. I wanted to go to him, enjoy the moment with him, but I thought better of it. Kim was such an odd man out; she needed an advocate.

"Hey," she poked me. "Thanks for that."

I smiled at her. "No prob." Then I widened my eyes in mock surprise. "Dang, girl," I said, looking at her hands, "You need to find a bar of soap!" They were crusted over with dirt and possibly even bruises, especially on the palms, which I thought was really weird.

She withdrew them and looked ashamed. "I know," she said. "I know, right?" She made a whooshing sound and said, "It's been really messed up, hanging out with you lately."

I felt really bad for her. "Kim, I'm so sorry…. Maybe we should have just taken you home."

"No way," she said. "I wouldn't miss this for nothin'."

I rolled my eyes. "Whatever, you. Don't try to act tough. It doesn't suit you."

"I'm not acting."

"Okay, whatever," I said, thinking. "Hey…I'm sorry for my part of what happened on the train." I thought back to how I woke up to find Michael missing, went to go find him and found Kim instead, and then… "I don't know what happened once Ellie showed up and started freaking out."

"Yeah, she's got her bags packed for a power trip," Kim said. "She's lame. I hate her."

I looked at her, surprised a little at her extreme tone. "Yeah, well, I guess I do too."

"Airel, I love you." She looked like she was about to cry.

"Kim, what's going on with you?" I blurted out. I didn't really want to know just then, I had to admit. But she was obviously emotionally unstable.

"It's nothing," she said, wiping at her eyes with the cuff of her dirty red sweater. She looked like a meth addict.

"It's okay to be weak, you know, to need a break. Even I need—"

"Even you, huh?" she said, the hurt in her tone pretty obvious. "Look, I know I'll never be like you. I'll never have cool angel powers. I'm ugly; I won't live forever…" she got a distant look in her eyes and put her hands in her sweater pocket.

"Kim, I didn't mean anything by—"

"Where is it?" she interrupted me. She sounded scared, her eyes darting all over the grass.

I laughed at her, but it came out fraudulent. "You're acting really weird, Kim. Where's what?" I looked from her eyes to the grass and back, judging the situation.

"My…my, um…" she fumbled.

"Your what?"

"I lost something," she said, her voice choked up. "I think it happened when we were wrestling…"

"What, you lost something…?"

"Yes!" she was suddenly very irritated. She pulled her bag close and unzipped it, keeping her body between me and it, peeking inside, rummaging around in it. "No, it's not here." She sounded desperate.

"Kim, honey, what's wrong?"

She stopped, frozen, her eyes distant. "Oh…" she said robotically. "It's nothing. I…I think I made a mistake."

"Kim, what the heck is wrong with you? What did you lose?"

"It's nothing."

"Nothing. Right. I don't buy it. Now what did you lose? Tell me." Now I was getting angry.

"I said," she looked at me speaking through gritted teeth, "it's nothing. It was just a little keepsake, and I—I found it. It was in my bag after all."

I regarded her. I knew she was lying, but I thought better of calling her on it right then. *Pick my battles carefully*, I thought. "Oh. Well...good. Glad we solved that riddle." I looked back to Michael. Ellie was walking back toward us, holding one hand up. Something dangled there that looked like keys.

I could already feel the shower running over me, washing away the dirt and grime.

"We use cash for everything," Michael said. "And no phone calls to home. I think that's how they found us." I watched his face. Something wasn't right. It was like he didn't believe what he was saying. His blank expression said more. I tried to tell myself he was just finally feeling tired, but then I didn't believe what *I* was saying.

CHAPTER XIV

ELLIE HAD PAID FOR two rooms with the cash Michael had given her. He wanted us all to share one room, saying, "We'll be safer if we stick together." Ellie vetoed that idea though, on grounds of decency. Her stock began to rise in my estimation at that point.

"Hey," I elbowed her as we left Michael to himself and made our way to the girls' room, a few doors down. "Good call."

"What, keeping you and your hormone-happy boyfriend separated? No problem."

"Yeah, no, it's not a problem," I reiterated. "And again, thanks. I'm not your average girl and I don't think it's cool to place myself in…awkward situations."

She stopped and looked at me, sizing me up again. "You're welcome, girlie. We've got to look out for one another, right? Besides, you're right. It would be a bit ticklish, that."

I laughed, and it made her smile. The sight of that expression on her face filled me with such a confusion of emotions that I couldn't sort it out at first.

It's like watching someone die: you know they're going to a better place, but you also know you'll never see them again. I didn't know how else to look at it; it weirded me out. *Why would I feel like that?* I chalked it up to my special abilities, which were still, after all, pretty new to me. How would I know when I had plumbed the depths of all the gifts my angel blood had given me?

We had arrived at our room. She turned the key in the doorknob, and before either of us could enter, Kim barged between us and bolted for one of the beds. "This one's mine!" she said and jumped on it like a little girl. She began peeling off layers, starting with her hideous red sweater.

We had to hurry inside and close the door before she flashed the whole parking lot from the second floor. "Geez, Kim!" I said.

"I'm first into the shower!" she ran into the bathroom in nothing but her underwear and slammed the door.

"The room's already thrashed," Ellie said. She groaned as she looked around us. "I'm not picking this stuff up; it's nasty." Kim had been a tornado of dirty smelly clothes.

I could hear the shower start up. I was a little jealous of that, but I figured I could wait. I kicked her shirt and jeans into a pile against her duffel bag, which had fallen into the space between her bed and the wall. "There," I said, "out of sight, out of mind."

"Did you see her…?"

"How could I miss her," I said.

"No, I mean the bruises. You saw it, yeah?"

I nodded. "Yeah."

"She looks like a user."

I was shocked at Ellie's frankness. "Wow…but that's weird. Why would you say that?"

"What?" Ellie said, pulling her own sweater off over her head. She pulled the hem of her white t-shirt down and sat heavily in one of the chairs by the modest table.

I lowered my voice. "Because I was just thinking the same

thing out there." I motioned to the grassy park outside, beyond the closed curtains.

"Look, it's no great stretch of the imagination."

"Duh," I said. "I'm just sayin'."

"Tell you what, Airel. Why don't you go next." She motioned to the shower. "I'll go get us some ice, maybe see if I can scare up a soda or two."

"Um, sure?" I gave her a confused look.

"It's not you," she said, trying to explain her abruptness. "I need regular alone time or I get grouchy." She smiled, again setting off the emotional fireworks within me.

What the heck, dude.

"You know what else…we're gonna need some new clothes, right? I'll be the search party for that."

"But I—"

"Don't worry," she said, "I'll get us some cute stuff. What, you don't think I know style when I see it?" She pointed to her blue mane.

I'm not worried about style, I didn't say, *I'm worried you're finding all kinds of excuses for seducing Michael behind my back.* "Whoa…" I was dizzy with the cascade of unexpected thoughts in my head.

"I know, I know. Good luck finding anything in this little country town, I know." She held up her phone. "I've got all kinds of fun toys to help me."

"Great," I said. "Gas-station clothes. Awesome."

"Aw, chin up. After bathing you'll feel properly sorted." She punched me in the arm playfully. "Promise."

Owwww! So much emotional pain! I wanted to die in the avalanche of it.

MICHAEL FELT EXACTLY LIKE a kid in over his head. He had poked the dog with the stick one too many times, and now the fence had broken and he was on the run, eager fangs giving chase and closing in. It was too much. He felt very heavy. Exhausted and worthless. He was waiting for some strong hand to rescue him— though his only experiences with strength had been commingled with unspeakable abuse.

Stanley had been…unkind.

He had enough faith to wrestle the doubt that kept throwing little pebbles at his resolve, pecking away at the belief that he had what it took to make it through this latest wrinkle, this latest setback, this absolutely insane upping of the ante.

"How could she?" he choked out, the tears coming. He was glad to be alone, he decided. *This is right.* It fit, though it made no sense and he had no idea how he was going to summon the strength to continue on. Though it was right, though it was…justice, he supposed, it still made no sense.

It was surreal. It was like he was watching a copy of himself when it had happened. He stood off, frozen in shock, and watched his body do things.

It had happened in the little park. Airel and Kim were being charmingly immature, roaring about eating rhinoceros or something, and then she tackled her and they wrestled and rolled around on the grass.

How could she?!

Airel and Kim rolled away, leaving it quite literally at his feet: the Bloodstone.

My God! "She's been carrying it this whole time…" his mind flew backward through all the places they had been, all the things they had done, all the plans they'd made, and all this time, the Bloodstone had its carrier. "Kim…how could you?"

She's a traitor…

No one had seen him pick it up. He had covered it with his shoe; *that's where the wretched thing belongs, under my feet;* and when Ellie took the cash to go get the rooms, he had bent and…and took it.

He cursed his awful father, cursed his memory, cursed the day of his own birth into this insanity. The *why* filled his head. El… *why? Can El be any good at all when His creation is so…so evil?* "Why do I have to be the one to carry this burden?"

He felt absolutely alone.

What will it do to me?

Michael felt pulled in two directions as the perpetually unhealing wound in his chest throbbed stronger.

CHAPTER XV

Boise, Idaho, present day

THE WHITE FBI AS-350 helicopter climbed quickly, accelerating to its cruise speed of 130 knots—about 150 miles per hour. At that rate, Reid would cover the roughly 300 miles to the scene of the incident in less than two hours.

Harry sat there, his nose buried in his Kindle eReader.

She wondered what he could be reading that was more interesting than real life. It irritated her. He was probably reading something hideously nerdy. She snatched the gadget out of his hand and glanced at the display. Seniority had its privileges, its prerogatives. On the "ePage," or whatever you called it, was something by some idiot Frenchman named Beaudelaire; something about *The Flowers of Evil* or some such rot. She snickered and handed the absurd device and its absurd content back to him with a sneer. He meekly took it without the slightest sign of protest, which made her despise him even more. *There are so few killers in the world,* she surmised. *Most people are just ignorant sheep.*

She was drawn back to the present situation, to what really mattered. It was such an incredible career opportunity, she realized.

She could ride in on her white stallion and claim to be concerned for Tom Rawlins, to offer to take up the loose threads of his investigation, all in the name of *esprit de corps,* for the FBI, for the team. Meanwhile, no one had to know that her real motivation was to look good to the bosses, be on her game, be the go-to gal, get things done in spite of her (slightly) evident grief for her (most likely) fallen comrade-in-arms. She had developed a feel for these things. Her gut was telling her that Rawlins was dead and that opportunity therefore awaited, yawning supinely before her.

Hey, she thought, *life's a contest and to the conqueror go the spoils.* And she could be a ruthless gangster when she needed to be. When it suited her. She reflected, a little egomaniacally, on herself: *What was your best moment, your favorite promotion, Gretchen? The next one,* she answered herself.

The helo slipped swiftly through the airstream.

Arlington, Oregon, present day

KIM HAD SHOWERED AND then collapsed into the bed quickly thereafter, falling into a deep but troubled sleep. She was comfortable now, lying there with the feel of clean sheets on her skin, her body heat reflected back to her, warming her to the bone. After so many hours spent on the run, in the rain, soaked and bedraggled, it felt so good to be in a real bed.

But there was something missing. She couldn't avoid it or deny it.

She reached under her pillow in her fitful sleep, feeling mindlessly, instinctively for the Bloodstone. It was not there.

Of course. She knew who had taken it; who now carried it. How

would she get it back from him? *What's the plan?* Airel, having
showered as well, napped beside her, breathing in and out with soft
sighs.

Kim was so exhausted she felt like she could sleep for weeks.
Yet she didn't feel the slightest bit refreshed. If anything, she felt
even more tired. Now that the Bloodstone had gone, she wasn't
sure what to do with herself. All she knew was that she was tired.
So very tired. The voices that called to her inside her head, once
interesting and full of ancient wisdom, now grated irritatingly
against her seared conscience, shaving away in layers every
forethought she attempted to coalesce into something—anything—
coherent.

She felt like she was going insane.

What was it that drew her originally to the little red stone? On
the cliff top, amidst the scuffle of angels and demons, while lives
and destinies were altered irrevocably roundabout her, it had called
to her in the warp of time…

She could hear voices. They spoke unspeakable usurpations
to her ragged mind, drawing her out of herself and into…into…
something that tasted sweet. Something intoxicating. *Something I
need.*

She wanted to kill something; anything. She grasped the
pillow with both hands and bit down on it with her jaws, her face
contorting in the darkness into a visage of rage. The world was *such*
an unjust place. But…she would make it right. *Yes…*

Besides, she thought, *the Bloodstone is mine.* She was weary,
yes, but mostly she was tired of being the third wheel in this band of
impossible personalities. With the Bloodstone she could see things,
feel things that had not yet come to pass, things she could not put
into words…

Was it so bad?

She was strong enough. At least when she had it in her hand. Oh, how desperately she wanted to hold it, to touch it once more. It was like sinking into the softest mattress on a lazy Sunday, curling up inside the womb of a thick down comforter, pulling the folds up over her head, muffling the world.

She would be the one to set things right. She would be the key.

It is my destiny. She had heard as much.

I will be patient. She agreed with the whispers in the darkness.

I will wait. The Bloodstone would return to her. It was irresistible, really. She would be the key to peace, a lasting cease-fire, the only one in all of history that would actually work, that would really last. There would be an end to all wars, and it would start in her flesh. She, with the Bloodstone, would be the catalyst. The spark. The first flame.

As her reward for her patience, for her labors, she too would possess long life and beauty. Like Airel, she too would be strong beyond her wildest dreams. She too would not only be able to heal her own flesh, but also the infirmities of others.

Her mind drifted once more. The Bloodstone's distant whispering call warmed her as she slipped into a world where she was not the dumb luck sidekick, but the hero.

"DESTROY IT. DESTROY IT. Destroy it," Michael whispered a subconscious mantra, his throat catching in desperation as he stared at the Bloodstone from across the room. It sat pulsing on the television cabinet, calling to him like a potential lover, offering everything, making promises, clapping blinders on his eyes that prevented him from seeing anything but itself. It was all gratification and no consequence.

He squeezed his eyes shut. He could not deny that he wanted what it offered him. *What red-blooded man could resist, anyway?* Anything and everything he could imagine and then some, it was all there inside the Bloodstone. Though he knew that the life it offered was fraudulent, that the healing of which it profanely whispered was bondage, that the sensual pleasures on display were paper-thin disguises worn by ancient principalities…

It was the kingdom of the Self, and he would be master, by God, and at last. He would bend no more to anyone other than The Alexander. He would inherit the mantle of his father and surpass him. In every conceivable way. He would crush all opposition, command his thousands upon thousands. He would usher in the final war, and in that obliteration of all that is, he would captain, finally, ultimate peace. There would be stillness. He would rule everything under the blackened sun.

Michael pressed his palms to his head and squeezed. *Destroy it…*

The wound he bore, that now had spread over his whole chest was raw and red; sickly fingers reached out in purple red spirals, enlarging its territory over his heart, grasping for more, still more. And it ached, wretchedly before, and now beautifully, now that he carried the Bloodstone.

He clawed backward desperately in his mind, but backward was forward and he was really confused. He tried to attain clarity; everything was so fuzzy, so…red.

RED.

Blood red.

I stood in a river of red. The color made me sick. The…water…

? …lapped at my waist, slapping at my belly as if it was trying to beat its way through me. If I had been a pillar of stone, and given enough time, pressure, flow, the sick redness would be content to erode me away into nothing. It had a consciousness of its own.

Why was it always red? Why always this dreaming about blood? I was so angry. I wanted to pull myself up out of the dream by the scruff of my neck, a *deus ex machina,* but I was powerless here. The redness was cold. *Thank God.* I didn't know what I would have done if it was warm. I gagged in my sleep. *Yeah, me and nausea go way back.*

I looked up, getting my bearings. A black sun, papier mache, was pasted onto the sky above me like a theatre prop. Everything became chilly. No vegetation to speak of lined the shores of this diabolical river. There was only black rock and the putrid stench of death.

This is getting old, darn it. I'm sick of having the same stupid dream and variations. Freud would have had ample material with which to work the alchemy of his psychoanalysis on me, *all up in my Kool-Aid and not even knowin' the flavah.*

I looked for my old "friend," the inevitable cloaked figure, star of all my fantasies, but I did not see him. I then felt inwardly for *She,* wondering if it was her sparking these dreams…or if it was something else.

"Listen and learn. Everything has a useful purpose, Airel."

I widened my eyes and shook my head, singing out, "Cra-zy," like an insane person had just said something to me that was completely absurd and I was going to walk away. It echoed back to me like I was inside an empty cistern.

I tried to walk to the riverbank but my feet wouldn't move. *Great! A river of blood with a quicksand bottom, and I'm sinking into it little by little.* "All right, Sigmund," I said aloud, really addressing *She,* "Have at it. Tell me what it all means." But there was nothing.

Does anyone know how to give me a straight answer? First it was Kreios and his cryptic non-answers, and now it was *She* taking up the mantle of obscurity.

"I guess I'll just stay here, then. In the river of blood. Sinking."

I looked more closely roundabout me, looking for whatever it was I was missing—and I knew I was missing *something,* for crying out loud. I was supremely irritated.

That's when I saw it.

The black Hell's-own-kindergarten theatre-prop sun was moving.

It was coming closer.

It soon spread from horizon to horizon, further blackening the dark sky. It rolled back gathering from bottom to top like a curtain.

I screamed in fright.

Revealed there was an enormous sickly eye, and it stared right through me.

MICHAEL SHOOK HIS HEAD, popping out of a dazed trance.

He was angry.

He wanted to hurl the Bloodstone into the depths of the Columbia River. It was, after all, only a short walk away. He walked to the window, his body containing a bundle of nervous energy. He parted the curtain on a sunset that had turned the river's waters into a red-orange torrent of blood. He shuddered, though he knew not why.

Then, like a lightning bolt out of a pitch black sky a simple thought came to him: *Airel.* Love. He breathed in deeply but it was ragged and spastic, as if he'd just been weeping his heart out. He exhaled and a tear escaped and ran down his cheek. He wiped it away with his hand and realized: he knew what he had to do. And why.

CHAPTER XVI

I OPENED MY EYES and stared at the ceiling. For the briefest of moments I could remember everything. Then it was gone, "like a fart in the wind," as Kim would say. *What did I miss?* I felt dirty, like someone or something was watching me. I knew we were being followed, I could *feel* it. Was it the Brotherhood? Was it right now? I didn't know.

Kim had snuggled up with most of the blankets in her sleep, leaving me chilly and naked on the bed. Becoming more aware of my surroundings, I panicked: *Is Michael in the room?* I covered myself as best I could and looked around. I spied Ellie in the bed opposite. She was sleeping. *Do angels sleep?* I guessed I had seen Kreios sleeping. I crossed my arms over my chest and sat up slowly.

I looked closer at Ellie. She was out cold. I figured maybe we would miss dinner. At least some of us would, anyway, and I was capable of getting some takeout for the rest of our little group so they could have something to eat whenever they woke up. As for me, I was hungry. Freaking starving.

But I was naked. *Yikes.* I looked around again. Ellie had been on a mission to get some gas station clothes, last I knew. Sure enough, there on the desk chair sat several shopping bags, and it looked promising: they were a big step up from convenience store quality. They were mall quality.

Go Ellie!

I grabbed the bags and made a dash for the bathroom. I never was the kind of girl who could walk brazenly across a women's locker room, whether anyone was aware of me or not. I didn't know how some women could do that. I was too shy for prancing in my birthday suit; it always made me uncomfortable. But what else could I have done? I wasn't going to get dressed right back into my filthy clothes after I had showered. *Gross.*

I shut the bathroom door behind me and flipped the light on, rummaging through the haul of stuff Ellie had brought back. I was stunned. It was like I had been out shopping myself. There were a couple of pairs of designer jeans, some really cute little tops, even some accessories like a little packet of hair ties. And—thank God—some high quality unmentionables. *Where did she find this stuff?* Did Arlington, Oregon have a Victoria's Secret? It was crazy, and everything fit perfectly. The other bag had some shoe boxes inside. *No way.* Again, I was stunned. I pulled out a pair of sturdy lightweight hikers with an aggressive tread on the sole. They fit my feet like they had been custom made. *Insane.* I ran my fingers through my hair and tied it back loosely with one of the hair ties. *Lookin' good.* I didn't know what to think.

I checked my reflection one last time and then turned off the lights.

I quietly left the room and went down to the lobby.

Michael was sitting in a chair by the coffee maker, reading a newspaper. He looked clean and fresh, wearing jeans and a button-up shirt. He saw me and smiled, folding the paper and setting it down. "Hey. You get a good nap?"

I nodded and hugged him, laying my head against him. I could hear his heart thumping in his chest. "You smell good," I said, relishing the familiar. "So…you're catching up on sports, or…?" I motioned to the paper.

His eyes sparkled. "Comics," he said.

I rolled my eyes. "Nerd."

He kissed my cheek, setting me afire. "Where's everyone else?"

I pushed him away gently. "'Everyone else' is still sleeping. I figured why wake them."

"Cool."

I could tell he was going to ask me something important, something potentially awkward.

"So," he said, "You want to try that date again?"

My heart skipped a beat when I realized what he had said, and my mind flitted back over all the—well, the Audrey Hepburn moments we had had. The awkwardness I had felt. It was like he was asking me out for the first time. Um, again.

"On one condition, mister. This time, no thuggish fights in the parking lot."

He laughed, a musical sound. "No worries. So, what'll it be? Pizza? Or pizza. That's, like, all they have here."

"Hmm," I rested my chin on my finger, thinking. "Let's see here. I'm gonna go for pizza."

He nodded as if I had said something very wise. "Good call."

"I could eat a whole one all by myself," I said. I loved that I could be a pig and not worry about…about being a pig. I could be me with Michael, and I loved that.

CHAPTER XVII

WE FOUND A TABLE near the back of the small hometown pizza joint and sat down. The place was moderately full; farmers, road crew guys, fishermen, and just-passin'-thru types filled various booths and tables. An ancient Rock-Ola jukebox hurled the occasional hatefully catchy 80's power ballad at all of us whenever someone dropped in some quarters, which was too often for my taste. The waitresses hustled from table to table with frilly little salmon-colored aprons around their waists. It didn't take much imagination to see them taking orders with pad and pen, lit cigarettes dangling from their lips, held fast by their filters in the bond of thick blood-red lipstick, thus completing the cliché. I mean, why not, after all?

One of them, a rough bulldog of a woman with pock-marked jowls and strands of gray hair rebelling against the bun that held most of it at bay, came and curtly took our order. She then swooshed away in a storm of polyester and Aqua Net hairspray.

"So," Michael began, "what do you think about Ellie?"

It was abrupt; it made me suddenly cautious. I brought my guard up by taking a sip of Coke, hiding behind the glass and speaking into it, "What do you mean?" My voice tumbled out amplified, it embarrassed me.

"Well, I mean...you two seem to have your differences, ya know? I couldn't help but sense the drama."

I huffed. It was mostly a laugh. "Yeah. Well, I honestly don't know what her problem is. Can we talk about something else?"

He looked frustrated. "Yeah, I guess."

I thought about how she had insisted on dividing us up along boy-girl lines at the hotel. "Look. I think she's who says she is, okay? I mean, like her or not, she's the real deal..."

Michael's expression was a clear question mark, and it hung over both of us. "But what was going on back there on the train?"

I thought about it, wanting to give him my best answer. "It was crazy. I don't even know. It's like all this...this evil...just came out of nowhere." I wiped beads of condensation from my glass down onto the table, spinning it counterclockwise as I did so. "I guess after the devil was done down in Georgia he decided to take a little train ride in Oregon, huh-huh," I laughed crazily at my own pathetic joke and made a face.

He didn't laugh or even crack a smile. "Yeah," he said, and that's all he said.

"What." I knew there was more.

"I don't know."

"Yeah, you do."

He acknowledged the truth with a little shrug. "Okay."

"Yeah?"

"Just okay."

"You're holding out on me."

This time he sighed heavily. "Sparkling conversation. First date."

"Second," I corrected him into my glass, taking another sip.

"Second," he acknowledged, drumming his fingers on the table.

"And don't try to change the subject. Go on, spill it," I said. I tried to sound encouraging, optimistic. It came out too harsh.

He sighed again. "I just don't know..." He looked like a little boy sitting there, like a little boy whose dog had just been run over and he didn't know what to do with himself.

I reached out and touched his arm. "What is it?"

We were interrupted by the waitress. She placed a hot pizza down on the table with a couple of plates, called us both "hon," and walked off after confirming we needed nothing else. We dug in greedily, forgetting the line of conversation for a moment. But it came back. I wouldn't let it die.

"Do you think we can trust her?" I asked.

"Ellie? Ha," Michael said, "Yeah, we can trust *her.*"

"What's *that* supposed to mean?" I gnashed another bite of gorgeous tasting pizza in my mouth.

"It's Kim you should be worried about."

"Mff?" I asked through my food. It helped me mask my shock.

"Kim. Dude. She's the reason..."

I swallowed. "What. Tell me."

He simply shook his head. "Can't we just enjoy ourselves for one evening, just the two of us? Why do we have to talk about this?"

"Because it's important?" I was a little incredulous.

"More important than taking a much-needed time out? Come on, we've been running from—" He lowered his voice and came closer. "We've been running for almost a week now. Running, like common criminals. From...from all kinds of...of things. And people. Can't we just have one night? A few hours?"

This time I sighed. I was exasperated but I took another enormous bite of my slice and began chewing it. All I could do was roll my eyes a little in expression of my frustration. "You're worse than my Dad," I finally said.

"Compliment accepted."

"Oh, FRACK," I said, which proved I was a *Battlestar Galactica* nerd.

He laughed at me and then took another bite. "I'm hungry," he said.

It was one of those things people said as they were eating; it made no sense really.

I knew he was done talking about The Issue At Hand, and in that sense what had happened just now was the spitting image of any number of conversations I'd had with my Dad. When it was over, it was over. He could be so stubborn!

Still, though. Something Michael said about Kim rang true and deep.

There was something about her that just wasn't sitting well with me lately, though I couldn't place my finger on it. *Why can he see it, and why can't I?* Was it just because I was so close with her? I ran over the hypotheticals in my head: the what-ifs.

What if you had a friend who…I mean, what if every evil thing in all creation was making a beeline to you, was bent on your destruction? What would be the best way to get to you?

A man on the inside.

I looked at Michael.

We've already been through this. The statement rang out in my head with an upturned questioning lilt at the end of it.

Who better to engineer ultimate betrayal, though? Who better than that person in whom there has been invested ultimate trust? I had seen a ton of movies, and in every one, the best friend was suspect number one. But this was real life, so was I just thinking this because of my movie habit?

Why is Kim here? I wondered. *Why would she be so eager to come along on what amounts to the worst imaginable version of a perpetual car chase scene?* I dug around in my feelings, searching for *She,* searching for El, searching for the truth, asking God for answers, reaching out once again for Kreios.

But there was nothing.

Part of me wanted desperately to defend her. Kim was my best friend from way back; nobody knew me like she did, and nobody could ever come between us. *Not even Michael....* Again, it resounded in my mind like a question, and it was difficult to know who had said it.

I shook my head and dug into the next slice of pizza. I was really hungry.

"Hey..." I said after a moment. My wheels were turning, moving on to different topics. "So... tell me again how we know Kreios is going to end up in Africa?" I had been wondering this for quite some time. I couldn't remember if it was Michael or Ellie who had said it first, and I had been meaning to get some clarification. Preferably from him.

"It's just what I'm thinking is most likely to happen. A hunch. The Brotherhood wouldn't have sent those twitchy little fast ones— the weird little fungus-covered ones—if things weren't deadly serious. I think Kreios is in big-time trouble. I think he's going after the roots of everything that is evil in this world. He's aiming for one of the most prestigious—I mean one of the most insidious strongholds of demonic power in the whole world. When I was in the Brotherhood...I mean...I know stuff, okay? I have memories that aren't even my own, because of James." He paused, breathing, apparently thinking.

"Those—those little twitchy fungusy ones are called Anti-Cherubs. They only come from Original lands. Like Africa. Or...

the Middle East. Like where Eden used to be. The Anti-Cherubs are some of the original rebels, like that big guy said. They are pure blood angels of darkness. Their usual function is to encircle the earthly throne of the Prince of Darkness himself with apostate traitorous praise." He paused and took a drink to fill the vacuum of silence between us.

"You talk about the devil. We had a brush with Satanic power the other night on that road. It's not a laughing matter. And your grandfather is, like, stirring it up because he thinks you're dead and he wants revenge. It would only make sense, based on what I've seen so far, that he has awakened powers in Original Lands either by threatening them or by actually *going there already* and fighting them on their own turf. It's the Nri Clan. They're legend among the Brotherhood. My f—I mean, Stanley…once when I was younger… um…shared with me…all this kind of stuff."

His eyes looked distant and haunted. I never wanted him to look at me like that ever again for the rest of his life.

"Anyway, I'm betting if we start in South Africa, we'll pick up one Hell of a trail. So to speak."

"You think we can find him?"

"Kreios?"

"Yeah." I swallowed and blinked back tears.

He reached across the table and grasped my hands, enfolding them within his own. "I sure hope so."

"Do you think he's…okay?"

He looked worried. "Of course."

"You're a bad liar." I attempted a smile but quickly looked down. There was the pizza. I wasn't so hungry anymore.

"You know why all this is happening, right?"

"Not really," I said, starting to cry now in earnest.

"The Nri are hunting us down because my father is dead. And

they're not the only ones, don't kid yourself. The one who retrieves the Bloodstone will become the next Seer." He stopped, allowing this new information to sink in.

"So…where is it?" I thought back to the day on the cliff.

"What, the Bloodstone?"

"Yeah."

"That is a really good question."

I narrowed my eyes at him. "What does that mean?"

"I'm not going to talk about it any further."

My jaw hit the floor in shock. Before I could shout abuses at him, he spoke again.

"At least not until you've had a chance to talk with Kim."

"Kim? What's she got to do with this?"

"You'd better ask her." He resumed eating. It was grotesque to me; I wanted to barf. *Oh, no….* Was my sickness coming back? And what did *that* mean?

"But," I began, "why would Kim have anything to do with…" As my voice did its decrescendo into nothingness, the light came on. *Oh, no.*

I watched as Michael rubbed his chest, grimacing like it hurt.

PART SEVEN
THE MARK

From the Book of the Brotherhood, Volume 3:
...

3. *The Brotherhood, dear Brothers and Hosts, had the
   honor to declare war against El from the beginning.
   The Fallen and their offspring, the Sons and
   Daughters of God, are traitors, not just to El—but to
   the original rebellion and the Leader, as well...*

CHAPTER I

U.S. Highway 97, Oregon, present day

THE DUST HAD LONG ago settled from the landing and the white
FBI helo sat immobile with its pilot just off the unusable roadway.
The wreckage of the accident under investigation was strewn in
lumps and shards more or less in a parallel line nearby.

It was a good decision, she thought, *playing the Federal
Investigation card.* Gretchen was glad that she had dismissed the
local yokels and cordoned off the scene as soon as she had landed.

But there were anomalies. Unexplainable things. *Like this
enormous dent in the middle of the road,* FBI agent Gretchen Reid
mused. "Holy…look at these cracks in the asphalt, how deep…" she
said to no one. Harry, whom she both valued for his usefulness and
despised for his subservience to her, trailed her around, his weak
hands trembling a little as he wrung them together at his waist,
picking his way carefully, awkwardly over and through the debris.

Gretchen lifted her pretty head and looked around, assessing
the situation. The log truck just up the road, Rawlins' car, or what
remained of it, pinned underneath. Then, in the opposite direction
on a line that passed through the dent in the road, the black SUV. Or

what remained of it. She made the calculations in her head, sizing it up. At first blush, it would appear that either the SUV or the log truck had crossed the double yellow and caused the wreck. Probably the SUV, because Rawlins had gotten too close, too obvious, and spooked the young man Michael Alexander. *High speed chase ensues. And Rawlins foolishly engages the youth. Stupid. I wouldn't have done that.* The youth, driving at triple digit speeds in the dark and in the rain, lost control.

"And caused the accident?" Again, said to no one.

Harry, still wringing his hands, met her eyes for a moment and she saw something there that didn't fit. But she let it pass, moving on.

The SUV had hit the log truck head on. No. *Not possible; it wouldn't have landed way over there,* she thought, estimating the distance from where she stood to the SUV at about 500 feet. No, that wasn't possible. After all, just look at what happened to Rawlins. Pancake city. No, something didn't fit.

"It's almost like it was thrown," she said. *How could it have been thrown?* Her hunch, that there was more to this incident than met the eye, was beginning to be borne out by events. She stood there in the silence, gusts of wind whipping at her hair, plastering her pantsuit to her athletic body, tugging at the fabric like jealous hands.

She turned around again. Harry had turned his back to her, looking off at the distance, his hand in his jacket pocket as if searching for a stick of gum, perhaps his eReader thing. Once more, she looked down at the dent in the road's surface. Then, with alarm she realized she hadn't been seeing what was right in front of her. *This isn't a dent. It's dents, plural.* There were two. Side by side, like—"feet." That's when she knew what she had been missing. Whatever had caused this accident…had fled the scene?

"Impossible," she breathed, looking down, wide-eyed.

Harry turned and she looked up. As he squared his body to her, his hand came out of his jacket. He brought it together with its opposite, raising them up. She then realized that his stance was all too familiar: that of an enemy gunman. And there in those hands was his pistol, real enough.

"Say goodbye, Gretchen."

"That's impossible—" The last sound she heard was only the first of two shots; a double tap that exploded her head like a coconut breaking open.

HARRY PUT HIS PISTOL, an original Colt 1911A1 .45, back in his shoulder holster. "Hollow points, Gretchen. Double tap to the head." He kicked her lifeless body lightly, playfully. "Bet you didn't see that coming." He laughed aloud. "Oh, well. Maybe, actually, you did. At least the first shot anyway."

In the distance the helo began to start up, the metallic whine of its single turbine climbing in pitch. The pilot, assigned to Harry and not working for Gretchen or even the FBI, had known what the signal would be and he was waiting for it. Harry knelt alongside Gretchen's body in the double depression of the "dents" in the road, the cause of which he had known full well, and all along. He placed a small RFID device down inside one of the cracks, below the surface of the road, and walked away.

Shortly, with Harry aboard, the helicopter took to flight, climbing. It hovered over the scene at an altitude of 1,000 feet. The pilot depressed the "pickle switch," a euphemism for the button that deploys munitions. A cylindrical device the size of a five-pound sack of flour released from the belly of the aircraft and fell. A retarder, like a miniature parachute, deployed from its tail, slowing its descent and homing it in on the RFID beacon Harry had planted in the road. The helo banked sharply and headed southeast at maximum speed.

When the bomb hit the ground it plonked dully, nonmetallically into the tarmac, its nose deforming and absorbing most of the force of the impact, causing the bomb to stick to the ground on the spot where it landed. Inside the canister, a kinetic firing pin pierced a thick membrane. Inside the membrane was a small amount of the chemical ethylenediamine, and as it mixed with the nitromethane that filled the rest of the bomb's canister, a violent explosion erupted. The two "dents" in the road were now an enormous single crater.

As for the rest of the "evidence," i.e. Gretchen Reid's body, it was engulfed, ablaze, torn apart and ejected in millions of fragments from the crater in a radius of more than six hundred feet. Harry smiled when the shockwave passed through him in midair. He sang a chilling little song: "Goodbye, Gretchen. Goodbye."

CHAPTER II

Ascension Island, present day

KREIOS RESTED ATOP GREEN Mountain, blandly and simply named in spite of its sublimely beautiful setting, almost 3,000 feet above sea level. Ascension Island, in the South Atlantic, was a good place to stop and rest, to collect his scattered thoughts for a little while, indulge in a stolen moment. This had always been one of his favorite places; a sanctuary of sorts for him. In the past it was always a destination. Now it was just a convenient place to stop, a waypoint on a journey elsewhere, and it made him intensely sad.

He faced south and east, away from Georgetown, his back to Wideawake Airfield, looking toward where he was headed: Cape Town, South Africa.

Kreios was so heavy with care that he was numb and staring. Wide-eyed, he let whole worlds pass by in review before his imagination.

Thoughts of the history of this place randomly crashed into and through him. Ascension Island, so named because of the date of its discovery on Ascension Day, a church calendar holiday. He knew its history of course, that some Christians had tried to redeem pagan feasts like Ashteroth by making them sacred—a millennially blind tradition that just as easily could be called sacrilege, depending on the perspective. *Good intentions,* he thought. He had been there at Babylon when the Tower fell, when the peoples were scattered. He had seen with his own eyes what that event had wrought under the sun.

What does any of it matter: he knew, for instance, and by personal experience, that Ascension Island was once used in what mankind commonly called the Second World War, in the Battle of the Atlantic, that the Allies had conducted operations against Nazi U-boats from the island. He knew it had served cross-Atlantic boatplanes as a refueling depot in the age of the propeller. He knew it once served as a coaling station for steam-powered transatlantic passenger liners.

He knew it all. He had seen one of the roots of the problem at Babylon. They had built a tower to their own glory. El had scattered them. Men were forced from then on to go their separate ways, to build their rickety empires with different languages. It was inevitable that different customs would emerge, that different ways of thinking would develop; different world views, alien to one another, would ensue. The chasm of worldview between men since Babylon was inevitable, he thought. *And beyond hope.*

The more of man's history he saw hurtling on past him at breakneck speed, the more meaningless and nonsensical it became. He had left paradise for this? *No. Not this.* In moments like these he prayed for the Brotherhood to come out of cowardly hiding and confront him. To take him. *After all, why not?* Perhaps then he might find meaning.

Honestly, he didn't care where he was, or even when. It was all the same perverse blur, an affront. He cared less too, in the final analysis, that the Brotherhood was sure to be tracking him.

Each flight, he knew, was like a cannonade at point-blank range. He thought of hiding from it all within the folds of time…perhaps going back to his little concrete room in the mountains of Idaho… walking through that door...

Perhaps, he thought, he was secretly hoping they would come. *All of them might converge upon me, thinking I possess the Bloodstone.* Then he might go down to Hell and take all of them with him. His mind flashed with Germanic legends of Valhalla, Gotterdammerung; the end of the world in a cataclysm of fire. He had known the demon Wotan, source of the legend. All these pagan legends had their dark angelic sources.

"The life is in the blood," he said, and he would spill it all. "Survival of the fittest," he said, mimicking Wotan's lie to the poor befuddled German philosophers, a lie that had now enraptured the entire world.

He ascended to the horizontal of a large white stone cross and sat upon it, an angel of El, hanging his head in desperation. His back to its post, he rested drooped on its arm, lifted up above the earth, and the tropical breezes filtered through him.

His thoughts relentlessly clawed back, torturing him: Airel was gone. Eriel was lost forever. There was nothing left. There was nothing but blood in the streets, running in the gutters, the blood of the Brotherhood…and finally, eventually…of Michael Alexander.

The traitor. The Judas Iscariot.

The warm breeze lifted him from his homicidal bent, brought him memories of his home. Millennia ago. It was indeed a different life. Filled to brimming with quiet, with solitude, with peace and fulfillment.

He smiled.

How long had it been since he had done that?

It was her face: Eriel. Oh! How she looked like her mother!

Wonderful. Beautiful, full of life and full of fire. It was she that had kept him going after his beloved wife had passed on. But how many countless years had passed over him in indifferent numb purposelessness since then?

He growled at the breeze. "It's all over now," he said aloud. She his beloved, and Eriel, and even Airel—every trace of his love and every reason for which he had abandoned paradise were now wiped away, obliterated. They were to be no more.

"But what does that matter?"

They were all gone. All three, gone. They would not return to him. He was abandoned, alone, dead, hollow. Kreios set his jaw and gnashed his teeth, his eyes narrowed to warlike slits. "We will meet again, young Michael Alexander. We will. And when we do…I will exact payment in full. And I will take my time."

The angel lifted up his head and stood to his feet on the cross. Looking east and south. The sun behind. Darkness before him. He was beyond intrepid; not even El could change his mind now. He had a very great many of the Nri to kill, and quickly.

Kreios deftly flexed his body and leapt into the air with a curse for the Brotherhood. The angel shot forward into the sky, leaving a misty contrail in his wake. The shape of wings, made of light and mist, hovered over his back.

Kreios drank in the elation of pure power and speed. There was something magical and holy about flying. Indeed, there had been a day when he was holy…but that was another time. Another life.

CHAPTER III

Arlington, Oregon, present day

"AND THE LORD PUT a mark on Cain, lest any who found him should attack him…"

I pored over this verse in Genesis 4, just one page before the one to which Kreios had guided me what seemed like an eternity ago. I was stunned at how much the Bible said, and with so little. The trouble was…what did it all mean? I was reading by the light of my Tracphone in the darkness of my hotel room, having grabbed the Gideons copy of the Bible out of the nightstand.

I had no idea why I had turned absentmindedly to this page. I was just sitting there reading it when it jumped off the page and grabbed me and wouldn't let me go.

Oh, Kreios…I really, really miss you. I wished more than anything then for my grandfather to come home to me. And home—at least as I had always thought of it up to that moment of my life—was now simply wherever he was. It's not that I didn't care about or miss my parents. I didn't have the luxury of time enough to reflect on them or what they might be thinking, how they might be worried about me. Truth be told, I was trying to avoid that subject; it was too painful, too far out of my control.

I was a prisoner again. A prisoner to circumstance. It sucked. *Is life really like this? Just all kinds of crap that happens to you? Or does a girl get to make a choice every now and then?*

She crowded into my mind. *"But you've already made all kinds of choices…"*

True enough. The realization made me hurt unbearably.

I was completely frazzled and confused and lonely and in need of somebody stronger than me. Though the tears threatened the edges of my eyelids again, I was sick of crying, sick of being carried along, sick of abdicating, sick of this slimy acquiescence that marked *me* somehow. And I supposed all of us, really, bore some kind of mark.

But I hated labels. I hated that my favorite books, for instance, had to be categorized as this or that or the other thing. Why couldn't they just stand alone on their own merit? Why did life lump everything together? "Grrr," I said to the lame hotel room painting hanging above the mirror.

Kim, snoring next to me on the bed, stirred a little but didn't wake. Across the room on the other bed, came a voice: "Date went that well, eh?"

"How 'bout you shut your face, Ellie," I muttered, with more than a little menace.

No reply.

I continued: "Or I'll come over there and finish the job I started when we first met." I was so peeved. How was anything about Michael and me any of her business? I just wanted her to go away. As I brought my knees to my chest and dropped my head into my folded arms, I willed for her to go away.

But then the bed moved and I looked up reflexively. I jumped a little. She was sitting there right in front of me, on my side of the bed. *How did she get over here so quick, so quietly?* "Whadda*you* want," I spat.

"Girlie, I was going to ask you the very same thing."

"Stop calling me that."

"Calling you what?" she asked in her insufferably cool accent.

"What gives you the right to poke your nose into everybody's business? And then act like nothing's happening, calling me by pet names. You're not my mom. Lay off."

"Sorry, girlie, it's just who I am."

I could tell she wasn't going to stop irritating me. It was too much fun for her. "Look, I'm not enjoying the game, okay? So bug off."

"You're perilously close to profanity where I come from."

I just rolled my eyes at her. *You're about to hear much worse.*

"Airel, what's bothering you? Do you want to talk?"

I just looked at her. I wanted to shout, "HA!" at her, but I didn't want to wake Kim. I looked at the clock: near midnight. "The only thing I want to do is sleep," I said lamely, hoping she would go away. "But I can't seem to."

Ellie placed a sympathetic hand on my knee, saying, "Shh. It's all right, now." And then that old weird feeling came back for me, the ripping apart of my heart and soul, and all I could think was *oh my gosh, she's crazy evil.* I brushed her hand aside, and as I did, something stabbed at my heart. It went deep; I didn't know what it was. It was just awful, that's all. "Just stay away from me, Ellie. I don't want to talk to you or see you or anything. Just leave me alone!"

I couldn't describe how she looked right then if I wanted to. But there was deep meaning and pain in her eyes. The source of it—I couldn't begin to know. "It's all right," she said again, standing.

She looked down on me with eyes that pierced right through

me, flesh, half-angel blood, bone, and marrow. "I'm gonna step out for a bit." She stood there for a split second, looking at me. It creeped me out, because for all I could make out of it her expression was one of love and acceptance.

Then she turned and slipped out the door.

I was so angry at her. How could she think I wanted to be her friend after she so shamelessly flirted with Michael, like, every five seconds. I saw through her. I could see that she was working some angle, was playing some game. I wouldn't play along, even if she pretended to play nice.

It all made me very tired. I fell back on my pillow and dreamed instantly.

It was the kind of dream that was difficult to judge; I couldn't tell if it was real or not. Dreaming or waking, this is what happened: I got up from the bed, peeked around the curtains through the window, and saw her. She was walking away with someone…it was Michael. After that everything was totally blank.

IT COULD HAVE BEEN hours, days before I woke. And when I did, I was so disoriented that I thought I was back home in my room before all my synapses were firing properly. It was jarring; that *where the heck am I* feeling.

And I woke with a start, like I had just hit the ground from some precipitous fall from dizzying height. I was pretty sure my spasm, which rocked the whole bed, was what woke Kim from the sleep of the dead as well. We both popped up from the pillows and stared at each other wide-eyed, wild-haired. She looked horrible.

"What's happening?" she asked.

"Ew, Kim," I said. "Dragon breath. What did you eat?"

She opened her mouth wide and hissed, "Piiiiiiiiizza, with loooooooooooots of gaaaaaaaarlic."

I gagged and turned away. I really did want to barf. She smelled like a freaking demon.

And that's when it all came thundering back at me. I heard Michael's voice in my head, urging me to talk to Kim about the Bloodstone.

It all made Hellish sense. Her motives, her behavior, her... smell...could all be explained by the one simple question that I didn't dare ask my best friend.

I hesitated. I didn't know where it would leave us once I opened this can of worms. A question like that couldn't be un-asked. Certain things couldn't be unsaid, just like certain things couldn't be undone. I thought about how my mom always used to tell me, "Adult decisions have adult consequences," urging me to be very careful as I tested the world with my newfound teenage powers of Choice. I thought I knew everything. Now it was starting to become clear just how little I knew and how much my parents—painful subject that that was to me—had known all along.

"Kim," I ventured, fearing the end of everything good and right in the world, "I...I need to talk to you."

She sat up and looked at me, pulling the covers up to her neck. Her face was serious. "Yeah, I guess we're overdue," she yawned.

You don't know how right you are. I decided to just go for it. "Um, did you happen to find a little red stone anytime recently?" I couldn't bear to look her in the eye, afraid of what I might find there. But I finally looked up at her.

A cornered cat. That's what she was. "Airel," she finally said, "I don't have it."

I had never seen her this way. This was not my happy-go-lucky Kim, my chatty Kim, my spacecase buddy from way back. She looked scared. I didn't know what to say.

"I swear, Airel. I don't have it."

"It was down in the park," I said, the light coming on, "wasn't it?" I felt so stupid. It was all coming together.

She nodded and then looked away in shame.

"So…" I was in disbelief. "So you carried it this whole time? All the way from…from…"

"I found it on the ground after Michael…um…after Michael—"

"Killed his dad?"

She was crying. "Pretty much." But these were not tears of relief, of confession.

"Kim, why are you so scared?"

She wouldn't answer.

I reached out and touched her arm. She gave a little start but then burst into tears.

"Oh, Airel! I'm so scared!" she sobbed. "I've never wanted anything so bad in my whole life!" Her body was racked with tears, but then she recovered. "I've never messed around with drugs or anything. But I can't tell you how bad this feels! I mean…it's like I don't even know my own thoughts; they just keep pounding away at me, I don't even know where they're coming from or why—I mean, I guess I know *why,* I just don't recognize the things that pop into my head, and now it's gone and I don't know where it is…" As she said this last part, she looked right into my eyes and I could tell it was a lie.

"Kim. Yes, you do. Fess up."

She growled at me. Showing her teeth. Her eyes were crazed.

"Kim. Don't. Mess. With. Me. You know I can handle you, no matter what." *Not that I want to fight my BFF, but dang.*

"I'm scared…"

"We've established that. Where is it?"

Nothing.

"Kim, I can't tell you how dangerous this is. Do you know what you've—" *Check that.* I didn't want to make her feel worse by implicating her as being responsible for all our miseries so far on this trip. "Listen. The Brotherhood wants that thing more than... more than a fat kid wants his next snack, okay? Can I let you in on a little secret?" I gauged her for a second. *How much do you want to bet she already knows this?*

She looked up at me. "What."

I plunged ahead, hoping my transparency would pay dividends between us in the long run. I missed my normal Kimmie. "You wanna know why they're chasing us down? It's not just 'cause Michael killed Mr. Alexander. Stanley, I mean." I looked at her more closely. "It's because... whoever picks up that stone...the Bloodstone...becomes the next Seer."

She seemed unfazed; I couldn't make it out. Maybe she had already figured that out, or heard whisperings about it, much like *She* would wind her way into my thoughts.

"Kim, that means power. Plain and simple." *She* popped into my head with this epithet: *"Deception equals control equals power."* It felt true enough. Especially just looking at Kim. I reached out to touch her once more.

This time she didn't jump. "He has it," she said simply.

"Who," I said, though the stab in my heart told me the truth.

"Michael," she said matter-of-factly, and I could tell it was partway intended as a jab. That wasn't Kim; it was the Bloodstone. My anger kindled. I was speechless. "What will he do with it, I wonder?" she went on.

"Kim..."

"No, hear me out," she said. "What possible reason could he have for wanting to keep it? And keep it secret? From, of *all* people, you? His so-called love?"

"Kim, you're starting to weird me out." I didn't add that I wanted more than anything to slap the smugness right off her face. *What is happening to us?* But I knew: it was the stupid stone. I growled and stood, pacing.

"What's the matter, Airel?" her tone was sickeningly sweet.

I bolted to her and got in her face, snarling. "Just you shut up, Kim. Seer. Whoever I'm talking to. You're not yourself, and you're out of your depth. No matter who you are."

She feigned mock surprise and awe.

I released her throat, which I didn't realize I had grasped in my anger, and stood away. "And for crying out loud, girl, would you brush your teeth before we have our next conversation?"

Thank God that broke the spell, or whatever.

Kim laughed out loud. She then walked in her underwear to the bathroom, her body covered with scratches, sores, bruises, and red marks. She looked awful. My heart sank for her. More than ever, I felt overwhelmed.

Worst of all…Michael. My Michael. *Now what?*

CHAPTER IV

I DIDN'T HAVE MUCH time to contemplate anything, because Ellie then burst into the room saying something about Michael.

I feared the worst and wondered why.

"Airel, I—wait, where's Kim?"

"She's in the shower," I said. "I know it's like 3 a.m., but she's weird. Anyway, why?"

She looked relieved for some reason. "I just like to know the whereabouts of my teammates, that's all."

"Some team," I muttered under my breath. Then I addressed her: "Ellie, what's going on?"

"I need help."

She looked so desperate that I was able to suppress my laughter. "With what?"

"I don't know what to do with him."

"Who?" I growled, suspecting the worst possible answer; the wrong one. *Why can't she just leave my man alone?*

"It's Michael. I need your help."

I shot up off the bed and got in her face. "How dare you! You know what, it's high time I told you off, little missy. How dare you.

How dare you! You stay away from him, you hear? Do you hear me? You stay away from him or I'll—I can't believe you're doing this, in broad daylight too!" *Never mind that it's the middle of the night...* "Anyway right under my nose, just flaunting your flirting. I'm sick of it, sick of you. I'm warning you..." I stopped in mid-rant because she turned away with a smirk, raised her hands and shook her head. What gall. I couldn't believe it.

All she said was, "Oh, the irony," and circled back around to face me. Her eyes were loaded with meaning I couldn't hope to understand.

I tried to speak but couldn't.

"Airel, listen closely, because I'm only going to say this once. I have no interest in your Alexander demon boy. At least insofar as it does not directly concern *you.* And for the record, I'm disappointed."

"About what?"

"That you've not guessed it yet. The intelligence I'd gathered up to now led me to believe you were smarter. Quicker."

"Look, you don't have to insult me, too—"

"I'm not, girlie. I'm just trying to help. Will you let me?"

It was just intolerable. One drop of kindness could defuse a nuclear bomb, dag nabbit. I scowled at her but relented. "Fine. But this conversation is not over."

"As I said: irony. Now, shall we go rescue your silly bloke together?"

Ooo, I hate this. Because now Ellie and I have common ground and it involves the love of my life. Darn you, sissy la-la Aussie electric blue pompom head girl! "What's he done now," I asked, the words chafing against me even as I spoke them.

"Um, yeah. You will have to see it to believe it. Unfortunately." She stalled for a moment. "I don't suppose this is the best time or place to confess this, but he and I were out and about together earlier. Just the two of us. It was a reconnaissance mission."

"Go on," I said through clenched teeth.

"He was concerned about signs of a tail, an enemy observation scheme. We ran them down together, stopped them. But it wasn't at all what we expected, and that's why I need you."

Before I could interject, Kim emerged from the bathroom nude, looking like the bride of Satan's spawn. "Kim," I said, "Would you wrap up in a towel or something?"

She simply yawned. "Oh, hi, girls," she said and walked to the bed and snuggled under the covers.

"Anyway…we've gotta run out for a minute," I said.

No response. Just muffled snores.

"Holy crap, is she out already?"

"Looks to be so, girlie."

I rolled my eyes. My life was officially ridiculous. Yeah, and things had kinda been skewing that way for a while now. "So what is going on?" I asked again, perturbed that I was still not getting it. It was like my mind had clouded over with a mental cataract or something.

"It's Michael."

"Duh."

"I need you to help me with him."

"Yes…" I arched my eyebrows.

"Look, it's easier if you just come with me now."

I didn't like that at all. I growled again. "You are the most exasperating person I know."

"Well, you can either come or not. You're still making the choices here."

Yeah, this whole freakin' thing stinks. I grabbed my room key and led her out the door in a huff.

WE APPROACHED THE PARK where, I could imagine clearly now, the Bloodstone had changed hands between Kim and Michael right under my nose. He hadn't told me about it at all. *But if he has it, why did he tell me to talk to Kim? She doesn't have it, he does!* I was incredibly worried that he was making some stupid brave decision, some chauvinistic act of noble duty and self-sacrifice to which men are so often and so foolishly predisposed. *Hello, hero boy, I don't need you to rescue me. I just want you to talk to me.* It made me even more irritable that he didn't trust me enough to share the burden of it with me.

"Darn you, Michael," I muttered under my breath, "what have you done now?"

I looked askance at Ellie walking alongside me. No clues there. Her lips were sealed shut in a grimace of strong determination as she walked through the grass with me.

Finally she stopped and pointed. "There," she said. It was clear she did not intend to accompany me further.

"Fine," I said, and walked in the direction described by her index finger. All I could see in front of me was the little roped-off beach area just beyond the trees and grass. There was a dark shape there, but I wasn't sure…it looked like a boulder to me in the dim light. I looked back to Ellie for confirmation, but she had already turned back. She was probably going back to the hotel for some sleep. *What a luxury,* I thought. *Why is she even here? To stir up all kinds of crap for me to deal with?*

I heard a noise from the beach and turned back toward the water. The shape that I had assumed was a boulder was subtly moving. The hair on the back of my neck stood up, and I groped around for *She*. Nothing.

Frozen to my place at the edge of the manicured grass, I waited in fear for more information. The shape was human. *Maybe.* It looked and sounded like someone was bent over, sobbing quietly in the sand. I decided to get closer. The choice wasn't made with the consent of my awareness; it was pure destiny.

I wagered a further risk: "Michael?" I took a few more timid steps toward the shape.

Then I realized what it was; the bubble of impossibility popped. *It's not one person. It's two.* Drawn out prone in the cold dark of the sand was a second person. The hair on my arms stood erect and my eyes widened, stark. Only one of the people was moving. The other was lifeless.

Please, God, don't let that be Michael! I thought Ellie had betrayed me, that she had lured him out alone with her and then ambushed, assaulted and killed him with one of her confederates. Who that might have been I had no idea, but that didn't matter. Then she had come for me, led me here so that I could be done to death as well, and then she went off to kill Kim as she slept. I looked wildly around in a panic.

I couldn't help but shout in a hoarse whisper: "Michael!" I was about ten feet away from either certain death or the love of my life, and it never once occurred to me to try to call the Sword of Light.

The shape moved, twisted toward me and I saw a face in the dark; a face I knew well. "Michael!" I ran to him, crashed to the sandy earth on my knees at his side and wrapped my arms around his neck. It was him.

I felt his sobs as they racked both of us in heaving grief. He did not return my embrace. I pulled away to see what was the matter. I then saw a thing that would change me forever, just like every little thing I had been made to endure since we had first met, since he had activated me, since we had sparked our intense bond to each other.

It was the face of a child.

Held in Michael's arms was a boy of no more than about ten years of age. His eyes were pallid and dull in death. Michael's face was drawn back in overwhelming pain. His sobs came in stabbing spasms as he moaned and cried.

I didn't know what to do. I had been thrust into a cup of such an impossible admixture of morbidity, pain, love, and sympathy, it felt absolutely crazy to be stirred up within it. It hurt beyond words, but I was with him. I knew that I could do anything, endure anything as long as I had my Michael. It was a fact, so I stayed there with him on that little beach in the darkness as he held the corpse of a boy.

Answers? They would come. I believed that, and it was enough.

CHAPTER V

MICHAEL KNELT IN THE sand, filled with grief. *What have I done?*

But it wasn't his fault. Surely not. *Why does it have to be like this? This is unbearable! Why do they have to do this kind of thing?* He raged against what had happened, and at his hand. Again. Regret, most bitter of all the emotions, rained down upon his heart and mind, soaking into the very marrow of all that he was.

He knew the methods, of course. He should have seen it coming. But he didn't imagine it. It took wickeder minds for that.

Airel whispered to him, "What happened?" She stroked his back, and it calmed him a little.

At first he was unable to speak. Once he tried, however, the words began to come easily. "They…I knew they had sent scouts. I just didn't think…I just didn't think the Brotherhood would do it like this. To send the…the Garrison of the Offspring!" Michael knew how horrid and evil it was. Demons manipulating the minds of the innocent, the children, making inroads against El by turning the children against Him. It had been a product of cold genius to him when he had first beheld it years ago. But now it was too real.

"They sent the children."

"What?" Airel said. "What does any of that mean?" She looked horrified in the darkness, looking back and forth from the dead countenance of the corpse to that of his own.

"It means," Michael tried his best to regain his composure, "that they have opened up the entire armory against us. And they want us to know it. Not that they're desperate. But that they will do whatever it takes."

"To do what, kill us?"

"Yes." He looked away from the dead eyes of the child across the river, to the distance. "And recover the Bloodstone." Tension, then. Heavy and sudden, full of unfinished business that would have to remain unfinished for now. "That's what they're trying so desperately to grab for. The Infernals don't care how much military capital they have to expend in order to gain it."

He looked at her. She seemed very scared, which was unlike her.

"Don't worry. At this point it's every man for himself in the Brotherhood. They're still not beneath the idea of killing each other in order to get the Bloodstone. With it comes the power of the Seer. They want that more than anything."

He looked back to the rapidly cooling body of the child in his arms.

"What happened?" Airel asked him.

He sighed. "I asked Ellie to help me ferret them out," he began. "I had begun to see some suspicious activity around the fringes of our movements here in Arlington. Since our plane isn't here yet, and since I also didn't want them to follow us when we leave, I decided we needed to confront and destroy them…"

Grief raked its claws across his wretched mind once more as he thought about the aborted life of the child he had killed, the missed unlimited chances it represented for life. For good or ill, the boy had a right to live. Michael had revoked all of that with a single act.

He tried to move on with the account of how it had happened. "With Ellie's help, we managed to isolate the tail. We had ascertained that there was only one. We cornered him here on the beach, against the water. I should have known before I took him down…" …*that he was too small to be a grown man…* "…but I took my shot anyway."

"You shot him?!" Airel hissed in a whisper, then recovered. "Wait…you shot him? I didn't hear any gunshots."

"The freeway's right there," he pointed straight ahead. The racket of interstate traffic, mostly trucks at that hour, became very loud once attention had been drawn to it. "Besides," he patted his ribs under his sweater, "Stanley trained me well. I know when to use a silencer."

It came off rude, like sacrilege, and he did not intend that. But he couldn't stop himself. "One shot. I took him down with one shot."

He then collapsed into more heaving sobs.

"I knew him, you know…" His voice softened as he brushed a hand over the boy's cheek. "This was James' little bro. I used to help change his diapers…" He choked on a sob and swallowed hard.

Airel prodded softly, "What was his name?"

"This was Marc." Michael was running out of tears to cry. He could feel anger beginning to set in.

"Did he…attack you?"

"Yeah, I chased him here. He was just beginning to change…I had to kill him. There was no time to think, really."

"I'm so sorry," she said. She was silent for a while. "But you had to defend yourself. You had to defend me—us."

"God, I killed him. I killed Marc. What else is there?" His voice was quiet. "When will it ever be enough?"

He stood, holding Marc dead and dangling. The boy was small in his arms. "I need some time alone. To take care of this, to think."

"What are you going to do?"

He looked at her. "Take care of it."

"Where should I go?" She sounded lost.

"Back to the room. Sleep. Ellie says her man will be here with a car at 8 a.m. sharp to pick us up and take us to the airstrip. That doesn't give you much time."

Airel looked very sad. "You want me to leave?" She stood off from him, hands in her back pockets.

He looked at her perhaps a little cruelly, he thought. "Yes," he said, hoping she would understand all that he had been through for her. For them.

Eyes brimming with tears, she left him.

I COULDN'T BELIEVE IT. Michael had killed a boy; demon host or not, he was a *boy*. And James's little bro, too. *Yikes*. And now he didn't want me around. I felt like I didn't even know him anymore. I didn't know how much to attribute to the Bloodstone, how much to all the crazy circumstances of our situation, and how much was just me doing my over-thinking thing again.

I walked alone, back to the hotel room. Back to Kim, the zombie; and Ellie, the weirdo. A little slice of Hell.

CHAPTER VI

Arabia 1232 B.C.

"HE HAS FAVORED YOU with a glance, Uriel! I think you have found favor in his eyes," Santura said. She smiled broadly at the young man, a little too much so for Uriel's comfort. She turned away from the boy Santura had indicated. He was tall and strong enough, perhaps, but his piggishly small eyes were much too close together.

"Him!" she whispered with disdain, "He's not what I should call handsome at all." Still, she was of age and she wanted a man of her own, if even as a plaything. Less for romantic exploits than to irritate her father, truth be told. Her uncle Yamanu gave her the kind of free reign only uncles could, the kind of liberties a father, in her experience, could not and would not ever grant a daughter.

Santura giggled as she flirted with the young man for herself. "Uriel, stop it! He is handsome enough." She gave him a little wave. "Besides, there's more to a man's eligibility than the construct of his face. There's nobility, for instance."

"Oh, Santura, you can rest assured. I know all about *his* line. Dear Yakob shall one day inherit vast riches not only from his father's bloodline, but also from his mother—the union of his parents was *most* wise *and* judicious." Uriel did not say that she found it deplorable for women to marry for dowries. For expedience. Was there not more to hope for under the sun?

"He is well liked by the elders," Santura said, running a hand through her long blonde hair and fiddling with the pure white flower of plumeria that she had tucked behind her ear.

"Power and lineage are not everything, Santura. I want to marry for love. I long for the embrace of the one I would breathe for!" Uriel looked out and away, across the rooftops of the city of Ke'elei to the red mountains beyond. "That is true love. I shall find him one day." Of course she knew of whom she spoke. But she would not speak his name. Not yet.

They stood at an upper window in her uncle's house. Yakob, down in the street below, blew them a kiss, delighting Santura, exasperating Uriel. She turned away from the scene, leaving her friend to her work—for work it was and work it would not cease to be. "Ugh," she couldn't help exclaiming.

She thought back to the strange and beautiful young man she had met not even a fortnight ago. Now *he* was something. There was something about him of which she could not rid herself in her mind. Indeed, in her very heart. Indeed still, he haunted her dreams and she found herself enwrapped within the soft welcoming folds of self-centered fantasy. *How could he capture me so, and in just one chance encounter?* He was all she could think about, all she wanted to think about.

Santura ducked back inside the stone arched window and sighed at her with big blue lovesick eyes. "Oh, Uriel! Isn't it wonderful? Life is amazing…"

"Santura, you are being unbearable again." Uriel smiled at her to soften the blow.

"I know, I know. There is...someone else you have in mind?" she squealed like a little girl. "Perhaps...the boy we met the other night?"

Uriel screwed up her face, trying to appear to be confused, but then turned away when her blushing cheeks betrayed her.

"I knew it! You *do* fancy him! Admit it, Uriel, you dream of him, do you not?"

"Santura, stop! He is a...a most fascinating young man, I will admit."

"Ha!"

"And if you must know, I do think he is amazing." She turned away and tried to busy herself with something, anything. "What I mean to say is that...is that he does have the most...the most captivating eyes." Intense redness swelled into her cheeks and forehead, making her feel slightly ill.

Santura shook her head like a sage old woman. "Ah...love!"

"Santura! Stop..." she begged, but did not mean any of it. She rather adored everything about him, even Santura's little tortures. All she could do was meditate upon his face, his features, his broad and very strong chest, his name. "Subedei..." she whispered the name and smiled wide.

He was not of the city of Ke'elei, of course. He was from out beyond the red mountains, a traveling merchant she guessed, perhaps some kind of nobility in his own right judging by the manner in which he carried himself, the quality of his robes, his headdress.

She had met him in the market. She had been walking with Santura, looking back over one shoulder to try to fend off a hawking fishmonger, when she crashed quite literally into him.

"Subedei..." He was so tall, so strong, so bronzed and handsome. His eyes were like the blade of the sword, and just as sharp. His frame lithe, supple, rippled with muscle, aglow with health and strength. Her imagination ran a bit wild thinking of him.

She had walked right into his powerful chest, stumbling over both his feet and hers, and looked up into his face as if awakening from a dream, his strong arms roundabout her. "Oh!" she had said stupidly, "I am so sorry!" She had dropped her purse, a little leather pouch of coins given as an allowance by her uncle for incidentals at the market. She glanced down at it in concern. The market was no place to go round dropping coins; anything could happen.

"Let me," he said as he reached down and picked it up, placing it safely into her open hands. They stood uncomfortably close for complete strangers, but neither of them made a move to separate for a long moment. Santura had been watching the whole thing unfold; her heavy breathing brought Uriel back around and she silenced Santura with a scolding glance.

Uriel turned back to the young man. "Thank you," she said.

"Subedei," he replied, and took her hand and kissed it, causing her to blush. This impetuous young man from parts unknown had the air of romantic adventure about him.

She fell instantly and surrendered her name on the spot. "Uriel."

"It is a pleasure," he had replied.

Uriel sighed at the memory of it. It was such a shame that they had decided for the sake of propriety to keep moving on, she and Santura. But after all it had been so embarrassing. It was really almost unbearable. She looked back in woeful regret. Would she ever see him again?

Reality came crashing back in upon her with even greater force as her uncle burst into the room. He wasn't ever one to come crashing or bursting into anything; he was so soft spoken. She knew her reaction of shock was owing solely to her state. Love. Fantasies. Self-absorption. "Oh, hello, uncle," she said in greeting.

"Greetings, my beloved niece, and her favored friend Santura."
He bowed to them. "Uriel, are you ready for your shadowing
lessons today?"

Her heart sank. All she truly wanted to do was to sit in
daydreaming speculation about the mysterious Subedei, ponder over
their wedding day feast, wonder at the power of his love, dream
about the home they might build together. "Oh. Why, yes, uncle.
Yes, I am."

"Good!" he said. "Meet me in the training hut two hours before
the evening meal. I have a special wrinkle I wish to throw at you
today." He winked and smiled at her. "I must go. Do not be late,
beautiful girl." He left as suddenly as he had come, pausing only to
grab an orange from the wooden bowl that lay perpetually on the
table of the house, the wooden bowl that she had gone to the market
a fortnight ago to restock with fresh oranges, figs and breadfruit.

She was heartsick. She had to admit it. Ever since that day…she
had not felt well. *This thing called lovesickness is quite real.*

Yet all she wanted was to see him again—and she would.
Perhaps I can turn these shadowing lessons to good use…. Perhaps
she could sneak out of the city under cover of the trade of the
shadower, and search for her man.

Subedei.

CHAPTER VII

Boise, Idaho, present day

"HONEY, I HATE TO do this to you, and especially now, but…" he searched for a way to say what he needed to say. "…But I've gotta take another sales trip."

She didn't react at all. That was not a good sign. If at least he could get a rise out of her he would feel better, feel like she wasn't completely overwhelmed with the situation. After more than twenty years of marriage, he knew her well enough to know that.

"Honey? Did you hear what I said?" He knelt down in front of her easy chair. This was her spot in the house. Nobody else sat here. She read her gardening magazines in this chair in the summer, crocheted in this chair when the weather was bad. "It's out of town…" He placed a hand on her knee.

She snapped out of her trance and looked away from the window, finally meeting his eyes. "What's that?"

"I said I have to take another sales trip. Out of town."

Realization dawned upon her features, and her countenance both brightened and fell.

It struck him that she was just as beautiful now, if not more so, than she had been on their wedding day. If beauty was in the eye of the beholder it was mostly up around the eyes, held within the light that dwelt there. It was love, it was intellect, it was…*well, it's kind of saucy. Sometimes.*

"I love you. I'm sorry to do this now. But I don't have much choice when the company comes calling. At least if we want to, ah—" he gestured to the house they had built "—live here. Still." He felt lame. He found it amazing that she could fluster him with a glance even after all these years.

"Oh," she responded finally. "Well, it's okay, hon. I'll manage." She didn't sound very convincing. "How long?"

"Well," he stood and rubbed his neck with one hand, looking contemplative, hoping she would buy it if he didn't overact. "It depends on what happens. The executive team will be there, the whole enchilada. The board, some important shareholders…so there's going to be a meeting of the minds, a strategy session; you know, and then a seminar when some of the more junior sales personnel get there. So it could take a week. Maybe two…. But you might consider calling your sister, honey. Maybe see if you can crash there while I'm gone. I just don't want you to be all alone right now. With all that's…that's going on, you know?"

"Do you think she's still alive?" she asked him abruptly.

Anger and pain pierced right through him. She wasn't talking about her sister. "Honey, the FBI is all over this. I'm sure Airel's fine." He knelt before her again and took her hands in his own. "Hey," he looked her purposefully in the eyes. "She's fine, okay? We're—those people are going to find her and bring her home. I promise."

She looked away and squeezed her eyes shut, pressing the tears out. She let them fall freely, unashamedly. "You really have to leave now?"

He tightened his lips into a straight line. "I wouldn't be doing this if I didn't have to."

She sighed heavily. A quiver of grief made it stutter as it came out. "It's out of town? How far out of town?"

"It's international, unfortunately. I have a long flight ahead of me. Plus I have to get down to Central District Health and get inoculated. These guys want to meet up in South Africa."

"Oh. Is it safe?"

He smiled. "Yes, dear. Of course, it is. But you really ought to call your sister, honey. Really." He stroked her hair away from her face.

"All right, then. I suppose…" She looked at him with brief vague suspicion, but let it drop in the end. She sighed heavily again. "I suppose you know best." Another sigh as she contemplated the situation. "I guess it would do me good to get out of here anyway."

He nodded. He didn't want to oversell it.

They stood.

"Okay, then. Africa? Amazing. I didn't know they did anything in Africa."

"Oh, wow, hon. You should Google it. You'd be amazed."

"Really?"

"Yeah. Use Google images. Search for Cape Town, two words. You'll be stunned."

"Really? Where are you staying there?"

"Oh, it's in a nice little out-of-the-way spot called Simon's Town. They've got a few little hotels there right on the water. Little café called Bertha's. Should be fun."

"Wives can't come?" She gave him an elbow in the rib.

Oops. "Ah…no. Sorry. The company just wants us men."

She rolled her eyes at him. "Just you barbarians. Fine, go. Go and smoke cigars and drink Scotch and gawk at bikini-clad women.

Just come home to me, all right?"

"Hey," he said, "have I ever told a lie?"

Again, the eyes rolling. She turned to walk to the kitchen for the phone, talking over her shoulder at him. "Just bring the man I married back home to me. That's all."

Conversation over. *Whew.*

"And one more thing," she said, wheeling back toward him suddenly and walking directly up to him. "I love you," she said, and kissed him savagely.

When she pulled away he was quite breathless. "Whoa. Nelly."

She turned back to the phone with a wicked smirk on her face.

He swatted her butt as she walked away, making her howl in shock. He cackled devilishly and then stalked away toward the den. God, how he loved to flirt with her.

But now it was down to business.

He ducked into the office and turned around quickly, listening for the sounds of his wife talking to her sister on the phone. Yes, she had called and they were talking. He closed the door most of the way and began to pack a single black duffel.

The bookcase pulled out from the wall in an arc, hinged like a door, revealing a hidden safe behind. He turned the dial of the combination lock. It opened to his touch, revealing his passports, his stash of various currencies, and a matched set of daggers. The South African passport, a stack of about a quarter million rand in large notes and the daggers—these all went into the duffel.

His passport was diplomatic, naming him as a South African national. Security checkpoints would allow him to pass completely unmolested when he flashed the document. He closed everything up, replacing the bookcase and rubbing his foot over the carpet where it had left a sign of its movement in a perfect semicircle. Smart was so simple sometimes.

The FBI had of course been either infiltrated or fallen prey to its own considerable bureaucratic girth. That was inevitable. *Idiots.* In any case, it was now time to take matters into his own hands.

His beloved wife would be safe at her sister's house, he would fly to Cape Town based on intel he had gathered from his own sources, and things would play out however they would play out. No matter what. Daddies didn't leave their children at the mercy of murderous kidnappers, slovenly predatory teenage boys, weird unexplainable news stories with bizarre common threads, or any other malicious force under the sun. He would rescue his little girl, by God, come Hell or high water.

Time to pack the clothes.

And you know what, it probably wouldn't hurt to pack the 12 gauge in there, either, on second thought. Follow up on that threat I made to that boy. He stopped and thought for a moment. *I'd better grab the pipe cutter in the garage and shorten the barrel.* With that, he also made a mental note to grab the hollow point rifled slugs for ammo. They could blow a pie pan-sized hole in a bull elk at fifty yards. *Imagine what one of them might do to a kidnapper.* Or an unfortunate boy, should he prove to be guilty of harming one hair on his little Airel's head.

CHAPTER VIII

Arlington, Oregon, present day

AFTER MUCH INTERNAL DEBATE about what to do with the body of the boy, Michael decided to steal a boat. He slipped into the water with the corpse and swam sidestroke, his trailing arm dragging the lifeless husk along behind. It was the only way to avoid the well-lit paths of the park, the lighted docks of the marina.

It only took about fifteen minutes of swimming under the Interstate bridges out to the docks. He found a wakeboard boat with a large platform on the stern and floated the body onto it. Pulling himself up, he climbed aboard and pulled the body with him, laying it flat on the deck. One minute more yielded the hiding place for the keys, the master power switch, and ignition. A few more minutes and he had cast off.

Allowing the boat's engine to idle, he piloted it out past the breakwater to the wide open and swiftly moving currents of the Columbia River. Turning the bow to the left, he let the boat slip into the downstream current and cut the engine.

"Goodbye, Marc. I'm sorry." It was all he could say.

He turned, stepped over the transom onto the rear platform, and lowered himself quietly into the river. He swam with the current, making his way slowly toward shore. By the time he reached it, the sun was beginning to peel the night sky back, opening the day wide at the eastern horizon. He stood on the southern shore of the Columbia about half a mile from the park and his hotel room. He faced the river and looked for the boat. It was drifting quickly downstream from him, farther out in the middle of the river. Before too long it would crash into the John Day dam, unless the police or someone else apprehended it.

"Good thing our plane leaves soon." He began the walk back, his pace rapid.

5 A.M. AND I was already in the shower getting ready for our flight.

I didn't sleep very well, or very long. I had weird dreams that I couldn't remember, and I woke up missing my family terribly. The ache I felt for them went beyond my parents, though. It was like I missed my extended family, people I hadn't seen since the last reunion—Mandatory Fun Day, I always called it. *Come on, I miss these people? Weird aunt Stella? Cousin Fred and his stupid Trans Am? Granny Beatrice and her flatulence? Really?* No, there had to be something more, something different. I wasn't seeing it; there was some weird blockage.

It had to be the stone. I wished I could have talked to Michael about it, but he was obviously dealing with enough already. I felt bad for him, but then again, if he was stupid enough to carry that stupid thing and think he could remain unaffected, well, I guess I wished him well. I mean, I had no proof of whether or not he had it, but I wasn't stupid; it was obvious. All it took was one glance into his eyes as he told me to leave him alone. Of course he had it. But I couldn't be a part of that decision.

Which really sucked. *She, what am I going to do?*

The answer came back instantly: *"Listen. Just watch."*

"Oh my God!" I said aloud to the shower tiles. "Cryptic and mysterious as usual. You know," I said, "it's nice that Yoda lives in my head. It's a little ridiculous, but I like it," I said as I scrubbed my hair with what was left of the wholly inadequate hotel shampoo. "But one question, master *She:* When do we get to the good part; you know, where I get to levitate you?" *Because I'm going to let you drop like a sack of rocks, babe. Deal with that.*

Then a single word popped into my head: *"Parables."*

Yeah, yeah, I get it. I get that you're like, teaching me in parables. But it's pissing me off, all right? I can say so and that's okay. I swear I could see the smug little smirk on *She's* face. Ooo, that made me mad.

I was out of shampoo and my hair, superhuman or not, wasn't clean. Dripping wet, I reached out from behind the curtain and raided Ellie's stash of toiletries she had bought from her run to the store. *Ah ha! Shampoo*...I drew it in with me behind the curtain. "Dang," I said, looking at it. "This is expensive stuff." *How did she come up with this stuff in podunk Interstate mile marker number whatever?* It eluded me but I used the heck out of that shampoo.

My hair finally clean, I stood there under the stream of running water and thought. What was my beef with Ellie, the electric blue-haired angel girl? I always assumed the worst about her. I assumed she was trying to steal my boyfriend; that she had killed him and set me up to come back and kill my best friend Kim; that she was the villain. But, hello, she was getting us out of town on a chartered jet. For, like, free. What was my problem?

I groaned. There and then I decided to try harder to be nice to her.

My thoughts swirled relentlessly. I felt bad for Kim. She had been used by that stupid stone. I couldn't imagine how she felt, how dumb and embarrassed she must have felt about all of it. She looked like she had been through a double-wide trailer park overflowing with angry alcoholic stepdads. Just bruises and scratches everywhere on her. Poor thing! I wanted to make it up to her someday, whenever I could. Because on some level, this was all my fault.

It had to be.

I stood there in the shower shaking my head in awe of how drastically my life had changed, and so quickly. It was all because of my Michael. My love.

I closed the tap and started to towel off.

How is this going to work?

Had he indeed chosen to be with me? To leave the Brotherhood? If so, why all this evidence to the contrary?

"Circumstantial evidence, you mean."

Okay, whatever. I mean, he was carrying the Bloodstone on him. If I had read my grandfather's book correctly, whatever man—or woman, I gathered—carried the Bloodstone was linked to unspeakable evil. Perhaps the dark prince himself. I shuddered. I recalled how the Seer in those old stories—in that historical record—had been linked to the demon Tengu. But Kreios had killed him. If demons could be killed. I had to admit to being massively confused.

I wished with all my heart Kreios were there with some answers. Because, of course, the real question I was asking brought me back around to the gigantic question mark that hung over my relationship with Michael: could a demon be reformed? Or, put more plainly, was there any hope at all for the son of the Seer?

Especially when he's carrying the stone that corrupted his father! To the point where Michael had to kill him to be rid of him!

I pondered all this and more. *What sort of legacy might the elder Alexander have handed down to his son? How much of that was above the surface, visible? And how much of it lay beneath, waiting to strike?*

I felt hideously selfish for asking what came next, but there was a fine line between self-preservation and plain selfishness. *What have I gotten myself into?* ...And I had crossed that line, apparently. *Dang!*

I looked into the foggy mirror for an answer. I wiped it off and peered into my new impossibly perfect face. Really, if I was honest, everything I was becoming was because of Michael. My new face was a gift from him. Part of the reaction, the activation he had triggered. The bond we shared. I saw now that at first what I thought was love or attraction was the bond that formed when I was activated, but it changed somewhere along the way. I was in love with him, even though I knew he hid some things from me. He was doing it to protect me; or so I hoped.

She broke in. *"Obviously you triggered something in him, too..."* I couldn't argue that. Something about me made him a little crazy. Crazy enough to kill his own father, crazy enough to try to kill himself when he thought I was gone. Dead. *As dead as that little boy. Marc.*

Then the thought entered my brain that no matter what, at some point I was going to have to face facts. Given what I had discovered about the change I had undergone, and indeed was still experiencing, I was going to outlive my lover by perhaps thousands of years. No matter what, I would lose him eventually. He too would be dead in my arms one day, his glazed-over and lifeless eyes looking up into the heavens.

Just like Marc. And I might hold Michael that same way and

weep the way he had done. And I might ask El why, too, just like he had. Ask Him if it would ever be enough. I wondered then: *Do I still want to go through with all of this?*

I couldn't believe my selfishness. It was repellent to me.

I had never known love. Judging by how I was acting, not really. I had never tasted true and abiding love, not once. *No, scratch that.* I knew I had felt it. It was when I was sinking into the deep, when I was dying. I had seen it in his eyes then. It was simple. Love was simply doing whatever it took. No matter what. That was all. And Michael had done it. When it hadn't been enough, when his best efforts fell short, he had kept on trying, he had persisted, even in spite of the fact that I had died. It was his brave and bold action that had brought me back, and against all possibility. Somehow he had attained something higher. I knew it to be true.

Further, and I knew this to be true as well, I had not. I hadn't shown him love. Not truly. Not if I was thinking of abandoning him in the time of his greatest need. I could see clearly then, as I looked into my own eyes in the mirror, the eyes that had come about as a result of his influence upon me— for good or evil, it all somehow had to submit to El's will in the end—that Michael had done everything for me, that he had borne much grief, many sorrows, so much stress, and so much pain and emptiness for me. All for me. It was impossible, really. Unbelievable. Incredible. How could I walk away from him now?

No way.

I set my jaw and glared at myself in the mirror. *Airel, grow up. Be a good girl now. And for God's sake: stand by your man.* If ever there was a time to do so, it was now.

I had some apologizing to do.

CHAPTER IX

WHEN MICHAEL FINALLY GOT back to his room it was 7 a.m. He was distracted and angry, the Bloodstone was gone, picked right out of his pocket, and he had a good idea who was responsible.

Ellie stood waiting outside his door, back leaned to the wall. "Come with me," she said.

They walked down to the park and sat under the bridge. "We need to talk;" she said, "Come up with some kind of coherent strategy."

He was starting to respect Ellie. She was pretty smart. He thought that thousands of years of experience might do that to someone. He still held back a little, as was his nature. If he had learned anything from the Brotherhood it was never to trust someone completely. The only person he let himself trust with all his heart was Airel. His heart swelled with love and pride for his Airel when he thought of the implications. He might not get to share all of that with her, but he would take what he could get.

"All right. But before you even get started," he said, "I know you took it."

"What of it?" she said.

"That thing is pure evil; very dangerous."

"Trust me, I know that."

"Why did you take it? You don't trust me with it?"

"That's not it at all, rookie. I'm following orders."

"From who?"

She just stared at him with a look on her face that said, "You know the answer to that." Then she said aloud, "I put it back in Kim's duffel."

He was stunned. "What!?"

"It has already started to bond with her. We both know that. Trying to keep it from her will only make things worse; some things are not up to us to decide."

Michael could feel heat in his chest. Part of him wanted to scream at her, take the Bloodstone back for himself. He felt that using Kim, letting her have the stone, was just cruel. "Why give it to anyone at all? Can't we just get rid of it; destroy it somehow?"

"Doesn't work that way, mate. It needs a host, it wants to roam the earth. The Seer is not dead. The spirit, the identity that is the Seer—your father—all of it is in that stone."

Michael searched his memories, thousands of years of them, for some sort of answer. He knew she was right, but the darkness he felt in knowing that Kim had the stone, knowing what it might do to her, made him feel like a traitor all over again. "And it's *your* place to interfere? Ellie, I had everything under control."

"Oh, yeah? Okay, when did you find out she was hiding it?"

He had no response.

Ellie's face softened. She put her hand on his arm and sighed. "It's not your burden to bear. I don't care what Stanley Alexander tried to pass on to you, mate. It fell to Kim. It fell to her and she accepted responsibility, whether that was done in ignorance or not. She's gotta live with the consequences of it now."

Michael sat back and digested this. How could he allow that to happen? Did El know what *He* was doing? How could He allow Kim's mind to be cursed? Michael didn't have a whole lot of personal experience, but he had his training, he knew enough about the role of the Seer in the great scheme of things to know that what Kim would have to undergo would not be good. In truth he didn't like any of it. "I give her a few more days. Tops. Before her mind snaps completely," he said, whispering.

"So be it," Ellie said with a shrug.

"That's cold for an angel of God."

"It's cold for one of your lot, demon boy."

He winced.

"Sorry," she said. "But it is what it is; it called, she answered. It is not up to me or you to try to fix it. We must use our heads and turn this terrible thing to the advantage."

"What do we do, then?" He was genuinely at a loss.

"First, we've gotta trust that El knows what *He's* on about. He sees the whole picture, we don't."

"Okay…"

"Second, we keep moving. Stick with the plan you yourself laid out. We take the battle straight to them. Drive right at the heart of the whole operation."

Michael sat and blinked, thinking. "Yeah, but…if Kim's got the stone, wouldn't we be taking it right to the hands of the enemy? It's like, exactly what they'll want. They just want the Bloodstone."

"Yep. And they'll do anything to get it, including fratricide on a whole new level. They'll kill anything and everything that stands in their way to be the first to get at it. That thing is a direct link to the Prince of Darkness himself. It means power, and they go mad for that sort of rubbish."

"I'm listening." He could imagine how things might play out.

"Plus, if we know anything about Kreios's whereabouts, we know that he's done the exact same thing, if for different reasons. He's taken the fight to the enemy citadel in Cape Town. If what I'm sensing is correct, we need to unite our efforts with his, and—and this is crucial—we need him to see that Airel is still alive. Or at least get her close." She sat forward. "We do that, mate…we do *that*, and it won't be long before the strongest Warring Angel of El, Kreios, awakens to *his* destiny."

His arms tingled. *Yes. Yes, there's something about all that, isn't there?* He could feel it. What was it? What could he call that feeling? *Truth.* He sat back, soaking it all in.

"So what do you think?" she asked.

"Let me get this straight. We run to the enemy because, one, it's the opposite of what they expect. Two, Kreios is there. Three, we're counting on them to basically defeat themselves because they're so insane for the Bloodstone?"

"They want it more than anything. Why not offer it up to them?"

"That's a huge roll of the dice, Ellie."

"You haven't seen what El can do, have you?"

"Still, it seems like an enormous risk. What if something goes wrong?"

She waved his comment off, irritated. "You only live once."

"Unless you happen to believe in things like resurrection," he replied, reflecting on Airel.

"Speaking of which," Ellie began, but then paused, looking at him.

"What?" He felt like she was withholding something.

"You'll never guess what else our little Kimmie is hiding from us."

"What is it? How do you know all this stuff?"

"I'm telling you, I keep the lines of communication open with El."

"So what is it?"

"Well, I'll allow that everyone's got their secrets. Everyone. But she's got a whopper in her little duffel."

Michael sat forward in anticipation.

"You know every angel's got a Book, right?"

Oh, no. He sat back and sighed.

"Yeah, she managed to get her little grubby mitts on a Book. I can only assume it belongs to Kreios." She looked at him gravely. "I can't imagine what she'll try to do with it."

"We should take it back," he was getting angry again.

"I'm afraid, mate, and again, there are rules for this sort of thing. And besides…we've gotta be shrewd about it. We can't just go barging in and swipe the thing. She can't know it's gone when we take it. Just like right about now, she doesn't know that the Bloodstone has mysteriously returned to her. Almost like it never left. But she'll know soon enough, and when she bonds with it this time, the effects will be obvious."

"There are rules? What rules?"

"It's similar to destiny. When those Books change hands, they must accomplish the purpose for which they've been sent into the lives of the possessors. If an angel of El loses his book…especially after having found it himself in the first place…well…life under the sun is about consequence." She quickly added, "And reward. Of course."

"Did you ever recover yours?"

"That's a long story, mate."

"But you're a full angel. You have a book. Right?"

"I'm not prepared to talk about it."

He looked intently at her. *Yeah, she's hiding something.* Just what, though, he couldn't tell. Still, she had been forthcoming enough in this meeting for him to continue to trust her. "Whatever." He let her off the hook. He changed the subject. "So we have our plan."

"Yep, and we're gonna let it ride, hey?"

"Agreed," he said.

They shook hands. She rose to leave.

"Oh, there's something else."

"Yeah?" He looked up at her.

"Do be very careful. This whole thing hangs by a thread." She then walked off, leaving him alone with his considerable burdens. He rose to his feet more weary than ever. He walked numbly back to his room one last time. He would be glad to leave.

KIM ROLLED OUT OF bed, her head and body aching. 7 a.m., the clock said. Not much time to get ready. She had to pee like a racehorse, so she shuffled to the bathroom. Airel was gone, the other side of her bed had been vacated. Ellie too had apparently left; her bed was empty as well. Kim stumbled, stubbing her toe on the leg of the desk. She bit her lip and swore loudly, hopping the rest of the way to her black duffel by the closet. She grabbed it violently and limped into the bathroom.

It was muggy, she realized, as she turned on the light. Airel and Ellie hadn't showered long ago at all. They were probably downstairs having coffee.

"Coffee…" she slurred. She had a craving. But if she was honest she would admit that coffee wasn't even close to half of it. She craved something else. Badly. Like a drug.

Naked, she reached mindlessly into her bag and rooted around for something to wear. Her finger brushed up against something exquisite, gorgeous and terrible. Instinct rose up and she clawed at it. That's when everything came unhinged in her mind, snapping her will like an old dry rubber band.

"I've always been here. And I always will be."

"Yesssssss," she whispered, drawing the object out from the duffel. The bathroom became red, pulsing with the light of the Bloodstone. Her bladder let go, emptying itself all over the floor, but she didn't even notice. She only gazed into the redness of the Bloodstone. With every ounce of her will, she wanted to dive into it, curl up inside it and die there, be unmade, find ultimate satisfaction.

In the meantime, the stone went to work. Patchwork. Remaking the outer shell of the one called Kim into something that might pass for beauty in certain circles. Appearances mattered a great deal. If nothing else, she would appear to be striking and different. In any case, the bruises and scratches were to heal. *NOW.* The kingdom of Hell didn't *suffer* violence. It *was* violence.

CHAPTER IX

Arlington, Oregon, present day

MICHAEL LAY IN BED staring at the ceiling, the sun piercing through the gap in the curtains, making everything plain and drab. It was nearly a quarter to 8 a.m., but he wasn't mindful of the time. He was riding in the painful place of existence where time didn't matter, where everything was meaningless.

He drew his arms up and rubbed the scar on his chest. It throbbed and ached and itched him deeply. It was getting worse. He needed help. "But there's no one," he said to the empty room. Not his dad, Stanley Alexander, who had been a selfish traitor from day one, leaving him an emotionally bastardized freak, all alone. Not Kreios, who had cursed him with unnatural bizarre demonic patchwork. Not even Airel. She didn't get it.

Would she ever?

He wanted to be rid of the connection with the Brotherhood forever. He wanted to move on, be done with it, be left in peace. But life wasn't turning out to be so simple. It was enormously complex and paradoxical.

Life would just be an endless sprint and they would run like animals, fighting to stay alive. There had to be a way to end it, to cut off completely from his past and start over with Airel. To love her, and that alone. That would be more than enough to satisfy him. His greatest fear, though, was that he had made too many decisions already, that those decisions had taken him too far down a path from which there was no return. Certain things, indeed, could not be undone.

There would be Hell to pay quite literally for what he had done to the Brotherhood. In that sense he was in good company, for that was where Kreios had ended up too. He couldn't pick a more powerful ally than that. Too bad the angel of El hated him. Michael chuckled bitterly at the absurdity of the idea; they would never be allies. It was impossible. Kreios was, truth be told, probably just saving him for last. Oh, he would have great fun with Michael. It made sense; it's what he would have done were he in the same shoes.

He coughed and held his chest. There was the unmistakable iron taste of blood in his mouth. But it was time to go. Maybe he could sleep on the plane.

WE HAD ALL AGREED to meet in the lobby at 8 a.m.

Ellie and I sat by the doughnuts sipping black coffee. *I could murder for my coconut latte.* "Bleagh," I said, scraping my tongue along the roof of my mouth like a dog eating peanut butter.

Ellie laughed, her spiky blue mane quivering in the rakish early morning light. "What's the matter? Don't like drinking off the bottom of the trough?"

"No," I said. "I miss my Moxie."

She smiled, bemused. "I've gotta take you to Europe some time.

There's this little shop in Rome that makes espresso that would kill you Americans with a single drop. And don't get me started on Turkish coffee. Cor!"

I just shook my head and smirked. Ellie was a pretty fascinating person, I had to admit it. Why was I so reluctant to let my guard down with people? *Probably because they sometimes turn out to be made of newspapers and photographs and other things that are not nice. And then they try to kill you. I guess that's why.* I rolled my eyes at myself. *Lighten up, girlie.* I smiled at that.

"Hey, Els," I said, shortening her name in an attempt to bridge whatever gap I had engineered between us. "Can I say something?"

"Sho," she said in her peculiar Aussie-ish Brit-like accent. "Fire away."

"Well," I began, feeling awkward, "I just want you to know that I've been…um…a real jerkhead to you at certain points…um, recently. And I'm sorry for that."

She laughed easy.

"I really am. And I'd like to tell you thanks for all your help. With, um…everything. With Michael. I haven't appreciated you like I should."

"No worries, girlie. I knew you'd come round." She rolled her eyes and smirked. "Eventually."

I laughed. "Dude, can we be friends now? Sheesh."

"Deal," she said, and we shook on it.

I took another sip of what tasted like cigarette butt soup. "Gawgh! What do they *put* in this stuff?"

"I don't know, but I'm pretty sure it's illegal where I come from. Here," she said, getting up and tossing a few little cups of French vanilla cream at me. "Try this."

"Ugh, are you kidding? That's like putting salsa on a turd burrito."

She spit her coffee out, laughing, trying to catch most of it with her styrofoam cup and failing. "Aw, look at that! Gross!"

We both fell over on our chairs, laughing like junior high girls joking about body parts. It was awesome. I felt like maybe this trip, this adventure would turn out okay after all.

We were interrupted by Michael. "Good morning, ladies," he said. "And I think you've probably had enough coffee. Already."

"Howzit, mate," Ellie said.

I smiled. I was glad to see him, glad to see he was in a good mood. "Hi. It's really good to see you," I said, hoping he could tell by the look in my eyes that I was as sincere as I could be.

"You too," he said, leaning down and kissing me on the cheek.

My temperature rose by degrees, coloring my face. I could feel it. "Hey," I said, grabbing his hand, "you really don't want to try the coffee. I promise."

He laughed as he sat beside me. "Okay, then."

"And by the way, first things first. I'm really sorry if I've been horrible to you lately."

He looked shocked. "If?!" He held my gaze powerfully for a moment. Then a smile broke across his face. He was flirting with me. "All is forgiven, my love. And thank you."

I just sat there and beamed. "So...you're doing well today then?" I didn't want to broach the subject of Marc and having to bury the bodies of little boys, however demonic they might have been. I didn't want to ask him about the Bloodstone that I knew beyond shadow of doubt he now carried. That he must carry, no matter how chipper he appeared to be. I was worried, but I let it go for now.

He squeezed my hand. "Yeah."

I looked at Ellie and she gave a little tick of the head in signification of the affirmative. All was well. I was learning to trust, even if I didn't know why Michael chose not to let me know about the Bloodstone. I loved and trusted him enough to know that he had a good reason for it. For now.

"Where's Kim?" I asked.

"Speak of the devil," came a voice from outside our little enclave. It was Kim.

She looked...well...sexy. That's the only way to describe it. She was wearing a cute sundress and sandals, but there was nothing innocent or wholesome about her look. Sure, she looked well, but there was something just slightly off about her. It wasn't necessarily a new look for her either; I had known her to use it on occasion before. But it was a marked change from how Ellie and I had seen her in the room just a few hours ago.

"Wow, Kim! Glad to see you're...you're up," I said, bewildered at how well... -ish... she had cleaned up. "I was just coming to check on you."

"Yeah, well, I'm here now, so no need." She yawned and stretched herself like a lioness, making the dress pull at her body and slide over her feminine curves.

I cleared my throat, embarrassed for her. "Coffee?" I thumbed over my shoulder in the general direction of the dispenser of hot brown industrial grade paint thinners. I caught Ellie's eye and shrugged with a grimace. What else could be next with Kim? *Welcome, Awkward Woman! Superheroine of the weird. Thanks for showing up to torture all of us with your undiluted and latently sexual oddness.*

"Oh, thanks! Yeah," she said, grabbing herself a cup and filling it to the brim. She took a sip. She growled with deep satisfaction, like she was selling breakfast cereal in one of those cheesy old TV commercials from when I was a kid. "Oh, man! This is *so* good."

"Do you want mine?" Ellie said, and I kicked her, trying hard not to laugh.

Kim didn't notice. "Oh! Hey," she addressed Ellie, "Thanks for getting me my new bag, Ellie. I really needed one and I really like it." She twisted around so we could see it. It was a bright pink backpack for elementary school girls, with an enormous Hello Kitty cartoon on it.

"Oh, you're welcome, love," Ellie said. "It suits you."

Kim dropped her jaw and gasped in pantomime excitement, "I *know*, right?!" She took another sip, gulping the coffee like a lumberjack.

Dear God, she is acting weird.

"Dude! Okay, who wants breakfast?" She was being just slightly too loud, and people were turning to notice the disturbance. "I do!" she raised her hand shouting like a cheerleader, and then burst into maniacal laughter.

"Kim!" I hissed, grabbing her hand and leading her toward the front doors. "What did you do, bathe in whiskey this morning?" *And drink most of it?* "What is wrong with you?" I looked over my shoulder to Michael and Ellie, signaling them to grab our stuff and come along. The last thing we needed to do was draw attention to ourselves. I wanted to get us out of there like yesterday. *Please, God, just let us get on the plane and get out of here.*

Kim skipped along holding my hand like a six-year-old playing double-dutch. Her ridiculous backpack knocked obnoxiously from side to side as we left the building.

"Jeez, Kim. Settle."

"OHMYGOSH I had the most weirdest dream, Airel. You totally have to hear about it," she grabbed both of my hands and took a breath. "See, there was this guy walking down the street, and all along the sidewalk there were these ladders leaned up against the buildings, but he was like totally walking along, like, UNDER ALL

OF THEM, and I was like holy crap that is a lot of bad luck he's rackin' up, HAHAHAHAHA!" she bent over cackling raucously at her funny joke.

I looked around desperately for a way out of this.

"Oy!" Ellie called from behind us. "Over here!" She was pointing to an old brown pickup truck sitting at the curb idling. A large man stood by the door with his arms crossed, smiling. "Pile in!" Ellie said.

Before I could move, Kim sprinted for the man, going boldly right up to him and introducing herself with plenty of posturing.

Gall, he must be twice her age. Gross. The man walked her politely to the passenger side door like a gentleman and saw that she was seated before closing it.

As he was walking back around to the driver's side, our paths crossed and he introduced himself. "Hex," he said with a gregarious engaging smile and a crushing handshake.

"Airel," I said, withdrawing my hand to brush my hair out of my eyes. I looked behind him to see Ellie and Michael tossing our bags into the bed of the truck.

"Don't mind this old banger," he said, gesturing to the pickup. "Necessity produces strange bedfellows." His smile was broad, revealing a wall of gleaming white teeth.

"Okay," I said, a little confused.

"That's Hex," Ellie called to me as she hopped into the back.

"Yeah, we met," I said, skirting around him toward Michael, who then traded me places and introduced himself, getting his metacarpals crushed in turn.

"He's my pilot."

"Oh, cool," I said. Michael then came back and, like a gentleman, helped me up and in. I let him think I needed that, for him. I grabbed one of the wheel wells as a seat. Rusty chains and bits of straw littered the bed of the truck.

"He makes instant friends wherever he goes," Ellie went on. "Quite useful, really. He could get a perfect stranger to write him into their will, I swear. That's how he got us wheels to the ramp today."

"Nice work," said Michael.

I couldn't help but smile. It was a perfect sunny day, the birds were singing, it was still early, and we were riding open air in the back of a farm truck to the airport, getting ready to fly to someplace totally exotic, somewhere I had never dreamt of. I was excited. It was easy to let Kim's weirdness slide for the moment. Besides, she was sitting up front with Hex and chatting *his* ear off.

Then it occurred to me: the mood Kim was in, we were sure to get kicked out of whatever restaurant we decided to patronize for breakfast. *Not that there's much choice here...* "Um, hey, Els? Where are we headed?"

"Brekkies," she said.

"Yeah, not a sit-down place though?" My face communicated the worry I felt as I jerked my head toward my slightly insane BFF in the passenger seat.

Ellie only laughed and pointed in the direction Hex was driving us.

I looked and saw my old childhood buddy: the golden arches of McDonald's.

"Thank God for Mackers," she said. "And drive-through windows, right?" She laughed, and I couldn't help but join her.

Maybe everything will turn out right in the end. Maybe, after all, it really will. I suffered myself a smile as I reached across to hold Michael's hand.

CHAPTER X

"THIS IS A G550. Top of the line," Hex said motioning to a big private jet as we all dismounted the faded brown loaner truck. "It's in a class of its own, really."

"Cool," I said. I didn't have a clue about aircraft. Nor did I have much desire to have a clue about aircraft. All I knew was that it looked very fast and very expensive, as if it had come from a world that existed for some people in reality, and for people like me only in storybooks. That my world was beginning to overlap that world was pure thrill for me.

I cast an excited look at Michael, who smiled at me. "Dude, this is unbelievable!" I sounded dorky, but then who cared? I watched as another guy, who was evidently a member of the crew, took our bags and loaded them. That is, except for Kim's new kiddiebag, which she wore over both shoulders and from which she refused to be separated.

"That's my co-pilot, Bishop. He's a Zulu man, very good at what he does."

"Howzit!" he greeted us from a distance over the din of the idling jet engines.

Hex stood at the base of the ladder and motioned us toward him. "All aboard," he said. "Make yourselves at home, please. I just have a few checks to make and then we'll be on our way."

I looked at Ellie, who gave me her little nod and motioned me aboard. Of course I couldn't beat Kim to the punch. She tromped up the stairs like a football player. I followed more sedately but hardly less excited. I just hoped Kim wouldn't white trash herself too much and embarrass both of us.

Inside it was all leather and wool carpets and exotic woods and technology. Lap of luxury stuff. Amazing. I turned back to Michael with a wowed expression. He returned it with a smirk and raised eyebrows.

Kim was being annoying, touching everything and rambling on. I wasn't really listening to her. I sat in one of the enormously comfortable chairs and looked out the window. The farmer, at least that's who I guessed it was, had come for his truck and Hex was out there talking with him. It wasn't much of a conversation as far as I could tell, with Hex, a towering black man, basically shouting into the ear of a wizened old salt-of-the-earth onion farmer and clapping him on the back. They laughed like old friends. *Dude. He is good.*

Ellie, who had been waiting nearby for the two men to finish their conversation, approached Hex and gave him a side hug, her little blue pom-pom head vanishing briefly in the crook of his massive arm. She was too cute. I decided I liked her. Having greeted her friend, she bounded away from him, jogging toward the plane. She crested the stairs gracefully and ducked in.

"What do we think?" she asked.

"It's sooooo rad," Kim said in admiration.

"Glad you like it."

"Can you, like, watch movies on that thing?" Kim asked, pointing to the massive display screen at the head of the cabin.

"Oh, sure," Ellie said. "What do you fancy?"

"Oh, I don't like anything fancy," Kim said, and I smacked my palm against my forehead. She went on, "My favorite movie is *Beauty and the Beast.* I think it's soooo romantic."

"Since when?" I howled at her. "I thought your favorite movie was *Miss Congeniality,* Kim."

She simply stuck her tongue out at me and sat down in a huff.

"No matter. We've got both of those and more," Ellie said. "We're connected via satellite all across the globe in this—"

"Beauty and the Beast! Beauty and the Beast! Beauty and the Beast! Beauty and the Beast!" Kim was hopping up and down in her seat, clapping her hands together like a spoiled rotten brat.

I pressed my hands to my temples and leaned forward. "Wow," I said, feeling desperate.

"Okay, Kim, settle down," Ellie said. "I'll put it on for you." She was talking to her like she might have talked to a small child. She grabbed a tablet sized control pad and deftly manipulated some settings. "There. It'll start streaming as soon as the decryption is finished." She turned back to Kim. "In the meantime, love, can I get you something to drink?"

"OhmyGawdyes," Kim replied. "I want soda pop! Soda pop! Soda pop! Soda pop!" She sat still, beaming at Ellie with crazy eyes and clapping her hands in rhythm to her chant.

The movie started up, telling the story of the ugly witch and the selfish prince. The music swelled in surround sound, filling the space of the jet with my preschool memories. What was up with Kim? *When did she become five again?*

Ellie approached me. "Hey, girlie. Can I get you a drink?"

"Yeah," I shot back, "What's the legal drinking age in international airspace?"

She chuckled and bent low to my ear, trying to talk over the preschooler noises.

Kim was now singing along with the symphonic score with a loud "Dum-da dum doo dah DUMMMMM-pum pum pum…"

Ellie said, "Don't worry, girlie. I'm going to slip a sedative in hers so you won't need one." She stood erect. "Unless of course you *want* to be sedated…to each their own."

"That's okay," I said. "Anyway, how quick does it work?"

"She'll be out like a light before we reach the end of the runway."

"In that case, I'll have a water."

Ellie, who had been holding her hands up as if she were writing my order on an imaginary notepad, dropped them to her sides, slumped her shoulders, and gave me a sharply sarcastic look. "Oh, that's imaginative." She stalked off. "Fine. Have it your way. We've got all kinds of expensive beverages on here, but never mind."

"Hey," I growled at her, "What about my boyfriend here?"

She didn't stop. Her voice came shouting at both of us from the back of the airplane, "He doesn't get anything!"

I looked at Michael and we both laughed. He pointed his index finger at his head and moved it in a circle, indicating that we had fallen in with the psych ward somehow.

"No doubt," I said back, laughing. It *was* insane. But I figured we all needed to let off a little steam. I grabbed his hand and kissed the back of it. He smiled and his blue eyes sparkled. I was so happy just looking into his eyes. I wanted to drown in them.

Ellie came back with a silver tray bedecked—yeah, bedecked in this case—with two ornate crystal glasses of crisp cold pure water, and set it down on the solid burled wood table between Michael and me. "*Madame et Monsieur,* your two hydrogens and one oxygen. Each." She turned toward Kim with a can of soda and fairly slammed it down on her table, making little drops of it blast out the opening.

"Ooooo, thanks! Soda pop soda pop soda pop soda pop soda pop," she sang along with the cartoon, forcing her words into the mouth of the bookish on-screen heroine.

Sedative, do your worst. I can't take much more of this.

The co-pilot, Bishop, bounded up the stairs. He was short and wiry and full of energy. As black as coal and beautifully pure African, he moved very quickly, darting all over the cabin and pumping our hands while smiling enthusiastically at us. He spoke in a very thick accent; it was difficult to understand what he was saying. I smiled at him and guessed he was glad we had come.

When Hex came aboard, Bishop shut the door for him. Then Ellie made the official introductions.

"This is Kim, Airel, and Michael Alexander." Michael's last name produced a subtle reaction in Hex. His eyebrows arched ever so slightly.

"Very well. It is my pleasure to meet you all. I welcome you aboard Miss Ellie's personal aircraft."

Whoa. This is hers?

My name is Hector LeFievre. You can call me Hex. Please relax, enjoy, and leave the flying to us." He gestured to Bishop, who smiled at us. "If you have need of anything, please just call the cockpit and we will do our utmost to serve you."

"Oh, Hex, just fly the thing. I'll take care of my guests," Ellie said.

Kim made childish noises in the background as she sipped at her soda pop soda pop soda pop and tapped her fingers on her little tray table.

"All right. Here we go," Hex said, and turned to the cockpit. Both he and Bishop entered through the flight deck door and took their seats. Bishop then reached back and closed it. Hex's voice came over the intercom: "Ladies, and our lone gentleman, please buckle your seat belts. This is the captain speaking."

Ellie sat casually in a seat facing us and kicked her shoes off, tucking her legs up under her. "Should I do the stewardess thing now?"

Michael laughed, "No, that's fine."

"All right then." Without looking, she reached back and snatched the can of soda from Kim, who at that instant was passing out and crashing. Ellie brought the can around smoothly as Kim plopped back and sideways over her own armrest, her mouth wide open. "See what I mean? Quick." She smiled and stood, walking to the back with the can of soda pop soda pop soda pop.

When she came back, the can was gone, and she carried a blanket and a pillow.

"What did you give her?" I asked, semi-concerned for my friend now.

"You don't want to know," was the reply. "But she's fine." She flipped a lever on Kim's chair and it lay down flat. She pulled her up by the armpits and righted her in the chair, propped her head up with the pillow, buckled her seat belt, and covered her with the blanket.

"Now that's hospitality," she said, admiring her work.

The plane began to roll, taxiing for takeoff.

Ellie picked up the tablet and gestured to the movie screen. "Anyone else watching this?"

"No!" Michael and I said in unison.

"'Kay, then," she said, touching the tablet's screen. The movie turned off. "Ah," she said, sitting in her seat again, "much better." She twisted to check on Kim.

Turning back toward us, she buckled her own seat belt. We followed suit.

Hex's voice came over the intercom again. "Prepare for

takeoff."

"This is my favorite part," Ellie said.

The jet engines roared and we blasted down the runway. As we became airborne it hit me: this was the first time in a long time I felt truly safe.

CHAPTER XI

Boise, Idaho, present day

HARRY, AFTER WAITING DAYS for the confluence of various
circumstances after the demise of one Gretchen Reid, sat on a
plane at the Boise airport, waiting for departure. The man next to
him was having a conversation on his cell phone. It sickened him
that people felt the need to parade all that weakness, all that idiotic
vanity, in public. Sure, the conversations were one-sided, but they
were also usually louder than ambient noise, and disturbing for their
disjointedness. Harry ground his teeth as the man prattled on.

"Yes, dear." A pause. "Honey, you're okay. Honest injun. Are
you enjoying your time with your sister?" Another pause.

Harry wanted to vomit. Either that or rip the man's phone
away from his hand and beat him senseless with it. Mercilessly, the
conversation continued.

"Of course. And how about you?" A pause again. "Oh, I'm just
waiting for the pushback so we can get underway here."

Pushback, Harry thought. *I'll give you pushback.*

"And I'll miss *you*. Well, it's only the civilized parts of
Africa…. Yeah! Of course…. Always."

Why must I endure all this nonsense? Harry thought. *Why couldn't I just kill the man in his own house?* He reflected on that. It would have been…less convenient. Orders were orders anyway. He understood rationally that it would be better to wait until Cape Town. It would look better. But emotionally he wasn't sure how much more he would be able to stand.

"I love you." The man in the seat next to Harry ended the call.

Thank you, Harry thought. *Perhaps now my day will improve.* But the man turned to face him directly, as if he had been reading all the hostility Harry had been broadcasting. Harry twisted in his seat, shrinking back from the man as he squared his shoulders and looked at his face.

"Let's not pretend we don't know each other, Harry."

This is not good. "I don't know what you're talking about," was all he could say in response. *Deflect this…*

The man lowered his voice and leaned in. "Oh, come on, Harry, let's not pretend anymore. I know all about it."

Harry chortled. "About what?" His body language communicated his distaste and contempt for the very idea.

The man lowered his voice still more. "About agent Gretchen Reid. And how you killed her."

Harry arched his eyebrows. "Oh, really? And here I thought you were going to be another boring dull stupid lazy mark."

"Not hardly," said the man, looking away and taking a sip of bottled water. "Not hardly. Why do you think I booked my ticket for this flight specifically?"

"Oh, my. This is getting good. But I'm afraid it's a chicken-and-egg debate on that score, my friend."

"What, you booked first?"

"So say some." Harry changed the subject. "So. Off to rescue our daughter, are we?" He gave a wickedly recumbent chuckle that would have weakened the knees of lesser men.

"Harry, I wouldn't tell you any more about my Airel if you held a gun to my head."

"That can be arranged."

"Tell you what, Harry—if I can presume to call you by your Christian name…?" Harry flinched. It made Airel's father smile ever so slightly. "How about this: how about when we refuel at Twin Cities, you don't move a muscle. How about when we change planes at Schipol in Amsterdam you behave like a good little boy or I'll splatter your guts across all those pricey cheese wheels in the duty-free. How about we pretend to be pals, okay?"

"And why," Harry couldn't help but laugh in his face, "why should I not kill you here and now?" *Oops.* Harry hoped he didn't say that too loudly. "And for that matter, why wouldn't you do the same, here and now?"

"Because, Harry. It's just not reasonably possible. Those idiot pretend mall cops with the TSA badges. FAA protocol. The Federal Air Marshall sitting in 17 D. The Boise PD. Ada County Sheriff. The fact that the door to the jetway is now closed and we're stuck on this tin can for the duration whether it's convenient for us or not. And then there's the question of your orders…"

Harry muttered strong curses under his thin veneer of cool. He gave a petulant little exhalation through his nostrils, scoffing.

Airel's father continued. "You want me to get to Africa. You need me to get to Africa. Unharmed. And I know it. And trust me, Harry, this showdown can keep until then."

"Okay," Harry dismissed him casually with a wave of his hand.

"Until then we're just fellow disciples in the tribe of…sales. On our way to the 'convention.'"

Harry laughed cruelly. "And just what do we sell?"

"Saleable things, Harry. Today it just happens to be a few extra hours of your life. Whaddya say?"

Through gritted teeth, Harry said, "Deal," and regretted bitterly his former audacity to have purchased a ticket on the seat next to the mark. He hadn't counted on Airel's father being so smart. That, he had never accounted for or even imagined.

Somewhere over North America, present day

MICHAEL WASN'T QUITE SURE how to broach the subject with Airel. He had been up since…well, he hadn't really had time to sleep at all, what with…all that needed to be taken care of. The body. And the Bloodstone turning up missing. He had been a little freaked out about that until his little under-the-bridge conference with Ellie. And now Kim carried it. *C'est la vie,* he thought cynically.

How could he tell Airel about Kim? How would she take it? He could tell by the way she looked at him that she thought he carried the Bloodstone. But he had to tell her. As if, by Kim's erratic behavior, it wasn't painfully obvious to everyone by now. But somebody had to call attention to the elephant on the plane.

And there was no time like the present. "Airel, can I talk with you?"

"Sure," she said.

Michael didn't even have to look at Ellie. "Excuse me," she said. "I've gotta make a trip to the loo." She got up and walked to the back of the plane.

"That was nice of her," Airel said.

"Yeah, she's pretty cool."

"So what's up?"

He hazarded a glance at Kim, who was snoring away in her seat. "It's about Kim."

"Oh, don't tell me. I know she's been acting really weird. What's with her?" Airel came off a little nervous. She gripped his hand tighter, as if holding on to him could bring her insane world into focus.

He looked at her. "I think you already know."

Fear crept over her face. She was quiet for a long time, looking at her sleeping friend. Finally, she looked back at Michael. "She has it."

He confirmed this truth.

"How long?"

"You're not going to like this one bit," he said. He tried to explain what Ellie had told him about destiny and choice and consequence and how it was Kim's burden to bear because, really, she had taken it up that day on the cliff top.

And he was right. Airel didn't like it at all.

She got up and paced the cabin, obviously fuming inside but keeping her tongue. "That's just not right," she finally said. "How can that be right? We can't let her have it—we can't do that to her! How is that fair?"

He sat and thought for a long time before answering. "You know, I don't have an answer for you. I don't know. What I do know is that she has accepted the burden of the Bloodstone fully now. She has bonded with it. She has chosen it over everything else."

"But how…how does a person come to that? How could she choose *that?*"

"Like anything," he shrugged. "You go far enough down the path of curiosity until you slide off. There's no coming back from some choices." He wanted to be careful now. "She's already beginning to change. It's taking her." He paused, wanting to choose his next words very carefully. "Airel, that's not even Kim anymore."

She tried to stay strong, but it only lasted a few minutes. She collapsed into a pile of sobs on the seat next to him. She covered her face with her hands and wept and he held her. He knew what she wept for. It wasn't just Kim. It was everything.

Eventually they fell asleep together, her head resting on his chest, his arms around her.

I WAS ABSOLUTELY STARVING. I wasn't quite awake yet, but I was aware of the hunger at least. There was something in the air too; a voice. It was tinny. I opened my eyes. We were on a plane. *Oh, yeah. The plane.* The tinny voice was the captain. Hex. *That's right.*

"…cruising at Mach point eight. We're currently slowing and on final to Ascension Island in the south Atlantic. We'll be landing at Wideawake Airfield in ten minutes for refueling. We'll have a layover of a few hours per Miss Ellie's request, so you can walk around a bit and eat a meal, perhaps see the sights. It's up to you. All the arrangements will be taken care of. Please buckle up and prepare for landing. This is the captain speaking." The intercom clicked off.

I looked around. Michael was stirring, but he wasn't quite up yet. Ellie sat across the way. She looked up and smiled at me. Kim was still out like a light. *Boy howdy. That must have been some cocktail.*

I looked out the window. All I could see was wisps of cloud and ocean. It was still daytime. *How long have we been flying? Did I hear him say south Atlantic? Wowza.* I couldn't figure it out in my head, but I was sure of one thing: it had to be tomorrow already. My stomach growled.

I could feel the plane descending and slowing, and my ears popped.

As we got closer and lower, I could see quite clearly the endless sea. There was nothing else out here. It seemed like we were getting really low and I hoped there was some kind of island or land out in front of us, because it sure looked like we were getting ready to crash into the water.

Just when I started to become really alarmed, a bit of rocky shore flashed by under the wing. I was instantly relieved to find that, no, we weren't trying to land on the open ocean. Touchdown came swiftly and gently.

Kim never stirred.

I elbowed Michael gently. "Hey. Get off me, dude." He had draped an arm over me and was drooling on the expensive leather seat. He gave a snort and blinked his eyes and looked around. "Oh. Hi. Sorry." He drew back his arm and sat up.

The airplane was slowing to taxi speed, and Hex meandered it over various runways to a row of big metal buildings where other planes like ours were parked.

"How long were we out?" Michael asked.

Ellie spoke up. "Fourteen hours. I guess you needed some rest, hey?"

I stretched luxuriously now that I didn't have boyfriend draped all over me. "No doubt," I said, peering out the window.

Hex's voice came over the speakers again. "It's a balmy twenty five degrees outside and the weather is perfect. Enjoy your day. This is the captain speaking."

Did he say twenty five?! "But it looks so nice out!" I said.

"Celsius," Ellie said.

"Oh. Duh." I felt so stupid. "Why did I not know that?"

"Because you've been snogging your boyfriend for over twelve hours, girlie. Anyone else wouldn't even know their own name." She smiled and I felt all gooey inside again. *What is it about this Ellie character?*

The plane stopped and we stood. Bishop came and opened the outer door with a huge smile and the three of us got out, blinking and squinting in the bright sunshine.

"What about Kim?" I asked.

"Oh, sweetheart, she's not going to wake for days. She'll be fine," Ellie said.

"Days?! Holy crap! Do we need to get her on an oxygen machine or something?" I asked, more concerned than ever.

"No, no. Trust me, girlie," Ellie said with a serious look in her eyes. "It's better this way."

CHAPTER XII

WE TOOK A TAXI to Georgetown for some grub. Of course when I say taxi, I mean tiny little minivan piled to overflowing with, like, almost twenty people in it and on it. It didn't help that the driver thought he was Enzo Ferrari himself, the way he blasted down the thoroughfares.

"I find you veddygood place to eat!" he said to us, flashing his pearlywhites.

And it was true. The food was astonishing. I had never had fish so tasty in my life. Fish! It was likely because most of my prior experiences with seafood were deep fried and square, served up with plenty of tartar sauce.

We sat at a secluded table in the corner of a little shop that sold light groceries and sundries, but that was also, according to our taxi driver, one of the best places in town to eat. I figured in that way it was a little like one of my favorite greasy spoons back home, Delsa's Ice Cream Parlor. Just a mom-n-pop shop.

After our main meal Ellie ordered us some samosas, little triangle-shaped pies filled with meat and veggies. She also ordered us some Turkish coffee, which was indescribable and amazing. We sat and talked, bloated with food. The ocean breezes filtered through the place through wide-open shutters that were thrown open against the sunshine.

"Well," Ellie said, "I suppose it's time to let you both in on a little secret."

The expression on her face didn't give away a bit of what she was about to tell us. I couldn't have imagined it. She just sat there with an adorable smirk on her face, like she was playing, like she was just going to indulge in a little girlish gossip. It seemed innocent enough at first blush, and I returned her half-mischievous little smile as she began to speak.

"I suppose I should just be out with it," she said, fidgeting slightly. "I'm not who I told you I am."

The smile faded slowly from my face. I looked at Michael. He was looking dead at her; he didn't return my inquisitive glance.

"I'm not an angel," Ellie said, dropping the bomb on us.

A moment went by unmolested, slippery. I couldn't get ahold of it. "Say what," I said in disbelief.

"I said, girlie, I'm not an angel. Not a full blood anyway."

Though I probably should have launched to my feet and shouted at her, I didn't have it in me. I just couldn't conjure up the emotion. I was instantly very tired, and I felt a large resignation coming for me, threatening to make everything I had ever done and ever would do completely meaningless. I searched for words and came up empty.

Michael interjected. "So you've lied to us this whole time."

She shrugged, "Pretty much!"

As far as I could tell she was having a great time with this new joke. *Surely,* I thought, *there must be more to it.* I probed inwardly for *She* and couldn't make out any signs of alarm coming from her. *Still. What's really going on here?*

I looked at Ellie's face and couldn't detect any malicious intent there. "So what are you saying?" I asked.

"You're not a full blood," Michael said. "Then what are you? Explain yourself."

"Yeah," I said, "because this…I mean, this is messed up. You've been lying to us the whole time!"

"Shh!" Ellie hissed at us, "we still need to maintain at least a little bit of order here." She sat forward a bit and directed herself only at me. "Airel, what I mean to say is that I'm just like you are. I'm a half breed."

"Wait. What? So you're a…an Immortal? You've been changed too?"

"Yeah." She sat back and looked at both of us for a moment.

"But you're not," Michael began, "I mean, you've never been a member of the Brotherhood?"

"That's an incredible question for you to ask me, kid. Like you have room to be suspicious. And, no, I'm not with the Brotherhood, though they've been known to recruit women from time to time. But you knew that, didn't you, otherwise you wouldn't have asked, right?"

This is just crazy sauce! Weirdly, in spite of what maybe should have happened in my heart and mind, instead of being angered by Ellie's confession, I was newly energized. *That's what it is! That's why there's this weird connection between us all the time!* I was exultant. "So wait," I said, "tell me everything. How did you change? What happened? How did…I mean, who activated you?" Suddenly we really did have all kinds of stuff in common.

"Patience, grasshopper," she said in her funny accent. "All in due course."

"Hold on," I said, interrupting Michael before he could get another word in, "I've been dying to know, since we're finally getting down to it here. Where are you from? How old are you?"

She giggled and obliged me. "I kind of lost track. If I'm honest. But it's fair to say that I've been around a long time. A very long time."

My mind raced.

"Anyway in answer to your question of where I'm from, I guess you could say I'm headed home right now. That's why I figured it was a good time to come clean. Cape Town is my own fair city. My own most recent fair city. I've been known to haunt Sydney and London from time to time."

"Wait, I thought you were from Portland. Or Seattle," Michael said.

"You assumed. I carry documents too numerous to list. What the documents say on their face is what allows people to draw their own conclusions in concert with how they think. And when you've got as much experience as I do, you know how to make connections and how to use them. At the moment, officially, I'm a dual citizen of ol' Zed-A and the USA—"

"Zed-A?" I asked.

"South Africa's official initials, girlie. Anyway, I guess you could say in regard to my American citizenship that I'm African-American. Though with skin this fair in an intellectual climate as intolerant and closed-minded as America is currently, I know it's the unpardonable sin for me to say so. If the world even believes in sin anymore."

I laughed at her little rant. I supposed she deserved it. "So you're from Cape Town? Is it cool?"

"Crikey, yeah. I've been all over the place. Quite literally. And Cape Town is one of the most naturally gorgeous spots on earth."

"Why did you lie?" Michael blurted out.

I felt a little ashamed at myself, feeling like a too-eager

turncoat. That, plus his question made me blush a little, but I nevertheless waited for her answer.

"That's easy, mate. You can't trust anyone these days. I have a lot to lose. There's a lot at stake here. Actually, you should feel privileged that I shared the truth with you even now. You ought to feel some measure of gratitude that I'm demonstrating enough faith in you to confide this."

"Okay, but why?" he persisted. "Why did you have to keep us in the dark at all? Are you even here because of El…and orders…or was that all just a lie too?"

Ellie leaned across the table toward us and lowered her voice. She pointed to me. "Airel knows the answer to that already."

After a split second of confusion it did indeed become clear as a bell to me. I looked at Michael and said, "She's here to protect me." *That's crazy! How could I be that important?* And of course it was beyond prudent for her to keep that to herself for as long as she dared. *She must think we're headed for something enormous, then… still though…little ol' me? She's here to protect me?*

But I knew. After all, I knew, and it was flooding into me. After all I had read in my grandfather's Book, after all I had experienced, after all the impossibilities of my own resurrection from the dead, my still-developing abilities, and the fact that I could now call the Sword of Light at a whim and wield it in battle, the very Sword my grandfather had been the only angel to possess… *well, perhaps technically it had belonged to his brother Tengu, before he had joined the rebell*—all of it came crashing into me with brute force. I grasped the edge of the table to steady myself. I was breathing hard, like I had just run a sprint. "Whoa," was all I could articulate.

"See? She knows," Ellie said. "Now, Michael, how 'bout let's fill her in on the rest of the plan. The *why* of it. The danger. She's gotta know. She's gotta know now."

For the next hour we sat at the table as they filled me in on how we were going into, basically, the lion's den. And how not just Kim was effectively the bait, but me as well.

Kreios, I thought desperately, *you had better freaking show up. We are taking some huge risks now. Risks that might change the whole world forever.*

WE BOUGHT A FEW little souvenirs from the street merchants before catching another taxi back to the airstrip. "Wideawake; what a cool name," I said. I was thoroughly engrossed, and as it turned out, clueless. I should have known better.

The bottom of our little world didn't drop out until we boarded the plane again: Kim was gone. At first I thought she had just woken up and needed to use the bathroom or something, that maybe she had gone into the hangar for some reason. Something temporary, something that meant she would be *back.*

But she was gone.

Ellie was as angry as I had ever seen her. "We've gotta find her. NOW."

"THAT'S A GOOD GIRL, Kim. You've done well. Very well."

Kim had been faking it for hours on the plane, pretending to be asleep. It was so crazy how the Bloodstone gave her the ability to do superhuman things, like resist powerful psychosomatic drugs intentionally slipped into her drink by psychopathic blue-haired trust-fund girls. How it gave her new desires she hadn't ever put together for herself. Take-over-the-world-type stuff. She felt, with it, that she could fly. *Perhaps I will…*

And time flew by too. Normally she would have been impatient. But the Bloodstone lent to her a different perspective; it was larger. She could see more of the historical picture with it, see that everything happened again and again in cycles of evil; that she only need wait for the next one. It would be along just as surely as the next bus to the end of the world. And that made her less jittery. So when the time became ripe she was ready.

But on the threshold of the total surrender of her will, she hesitated. Destiny loomed over her in the form of pure doom; there was no hope save for her last free decision: *Is this what I really want?*

"Hush my dear," the Bloodstone cooed, *"and savor the taste…"*

It does taste good….

Under the carnal influences of the Bloodstone, she sprang from her seat and bolted from the plane. No one saw her; the pilots were indoors filing their flight plan and checking the weather. The ground crew was busy elsewhere. The gang of three, those troublemakers, those molesters, those kidnapping liars, would be back soon, so she took off at a dead sprint.

But she wasn't really Kim, was she? *No, not anymore. Now I'm better than Kim. I'm Kim as I should have been. And I will evolve into something truly magnificent. Something immortal.* Kim told herself that her root motivation wasn't jealousy; that she didn't really just want to be like Airel, to have what she had, to be beautiful, to live forever, to have Michael for her own. But it was all lies. Fighting fire with fire, she told herself lies that countermanded the previous lies. In fact, the truth was, *everything* was a lie.

None of it mattered.

She would be beautiful.

Untouchable.

SHE WAS BEGINNING TO wheeze, to pant, to convulse as its—her—legs pumped up and down over the dead moonscape of lava rock. She was spewing forth more evidence of the presence of the Bloodstone: gooey black tar oozed from her nostrils and a fume of that vapor poured out from her mouth in puffs.

For an instant one of the legs failed to pump properly, stumbling over an irregularity in the field of rocks. Down she went. There was no pain; only the Bloodstone's manufacture of an all-consuming elation that dwarfed all other indicators of pain or reality. There was blood on the hands now though.

Slipping the straps from each shoulder one at a time, it took the pink backpack off and reattached it to the front, running her arms through the straps again so that this time the bag rested on her chest.

A ripple appeared on her back as razor sharp wingtip talons skillfully pierced the skin and the fabric of the dress, protruding slowly like a plant growing out of fertile ground and then unfurling like the petals of a diabolical flower. At first green, the wings quickly changed to brown, matching the lava rock landscape that was spread roundabout.

"Tengu deserved his end," the Bloodstone—Nwaba now—thought. *"Now it is my turn…"* Swiftly the wings descended, and the hybrid creature shot into the sky as if launched from a catapult. The wings of something, anything, that could fly; the face of a human. *"Well…as far as is reasonable,"* Nwaba said to himself. After all, this chameleon had never quite been fully anything.

Nwaba flew, his wings protruding from the spine of the one named Kim, toward the peak of Green Mountain. He could detect the stench of one of his oldest foes. Kreios. He might know Nwaba better under younger names. Only if Kreios had truly been paying attention would he know him as Nwaba. *"We shall see, Kreios. And we shall see you soon."*

The one named Kim spread its arms wide in menace as the wings shot her swiftly through the air, pink backpack first, toward the place where Kreios had last stood upon the earth. That place with that accursed symbol, the cross.

CHAPTER XIII

Cape Point, South Africa, present day

KREIOS DECIDED TO MAKE landfall in an isolated spot. Cape Point provided that in spades.

An isthmus that projected from the continent, it was the south-westernmost point of Africa, and it divided the Atlantic ocean from the Indian ocean. The land raced upward from sea level like a scalded cat, its steep slopes creating precipitous and sheer drops from dizzying heights to the crashing surf below.

Kreios swooped in along the tops of the waves as he approached, feeling the salt spray in his face as he went. Considerably far below the Cape Point Lighthouse, he alighted gently on the cluster of rocks that El had heaped up here as a boundary to the deep.

"This far and no further," he said to himself.

He scrambled quickly up the rocks toward safer altitudes, reflecting on the sheer boldness he had employed to rescue Airel's body from the water, what seemed like only yesterday. *Too late.* Still, he wondered. *Why had I not drowned then? I should have been utterly swamped and useless.* He wasn't sure why, at this point, he had even attempted it. He had known it was suicide. *Perhaps that was why.* And yet El in His infinite wisdom had tweaked the situation, as He so often did. *But why?*

Kreios climbed upward away from the dangerous crashing waves to safety. He could remember: as he had rescued Airel's already dead body, the way he had actually *gained speed underwater.* It was impossible.

"With El," he said, finally gaining a rude little path on which he could walk from there on, "all things are possible."

"And impossible that an angel should be saying so," he added as an epilogue. *Ah, if she could hear me now.* Which she? *Any of them. All of them.*

Rage once again took him by the heart, stabbing its poisoned blade deep into the center of his will, radiating out from there manipulative currents that told him where to go, what to do.

A noise in the hardy shrubs off to his left set him on edge, and he drew his sword.

Just in time, too, because a baboon leapt out at him for crowding its turf too closely. Kreios reacted swiftly with his blade, hacking the unfortunate beast clean in two. It was a pity. He was hungry, but baboon was not a sweet meat. Terrible for food, carnivores. *These are the work of the devil anyhow. Brute savage things.*

He left the useless bits of carcass where they lay and didn't bother cleaning his blade, resheathing it in the scabbard on his back, under his hoodie. The next member of the Brotherhood he encountered would commingle its blood with that of the baboon. It would be two of a kind, then. Fitting. Kreios continued on up the path.

Ascension Island, present day

"WHERE DO WE START?" I asked, bewildered.

"Witnesses," Michael said.

"Wait," Ellie said. "I need a moment." She closed her eyes and sat down on the tarmac. Several minutes elapsed.

I nudged Michael. "Dude. What is she doing?"

He rolled his eyes and shrugged. "Communing with her ancestors?"

"Shut up, you two. I'm trying to feel which way it went. I'm trying to do something here."

"Feel…which way…it…went?" I asked.

Ellie did not look up at me as she rebuked me. "Listen, mate. You have your gifts, I have mine. Don't interrupt me again; you're wasting time."

Humbled, I leaned into Michael's chest and said softly, "Uh-oh. I've gone from 'girlie' to 'mate.' Now I'm lumped in with you." I grimaced at him.

"You're totally screwed," he whispered.

More agonizingly silent and motionless moments went by. It killed me. Never mind that my friend Kim wasn't even herself anymore. Never mind that whatever part of her I had loved for so many years was now probably lost forever in the smashing of her mind. She was shattered now, but I still felt crazed about finding her. Even if it was only her body, even if she was just an unholy habitation for some overly ambitious demon. Even if it meant mortal single combat between us, I was desperate to find my Kimmie.

Ellie broke the silence. "East," she said, her eyes still closed. "It's east."

"I know why you're calling her *it,* but I don't like it."

"I'm not calling her *it.* I'm calling the Bloodstone *it.* There's still a difference."

My heart was actually hurt more by the prospect that Kim was somehow still there, still suffering under all the garbage being poured out on her. "We've gotta *find* her."

"Working on it," Ellie said, sitting still. Her tone of voice was as if she was sitting at some control panel, working dials and switches as she gazed deeply at some readout or something.

I was dying to ask her what she was doing and how she was doing it. But my love for Kim, whatever remained of her, surpassed my curiosity.

"Okay, we're good," Ellie said finally, opening her eyes. She sprang up from the pavement and grabbed my hand, pulling me along. "Walk and talk, girlie. You too, commando Joe. We need all hands on deck now."

"What's going on?" I hazarded a question as we ran toward the hangars.

"Kreios was here," Ellie said.

"What?! When?"

"Day or two at most."

I wanted to skip for joy. We were getting close. I wondered why I couldn't feel him, couldn't reach him in my mind. It annoyed me that Ellie could and I couldn't, but should have been able to.

Ellie continued to drag me along; she was faster than she looked. Michael was falling behind, though he was sprinting and trying his best to keep up with us. "Hey," I said, "wait for Michael. Hey!" The pace wasn't slowing. "Hey, Ellie, where are we going?"

"I'm looking for a tool!" she shouted at me, exasperated.

We ducked in and out of open doors, around corners, looking for this tool, whatever it was, in every shed and hangar in the area. Occasionally the odd mechanic or private pilot would look up at us as we sprinted from one place to another, popping our heads into and out of doorways.

Finally, around the back of one of the hangars, there was a small shed rotting away in a state of rusty dilapidation, its corrugated metal sides and roof evoking something out of a role-playing video game. Ellie, still grasping my hand, gave a final burst of speed for the structure and kicked the door down. "There!" she shouted in triumph.

I didn't get it at first. I was looking for some kind of hand tool, falling for, as Ellie had put it earlier, basically whatever my mind expected to find. I didn't understand fully until Michael finally caught us up, panting furiously.

He placed one hand against the doorframe and looked into the darkness within the shed. "Whoa," he said hoarsely, "A Bowler Wildcat!"

CHAPTER XIV

LIKE I HAD ANY idea what a Bowler Wildcat was. Boys and their ridiculous off-roaders. And of course it was looming hugely in the shed, unmistakable had I known we were looking for a racing truck.

But I found out soon enough that it was indeed a tool. A tool for seriously fast going on any terrain. How did I find that out? Easy: Five minutes after we found the thing, we were racing east across a bumpy field of volcanic rock like it wasn't even there.

Since it was a two-seater I had to sit on Michael's lap the whole time, and contrary to what I might have thought, it wasn't even close to fun. My head banged against the roll cage and the windows, my butt banged against his lap, my head pounded with the noise, and Ellie never slowed down through all of it.

"You're a crazy driver!" I shouted at her. But I endured it for the possibility of being able to help Kim.

All Ellie did was drop the hammer, accelerating across the rocky undulating hills until it felt like we were either flying or sailing; I couldn't tell which.

"So where are we going?" Michael asked, his voice cracking against the noise and heat of the cramped enclosed space.

Ellie pointed straight ahead and straight up. "There! Green Mountain! That's where Kreios was and that's where the Bloodstone is!" The racing engine roared even louder and we were gone in a cloud of dust.

Schipol, Amsterdam, present day

SCHIPOL AIRPORT IN AMSTERDAM was one of the busiest air terminals in Europe. Flights came in from and departed to nearly every continent. Great walls of steel and glass enshrouded it in a shrine to the sleek and modern. People from every tribe and nation walked its corridors every day.

Among them were two men lately of America, specifically Boise, Idaho. They walked and talked. Their layover would last only about one more hour, then they would have to board their plane for Cape Town via Johannesburg.

"You know, at some point I'm going to have to use the restroom," Harry said to his companion. "What will you do then?"

"You wanna go? Let's go."

"What, together?"

"Certainly. Might as well get it over with."

Harry shrugged and kept walking toward the sign for the men's room. "What're you gonna do? Lend me a hand as well?"

"You're not funny at all," Airel's father said.

"I think it's a fair question, since you're nannying me."

"No, Harry. You're a big boy. I trust you not to soil yourself."

Harry grinned a little at the perverse *tete-a-tete,* but mostly he grinned at the idea of what he was planning. "You know…friend… I'm going to need a minute or two here…"

He looked at Harry. "Fine. That's fine. You go back one out and take your time with it. I'll be waiting at the sinks when you're done."

"It's a lot of paperwork. If you know what I mean," Harry said. "I tend to take my time in only two areas of my life, and this is one of them."

"I'm not asking what the other one is."

They walked into the restroom, Harry leading the way. He selected the farthest stall and walked straight for it. As he turned to close the door, his hand absentmindedly grasped its sleek metal top edge. He did not have time to latch it.

Airel's father, following Harry, did not hesitate an instant. He removed his pen from his shirt pocket in mid-stride and aimed the point discretely at the door. The other men in the large restroom went about their own business as men do, making no conversation and not desirous of it. He pressed the pen's engage/retract button as it made contact with Harry's stall door, releasing a bio-EMP pulse into and through it, energizing the door with a carefully engineered amount of voltage. It was just enough, and not too much, to accomplish a predetermined effect. It had taken years of R&D in three labs spread across two continents to develop the weapon. But of course, these were all just bullet points in a sales pitch, one Airel's father had cycled through with many a secret and elite client.

The bio-EMP pulse terminated its fury in the center of Harry's chest, instantly arresting his heart and contracting selected slow-twitch muscles on his body—the specific muscles that produce the fetal position.

Harry thudded into something. Airel's father opened the stall door to confirm the kill.

Harry was seated on the toilet; he had involuntarily soiled his expensive trousers. His torso leaned back to one side, propped up by the toilet paper dispenser. His head had knocked against the tile wall, his eyes wide and glassy. A trickle of blood escaped the corner of his mouth.

He was dead. Airel's father retreated, closing the stall door.

It had only taken half a second. Airel's father swept the room with experienced eyes as he moved smoothly toward the adjacent stall, as if that was what he had been doing all along. When he turned he noticed one man looking in his direction, disturbed by the racket Harry had raised as he had so violently sat down. He shrugged at him, hiked his thumb over his shoulder at Harry's stall and said, "Lots of paperwork," and smiled. The man rolled his eyes and left.

Airel's father entered his own stall and closed the door. Perfect timing. He had to pee like a maniac. He would be landing in Cape Town in about 16 hours. He could maybe catch up on some sleep. He caught a whiff from next door. *Whoa, Harry. You stink.*

Cape Point, South Africa, present day

KREIOS STOLE SOME WHEELS from the car park, the British way to say 'parking lot.' Details mattered, and he made mental notes to himself to blend in as much as possible. It was an old Toyota Land Cruiser pickup. Decades old, the design didn't stand out on South African roads and it didn't have much in the way of anti-theft measures. Just get in and go. He drove calmly, just like he owned it, right up the M64 to the M4, headed for Cape Town.

He was headed for one particular building. But he didn't want to allow his mind to rest on that too long.

What's the plan? He had to admit, he didn't really have one, beyond one of two scenarios: one, go in guns blazing, figuratively or not, and take as many of them with him as possible. Two, he would take them out surreptitiously in small groups, keep them guessing, keep them afraid. After all, they had to know he was coming.

Yes. That could be a problem, too.

This was what was left of the whole range of choices he had had not too long ago. He had whittled them down to two primary options. One of the most portentous choices he had made right from the beginning was to submit to naked rage, and this is what it had left him. But had he not been justified in giving in to it?

Was it not a just war he now waged against the Brotherhood? Had they not taken everything from him?

How can it be? He reflected on the very reasons he had had for abducting Airel in the first place. He knew how special she was; that's why he took her. He knew she had to be set apart, protected, watched closely, instructed, trained. He had heard clearly what El had told him, that she was absolutely crucial to the turning of… historical events. He dared not allow his mind to dwell upon these, even in brief.

But all was lost.

How can that be possible?

Have I missed something, El? He drove on in silence as the sun set in the sundering west. *I thought it would not be possible for her to die, ultimately, given what You told me. I thought I could protect her. I thought my efforts would be adequate.*

He could think of the situation no longer. He had a limited endurance these days. He could take only so much reflection on Airel before he sank either into despair or rage.

He had to find someplace to stay that was crowded, somewhere he wouldn't be noticed, somewhere the stolen Toyota would blend right in if parked for several days. He needed time to strategize and think.

He turned right with the light onto Atlantic in Muizenberg and drove a little way.

Then, on Alexander Road, he veered left. *This is as fitting place as any.*

There would be murders here; it was inevitable with Kreios. Soon.

CHAPTER XV

Arabia, 1232 B.C.

IT WAS DARK. PERFECT.

Uriel sat on her bed and concentrated on the lesson uncle Yamanu had taught her the previous day. It had been incredible when he showed her how to use the gift of the Shadowers. *Perhaps it is not the only gift I possess. But it is the most fun I have had in a long time,* Uriel thought to herself.

Slowly as she focused her mind, the dense fog of the art descended upon her physical features. Unlike her uncle's signature manifestation though, no mist, no cloud, no vapor attended it. No. As for Uriel, she simply disappeared from physical sight, even from spiritual sight. She was simply not there.

In time she would learn how to make other things disappear. Soon she would be able, with practice, to be able to render physical objects immaterial; she would be able to walk through drawn shades, closed doors, even walls.

But not tonight. Tonight was just a beginning.

Tonight she was not visible to the naked eye, whether that eye illuminated the face of man or angel or beast. Therefore, she crept as quietly as she was able to do from her uncle's house, down the deserted city streets of Ke'elei, past the guards, up the inside of the main gate tower steps, across the city wall, and down the outside of it. The skidding scrambling noise she made as she slid down the face of the stones did attract some attention, but when the guards were unable to see anything, they continued on their rounds.

Overjoyed and elated with her new freedom, she set off in search of her beau. She didn't know where to start other than right outside her doorstep. She had faith that the road would carry her there. Somehow. That was more than enough for her.

Though the tall redwood forest concealed her in its deep shadows, allowing her to rest her gift easy, conserving energy—for it did take a great deal of concentration for her to use the gift of shadowing—still, the deepness of the forest was threatening. In the back of her mind she was unsettled.

She talked a good game, especially to her dear father Kreios. If the truth be known though, she was still a scared little girl inside and she missed him terribly.

But what was done was done; what could she do now? There was no going home. She was a woman now and was restless to make her own decisions. Her father had to let her go eventually in any case. Perhaps she was like the tulips that pushed the late snows aside in early spring, sending their tender green shoots up to bloom audaciously before the season was quite yet ripe. It was not her fault that Kreios was not ready for her to depart. To bloom.

He would certainly not be ready for her to marry, either.

Ah, Subedei! She longed for him more than she could begin to say. As she reflected on her fantasy lover, her mind drifted and she became unguarded. She forgot that the great city of Ke'elei had walls for a reason. She failed to remember that, especially at night, there were things without the walls that were darker than the night itself. And more powerfully frightful.

The awakening she received was rude.

They swung in from the trees. They jumped up from under mats made of massive fern fronds that they had laid on the floor of the forest. They wielded spears, swords, the knives were out. She didn't have time to do anything but scream and cower like a child. Instantly she was full of regret, wishing to undo a great deal of her life up to this moment. But such a thing was not possible. She tried to remember her training, to shadow, but it was all still very new. And she was very scared. Too scared, in fact, to focus properly.

Then, from the recesses of the dark hollows that lay on the path before her, a figure emerged. It was Subedei.

Ascension Island, present day

MICHAEL TRIED TO HOLD on to Airel as best he could, but the V8 powered beast was bucking and snorting relentlessly as it climbed and clawed its way toward the summit, bouncing them all over the place.

Finally, after more than an hour, the ride ended and Ellie pulled up, stopping on an overlook. She hit the kill switch and then the engine was still. The whole mass of the truck sizzled with energy and dust and bits of dirt, the radiator ticking madly.

"We're close," Ellie said as she opened the door and got out.

"So what are we gonna do, sneak up on her now that we've arrived at five thousand decibels in a cloud of dust?" Airel said as she opened the door and then practically fell out. "Ugh, I feel sick." She crouched down in the tall grass and held her head in her hands.

Michael went to her and put a hand on her shoulder. He turned back. "Ellie, where are you going?"

"I've gotta find her before she leaves."

"Leaves?" Airel was suddenly back up and running; the change was dramatic and instantaneous.

"Airel, are you okay?" Michael asked, concerned and chasing after her. They both ignored him.

"Yeah," Ellie said to her, "The Bloodstone has found the next demon prince in the line of succession. It has conjoined with it and only needs one more thing: it's up here looking for sign. It's like it's tracking Kreios. It's looking for clues as to his whereabouts. Once it's on his trail and knows which way to go… " She stood halfway up the next rise, one foot uphill and one down, her body twisted back toward them. "After that I'm afraid all that'll be left for Kim is the fat lady."

"The fat lady, the fat lady," Airel said quietly, climbing after her. "It's not over till the fat lady sings."

"I'm coming with you," Michael shouted after them.

"Try to keep up," Ellie said. "Just follow our dust trail."

She wasn't kidding. The two girls were rockets. Michael was left to pant along alone as he climbed the remainder of the mountain.

That was the trouble with summits, he knew. *Just when you think you're there, you look up and there's a whole new mountain in front of you.* He dragged his battered and tired body upward, though. The sleep hadn't done him much good. Not that sleep on a plane ever made anyone anything but more tired. Travel by air, like anything, had its drawbacks.

The girls were long gone, but he could see the line in the grass they had left behind. A cluster of shrubs lay just off the path ahead. Beyond that, there wasn't much up here. He looked down to be sure of his footing.

When he looked back up, the path was blocked. It was Kim. Or what was left of her. She was posed suggestively, holding the Bloodstone out to him like temptation itself. "You know you want this."

Arabia, 1232 B.C.

"SUBEDEI?" URIEL SAID. "IS that you?"

He came closer and extended his hand to her, helping her to her feet. With the other hand, he unsheathed a dagger and held its point at her throat. "So pleased you are here, Uriel." He gestured to those around him, his entourage, his band of warriors, his collection of thieves. "Honestly, you caught us by surprise; we weren't quite ready for you. Not this soon."

She swallowed, but the movement of her throat against his blade drew blood. A drop of it flowed slowly downward toward its hilt. "Subedei, what is happening?" She began to cry.

He blinked, a momentary enigma. This was not the face of a lover. It was the face of a hardened warrior. But something passed over his countenance. What was it? Indecision? But then it was gone.

Uriel was confused and lost. She thought she was going to begin a new chapter in her life, strike out on her own, make something of herself, prove the whole world wrong with the strength of her love. But when she had drawn the curtain aside, instead of revealing her wildest dreams, she beheld dawning horror. Subedei was nothing like she had imagined he would be. *Stupid, stupid, stupid!* She had let her mind get away with her.

She felt it coming, too: the sickness. She had been feeling the same way now for the past few weeks, but it was strange, it came and went. It seemed it was connected to something, but what? *I usually only feel sick...when I think of...Subedei...*

"Oh, no," she said, and promptly vomited.

She closed her eyes in shame. Now she knew: she was surrounded by the Brotherhood. And she had been activated. Her father had been right about everything.

The sky caught fire. She was plucked up by something swift and bright, it swooped down and lifted her up into the air. When she opened her eyes she knew she was in trouble: Kreios had rescued her. Now there would be real trouble—for everyone, but mostly her.

Ascension Island, present day

MICHAEL KNEW HE WASN'T looking at Kim, though his eyes and his memory conspired against reality to manufacture the lie. And when she had said what she said, there was something bestial about it that repelled him.

His first instinct was to stall for time. "Hey…uh, Kim. What are you doing here?" But he knew very well.

"Shut up, pawn. Kim knows that you shroud your thoughts in deception; she does not believe a word you say. Kim is no fool. She cannot be tricked." She licked her lips, coating her tongue with the sticky black tar that encrusted them.

Michael quickly analyzed his position. He stood downhill from her. The base of a little sheer cliff was to his left, a steep rolling drop-off to his right. He knew further that he was facing down one of the original manifestations of evil. No one knew for sure if the Bloodstone was Lucifer himself or merely a connection to him.

There was a possibility that the Bloodstone wasn't either of those; that it masqueraded as such to cause tremors of fear, upon which it fed like a ravenous beast.

Whatever the case, Michael knew his situation had become very serious. "All right then," he said. "We won't kid ourselves."

"That's right, seed of Alexander. We won't." She tucked the Bloodstone away inside the palm of her hand and held it stiffly at her side.

"You obviously know who I am."

"Yes!" The one called Kim padded lithely back and forth, sizing up her prey. "You tried to kill me the last time I saw you." She licked her lips again, her voice a razor's edge.

"I failed." Michael tucked his chin and spread his stance, readying himself. "Tell me, demon. What is your name this time?"

Kim roared violently, ejecting bits of black slime from her enlarged mandible-like mouth, spewing forth like a volcano. Bits of it sizzled wherever they landed. "The Alexander asks our name, does he? No! No, we shall not be tricked!" Kim's skin was turning green, blending in with the tall grass in which she stood.

"Fine," Michael said, and promptly drew his pistol and fired. The shot had been aimed squarely at the Bloodstone in her hand, but as the bullet neared its target its trajectory became twisted and bent, pulling it into compact orbit around the stone. It slowed and then fell to the earth harmless.

The demon laughed, a wretched constrained sound. She began to prattle on in an incoherent stream of meaningless words. Michael pretended to pay attention to her, wore a false look of dread on his face. But he knew what effect the unsilenced gunshot would have. He needed only to wait now for Ellie and Airel. Then it would be three to two. Unless Kim's weird third-person monologue included more than one demon.

Arabia, 1232 B.C.

KREIOS SAT ERIEL ON one of the topmost branches of one of the
tall redwoods outside the city walls of Ke'elei. He did not have the
time to scold her or even to confirm if she was all right, nor could
he take the time to tell her what surely she already knew: that she
must hold on tightly or fall to her death. But she wasn't a little girl
anymore. She knew these things now. It was clear to Kreios, just as
clear as the fact that she had stubbornly chosen her path; she had
been activated. Now nothing would ever be the same.

He then descended upon the demon horde below with ultimate
wrath, sword first. A father's love for his daughter manifest as a
tower of rage if she ever faced harm from the hand of another.

Demon and weird beast alike fell under his blade. Horses,
bizarre apes with smashed-looking faces, unchained jungle cats
that had been saddled for combat, even one enormous lizard-like
monster from the early days, when men lived to be a thousand
years old, before the flood, before creatures like this had been
mostly exterminated, evolving into dragon myths. The entourage of
Subedei was decadent indeed for him to possess one.

But it made no tactical sense for such creatures to be here,
which made Kreios despise his foe all the more as a fool. There
were shouts as the single-handed slaughter continued apace.
Subedei was rallying them into formation. But it was too little
and too late. The guards upon the city wall, less than a league off,
sounded the alarm and angel sorties had already organized into the
air. Subedei's little detachment of troops was doomed. It was now
his turn to rue the recklessness of a foray into the woods so near the

great city.

Kreios looped into the air with his kind and sized up the final blow, looking for the captain of this force. Sword to the fore, Kreios searched for Subedei. But he was not to be found.

Kreios shouted in rage. He had missed too many opportunities of late.

Ascension Island, present day

THE SWORD OF LIGHT made one heck of an entrance, especially when it came out of nowhere like it did when I wielded it. I leaped from the cliff top above Michael and Kim with a primal scream, sounding like a Valkyrie or something; it scared even me. I landed in between them Sword first, plunging the blade deep into the grassy earth, ejecting bits of geological shrapnel in every direction. Light spiraled around the Sword and up my arm, swirling with great energy.

Ellie took a different tack, deciding to come at Kim from the uphill side along the path, from behind her.

Michael crouched down in the blast radius of my landing, shielding himself just in time. Kim was forcibly knocked down. She never saw Ellie coming.

Kim, if you're in there I hope you know I'm sorry for this...it's not how I wanted you to go.

In an obscene movement, as if her body was a marionette on strings, she sat bolt upright in the dirt. Her head twitched a little as she looked at me, like her thoughts were a skipping record or like she was having trouble rebooting.

I approached her, Sword at the ready. "Kim—"

A beastly voice answered, "Kim is not...Kim is not...Kim is no more. It is only the Nri..." The tent of Kim's body hiked itself to its feet in a crouch and looked up at me, baring its blackened teeth, twisting to acknowledge Ellie's presence behind.

"You have to end this," She said within, in a very clear tone. I charged, but it was too late. *I* was too late.

Kim—it—leapt up to the top of the cliff above, inhumanly, a jump of thirty feet or more. Its ungodly wings unfurled in a huge sweeping motion, drooping down from the cliff to where we stood. The face of Kim smiled the wickedest smile I had ever seen and then looked to the sky. The wings were slowly raised.

Then the thing, the housing for the Bloodstone, bolted into the sky and was gone.

CHAPTER XVI

"FIRE IT UP, HEX!" Ellie shouted at her questioning pilot as she walked right by, straight to the door. Michael and I followed suit, glad to be done with the return trip to the airfield via the Bowler insanitymobile.

Hex asked Ellie, "Where have you been? I thought you were only going to be a few hours at most!" He scolded her like a worried parent, following along behind.

Ellie stopped abruptly, turning on him. He nearly bowled her spare frame over, but she stood fast. "Listen, Hex, just get us preflighted and out of here like yesterday, okay? I mean, light it up." She turned and quickly bounded onto the G550.

"Yes, ma'am," he said.

"Excuse us," I said. Michael and I made our way around him toward the door.

"Sorry," he said. He then turned to his work as we boarded and began doing all those little checks that pilots have to do in order to get the airplane ready to defy gravity.

Cape Town, South Africa, present day

AFTER THE REFUELING STOP in Jo-burg, as the locals called it, the plane carrying Airel's father had only about another hour's flight to its final destination.

The 747, a city with wings, set down on the tarmac in Cape Town on a mild afternoon. Massive thunderheads loomed in the distance and a shroud of ribbon-like clouds were draped over Table Mountain. There were patches of sunshine that lent places like Hout Bay an aspect of having been lit from beneath, the turquoise color of the sea iridescent.

Though it looked like paradise, Airel's father knew this was when the real heavy lifting would begin. As the lone sales rep for a clandestine arms and technology house, he did indeed have many tools in his arsenal. And he knew how to ply his trade, as well as the trade of those who bought his wares.

But he didn't know where to start looking for his little girl.

He knew she had to be here, though. It was clear enough, looking through news reports like the ones he had seen that led him here: *Graveyard Massacre. Seventy-five men, two women brutally murdered...Schoolyard Ripper...*and all of them with something in common: the same man. Whether it was a grainy photo or a still from security camera footage, he could recognize the blond killer from the BPD report on the original incident at the movie theater. When he finally put it all together it was like a parting of the clouds to reveal pure sunshine. This mysterious blond-haired man had crossed paths with Airel once too often. Now he would cross swords with Airel's father. *To the death.*

He didn't know what the killer wanted with his daughter. He could only assume she needed help and that the killer, if backed into a wall, would eventually lead him to wherever he was keeping her. He had all kinds of tools he could use that made people talk.

Now one problem remained: *Where to find the bastard?*

Somewhere over the South Atlantic, present day

BEFORE I KNEW IT we were airborne, bound for South Africa, Cape Town direct. It wouldn't be more than a few hours; Hex was flying us close to mach, the speed of sound.

I was worried about Michael. He had obviously not fared well on our little adventure up the mountain. He sat scrunched in his seat, his eyes closed, beads of sweat on his brow. I adjusted the ventilation so that a cool stream of air washed over his face. I loosened the collar of his shirt a little so his skin could breathe.

That's when I first noticed the mark on his chest.

My mind flashed with anxiety, my hands pulling at the buttons of his shirt in desperation as more and more of the weird wound showed itself. It was like a star, purple-black at its center with spiral tendrils radiating out from there in red and yellow, that ugly bruise-yellow that attends blunt force trauma.

"Michael!"

It took me a moment to realize he wasn't responding. He wasn't just tired. He seemed like he wasn't all there, like he was…I couldn't go there. *Oh, no. What's happened?* I was going to lose it.

My hands grasped each other and I brought them reflexively up to my chest, next to my scar. Then *She* crowded into my mind. *"You have a wound from the same blade."*

I was stunned. I remembered it, my hands now clasping my chest, rubbing the only scar I would wear forever. It was clear: I could heal. Michael could not. I searched inwardly, racking my brain for an answer.

That's what happened. I remembered what I had seen in my vision, when I was...*what, dead? Kreios healed him with the Bloodstone.* I remembered everything; how Michael had howled in pain and confusion as my grandfather brought the Bloodstone to his chest. I sat back in remorseful silence. There were no tears. I just shook my head.

"It was a curse that he laid upon him," She·said. *"But he thought that was what you would have wanted...for Michael to carry on...however possible..."*

I could tell *She* was sad. I had never known her to be like that. And it was a heavy thing indeed for a girl to have a broken-hearted conscience.

But what kind of life would that be? I protested to her. It was clear that Kreios didn't really know me. Not if he thought I wanted Michael to live under some irrevocable curse.

Ellie was now at my side, a look of concern on her face. She said nothing. I was glad. I wouldn't have known how to deal with a conversation then.

Michael stirred in his fever, muttering one word: "Kasdeja... Kasdeja..." He said it over and over.

Finally Ellie said, "I'm sorry, girlie. I think that last run-in with the Bloodstone really did a number on him."

Yes, it had. It was all that and so much more. Michael had been carrying the load, he had been doing the heavy lifting for all of us. He never sought the limelight, never did what was best for himself, never wanted for anyone else to be too worried about him. He had kept it all to himself.

Meanwhile I ran around like a chicken with my head cut off, bouncing from one crisis to another. But he was steady. I cursed myself out loud. *No. I won't believe it's too late. Not after all this. Not after all we've done, all we've endured. We're almost to the finish line!* I couldn't quit now.

Kreios would know what to do. If anyone would, he would. "Ellie," I said, "I think he needs water. I'm going to go get him some."

She nodded. "It's in the back there. In the cupboard."

"All right," I said, getting up and walking to the back. *Cupboard, huh?* Everything was stainless steel and latched shut against the possibility of turbulence. There was nothing to it but to go through all of them methodically. Top to bottom, left to right. I was glad for a menial task to take my mind off how badly Michael looked, how I was powerless to help him.

The smaller doors hid first aid stuff. Then there were cups, glasses, all of them crystal or sterling silver. There were napkins, plates, and so on.

Across from these my search for bottled water got colder. All that was in these cabinets was what looked like Ellie's stash of military spec survival gear. I had opened every door on the stupid plane, I thought, until I came to one that was bigger still than all the others. *Warmer. I should have started here; this looks like a fridge.* And it was.

Once I released the latch and opened the door I stood back bewildered. It was stocked with every imaginable kind of chilled beverage. Plus there was cheese. Lots of it. Exotic stuff like Muenster and Camembert. The bottled water was near the bottom toward the back. I grabbed a couple bottles and made my return journey toward the nose of the plane.

I walked up to Michael and Ellie. "Here you go," I said,

offering her the bottle.

She took it. "Thanks."

I sat back down next to Michael and tried to get him to take a sip of the cold water. Turning to Ellie, I said, "Dude. What's with the cheese?"

She laughed. "There's a lot of it, ain't there? It's a weakness. More of a hobby, really."

"You're really weird," I said, and I meant it.

She took it as a joke and laughed, making us both laugh. It was a bittersweet moment. If I couldn't laugh I knew I would start in with the waterworks; Michael looked like death.

Bishop interrupted us. "Everything okay?" he asked in his thick African accent.

Ellie answered for us. "Yes, Bishop, of course." She smiled at him and he returned it redoubled, his pure white teeth and pure white crewman's shirt gleaming against his deep brown skin.

"I've just got to make sure you people are well attended to, that's all." He smiled and excused himself to the rear of the plane.

When he had gone I said, "I really like that guy."

"Oh, girlie, Africans are superb. I love them. Did you know there are ten official languages in Zed-A?"

"Ten?" I was flabbergasted.

"Yeah, most of 'em are tribal; either Zulu or Xhosa or Sutu. Bishop is Zulu. He's only been with me a little while, maybe four months, but I've been really impressed with him."

I laughed and allowed my gaze to wander to the open door of the flight deck. I had never been allowed to look out the front of an airplane while it was flying. I looked at Michael, then at Ellie. Michael was resting, he had taken a swallow or two of the water and was no longer muttering incoherently.

She must have read my mind. "I'll look after him, girlie. Go ahead. He just needs rest; I don't think he knows how to take care of himself." She motioned me forward toward the cockpit.

"Hex won't mind?"

"Hex? No, in fact he'll be glad for a change of company. I'll keep Bishop occupied back here."

This is cool. I stepped forward, glad for a diversion from all the stress. "I'll be right back."

Muizenberg, South Africa, present day

KREIOS WALKED BAREFOOT ALONG the cool empty beach in Muizenberg, the colorful swimmers' stilt house changing rooms lining the wide sandy expanse above the high tide mark. He could no longer ignore the huge drain on his mind, his body, his will. New thoughts started to take shape in him, new ideas. They were different. Dark and ugly.

It could be that I have overstepped, he began. Like the gentle waves along the shore of Muizenberg, the thoughts were small but consistent and relentless.

He felt the draining pull toward it.

But he also felt El somewhere in the midst of it all. He couldn't tell if El was the source of the new thoughts—which called him home to paradise, or so it seemed—or if El was in opposition.

Kreios allowed himself a bittersweet indulgence and set his mind searching along all the old corridors of pain and loss within. His bride: the day he had held her in his arms as she expired from a long and fatal childbirth; the day he buried her in the frozen ground. His Eriel: the day she had simply vanished and he could not know if she was alive or dead. Or worse, if she had been ultimately turned by the Brotherhood that had activated her. And Airel. Sweet girl. Too short, his time with her. That had been the case every time.

The depths of his broken heart cried out to El for an answer, and this for the first time since before all this insanity had been set in motion, before the episode at the movie theater, before he had been forced to intervene in Airel's life. As the heart of the angel of El broke, as he became utterly desperate, as he asked foundational questions, a ready answer came to him.

"Stand and knock." Kreios heard the voice of El as clearly as when he had been with Him in Paradise. He was alone on the beach, except for a few lone figures in the distance. He wriggled his bare toes into the sand and waited for more. *There is always more.*

He closed his eyes and willed his mind to become clear and oriented solely on El. Moments passed. And then it appeared: the door.

It was the selfsame door behind which Kreios had always been able to find answers. Of course, it had usually happened that the answer was in the form of a weapon. But this time it was different. This time it was not a weapon. It was an enjoinment. The frameless door opened to him.

The mind of El poured pure light into his angel of death, calling to remembrance all the instances of purpose and power for which he had been created and to which he had been called. Kreios recalled his forgotten itinerant works, especially in Egypt on the night of the first Passover, the night he had moved through the streets of the city of Pharaoh in the middle of the night, looking for lamb's blood on the lintels, slaughtering every firstborn son. He had forgotten. Until now.

He had forgotten about the conquest of Canaan, too. He had forgotten about his help to the commander Joshua, to the great king David. These were righteous warring men with great quantities of bloodshed on their hands. Kreios was of the same construct.

As El poured understanding into him, Kreios remembered it all. And then the perspective shifted in regard to his current mission. It was not a desperate lone-rogue bursting fit of rage, a reaction to unconscionable Brotherhood transgressions. No. It was instinct. Kreios had been made for such a thing, such a time as this. He had been created for it.

As Joshua had held the javelin aloft, so El now lifted Kreios up. And then El said the rest; what Kreios had been waiting to hear: *"See, I have given them into your hand."*

The door faded and he opened his eyes. He could feel his strength begin to return.

"Lift up your eyes."

Kreios did, and beheld a swarm of birds darkening the sky.

They were headed west. He looked closer at the unusual sight. *No. Those are not birds.*

No, indeed. They looked like bats, more like. But there was some trickery going on, some sleight of hand, some manipulation of the willing.

There were only two possibilities. One was that the bats were flying low, perhaps no higher than two hundred feet above the ground, and that their wings beat slowly, not enough to keep them aloft. The second solution was that he was not seeing bats at all. He was seeing a hundred enormous demons, their wingspans not mere inches across but whole yards, beating in time against acres of atmosphere, and they were flying considerably higher.

The dark cloud moved west, against prevailing wind, out to sea as the sun set. It was a new wrinkle, and it pulled upward at one corner of Kreios' mouth.

CHAPTER XVII

Somewhere over the South Atlantic, present day

I KNOCKED LIGHTLY ON the doorframe.

Hex looked up and back at me and smiled. "Come on in."

I ducked into the cramped space. There were more lights and buttons and screens than I had ever imagined. I climbed into the empty seat to his right as delicately as I could manage, scared to death I would accidentally hit the self-destruct button. *After everything that's happened so far, I wouldn't be surprised if there was one.*

"Are we getting bored?" Hex was relaxed.

"No," I said, unsure of what else to say. I looked out ahead of us through the windscreen into the darkening sky. There were clouds peppered below in the distance, the vast dark sea beneath them, an endless backdrop.

"Pretty soon the stars will be out. Have you ever seen the stars from up here?"

"No." I was really struggling for words; I felt my heart constricting in my chest. I was worried about Michael.

"Well...pretty soon you'll see them. We land soon. It will be something you can never forget."

"Are we there yet?"

He laughed. "As I said, soon. Maybe we start to descend in twenty minutes."

I was glad about that. Michael probably needed a hospital. I pushed the fear down and looked around at the cluster of controls. There were screens with complicated readouts on them, gauges, levers, buttons, knobs. "How do you keep it all straight?"

Hex laughed. "Lots of practice! It appears to be worse than it is. Look, the altimeter says we're cruising at forty thousand feet. Airspeed, here, indicates mach point eight. And here," he said, motioning toward the handlebar thing, "that's called the yoke. You have one too," he said, pointing to the one on my side.

I shrank back from it slightly, afraid I would inadvertently crash us. Still, it was really cool and I looked out the windows into the darkness, trying to see land. Ahead, way ahead and down, I could just barely see pinpricks of light through the clouds near the horizon. *It must be Cape Town.*

Hex went on, "Pull back and we go up. Push forward and we go down. It is easy!" He smiled broadly at me.

"Easy, huh." My eyes swept over the truly bewildering array of information and controls. I couldn't see how anyone could fly a plane.

"Just like a car, but we move in three dimensions, not two." His accent got thicker. "De Wright braddahs, dey tink of dis. Veeeery smart, dem."

I flashed back to the rain-soaked accident on that Oregon highway. The big African I had killed had talked with the same accent. Far from being charming, as it might have been to someone more innocent, it chilled me. I looked out the window to the right and saw a cloud below us. It was different from the others; it was dark and moving in the wrong direction. The other clouds were all moving slowly front to back as the plane rocketed forward. The dark one was moving with us. *That's weird.*

I glanced at Hex and he shot me a big smile.

I heard a noise from the back. *Maybe Michael is coming around.* I turned to look. I saw only that, if anything, all was not well back there. Michael hadn't moved, but Ellie and Bishop were entangled in what appeared to be some kind of wrestling match. *No, check that. It's a fight!*

I looked back at Hex, a smile still plastered on his face. That's when it finally hit me that we had been completely set up.

The Brotherhood.

No sooner had I thought it when Hex's sharp and massive elbow collided with my temple. I collapsed. The lights were going out.

"You cannot hide from us," Hex said, and then everything went white.

NWABA WAS A CHAMELEON spirit. He could be anything he dared, and he was old, very old. He was one of the original rebels that had sided with the dark prince from day one. He too had been cast down from Paradise to the Dominion under the sun.

With that kind of pedigree, there were certain carryovers. He could fly faster than any other Brother, for instance.

He had been waiting in the line of succession for his chance at the Bloodstone for millennia. When it had finally come calling, he was ready. It was electrifying.

Nwaba had to confess one thing, if at all: that he was addicted to the unexplainable, the cultic ritual, the mystical. As such, his experience with the Bloodstone was unprecedented and satisfyingly addictive. From the time he had first heard the call, to which he had instantly given his consent, he had been in two places.

Part of him had remained in Africa, but part of him had been pulled to the host, the frail girl named Kim. And he had existed in duality until she had finally succumbed to the inevitability of his wooing sentiments that in fact were mere echoes of what the Bloodstone itself was saying. Once he had gained a foothold—no indeed, once the Bloodstone had gained a foothold in the host girl— he was truly master and commander; he had been sucked right in. It had happened there on the tarmac in that plane: confluence.

It had all come together there.

He had seen the look on the boy Michael's face, knew he was too weak to continue. And he had seen the daughters of El there with him. He had seen that one with the Sword of his erstwhile companion Tengu, the weapon the outsider Kreios had stolen away from the Brotherhood. Nwaba would prevail, and the Sword would return to the fold.

To that end he had gathered up a welcoming committee. A small part of his Nri army. One hundred of his fittest and strongest that could fly out to meet the three in the air. It would be easy work. There were, after all, already two of the Nri Clan of the Brotherhood on board the plane.

"GET OFF ME!" ELLIE shouted, kicking Bishop in the face. But he tackled her again, this time taking her down onto the floor and straddling her.

He reached into his shirt pocket and retrieved a folding razor knife, opening it up. "Daughter of El, it is time to send you home forever!" He drew back to strike.

Taking advantage of this opening, Ellie punched him in the throat twice, making him gag. He weakened for a second and she scrambled out from under him. She stood and kicked his face with her heel, knocking him backward.

As Bishop howled in furious pain and groped at his eyes, she walked over the top of him shouting, "Airel!"

But Airel was down.

Hex twisted in his seat and looked directly at Ellie, pure unleashed hatred fueling the fire of his eyes.

NWABA WAS EASILY THE biggest of the Nri clan. His wingspan was over two hundred feet, when he felt like flaunting it, when he wore the right suit of clothes. Or when it was useful. Like now.

He shot ahead of the pack, upward, aiming to intercept the G550. The Nri detachment had flown west from mainland Africa and then begun to loop around and climb as they closed the distance. He would have only one shot at this. The body of his host—the one named Kim—was with him, securely bound to his belly inside the cocoon he had woven for her, pink backpack and all. He pumped his enormous dark blue wings furiously, anticipating where he would cross paths with the plane.

Shrieking by at nearly mach when he made contact, it was all Nwaba could do to rake his claws along the fuselage, grasping for it. He flicked his leg out and up. A great rapier-like talon shot upward against one of the engines as he slid by, his tail to the rear along the plane's belly. The engine instantly flamed out and exploded, sending bits of shrapnel everywhere and producing a massive plume of smoke that stained the sky. He folded his wings tight against his body, flattening, reducing drag.

Nwaba wanted to do more. The heat of battle descended upon him, bloodlust filled his mouth, and he grasped for more of the slippery aircraft. He pierced through the fuselage with the claws of one hand, holding fast. He flipped his body around, head to the rear, and climbed backward and upward along the rear of the airplane. He wrapped his prodigious barbed tail around the vertical stabilizer. He then sunk the talons of both feet deep into the tapered rear of the fuselage.

As his clawed hands grasped the tailplane, he was ready: he unfurled his great wings.

The effect was like deploying a massive parachute on a dragster. The plane groaned and snapped in protest as Nwaba wrestled it from the sky.

As he violently slowed the plane, the Nri welcoming committee caught up.

The aircraft then split apart at the massive incisions made by Nwaba's taloned feet.

Both pieces began to plummet to the sea below. He let the tail section go; it sputtered and spiraled, smoke pouring from its remaining engine. He drew his wings back and chased the front section, looking for flailing humans in the darkening sky.

CHAPTER XVIII

Cape Town, South Africa, present day

THEY CALLED HIM MR. Emmanuel. It was the perfect moniker for him. It spoke to his penchant for self-important sacrilege, his megalomania, his fervent belief that all roads led to him. Sooner or later. Wearing a very stylish white fedora, he leaned against the wall in the international arrivals terminal and waited for the mark.

It had been boring, really. He had known Harry would fail. Like a tool, he had served his purpose and then outlived his usefulness. And that was perfectly fine. It was the same with Apartheid, for instance. It had served its purpose well enough for him and his associates. And sure, it was dead, but mostly just on paper. Blacks and whites and coloreds still distrusted one another, still collected in their ethnic cliques. In that sense then it was more alive than ever, and the people now carried the walls with them wherever they went. Success.

Mr. Emmanuel suffered himself to yawn openly, to check his wristwatch. He knew few men wore them anymore; they had become redundant with the advent of the mobile phone, but that was precisely what had brought them back into fashion as far as he was concerned. He noted the time. Any minute now.

His mind wandered, as it did habitually. Perhaps he would change his fashions and use a pocket watch instead. But that would require that he wear a waistcoat, which would necessitate a change of his personal style. Waistcoats weren't worn with jeans. Not by him, at any rate. And then there would be the question of comfortable shoes. If he had to wear a suit everywhere he went, he would not be able to get away with comfortable shoes any longer, and that would inhibit performance. Perhaps he would have to change his car, maybe even his house as a result. No, the pocket watch was not pragmatic.

And Mr. Emmanuel was deeply pragmatic. He knew the old schools of classical philosophy and he picked and chose what he would adhere to. Was that not pragmatic? And after all anyway, he was a god, so whom should he fear? At least he believed he was. And if he believed, was he not a god? Who could say otherwise? Who would dare correct him?

Except the master.

Yes, but that went without saying. As a matter of fact, he preferred it went unsaid.

To all who resided on the downwind slope of his affectations, he was and would be a god. And that was enough.

His nostrils flared.

Here comes the mark.

Mr. Emmanuel allowed him to pass him by and then followed nonchalantly at a discreet distance.

The mark didn't know it, but he was completely caged. Mr. Emmanuel flicked a finger and the teeming crowd swerved, carrying the mark toward the mouth of a corridor where he was quickly and inconspicuously tased and then snatched by three strong men. Mr. Emmanuel smirked. *A taste of your own medicine, John.*

The three thugs were faithful servants. They would bundle John, the mark, into the back of a kombie and deliver him as ordered, to the building.

And Mr. Emmanuel would take the helo to the top of the city tonight, in the same building, the skyscraper his petrol company owned. It was all a shell game; it was delicious.

Sure, sometimes it bored him, but did not the gods suffer boredom from time to time? It was no matter. He would smite someone from his Olympus and then he would feel better. Sleep like a child.

AIREL'S FATHER NEVER SAW it coming. He should have, if he really knew what he was up against. But he couldn't dream of the wickedness arrayed against him.

The crowd in the international terminal was close, and like a mob at a sports event one simply went with the flow. When the flow forced him toward the mouth of a nearby hallway, three goons came out of nowhere and tased him. IIis body went limp, they gagged him, bagged him and snatched him up. Then they stuffed him into the back of a van.

Very professional. But now he was at the mercy of some real baddies, and he knew it. What was more, he probably knew them. He could recognize the effects of the weapons he sold. Which client had turned on him? He had some ideas.

But then he felt the prick of what could only have been a hypodermic syringe. *Great, John. Now what?* Everything went dark.

Arabia, 1232 B.C.

KREIOS HAD BEEN PREPARING a lecture for her in his mind as he killed the last few members of Subedei's stupid entourage. Of course he had known; what father would release his as-yet unformed adult daughter into the wilds without at least watching over her? He had known she was headstrong, even stubborn, but this...this had been a surprise.

Had he not tried to instill more sense into her? Had he not spent himself in her childhood, trying his utmost to raise her to be prudent and wise? What she had done this night felt like betrayal.

He swooped upward toward the treetops, thinking on all she had done. She deserved a stern word or two, and he would not fail to deliver. But as he approached the bough where he had left her, he knew she had gone. He cursed himself. He had placed her there in the hope she would be both safe and unable to flee easily from him. But she had found a way.

How had she managed that?

Unless she had been taken. His heart suffered the pang of anxiety as he circled the treetops in the vicinity, double and triple checking that she was indeed not there. He descended to the path below, where the leaders had circled to discuss the incident.

Yamanu was among them. "Have you seen Eriel?" Kreios grabbed his tunic gruffly.

Yamanu turned to him, surprise and concern showing on his features in the darkness. "Is she not safe?" he asked.

"I do not know," Kreios said, panting a little. "I thought I had left her in a safe place during the skirmish."

"The one called Subedei escaped," Yamanu said. "That was the one Eriel had come out to meet..."

As he said the words, Kreios knew in his heart what had

happened. "What are you not telling me?"

Yamanu did not speak immediately, and still more angels gathered roundabout, awaiting further orders, further action.

Kreios extended a hand and placed it on his shoulder. "Tell me, friend."

Yamanu shook his head. "I am afraid, Kreios, that I am responsible for this debacle."

"Why do you say such a thing?"

"Because, friend, I had been teaching her how to use the gift of the Shadowers. Perhaps before she was yet ready." His face was downcast. "I could not help but see a predilection in her for the gift. She has much potential, Kreios; you should be very proud of your daughter. After one lesson, she escaped through the defenses of the great city and found her way to liberty."

"Are you telling me that she is still somewhere near? Perhaps hiding from us even now?"

Yamanu's face betrayed the deep fear and pain he felt in regard to Eriel. "My friend Kreios, there is more that remains to be revealed to us. I am sorry. I started her training too soon. She was not ready! She does not yet understand the purpose of the gift; she cannot properly bear its attendant burden."

Kreios grasped Yam by both shoulders and looked deep into his eyes, his own eyes begging without words for a morsel of bare truth.

"I am afraid she could be anywhere, Kreios."

"We must find her!" Kreios turned to bolt; he wanted to begin the search and make sure she was not taken by the boy.

"Kreios," Yamanu said, touching his arm from behind, "we cannot."

"What do you mean?!" Kreios asked him incredulously. "This is absurd! We cannot?"

Yamanu nodded quietly.

"Why?"

Yamanu paused before answering. "Because, friend, she does not want to be found." He waited yet another moment for this new and profound information to settle.

Kreios slumped.

Yamanu grasped his shoulder. "She is that good. Until she wants to be found…we will never find her."

CHAPTER XIX

Somewhere over the South Atlantic, present day

EVERYTHING EXPLODED.

I had been knocked unconscious.

When I came back around to myself, the air was filled with an enormous roaring sound. From the instrument panel behind me there were a gaggle of loud buzzers sounding off. I peeled my eyes open and they were instantly stung by a thousand needles of thin atmosphere. I was dizzy; it was difficult to breathe. One arm was hooked through the supporting structure of a seat, one leg was cocked up and wedged behind me in the doorway to the flight deck. I looked out the closest available window: one of the windscreens in the cockpit behind me, and I saw what looked like blackness with an occasional pink-orange stripe passing vertically from right to left.

Then I realized: *that's the sunset. The horizon.* We were sideways and cartwheeling through the air.

My body was being pulled. I looked back to the direction I was facing, the direction I was being pulled. There was Michael, still buckled to his seat and passed out. More importantly though, there was wide open nothingness where the back of the plane had been.

And I was being sucked toward it.

Where is Ellie? Hex and Bishop were gone. I could see Michael, and I tried to make my way toward him. I knew I would be able to use the sucking momentum to get to him, but I had probably only one shot. If I messed up I would be sucked straight out the back without him. And I needed to rescue him.

I wasn't sure of the details, but I knew I had to get him out of the plane.

Pressure pulled relentlessly at every part of me. I had to get across the aisle and move…fly… about ten feet toward the rear of the plane in order to connect with him. It was very difficult to breathe. I felt my body flirting with another blackout.

I had to make my move.

It was ugly. When I let go, everything happened so fast. I became airborne and hurtled toward the wide open. I almost missed my shot. If I hadn't pushed off with my legs a little I would have gone straight out the back.

But I didn't. I collided with Michael's chest like a 98 pound football, startling the crap out of him and waking him up. He grasped me in a bear hug, looked around with wild eyes, saw me, saw the foggy atmosphere in the plane and craned his head all over the place like a bird. "Airel, wha…" His eyelids grew heavy, his grip on me weakened.

He passed out again.

Oh, no. I clung tightly to him, trying with one hand to reach the release on his buckle.

"Hey!" Ellie screamed into my ear and I jerked back a little in surprise. My eyes asked the question for me. "Never mind!" she screamed above the roaring noise. "Just grab the parachute!" She was standing in the aisle, her feet braced hard between two seats.

*Parachute. I didn't think we would need those…*I thought about the inflatable raft I had seen in the cupboards as well; the survival beacons. Everything suddenly became far too real. *This is life and death. In a wrestling match.*

I grabbed the chute from Ellie; it was an enormous thing. I slipped my free arm through the straps, grabbing Michael with the other.

"Ready?" Ellie screamed again.

I nodded.

She let herself go. She was sucked violently from the plane. I decided it was a very scary thing, but I didn't want to die, either.

Holding fast to Michael and the parachute, I found the seat belt release and pulled.

Cape Town, South Africa, present day

KREIOS FELT THE DRAW on his strength as he neared the center of the principality of the evil prince Nwaba, the enormous high-rise citadel of the Nri. He did not wanted to admit it to himself, but he could feel himself weakening, feel the longing for the Sword, wondered why he could not retrieve it now of all times. He consigned himself to the strong possibility of a suicide mission.

But now everything was different.

When he had seen the great demonic horde flying west, he was struck. In his impetuous youth he would have given chase, which would have ended in a sound defeat. Instead he bode his time and thought it over.

He had guessed Nwaba was at the head of his westering detachment then, and now he was quite sure. He felt his strength returning in waves. The prince was away. The city was unguarded.

And Kreios could attack in strength.

He would do what El had done to Sodom and Gomorrah. He would burn it to the ground.

CHAPTER XX

Somewhere over the South Atlantic, present day

IT WAS LIKE WE were shot out of a cannon. Everything around us was completely dark, and if it was difficult to hold onto both Michael and the parachute in the confines of the plane, it was seriously close to impossible while falling through the sky. All the problems I had inside the plane were now magnified: it was louder, harder to breathe, more physically demanding, and I couldn't see because I couldn't open my eyes.

She said, *"Let Ellie help you."* It was a good thing I had ample warning, because before I knew it Ellie was shouting in my ear again. Something about getting the parachute on. Clumsily, I gave her one arm at a time as she helped cinch everything up. *This is insane.* The straps were either big enough to bundle me together with Michael or there was an extra set. I didn't care about details, I just wanted the madness to end.

I worried that we were going to hit the ocean at any minute, that I wouldn't see it coming. It was really bizarre that my number one instinct was to see it coming when it came. Now that there was at least a parachute though, everything should have balanced out. But it didn't.

She was going berserk I my head, Ellie was shouting, the wind from our descent was debilitating.

I forced my eyes to open. My tear ducts were emptying themselves in the fierce wind and my vision was blurry. It didn't help that we were falling through the last dying embers of the sunset, either; it was almost pitch black.

Except for a weird cluster of light off to one side, that is. As my brain tried to process this new information, I became sick with fright: I was looking at the city lights of Cape Town. From like, thousands of feet above it. I could see the outline of the coast of South Africa below, but it wasn't directly below. It was below and far away. We were going to fall into the ocean.

Ellie shouted something into my ear again, grasped something on the front of me and then pushed off violently, yanking hard on the straps as she went. "Hey!" I shouted in total impotence, the pelting wind sucking all the volume from me. And then I realized something new. Ellie had pulled my ripcord.

It was like hitting pavement. *Or maybe like getting your arms ripped completely off.* Whatever the case, the chute opened above and Michael and I were saved. I realized how thankful I needed to be for all that had happened at Ellie's hands. I couldn't have held onto Michael if I had wanted to. I was very glad to have him strapped to me.

I looked around me, trying to orient myself by the lights of the city and what remained of the sunset behind us. Below, I saw Ellie's chute deploy in a bright red and white flume, filling with air, arresting her descent as well.

I breathed a sigh of relief and wept silently to myself. *This is totally crazy. I can't believe Hex and Bishop! Is Michael okay? How do we get out of this one? Are we going to just crash into the ocean?*

Who will save us then?

I looked out to the horizon again, glad for a moment's peace. A bloom of white and orange erupted far below us. *That was the plane. It just crashed into the ocean.*

Then something flew by me. Something big and dark. *Dark.* My mind returned to the dark cloud I had seen from the cockpit before everything had gone horrible.

"Get ready," She said.

Cape Town, South Africa, present day

IT HADN'T TAKEN LONG at such a late hour for Kreios to drive the little Toyota bakkie from Muizenberg to Cape Town's business district. He had parked about a half a kilometer from the building.

It was a major landmark, one of the tallest in the city. The ruse was that the company drilled for, refined, shipped and bought and sold speculative shares of oil. And that provided its masters with the resources they needed to ply their real trade. Kreios knew it all; how could he not? The wicked hands at these controls belonged to fallen angels with whom he had once dwelt in paradise. Before all the stars fell.

He decided on a direct course of action. Something bold, impetuous. He would see how many he would have to kill before the Nri Infernals noticed.

As he walked along the sidewalk at the front of the building, he looked inside the massive lobby through the glass. There was a lone security guard at the enormous desk, which rose like a sailing ship's quarterdeck above the lobby. Beyond it were the main elevators, eight of them.

The guard's head jerked up as Kreios neared the main revolving doors. Slowly, as the truth descended upon his features, the guard's face went white with abject fear.

Kreios carried with him no natural weapon. It wasn't his appearance that had given the guard cause for fear. It was simply that Kreios, now fully aware once more of his body of work over thousands of years, was in close proximity now. And when El's angel of death was upon the doorstep what happened next was inevitable. Final.

The guard stood and began to tremble like a frightened child. Some of his trembling was due to the fact that his Brother was ripping out of his flesh, becoming fully manifest.

Kreios stopped at the revolving front doors, of which there were a pair. Their partitioning panes of glass were arrayed at ninety degree intervals along their axes of rotation and extended out from there in a radius of at least eight feet, all glass.

Inside the glass façade there was the security desk, set up like a fortress, a command post in the midst of the lobby, and behind that were the elevator cars.

Kreios turned to face his objective. He saw *beyond* the glass, the polished tiles, the electronic surveillance and security measures, the steel-reinforced concrete. He saw, much like he had seen on the night of the original Passover, not just that there was no signal of atonement on the "lintels," such as there were. No, indeed, not only was this building *not* excepted from him, it was covered with sign upon sign and symbol upon symbol of its effrontery to El, the enmity it not only represented but embodied. It stood as a monument to itself. It was therefore precisely identical to Lucifer, which was intentional on the part of its masters.

Kreios widened his stance, bending at the knees, and removed his hands from the pocket of his hoodie sweater.

Somewhere over the South Atlantic, present day

"RESERVE CHUTE." IT WAS cryptic even for *She.* But it soon became clear.

The dark cloud, a.k.a. a huge cluster of freaking demons, was swarming. They were coming out of nowhere, they were everywhere, swooping in, through and around us at all times. Meanwhile Michael and I were just hanging there in the sky, a punching bag, a dangling bullseye.

I could tell one of them was bigger than the rest. Worse, it was hounding me. I could feel it circling us, feel the massive bursts of air pressure from its wings, and I caught glimpses of its hideous shape as it passed under me.

In one fell swoop, all the cords holding us to our parachute were cut. We were falling again. And though I couldn't see much, I could see enough to know that we didn't have much time.

My first reaction was stark fear. But something within me rose up and protested against it, told me I was tired of it already. I became contemptuous. That was the only word for it. Letting go of Michael, fully trusting the straps for the first time, I held my hands out.

This stabilized our flight, sending us on a straight trajectory. I scanned what bits of the sky I could see. There were dark shapes flitting *everywhere.* I couldn't see Ellie's chute. I assumed she too had been cut loose. I also could not see the jerk that had sent us plummeting again.

I quickly realized that I could steer by shifting the position of my limbs. If I put my feet together and held only one arm close to my body, my outstretched arm produced drag and we spun in a barrel roll. Using this newfound trick, I wheeled us clumsily around to face the heavens. I squinted, trying to see, looking around desperately for my prime offender.

I wanted something from it. A wing would do. Perhaps a leg as well.

My mind pulled into wild abstractions, I digressed from this macabre list of menu items to my last conversation with Hex. *Have you ever seen the stars? They are beautiful up here....* It was true. Though I was hurtling to the earth at probably hundreds of miles per hour, strapped to my boyfriend no less, I had to admit it. The stars *were* beautiful.

But there was a massive hole in them. A vacuum of light. And it was getting bigger. *Or nearer.*

"Come on!" was all my mind could produce from my lips as the Sword of Light blazed forth, coming to my hand, ready for battle. In its piercing acetylene light I saw the menacing outline of my enemy.

CHAPTER XXI

NWABA HAD ALLOWED THE others to harass and seek and destroy the inconsequential one while he snipped the wings off the daughter of El who possessed the Sword.

Simply put, he wanted to add the Sword to his arsenal. With that, the Bloodstone, and the other item in the host's pink backpack, he would begin to fulfill his potential.

But first he must procure the weapon, which meant she must die. He adored the fallen domain, how it was brutally animalistic, how there was only the hunter and the hunted. He swept his wings back and lunged forward and down upon her plummeting form.

Just when he was within striking distance, she unsheathed the Sword with a shout.

He extended his talons.

IN THE BLINDING AND sudden light of the Sword, I had even more trouble seeing my enemy. All I was able to do was brace for impact and pray the blade would make its mark.

As it approached, all I could see were wings as big as an airplane, wicked talons, and a shriek that filled me with terror. I swung the Sword around, praying it would make contact, that it would telegraph information to me like it had on the side of the road in Oregon. But this time everything was vague and masked. I couldn't tell for sure what had happened; only that I had cut *something* and that as a result Michael and I were sent tumbling out of control.

The next shriek that rent the night sky was delayed, and that told me that I hadn't delivered a death blow. No, something else had happened. But that didn't matter right now. I was fighting for my life, for our lives. There were so many demons left, circling, that wanted to kill us.

As my mind refocused on our more immediate perils, the Sword disappeared. I tried to call it up again but it was no use. *Great!*

That's when the last thing *She* had told me resounded in my head once more: I began frantically searching for the release for the reserve chute.

Desperate, desperate, desperate. I groped, fumbling in the dark as we spun out like a one-winged bird.

I caught a glimpse of the water below. I gasped as I realized how close we were to hitting the surface. It would be bad if we did, at this speed. Water or concrete, it didn't much matter. Both were just as deadly.

We couldn't have been more than five hundred feet above the surface of the sea when my right hand finally found the release. I pulled as fast as I could. There was a great sweeping rushing sound as the reserve chute deployed into the darkness.

But we were still falling very fast; I could see the waves distinctly now and we were not slowing.

At last, when I felt I could reach out and touch the sea, when I, eyes wide, beheld our end and was powerless to effect it, there was a big pop above us. My limbs were wrenched again and I saw stars.

I reached up to the control handles and pulled them both very hard, flaring the chute.

Our feet kissed the waves; the deep reached up and pulled us in. Down.

PART EIGHT

THE AWAKENING

From the Book of the Brotherhood, Volume 3:

4. *Dear Host, it is your privilege to further any advance of the
    Leader's Kingdom. You hold your very life forfeit for the
    cause. You are to obey orders instantly and without question.
    For when you are finally unmade, you will find the nothing
    you now seek. The Leader wants to give it to you, but you
    must obey to the death...*

CHAPTER I

Somewhere over the South Atlantic, present day

NWABA WAS ENRAGED. THAT cursed idiot girl had brandished the Blade as if she had known more than she *could* know. It filled him with perverse admiration, for it was the kind of blow he would liked to have struck. But he had missed her entirely.

The daughter of El had proven cunning. *But how could she have known, been so precise?* She had wielded the Sword expertly, had cut the cocoon away from his belly, had separated him from the host, Kim. Plus she had raked the righteous tip of the Sword across every rib on one side, a clean slice that oozed black blood.

He quivered with deep hatred and anger, looking around frantically for the body of the host of the Bloodstone. The one named Kim was falling like a rag doll to smack upon the welted surface of the sea, lost unless he snatched her in midair.

Worse still, she carried the precious cargo.

Squinting his eyes he searched, crazed.

There. He saw her flailing and pathetic form below him.

Growling in scalding curses, he launched himself with his great wings and then folded them to intercept her. He could not damage the body of the host; he must get under her and slow her fall gradually. He shot past her like a bullet, spread his wings, nuzzled her onto his back and then flared just above the surf.

He spread into a glide and slowed, reaching back with a claw and pulling her down to his feet where he could grasp her, look her over, ensure the precious cargo was safe.

The host was intact; in a kind of hibernation mankind called a coma now. The host was, in fact, never better. But the pink backpack was missing.

An unholy roar erupted from the heart of him. *That insufferable girl must have cut the backpack off as well!*

So now Nwaba had two choices, and he hated them both equally: He could either spend himself fruitlessly searching for the wretched backpack, the Bloodstone, and that other valuable cargo— which by now had certainly been swallowed up by the sea—or he could return to his stronghold and attempt to mend and regroup. He could then return with fresh troops, specialized men and Brothers who could retrieve the object of desire from the bosom of the perilous deep.

He called his captains to him and issued new orders: "Pluck them from the sea. And bring them to me."

Cape Town, South Africa, present day

MR. EMMANUEL SAT AT the top of the world and clutched his side. This was not good. And it would ruin a perfectly good shirt. Though his laundress could certainly get bloodstains out, it wasn't practical to introduce the problem in the first place. Too many questions would be asked, he would become quickly bored with it and then certainly have to kill her, and then he would have to go to the trouble and inconvenience to find a new laundress. And he particularly liked how she turned out his shirts.

Exasperated, he stripped it off.

The master must be suffering. And he will arrive soon, no doubt. Mr. Emmanuel sighed and employed the wasted shirt as a bandage, slowing the flow of the blood. It would do for now.

He walked through his fiftieth floor penthouse toward the gymnasium. This would sting a bit, but the life was in the blood and he didn't want to go 'round losing too much of it. Whatever had happened, it was big. The gash was about a foot long, spanning the distance from just under his right pectoralis down one side to just above his pelvis. The inner flesh of all the ribs on that side had been exposed.

In a cabinet in the gymnasium, there were various medical supplies. There were also cans containing an aerosol liquid that he hadn't quite yet taken public. It was too good for that just yet.

He sprayed it over his wound, the edges drew closed, and the bleeding stopped. It did leave a scar, and it certainly hurt a lot, but it repaired the damage.

The mind was powerful, so much so that the connection between demon and brother would bring about real enough wounds if one or the other were injured. It was psychical, spiritual, so powerful that it crossed with ease into the natural. But Mr. Emmanuel fancied himself a god, and gods were eternal beings. He was in control of his own mind. Even if his demon died— the one for whom he played host—he would yet live. Besides, the Bloodstone was calling Nwaba onward now, and once they possessed it together the rules could change. *Possibly in my favor;* but he dared not think such things out loud yet.

For now the only change he needed was in regard to his shirt.

He slid the old one down the chute to the incinerator.

False Bay, South Africa, present day

I HEARD SHOUTING IN the wet dark, but it came and went and was distant. The waves were relentless and unpredictable, crashing in on us, entangling us in the lines of our chute, which, now that it had completed its job of grabbing air, was grabbing currents in the sea, threatening to pull us under.

I flailed. Though he was strapped to me, it was very difficult to keep Michael's head above water. The only way I could do it effectively was to lie on my back and thrust my belly up, but it was a herculean effort. Even with my superhuman abilities, I would not be able to continue like this for very long.

The shouting came closer, but I still couldn't make it out. *Something about a propeller? Or something called shoo-daway?* It didn't make sense. Besides, I had other things to worry about. *Great. We're saved from certain death at the hands of Brotherhood traitors by an enormous plane crash, which thrusts us into certain death at the hands of gravity. And an airborne horde of demons.* I went down the list, thinking that if I were a cat I would almost be out of lives by now.

My top priority was fast becoming finding a way to release the chute from Michael and me. I thought it certainly had to be like the ripcord pull, only different enough to eliminate confusion. I tried to scramble for it with one hand, but every time I did that we sank under the waves. I was seriously worried about Michael. If his airway became restricted in his unconscious state, he would suffocate and drown. I didn't know how to release the pack straps; I searched in vain.

Now the shouting was near and very clear. It was Ellie. "…your chute away!"

I figured she was telling me to cut the chute away. *Like duh. Trying that, genius.*

"Airel, cut your chute away! Use the Sword!"

The Sword! "Duh!" I said, and focused as hard as I could on my grandfather's blade. It was obvious when it appeared; the sea lit up all around it, fizzing like crazy. I did my best to cut us loose, being careful not to injure Michael or me. But the cords of the chute were on all sides now, tangled with us. After the first few swipes of the Blade we were in better shape, which was good, because I didn't have both arms to keep us afloat. I kicked my feet as hard and as quick as I could to keep us up, but I was running out of energy fast.

I looked around for the largest remaining mass of cords and took one final swipe at them. The Sword made the sea boil around us; I could feel the warmth coming across us in alternations of cold and hot. But at last we were free; the parachute fell away and drifted off.

I had figured out by now how to put the sword away with a thought, and I did so. I basically just had to think of something I needed more desperately, and what I needed then most of all was to keep us afloat. The Sword returned to wherever it had come from and I treaded water furiously, hoping Michael hadn't gotten too much seawater in his mouth.

Then I heard Ellie's voice. "We've gotta stick together! Stay close, okay?"

I was breathing very hard, working even harder. "Okay!"

"We're in real danger, all right?"

"Well, duh! Unless I'm missing something?"

She spat salty seawater out of her mouth audibly. "Yeah! You are! We're in False Bay, girlie. There's no greater concentration of sharks in the whole world…"

As I treaded water, I rolled my eyes. *This is impossible. Just one thing after another.*

"Is it?" She answered me. *"Just watch."*

"So stay close!" Ellie continued. "And here." I heard a pop and a whooshing sound, like something being filled with air. She slapped the water with it in front of me and I peered at it in the darkness. "Grab it!" she shouted.

I did. It was a float. Now I truly understood the meaning of the words "life preserver." I didn't know where in the world she had gotten one; I figured it had to be just another part of all her fancy survival gear I had seen stashed away in the back of the plane. *The plane. Holy crap, we just survived a full-on plane crash!* But I couldn't take the time to be amazed at anything. I had to keep Michael's head above water.

"And stay close, remember?" Ellie shouted.

"Okay!"

I tried to get Michael higher. I stuck an arm through the inflatable life ring and shifted his weight around, pulling the ring under us and floating us both. I slowed my kicking, just trying to keep us close to Ellie. And breathe. I needed to breathe.

"Now," Ellie said, a little calmer now that the situation was more in hand, "we just have one more thing to worry about!"

Through my gasping ragged breaths I managed to ask her, "What now?"

She pointed up. About a hundred demons were circling above us in the night sky.

"Great."

Cape Town, South Africa, present day

KREIOS WATCHED UNMOVED. THE man and his Brother inside were scared, they knew that everything they did from this moment on was in vain. They ran in circles, maddened by his proximity to them, their minds driven to tatters in the drawing out of the moment by the angel standing, waiting at the doorstep. For here now was real authority, and their rebellion had found its end.

But Kreios would wait for the signal as he had waited for Joshua at Ai.

Then the two inside stopped their madness and faced him, cowering, finally bowing down and begging as they had been destined to do. For they had been devoted to destruction. Untouchable by any but the angel of death. When Kreios touched them they would find an end—and a truly terrible beginning; one they both knew and dreaded. Kreios was not the Judge, he merely went before Him to prepare the way.

The moment drew near, he could feel it.

NWABA COULD FEEL SOMETHING too. Ordinarily his master Lucifer, the prince of the power of the air, owned the very skies. But something was changing. Something familiar drew near *in the air*, but he could not isolate it and identify it. *Who would dare to challenge Lucifer's principality?*

But he knew the answer to that question. At least he thought he did, because still, specifics eluded him. It was a true authority, which meant the artifice of his own was soon to pass away. Oh, how he hated to be reminded that the favor he enjoyed was merely temporal. And it *was* favor, curse it all. He hated all of it.

He flew on, toward his citadel.

FALSE BAY WAS A bubbling cauldron of activity that centered on three huddled individuals treading water. Demons circled above, swooping down upon them, trying to make a play for snatching them out and carrying them off. They descended as near the water as they dared, being as mortally afraid of it as any angel under the sun might have been. Some pumped their wings furiously as they tried to hover, some swooped and dove in massive arcs, aiming for the helplessly swamped daughters of El, and the Alexander, the traitor. All they needed to do was finish, snatch them up and be gone.

But this was only one component of peril. The Great White shark, terror of the sea, was circling as well, and in numbers not found in any other body of water on the planet. Smelling fear, smelling prey, they closed in.

"JUST WATCH," SHE HAD said.

Well...I'm waiting. I was exasperated. I looked heavenward into a midnight blue sky, peppered with points of starlight and afflicted by evil beasts that wished only to end us. *El...help!* We were spent, surrounded, and my Michael needed help.

I heard an unholy shriek from behind me. I turned quickly. In the light cast out into the bay by the millions of city lights, I saw a demon struggling to stay airborne. Then another Hellish scream resounded from another direction, and I turned in time to see one of the horde splash down, struggling violently in the sea. There was a frenzy that accompanied it, and I couldn't make sense of what was happening at first.

Then Ellie said something, awe in her tone: "Airel, look! Watch." She pointed into the darkness.

Lit in silhouette by the lights on shore, we watched in amazement as an enormous Great White shark breached, rocketing out of the water, its terrible mouth clamping onto the hovering body of one of the demonic horde. This one didn't have time to do much but vomit forth a pathetic yelp before it foundered in the sea, sinking to its death.

I gasped but was otherwise totally speechless. The sharks were all around us. Contrary to what I had thought, though, they weren't a danger to us. They were like our vanguard. I wept for joy as our brave cohorts began to defend us.

CHAPTER II

Cape Town, South Africa, present day

KREIOS SMILED. THERE WAS the signal; he could feel it. El was on the move.

He stepped forward toward the doors and extended a finger. The glass returned to dust at his touch and scattered to the floor, some to the wind. The door's metal frame, which had held the glass, oxidized and corroded in seconds, crumbling into blackened slag and falling into a heap.

Kreios looked left and then right, withering every window and frame on the main floor into nothingness; dust. He stepped into the lobby, his body emitting pure white light that pulsed with his heartbeat.

His footsteps left no trace, not even the residue from the soles of his shoes followed him. Indeed, the base elements fairly cried out and abjured him, grains of sand becoming animated and scurrying off to avoid his touch, his vicinity. He moved across the lobby smoothly, without observable evidence.

The man and the Brother cowered powerless before his approach. In his wake was woe, the screams of the damned, the dust of the earth. As he passed by it overtook the two, and they were no more.

Kreios moved into the heart of the building. Up. There were no barriers.

THE BATTLE BELONGED TO El, and it was magnificent. Now on every side of us there were hundreds of sharks breaching, pulling demons out of the sky, dragging them into the sea and then fighting over their remains. Black demon blood roiled in the salt water, producing a horrible stench that could not be described.

THE REMAINING DEMONS RETREATED with screeches of rage. They would not return to their master: to fail was to die. This night was death; a sound defeat. Something had changed. The few that remained turned to the west, disappearing over the wide expanse of sea.

KREIOS MOVED THROUGH THE corridors of the skyscraper, working his way up from ground level. There weren't many here tonight, but those that were wished they were not. He would oblige them, then. They would be no more.

A man in a corridor staggered away from him, blood soaking into his clothes from underneath. Kreios passed him by; he was gone. Another man in an office met his eyes and then fell to his knees, begging mercy. A semicircle of blood soaked through his shirt. It was the size of his entire abdomen. For a moment it appeared that a shark had made a single bite out of the man's torso. He collapsed and died before Kreios got to him, but in the wake of the angel he became mere dust.

More. Upward. To the top.

NWABA LANDED BY THE enormous elm tree in the rooftop garden of his skyscraper citadel. He opened his jaws and spoke to Mr. Emmanuel, who had been waiting with salve for his wound. "We have had a change to endure." He dropped Kim's comatose body on the floor. "This one cannot yet be discarded. The Bloodstone is…temporarily lost."

Mr. Emmanuel said nothing, merely stepping forward and spraying the salve on his master's wound. It stung Nwaba like mad, but it repaired him.

Nwaba the chameleon then selected a smaller form; his favorite. The massive wings retracted and diminished, the color of his skin changed to pure white, and he became more like a lizard with the face of a man. The massive talons on his feet became mere claws, the claws on his hands became grippy pads, the wings became more like a cloak, shrouding his newly spare and diminished seven foot tall frame. His tail reduced its thickness to a mere wire, long and thin.

"The daughter of El somehow knew," Nwaba said to his slave. "She cut the cocoon; we nearly lost everything."

Mr. Emmanuel shrugged. "I can wait." He placed the can of salve on a stone seating area. They stood atop the roof of his building, his skyscraper, in the garden. It was anchored visually by a large elm, easily one hundred feet high, that had been transplanted via helicopter. Roundabout this were geometrically arranged rock beds, grasses, and thorny plants. He continued, "Is it not worth the wait?"

Nwaba grunted sweetly. He made no other comment.

"Still..." Mr. Emmanuel said, "I must do something with this." He kicked Kim's inanimate body.

Nwaba grunted his affirmation and turned away in disgust.

"Just so you know," Mr. Emmanuel said, which gave Nwaba a moment's pause, "I'm actively working the other angle."

Nwaba responded with bestial voice, "Let me know if you need me," which was probably the most frightening thing a creature like him could have said in that moment.

But not for Mr. Emmanuel. He responded with a simple, "We'll see."

MR. EMMANUEL HIKED THE prodigiously stinky body over one shoulder and walked into the house. Through the living room, with its twenty foot tall windows looking toward Table Mountain, and into the kitchen, with its walk-in freezer. Unfortunately for his diet, this was the best way to preserve the body of the transition host—wedging it in here among his foodstuffs.

Even at the top, there were times concessions—compromises—had to be made.

Besides, as he had said to the master, would it not be worth it?

Their plan had been to procure the Bloodstone with its current, or transition host; the one that had inherited its authority by chance from the elder Alexander. Then when all was in hand, ownership could be transferred by blood sacrifice. The body of the one named Kim would be bled and burned with fire, Mr. Emmanuel would perform the rite, and then he and Nwaba would be conjoined to the Bloodstone. Simplicity was beauty.

But unfortunately, the rite required the Bloodstone to be present.

So they would have to wait.

Mr. Emmanuel closed the freezer and locked the door, thinking clandestinely of a way around the problem of power, and more of it. Perhaps the man John could provide something to him. To him alone.

CHAPTER III

NWABA RETIRED TO RECOVER his strength, calling in one of his subordinates for the issuing of supplemental orders.

Losing the Bloodstone was intolerable. Worse, he had no one to blame. No one, that is, but the daughter of El who had instigated the deed. He was inwardly furious, but he held himself in check for now.

The lieutenant reported, something like respect and fear in his eyes. Mostly it was fear. Nwaba did not look at him as he issued the orders.

"One hundred more. Search the waters. Find them quickly and bring them here. Do not neglect the island; in fact, start there. Dismissed."

Wordlessly, the lieutenant acknowledged the orders and left.

Nwaba could now soak in his regrets for a moment, awaiting the arrival of the Sword. Then things could change for the better.

False Bay, South Africa, present day

IT WAS UNBELIEVABLE THAT we had survived a plane crash. Crazy that sharks had killed all those demons. But it was absolutely insane to find land in the middle of the ocean. Ellie, since she was familiar with her home, led us onward.

"We're just gonna take it nice and easy," she said. "Sidestroke."

"Where are we going? Aren't we miles from shore?" I asked. I could see the lights of the city lining the edge of the bay all around us, but they were very distant. I guessed it would take days to swim the distance.

"No, we're not far," she said. "There's a little rock up here called Seal Island. We can regroup there."

We swam on through the darkness for a while.

"I'm assuming," I said in between breaths, "they call it Seal Island because there's seals there?"

"Yeah," she said. "Cape fur seals. They like to hang out there. And that's why there are so many sharks."

Flabbergasted, I said, "Stupid seals. Why don't they move on?"

Ellie was silent for a moment. "Well, I guess they really like it. Either that or they believe it belongs to them. That it's rightfully theirs. And there's lots of yummy fish here for them, too. So they endure the sharks."

Got it. "Sometimes you need something bad enough that you gladly suffer the consequences, huh?"

"Sho," she said. I guessed it was sort of slang for "totes," or something, which made me miss my Kim. *Poor Kim!* Would I ever see her again? But I couldn't allow myself to think too much; I had to be disciplined and concentrate on one thing at a time. That was really hard for me.

We swam on. The waves tossed us every which way, and

prevailing currents did their worst as well, but we finally made landfall on the "rock." I estimated it was about an hour after sunset.

Ellie hadn't been kidding about the island being a "rock." It wasn't much more than that, about a city block in size. We had to fight the crashing waves, the slippery surface, the darkness, and the idiot seals as we clambered up. But we staked out a territory nevertheless, and eventually sat down. The ocean was inches away from us; Seal Island didn't poke up out of the water by very much at all. But it was a resting place, for which I was very grateful.

Michael, thank God, was still alive. He was breathing, at least. We all three had to huddle together for warmth, soaked on the cold rock.

"So what do we do now?" I asked Ellie.

"Wait," she said.

I CHECKED ON MICHAEL'S condition about every fifteen minutes. Meanwhile, Ellie looked at the seals like she was hungry. So it seemed, in a way, that we had gone from bad to worse. *Are we now prisoners on this little island?*

Still no rescue boat, though in truth it probably hadn't been that long, plus it was the middle of the night.

I was getting antsy for results. Michael's condition wasn't improving. I was glad he hadn't gone hypothermic on me in the water, but it wasn't like he was some kind of superhero—he needed professional medical help and I wasn't that. I could barely keep him warm enough. And even if I could get him to a hospital, would they be able to save him? Did modern medicine have a cure for something that the Bloodstone had originally produced?

Most likely the answer was no, I had to admit it. A strong "no," because stuff that happened to Michael and me was pretty much impossible, and that made it impossible to explain. But there might be a slim chance the doctors could at least treat the physiological parts of what ailed him. That meant, however, that they could only treat his body for symptoms, which wouldn't be enough.

"Ellie," I said, jittery with anticipation, "I need to do something."

"Fine; get out that fancy Sword of yours and kill us a seal so we can cook it and eat already."

"No, not that. I can't just sit and wait for something to happen." I pulled back the fabric of his shirt and looked at his wound. It was like some horrible shield, taking up his entire chest. It was beginning to harden, developing cracks. It looked like hard earth. I whimpered in despair for him; I didn't know what to do.

"If I don't do something about this, I'll feel horrible forever." That was the gist of it. I sounded like I was only really concerned about myself, and that just wasn't true. "Els, I've gotta do something to help him."

She looked up at me from her zoned-out stare for the first time. "I know what you're thinking. But if Michael was still in any way connected with the Bloodstone, his wound would be healed. He is rejecting the healing. His mind and body are fighting the call, but it wants him and it will do whatever it takes to close the sale. So to speak. He has to give in to it if he wants to be healed."

"What if he doesn't...doesn't give in?" I knew the answer, but I needed to hear it from her.

"He will die, girlie. The infection will keep spreading until he's dead. I'm sorry."

"But he's alive right now. Michael is alive. I can help him— well—not me, but...but Kreios can. I need to find him! I've got to find him and bring him to Michael. He will know what to do."

We had a moment then. She looked like she was thinking something over, something important. After a long awkward silence, she finally said, "Can you swim?"

"What, you're asking me if I'm a good swimmer?"

"Yeah, girlie."

"Well...if you don't count that one time I almost drowned as a kid. And that other time I almost drowned because I died. Then, yes, I'm a great swimmer."

"Champion. Get cracking then." She pointed toward the lights on the horizon. "Right away."

I jerked backward, momentarily shocked. "Dude. Who peed in your corn flakes?"

"Nobody. That's the problem. When I don't get enough to eat I get grouchy. If there were any corn flakes at all, soiled or not, I would've scarfed 'em for sure."

"Ew."

She smirked but didn't laugh. "Really, Airel. Sounds like you've made up your mind already anyway. It's the only option you've got left here and there's no time to argue. So you'd better get cracking, as I said." She pointed again.

I took a deep breath and then let it out heavily, looking out into the dark waves. "Great. Just great." Ellie looked fearful. *What, is she scared of the water or something?*

"You're gonna wanna go starkers, trust me."

"Starkers?"

"Nude," she said.

"What?!"

"On a swim like that, clothes will needlessly tire you."

"Huh, no way," I said. "Not a chance."

"Then at least you'd better get a running start, girlie. Otherwise the waves will smash you to bits against the rocks and it'll hurt."

"Gee thanks, Els." I paused. "Hey. Look at me."

"Yeah?"

"Will you please do all you can to help Michael?"

"I will. All I can."

"Promise?"

She grasped my hand. "I promise, girlie. Now. Get the heck outta here."

I shook my head. I looked at Michael. I knelt to his side and kissed his lips, struck by how weird it was to kiss someone when they didn't reciprocate. This was nothing like I had imagined our lives would be; someone had thrown us a major curveball. It hurt more than I could bear—the idea of what *might* happen—but I couldn't think of that right now.

As I knelt at his side I prayed desperately that I would see him again soon, alive and well; that this was not our final moment together. My eyes welled up with tears and I shook my head in disagreement. *This is not the end.*

I stood and said, "Goodbye," and then took a running jump into the darkness.

CHAPTER IV

THE PLUNGE INTO THE ocean again was rude, shocking, dispiriting. Almost depressing. Why? Because now I was alone again. That meant I couldn't fool myself into taking less responsibility for what happened by blaming other people's actions for the bad stuff. It was all on me.

Plus I was cast out into the unknown, into the dark ocean where unseen sinister things glided along within its blackness, ready to attack me. I didn't feel like a superhero, a half-breed, an Immortal. I felt like fish food.

I hadn't really thought about the distance between the island and the mainland before I jumped. It was one thing to swim laps in a pool. That body of water was, though liquid, still static in a way. In the ocean there were huge waves that swept over the top of me, there were currents that took me where they wanted to go, and that was not where I was trying to get. Whenever I looked up to figure out where I was, it looked like I was headed in the wrong direction.

Plus there were the seals, whose territory I had invaded both on land and now at sea, not to mention the sharks that patrolled here. And the darkness. What else might there be? I didn't want to think about it.

But there *was* another thing: my clothes. They were holding me back, pulling me down. Ellie had been right. I needed every advantage I could get. I needed to take on the slippery shape of the fish, at least as much as possible, if I was going to survive this. I wasn't just side stroking with a life ring anymore. I wasn't in survival mode. I was swimming for as much speed and distance as I could muster. The longer I swam with my heavy restrictive jeans on, the more it became clear to me that it was either going to be me or them. So I ditched them.

That seemed to improve things, but then it became obvious that my shirt was dragging me down. Ellie had been right. *You have got to be kidding me. I am not going to be seen in public in my underwear.* I could just see the news broadcast featuring me scrambling awkwardly out of the water into a boat, or being hoisted up to a helicopter in my skivvies. Or my "knickers," as Ellie would have said. But it was clear: the shirt had to go.

As I ditched that too, I made a mental note to draw the line there. I wasn't going to be swimming in the buff, no way. If I died, I would die at least partially clothed. A girl had her dignity, however much of it. And as I swam on, I was glad that, if I was going to be parading around in my underwear, at least I wasn't wearing granny panties.

I HAD TO REST occasionally and just let the sea take me, trying hard not to think about sea monsters coming to get me.

I slipped onto my back and stretched out as much as possible, allowing the ocean to carry me along. *One thing's for sure, I am not a fish.* I looked up at the dark sky and tried to think positively. I tried to think of how Michael would be better, how Ellie and he and I would all be reunited in happy embrace, how I would somehow find the mainland and a towel or a blanket and get help for us.

But it had all gone horribly wrong. At every step of the way, we had been met with unreal opposition. Whatever could go wrong, did. We barely had time to breathe before the bottom fell out again and we sank.

I had to get ahold of myself. I was so hungry and thirsty. It felt weird to be surrounded by water and not be able to drink. By now my body was beginning to consume itself, and that wasn't good because there wasn't much there to begin with. And this was a mission I had undertaken with no option for failure or incompleteness. Both of those would be permanent if they occurred. So I kept on swimming and floating, floating and swimming, trying to make some kind of progress.

By degrees I would occasionally look up and see that I had moved across the bay and had indeed made progress. The mountains that ringed me in were growing larger on one side. Unfortunately, due to currents and waves and wind, it looked like I was taking the long way. The shore that had looked so tantalizingly close at times was sliding by alongside me. I wasn't going to get to land that way. But it did appear I would do so eventually, given my path up to now. The only problem was, if I gauged the distance right, I was only halfway there.

Oh, this is so much fun. I should write home and tell them all about—I couldn't go there. No way. I could not allow myself to think about home. But it all came crashing down on me anyway, yet again. I missed my parents incredibly; especially my dad for some reason. I missed Kreios. I wished all the crap that had happened to us would just go away forever and leave us in peace. It rained down on me, isolated and alone and drifting in the void.

ONE HUNDRED FRESH NRI demons, sent out on supplemental orders by the lieutenant, circled the skies over False Bay. They were looking for prey, looking for—if it came to that—remains. The master hadn't specified.

They had started at the island though, which he *had* specified. They had scattered seals and seagulls to the water, scooping some of the seals up and ripping them apart in midair for sport. But there were no humans on the island.

Reportedly there had been three of them, at least according to what little had been communicated through the ranks. But if there were indeed three, there were no longer any. They were either gone or dead.

The master would not be pleased with that report.

As a result the detachment flew sorties all over the bay, throwing caution to the wind, ignoring normal protocol and rules of engagement, even allowing themselves to be seen and heard, observed by some citizens, fishermen returning home in the dark.

But it was clear to the lieutenant from the moment they had discovered the island was unoccupied: the three had slipped the net.

CHAPTER V

BASED ON HOW LONG it had taken me to get to where I had been at the halfway mark, I had crudely estimated that I might make landfall by dawn. That is, if I wasn't eaten by sharks, seals, the Loch Ness monster, stung by jellyfish, run over by a gigantic ship that didn't know to look out for crazy girls swimming in their underwear in the dark, or even some rogue demon that had been watching and waiting.

The life of a half-breed. So exciting.

But at last, I finally looked up to see not an abstract far-off cluster of light representing some unreachable town or city, but genuine individual lights and shapes and buildings and cars. Even a train went by, its light swinging a wide arc over me in the bay, and I could hear its horn sound off. I gave a muffled cry of hope.

I swam. Kicking and paddling, I moved my arms and legs with purpose. This was the finish line, and I would make it.

Cape Town, South Africa, present day

IF THE BUILDING HAD been observed from the street it would have appeared that the lights within were being snuffed one floor at a time from the ground upward. It was not some bizarre atmospheric fog or smoke from some impossible fire. It was just nothingness. Taking over. Moving methodically. Quick. Unexplainable.

The presence that stalked floor by floor through the skyscraper citadel was killing off host after host, and by extension stalking the Nri Brothers—the demons who were still, as of this moment, scattered across the principality engaged in their own mischief. Though the Nri were powerful, being bound by the superstition they so willingly exploited to advantage, they also could not escape its consequences. Their subscription to the religious tenets of ancestor worship created a very strong bond between Brother and host: if one suffered an injury, the other one did as well.

But the demon mind was a powerful thing; sometimes in the individual it could produce unforeseen anomalies. Some of the Brothers were strong enough to will their way out of mortal danger. Those were a rare breed, and what few were able to flee to more hospitable parts of the world did so—to the west.

In reality though, that was a mere deferment, a trifle. There was nowhere for the Nri Brothers to hide, no matter what temporary allegiances they might make. The full force of that which worked its way through the tower was striking the Nri with duplicative effect all over the city. Not since the early days had such a thing been seen under the sun. It was reverberating through the atmosphere in tremors, signifying the beginning of the end; that terrible reality that all fallen angels had denied for millennia.

The angel Kreios was ushering it in. And El was beginning to assert Himself.

NWABA COULD FEEL IT now, it was unmistakable. For the first time in thousands of years his fear became genuine again. It was a flash in the pan, fleeting, but still: deny it as much as he might, he could not tell lies to *himself.* Such a thing made fools of the sane; he would not cross over.

If this is indeed true, he thought, *if El is beginning the final judgment...?* He stalked the floor of the penthouse living room, his resplendent shimmering white form, both hideous and beautiful, covered in scales as well as skin, a lizard with human face, a fully intentional contradiction in terms, designed to be an affront to truth and beauty. To El Himself.

What shall I then do...? He mulled the possibilities over.

If the list of possibilities was narrowing, he would eventually be left with two choices. These two choices every fallen angel had known from the time the manifestation of El had fulfilled all prophecy. Before that they could only guess, but now they knew: they could either fight or die.

For thousands of years they had chosen to fight. Still in rebellion, a third of the host, the full number of them that had chosen to rebel and cast their lot with Lucifer, had for thousands of years been fighting a war of mitigation. Though they had failed to defeat El at every point along the way, still they fought, they resisted. They knew they were doomed to lose. That was why they fought. That was what made their cause ultimately moral, ultimately just.

They fought against the great heavenly tyranny, and at heavy cost. So many of their number had been snatched off to eternal punishment over the centuries, and so few were now left.

Nwaba's anger kindled afresh as he thought of the Sons of God. They too were fallen. Yet El favored *them*. They *claimed* to leave Him for love, for women. But the Nri at least had just cause, rights, they worshipped their own morality. They occupied the high ground, and for this reason the Brotherhood would never stop hunting down and killing the Sons of El. Not until they were all dead.

CHAPTER VI

"COMFORTABLE, JOHN?" MR. EMMANUEL asked the girl's father. It was one of those things people said. He actually wasn't the slightest bit interested in John's comfort level.

John made no response; he lay on his back under the restraints.

Mr. Emmanuel had known all along, of course. He had many levers to pull, and he had pulled enough of them in America to get Harry—his agent and a member of the Nri—inserted, with another, a helo pilot, into the FBI investigation on the girl Airel. It gained him the inside track, got him closer to the daughter of El through her desperate and unsuspecting parents.

It was a thing of beauty, really.

There had been considerable collateral damage, about which Mr. Emmanuel was completely indifferent. And of course Harry had always been expendable, which Harry didn't need to know. He had served his purpose; he had lured the bait man John all the way to Cape Town. Soon, the girl would come and the Sword could be… appropriated from her.

For Mr. Emmanuel the ends justified the means if they were pragmatic to him. There were those born to serve, others born to lead. And then quite apart from all that, there were those who crushed both the servers and the leaders and enslaved them to a whim.

History was replete with examples of the stupidity of sheep. *Ignorance is its own drug,* he thought, *it needs no catalyst. It simply is.*

He chuckled.

There sits the mosquito, engorging itself upon human blood, completely ignorant of all peril. It does not know of the vampire spider, hunting for human blood by proxy. The mosquito does not know that by indulging in its drone-like instinctual tracks of behavior, it is in fact attracting, by the very scent of the blood it consumes, a most fearsome hunter. The spider cares not for the mosquito, only the blood. But sometimes the circle of life produces a two-for-one deal.

The mosquito could not know of the trap that had been laid for it. But indeed, dear friend John had stumbled into the web, and perfectly.

It was a funny thing, coincidence. It was too good. Who would have thought that John, Mr. Emmanuel's special weapons sales rep, would be the blood father of the girl? *Speaking of blood, that is.* Anyway, it was staggering; it was indeed a small world. These things simply happened sometimes, and it was best to just let them play out, let them detangle on their own.

As the various pieces of the puzzle showed themselves, they fell perfectly to the spider's hand. "Well? Aren't we on speaking terms, John?"

John, finally waking up enough, finally regarded his captor, though he did not look at him. "Mr. Emmanuel, I regret to inform you that I am no longer your sales representative."

He was interrupted by a burst of laughter from the spider.

He continued, "You're going to have to call the company and make the necessary arrangements."

"Oh, John! You *bossie;* crazy man. I knew there was some reason I liked you." He sat down in a chair by his bound captive. "Still…" he looked around the room, "we simply must come to a meeting of the minds."

Mr. Emmanuel was gazing at the hypnotic dance of fire. The room in which he sat—at the side of the examination table to which John was bound—was big and dark. Its ceiling was dark and domed, a large hole at its center that emanated darkness. Its circular perimeter was only delineated by a trough of white stones, in which orange-blue flames licked mildly upward at the highly polished black stone walls all around. It lent an evil cast to the atmosphere of the room, for there was no other source of light there. In fact, it looked like Hell's own drawing room.

"I'm just looking for a little bit of intelligence, John. Surely if you've come this far, you must know something I don't. Surely you must have something with which to barter her life." He paused. "Or yours; I don't care. Come now. Can we not compare notes?"

John did not look at him. "Nope."

"John, you must know me better than that. After all these years providing some of the most delightfully effective weapons in the world? I wish your daughter no harm. No, certainly not. It's simple. She only has something I want. I wish to find her and then retrieve it. It's just a little trinket; a souvenir."

John cursed at him. "I do know you, Mr. Emmanuel. That's the problem. I know all my clients."

For the first time Mr. Emmanuel began to show irritation, because the ruse wasn't working. His facial features dropped into a scowl. "Be careful, John." He stood so that he could pace, lecture. "I have some choice items from your own catalogue. I might use them on you; I might not. Listen. I'm being serious. Just tell me where she is. Then I will recover the item and bring her to you, and you both can live."

John sighed.

In truth, Mr. Emmanuel had always planned on using John as a hostage. He was terrific leverage, and the girl would certainly come running if daddy needed her superheroine help. Of course, John didn't need to know that; even if he had already deduced as much, he didn't need to hear it from his own lips.

But Mr. Emmanuel changed tactics again. "The fact is...I will find your daughter before you do. Just look at you! You're bound to a slab, John. It was a game; you've already lost. I *have* you. We pitted you against me, your motivations against mine. You lost because you seek to preserve..." He shrugged, thinking of a new button to push. "Seems noble. To preserve the flower of her youth, her...purity."

John struggled against his bonds but said nothing.

"But my motivation is stronger. And I have many, many more resources." Mr. Emmanuel drew near and began to talk into John's ear. "And...I know something you don't know." He said it in a singsong voice. He couldn't resist.

John looked up at his captor now, hatred and a lust for vengeance burning through his eyes at the man.

Mr. Emmanuel feigned shock, gasping. "Oh! What. Did you think I was going to tell you?" Laughter. "Oh, no, John. Oh, no." He turned aside briefly and drew an object out of his pocket. "You know what this does, right?" He held the object before his prisoner's face.

John's expression revealed the slightest amount of recognition and fear, but it was gone just as quickly as it had appeared.

"Yes, you do!" Mr. Emmanuel laughed insanely. "Yes, you

know precisely what this does. It applies pressure. Gets me what *I* want."

"Tell you what," John said, "How about we make a deal."

Mr. Emmanuel arched his brows and leaned over his prey.

"How about this: How about we dispense with the theatrics, you release me from this table, and then I kill you with my bare hands? How about that?"

Mr. Emmanuel shook his head in amazement. "Wow, John. You surprise me." He removed the protective cover from the syringe he held in his hand, primed it, raised it high and then slammed it straight down, the needle piercing John's heart, injecting the drug straight into his system. Through bared teeth, Mr. Emmanuel said, "It's always the quiet ones, isn't it?"

John gasped for air, eyes wide.

Mr. Emmanuel withdrew the syringe with contempt, throwing it across the room.

John faded and then passed out.

Mr. Emmanuel kicked the chair over, walking for the door in fury.

CHAPTER VII

IT WAS UNAVOIDABLE NOW. Nwaba stood to his feet, alarmed. *Alarmed?! No. Surely not.* He was not alarmed. Not even concerned. His troops would soon bring him word, bring him the girl, bring him the Sword of Light—that cursed and wretched blade that had been stolen from Tengu by the interloper Kreios.

But he could feel the presence of El now, and indeed he was concerned. Even alarmed. Because for Nwaba, the presence of El was not a good thing.

He began to lose control, to act irrationally, to succumb to inevitable fear. He felt like a small child, a child unattended who'd been intentionally disobedient while Daddy was gone, in full knowledge of the coming punishment.

And now Daddy was home.

Nwaba scurried from his chamber down the corridors of the penthouse, toward the room where Mr. Emmanuel was keeping the bait man, John.

Nwaba met his host at the door; he was just closing it.

"We have not much time!" Nwaba spat at Mr, Emmanuel, his color and form becoming slightly blurry as his mind wavered over the possibilities. "What are you doing?"

"Applying pressure."

"Fool; El's agent is coming! WE MUST ACT NOW!" He roared and flung the door open.

As he entered the room he saw John in deep unconsciousness, bound to the slab. He was enraged. "What did you do to him?" He made large strides across the polished black tiles.

Mr. Emmanuel was following close behind. "He will be all too ready to spill his guts soon," he said. "The drug needs time to take effect."

"I need him to be coherent now, pawn!" He cursed, roaring his displeasure at Mr. Emmanuel. Nwaba had closed the distance to the bait man John. He grasped the edge of the altar slab, threw back his head and let out a shrill and terrible call, like a bird immense enough to roar. In response, the flames rose in the trough that ringed the room, licking upward on the wall. Nwaba's wire-thin tail whipped around.

From a dark recess in the ceiling there descended eight dark shapes crawling downward. They scratched their way outward in a radius from the hole, making a circle as they hung upside down above the room, enclosed within their blood-red wings. Joining these were three jittery fungus encrusted Anti-Cherubs. They crawled upside down on tubule fingers that suctioned them to the black domed ceiling, creeping in spastic movements, their faces sniffing at the putrid air, observing what could be observed.

"Mr. Emmanuel," Nwaba said, his gaze unflinching, "Bring the transition host. Whether we have the Bloodstone or not, we must begin the ritual."

The eight figures on the ceiling then began their animalistic chant, the three Anti-Cherubs vibrating with pleasure at the spectacle.

THE MASTER WAS CALLING.

From Nordhoek to Muizenberg, from Simon's Town to Morningstar, Strand to Camps Bay, the call rang out. From behind rubbish bins in alleyways, from under rocks, from the vineyards of Stellenbosch to the urban wilds of the Tokai Forest, men joined with their Nri Brothers and rallied to the call of the master Nwaba. It was time. The Nri would rise.

KREIOS HEARD IT. HE knew what was coming. Ten stories below the penthouse, he stopped and waited, listening. He had only taken a few, perhaps a hundred. There would be thousands more now, and they were all converging upon their evil master Nwaba.

Kreios quieted himself and waited for El. Everything hung in the balance now. What he did next would seal—or unseal—the next thousand years. And it would only be a beginning, but…it must be the right one.

MY FEET HIT BOTTOM. A wave rolled over me, toppling me forward. I had to give one last burst. *Come on, Airel, you can finish. Push it.* I did. With a few more strokes I was in the shallows and the surf was receding. I made a clumsy exhausted run for it to avoid the next incoming wave, stumbling up onto the beach until the waves could only kiss my ankles, no longer a mortal threat.

I was breathing very hard. I was completely spent. I sat down on the beach in my underwear in the darkness and rested for a moment. I couldn't believe I had done it. Now I could concentrate on trying to get some help. *And some freaking clothes?!* I was glad it was dark.

Judging by the state of activity around me, I figured it was well after midnight. The witching hour. When all the freaks were out.

I looked around me, trying to figure out where I was. I was on a beach that was studded with massive rocks and boulders. There was all kinds of activity going on; little shapes darting here, there and everywhere. Penguins. *Okay. That's weird. Penguins? Really?* They were kind of cute, though. Little black-and-white waddlers. I had to smile, even though I was just about as naked as they were.

How am I going to find clothes? At least before I went off walking down the street shouting for help, I needed to cover myself.

She spoke up. *"Bertha's."*

I sighed. I shook my head and stood up, trying to dust as much wet sand off my butt as possible. I had to play the game. Take what I could get and watch my attitude. That was all. I looked around me. There were some buildings standing off a ways. Some of them looked like hotels, others like private houses. In the other direction there were some huge docks poking out into the water with a big navy boat parked at one of them. *Parked? I guess a Navy guy wouldn't say 'parked,' but that's my story and I'm sticking to it.*

I decided to start walking. Away from the Navy guys and their battleship or whatever. Perhaps I could use their help *after* I found clothes, but not before that. Perhaps I would find something at Bertha's like *She* had said, which, I assumed, was a clothing store with an open window or something. Trying to understand *She* was a monumental task sometimes, but I was glad for what little info I got.

After I walked up the beach a little way, past a sign that read: Simon's Town, I saw a big, long canary yellow building with gabled green roofs pitched over its windows. It looked like a resort, so I thought it was a good place to start. I kept walking until I saw the sign hanging out over the boardwalk: *Bertha's.*

"Sweet!" I said, breaking into a run. I tried to keep away from the pools of light made necessary by civilization, but it was not easy. The closer I got to the hotel, the harder it became.

Finally I ducked into a little nook in the wall made by the shape of the building. I was wet, covered in grimy sea water, and a little desperate. I racked my brain, trying to think over what I was going to do. I was at Bertha's; I had made it that far. *Now what?*

My hand brushed the corner of the wall as I peeked out from my not-quite-dark-enough hiding place. I scanned the area for clues. And then I saw something. Not far off, draped over the fence that surrounded a large pool area, were some towels and what looked like some clothes someone had set out to dry.

Come on...be something I can use!

I ran to the fence and looked through the stuff. I didn't hear anyone shout anything at me; it didn't seem like anyone was out at this late hour as I glanced around. I just focused on the clothes.

A towel, another towel, some cargo shorts... I rummaged like mad. "Yes!" I said a little too loudly. I had found a white button-up top. Sure it was a little too big, but for crying out loud it would work for now and that was all I cared about. I quickly shrugged into it and then, grabbing the cargo shorts, barefooted my way back to my little cubbyhole. I buttoned up the shirt—it was way bigger than I had originally thought, but a quick knot in the bottom hem fixed that problem.

I crossed my fingers as I pulled on the cargo pants.

I giggled. They were about a foot too long and just as wide. I pulled the drawstring as tight as I could and cuffed them up to my knees. I looked like a refugee, but I was thankful at least for clothes to wear.

A burst of laughter shot out over the boardwalk, knifing through the night. It spooked me, but I realized it was just a bunch of people partying into the wee hours of the morning in their room, the balcony door wide open. They hadn't seen me.

I turned up the path toward the café, trying to act like I belonged there.

My hair felt slimy and gross, but I was once again a girl. It felt awesome.

Now to find help.

I stumbled a little; my head was spinning. My stomach growled. *Okay, first things first: I desperately need something to eat.* "All right, *She*. Whatchagot?"

CHAPTER VIII

Cape Town, South Africa, present day

NWABA UTTERED GUTTURAL CLICKS, a language of the damned, of the fallen. He stood in the center of the circular room, the fire ringing its perimeter augmented now, the flames enlarged and intense, licking ever higher at the tops of the walls. The eight red-winged creatures hanging above echoed the ritualistic song, amplifying its effect, the three Anti-Cherubs issuing forth upside down with exhortations in unknown tongue.

In the center of the floor below, the body of Kim lay on the slab. Mr. Emmanuel, now robed in black, read incantations from an ancient book. John the bait man, still unconscious, was now suspended directly above Kim's body by chains that descended from the black hole in the ceiling.

Outside, thousands upon thousands of Nri demons deposited their hosts on the roof and then clustered upon the building like an ant hill, crawling downward on its obsidian glass surfaces, penetrating through every aperture and crack to its interior, trembling with caustic delight at the prospect of conquest.

The master had issued the call to arms. That hadn't happened for a thousand years.

INSIDE THE BUILDING, NOW just one floor below the penthouse, the angel Kreios stood nearly omnipotent, in submission only to El. He awaited instructions.

Then in the middle of the night, as a closed door suddenly opens upon a new way—a path anticipated by faith—Kreios understood what he would do. El had made sense of his vendetta for revenge on the Brotherhood; He would make sense of this new thing as well.

Kreios was off like a shot, a bolt of pure lightning.

He pierced straight through the remaining structures that remained overhead, into the sky. The report of his flight was visible for miles around. He flew straight up, the trail he left behind pure white light.

NWABA'S PATHETIC LITTLE RITUAL was thrown into chaos as the building shook. The demons on the ceiling chattered nervously, the bait man swung to and fro in his chains, and even Mr. Emmanuel was flustered in the reading of the incantations.

The three Anti-Cherubs wasted no time. They scurried back through the opening in the ceiling, gone. Gone.

Nwaba shrieked his displeasure and rage to the four winds, issuing immediate orders to seek and destroy the angel Kreios. What Brother could bring back his head would be promoted to second in command.

The swarming frenzy of Nri demons that had shrouded the

skyscraper in a surging mass of hideous activity now peeled off like wasps, following the trail left by the angel.

I FOUND PART OF a sandwich on one of the outside tables in the café, which, by the way, was what Bertha's was; a restaurant. I had assumed it was some kind of clothing store, given how cryptic *She* had become.

My mouth watered as I looked at the half sandwich. I looked around like a thief before wolfing the whole thing down. I figured I could be grossed out later. My body was reminding me of my equally strong desire for a drink of water just then, when my eyes were drawn to something in the distance.

Then I saw it: Something pierced the sky in the distance like lightning. Except it was going straight up.

What is that?

KREIOS WAS DRAWING THE entire Nri clan out from its high citadel, the physical amplifier for its Babylonic power. The skyscraper had served from the time of its construction as a conduit for the transfer of power from the spirit realm to the natural. As such, Kreios reasoned, if it could be destroyed or at least minimized in the battle, the Nri would scatter like roaches when the lights came on. He trusted that El had a plan.

If the feint was to work properly, he would have to slow down and give the demons something to attain. In other words, he would have to let them catch up a little. Once more, he had to demonstrate what he believed with action.

But as he did so, he felt an old familiar drain on his angelic abilities. His heart sank. This could simply not be so.

Now he was entirely exposed in the sky, nowhere to go, nowhere to hide, no weapon in his hand and no clues from El as to what to do next. The more he fell back, the more his strength was sapped. He had gone too far this time. Past the tipping point. They would have him soon, and when they did, his life would indeed end.

Unless El does something.

Kreios fell still farther back. He reached out to El, questioning.

"Just watch," was all he heard.

NWABA WATCHED HIS ENTIRE army depart, giving chase to a single angel. He began to have second thoughts as to the tactical sustainability of his last orders. He considered a countermand, but in the end dismissed it as impractical. Besides, he didn't have even a single courier to send so that the order could be rescinded. He growled and let it be.

The tower could remain unguarded as long as the primary foe was completely engaged in battle, and that was Kreios.

But is it? Doubts filtered in around the edges of his mind. Was Kreios indeed the primary source of enemy power, or had Nwaba fallen for a ruse of war? It was too large for him to understand. Nevertheless, he had his instincts. And they were telling him to fly, that it was no longer safe to stay in the tower now. It was a target, and he, if he was smart, would get away from it as quickly as possible.

But where to go? *Somewhere with leverage, that's where.*

He whipped his long thin tail around, skillfully cutting the chains that held the bait man aloft. He fell to the floor a wreck, beside the now fully thawed body of Kim. She was nothing but a cadaver.

The only pulse that remained within her now found its source in the Bloodstone. When the two were united and the transition ritual performed, she could be discarded. Until then she would remain useful, however.

"Mr. Emmanuel, we depart now. Gather these slaves."

CHAPTER IX

I STOOD ON THE ground slack-jawed, looking at something impossible.

A bolt of pure light, evidence of heaven, shot straight up into the sky.

Kreios.

I spoke my grandfather's name in awe: "Kreios!"

When I first saw him blasting through the atmosphere on a trail of light, my heart took to flight as well. I remembered his training; that love is the most powerful force in the universe. Indeed, love was all I *could* feel when I saw my grandfather. It was an awesome thing to see him take to the skies.

I let the waves of emotion roll over me. I allowed my heart to roam free in the excitement of knowing that my grandfather was still alive, that I might soon be reunited with him, that he might soon learn the truth about me—that I, too, was still alive. I had to get to him.

I realized then in my reverie that I had closed my eyes.

I opened them to discover that I was more than twenty feet above the pavement.

What the heck?!

Thankfully, *She* interrupted my alarmed thoughts.
"Concentrate!"

I obliged, wide eyed. I thought of the last thing I could
remember before I found myself hovering above the street. *Kreios.*
I was thinking about seeing him again. Our reunion. I stared at the
horizon, at the vertical line described by my grandfather's incredible
flight through the air.

I glanced down. I was now more than one hundred feet above
the ground, in the darkness of the predawn sky. *Whoa.* My mind
calculated things I hadn't needed before. It made accurate tallies
of altitude with a glance, brought me trajectories and g-force loads
and sharpened my vision incredibly. While I was taking it all in, *She*
interrupted me again.

*"Change of plans. Kreios needs you more than Michael right
now."*

I was a gigantic question mark inside. *What?*

*"Use the Sword. Defend your family. Airel...you were born for
this. Awaken!"*

Something inside me took hold. It was beyond thought or
explanation. It just was. The word she used—*Awaken*—was perfect.
I felt like every part of me, both human and angelic, once mere
averages and mostly asleep, were now wide awake and aware of
everything in my environment.

Wideawake. That's what I was. It struck me that there simply
was no such thing as coincidence anymore.

My eyes, once wide with new realization, now narrowed into
the hard countenance of the warrior. Whatever had happened, *She*
was dead right. I could do this.

I concentrated on one thing: speed.

If I could have seen myself, I might have fainted. I was starting to come into my own. The awakening process, much different from mere activation, had given me my wings. I couldn't see them, but I could feel them. With that change had come new powers of observation, like altitude and airspeed over ground, stuff like that. But I had also gained a new set of eyelids. It sounds gross, but they were cool. They slid down to protect my eyes from the sheer force of the wind rushing against them in flight. They were a little like those nighttime driving glasses, only far cooler and much more useful. They sharpened my sight, protected my eyes, illuminated everything.

I was definitely coming into my own.

I focused on where I needed to be: straight ahead ten miles and about twenty thousand feet straight up. I set my jaw and leaned forward.

I was gone, out of there.

THE SPEED I GAINED came quickly. Before I knew it, I was passing five hundred miles per hour and still accelerating. I was going to go supersonic. I looked ahead, toward Kreios, trying to concentrate on flying. *Flying!*

A few seconds later there was a big boom, and everything went quiet. I was outrunning sound itself.

I stole a glance backward. Behind me was a trail of pure blue light.

KREIOS WAS BECOMING DESPERATE. He was getting very close to the edge of what he could handle. He would soon plummet to the earth, out of control, easy pickings for the Nri vultures. He closed his eyes and fixed his heart completely on El now.

"Though He slay me, yet I will hope in Him."

Kreios flamed out. He was out of energy, spent. He curled up and fell. It would not be long until the Nri intercepted him and tore him to pieces. There were no questions. There was no why. Whatever happened now would happen, and he would be at peace with it.

With this thought, shadows closed in upon his mind. He thought of his beautiful wife. He had told her thousands of years ago that they would be reunited. He longed to fulfill that promise. Perhaps now...

I WAS GETTING CLOSE. I could see clearly from one mile away that Kreios was falling. It looked like he was out of control. *What is he doing?*

"He needs your help."

Kreios tumbled as if unconscious. A skinny demon with wings much too big for its body took a swipe at Kreios, grabbing him for a moment. I gasped and watched as he tossed my grandfather like a rag doll to another demon, much larger, who then turned back toward the earth.

I knew what to do. If my grandfather was a fearsome warrior, so was I. If he had killed his ten thousands of demonic infidels—which I knew from my own study was a word that meant "unfaithful"— then I too could, and I would. I thought of the Sword.

It sprang instantly to hand.

I opened my mouth to shout. The battle cry that came out shook the very skies, it was a shriek terrible to witness, sounding like a hawk diving for the kill…only I was ascending into the midst of a black cloud of Nri demons.

"This is the entire Nri horde," She said.

They should have thought twice, I responded.

I did not see the masses of Nri wings and talons, just Kreios. He was my grandfather, he needed me and I would not let him die.

On my first pass through their airborne mob I sent one hundred and forty two of them to Hell.

I circled back around for more.

Kreios was still in the grip of the demon who had last grasped him, only most of that demon was gone. All that remained of it was a severed leg. The Sword was doing its job. The limb burst into ash, and my grandfather was free. But still falling.

Now at twenty thousand feet up, before Kreios fell to his death, I had quite simply a crapload of demons to kill. I faced the Nri horde alone, the Sword blazing in my hand.

CHAPTER X

KREIOS BEGAN TO FEEL something new. Rushing wind in his ears. The sensation of falling. He was not dead; he would not awaken to see his beloved bride. *Not yet.*

He opened his eyes. He was still alive and falling.

The drain…it was ebbing away. What was it he felt now? Vague but familiar. It was like the Sword of Light, only different. It was profound; it felt so similar to his beloved old weapon, yet it was clearly *not* somehow. He looked at his hands. They were empty. He felt it, though. The drain had stopped.

He was gaining strength.

He could fly again.

He corrected his descent and shot into the air, feeling all his strength beginning to return; he was being filled with power. *El?*

"Just watch."

Then he saw what El was talking about. A blue streak cutting through the Nri horde. It was supersonic, and an attendant pure white light went with it. A great number of Nri demons were struck in the collision and began the long fall back to earth. They broke apart, turning back into ash. The blue streak circled back around again and again, taking more with every pass.

El, what is that? Kreios was genuinely bewildered, and what caused him to shake his head in amazement was that he had not felt bewildered for ages.

He could feel the delight in El's voice: *"Just watch."*

He did.

KREIOS WAS SAFE. HE could fly again; he was awake and aware, I could tell that much with my new super eyes. That left me free to use the Sword on the Nri.

And use it I did. *Squalembrato;* I sliced diagonally across the torso of a hideous and stinking wretch, then brought the blade back around and up, ready for the next one. *Fendente;* from 12 o'clock at the crown of its horned head with the *temperato* of my blade straight down the nasty thing, splitting its miserable carcass in two clean halves. I roared in vengeful fury, letting my love for my grandfather power my every move in midair.

Light from the Sword interlaced in three streams on the flat of the blade, winding down onto the hilt and onto my hand, up my arm. I was conjoined to the weapon; for the first time I felt that it belonged to me, that I possessed it, that it was mine to wield, mine to use. Together with it, I was aglow in the ash storm of demonic debris it created by my hand. None could withstand what I had now become.

Already supersonic, I began to pick up speed.

THE STREAK OF BLUE light wound its way around the cloud

of the Nri, hemming them in on all sides; they had nowhere to go. Gradually as the streak went around and around, it began to take on the shape of a glowing blue globe, the trail of blue light passed through them so quickly. Huge amounts of demon detritus were grist in this mill. They fell out from the bottom of the globe as wings, trunks, limbs; now prey only to gravity and the surface of the earth miles below.

Kreios was overcome with emotion, coughing out an incredulous guffaw. El had utterly routed them. And quickly. "What is this new thing?" he asked.

Then he heard, *"Just watch!"*

Kreios waited and watched still more, and then the blue light slowed as the last of the Nri clan fell away beneath. The streak became still, a point of light, a round blue aura beneath pointing downward, the unmistakable pure and bright light of the Sword of Light above.

Kreios was stunned for the second time that day. The Sword!

"Go," he heard, so he went to it.

The sun was beginning its ascent in the east now. It threw its first rays upon the clouds where the battle had taken place, lighting them on fire in brilliant silver, red, and deepest midnight blue. Set like a jewel in a crown of magnificence was the radiant blue light, now just visible as a figure. It held aloft the piercing and pure Sword of Light, symbolic of victory.

He could not have imagined for anything in the world what he would behold when he drew near. There, with face burnished to glowing in the warmth of the Sword, was Airel. She smiled proudly at him.

He could do nothing but go to her and weep for his beloved granddaughter, his darling girl. She was dead, but was now alive. He shouted to the heavens with exultant joy, "She is alive! She is alive!" He fell on her shoulder and wept more, wept like a small child. The sun cast them in relief, a shimmering and pure sight.

CHAPTER XI

AS THE SUN ROSE over Cape Town there was a problem with the Table Mountain cable cars. The system was down, the cables jammed, and a car was stuck up near the top wheelhouse, dangling motionless from the cable 3500 feet above sea level.

Workmen doing the checks that morning in preparation for the open at 8 a.m. had gone missing. Clocking in, one of them was snatched screaming across the industrial floor of the mechanical room into the predawn darkness by something powerful and hideous. His cries were stifled shortly. The next one, alerted by the disturbance, had run into the room and been blindsided, grasped about the midsection by a massive clawed hand. Before he could draw breath to cry out, he was thrown out into the ether off the sheer edge of Table Mountain, falling to his appalling death after a very long drop into nothingness.

Something dark and huge then mounted the cables, draping itself over the stopped cable car like a shroud.

As the sun began to rise, a fearsome cry rang out over the city. It sounded bird-like, but it was loud and it radiated darkness; it broadcast fear and rage. To the few early morning observers on the ground below, who could not see much, it looked like there was a massive tree tangled in the mechanism and dangling down from atop the lone stuck cable car. It fluttered and waved in the breeze.

But it was not a tree, and it was not passively fluttering.

It was the enraged prince of the Nri, the last of his kind, wearing his finest and largest suit—the one with the big wings and claws—*"the better to kill you with, my dears"*—and he was issuing the call for vengeance.

WE HEARD THE CAWING croaking birdcall of the master of the principality from twenty thousand feet up. Though I had to shake my head at the relentlessness of events, I had learned to set aside my sometimes admittedly bad attitude and just buckle down. Besides, I had my grandfather back, and it was beyond awesome to be alive.

He was more than a little surprised to see me, especially up in the rarefied air he normally tread without me. He had so many questions that I was overwhelmed at first. I tried to begin to explain, but then this creature—Nwaba, Kreios called the prince of the Nri— had bellowed at us and we had to put the conversation off for the time being.

I couldn't help but grin at Kreios as we flew together for the first time.

"I knew you were special, Airel, but this...I cannot believe it!" That just made me grin at him even more.

But the grin was wiped off my face when I saw what Nwaba had done.

There, on a cable car strung out above the city far below, was the biggest demon I had ever seen. He dwarfed the cable car on which he was perched, shrieking at us. In the carriage that dangled below were two figures that at first I did not recognize. One of them was in charge, the other was a hostage. It was obvious from their body language.

But then my newly enhanced eyes picked out something else inside the cable car, stretched out on the floor behind them. I recognized the dress. That little sundress. And the red hair. It was Kim. She looked horrible, like a corpse, and I wondered if she was alive. *If they have killed her*...I began to think of ways to punish the villains for their crimes, but then Kreios touched my arm. I looked at him and he shook his head. He had seen too.

"Remember your lessons," he said.

I nodded and settled down.

The demon prince spoke.

"Kreios! You have been on a little killing spree, my old friend. Some of the strongest clans fell under your hand. And now you come here. To my house." A guttural laugh. "And the daughter of El! She has found some new tricks to turn." The demon looked down into the carriage and said something about a "Mr. Emmanuel" or something.

I looked into the carriage as it rocked under the weight of the monstrous demon. The wings of the beast drooped down far below the bottom of the car, and against the backdrop of the wheelhouse perched on the edge of the mountain, with its massive arched mouth waiting to receive its travelers, the sight was medieval. Dragons and castles filled my mind.

But then two and two clicked together to make four: I recognized the hostage.

No. It can't be him. "Oh, no! Kreios! They have my dad!"

"Yes!" Nwaba cried. "Yes, I do! And I am unafraid to snuff his pathetic life!" He bared his teeth and hissed at us.

"Be careful, Nwaba. You are not in a position to make threats,"

Kreios shouted at him.

"Am I not?" the demon said.

With that, the goon in the car, who I guessed was Mr. Emmanuel, then shoved my dad almost entirely out the window, holding him back at the last moment.

"DAD!" I shouted, and then noticed that something wasn't right. My dad was standing, true. But he looked like a puppet on a string, asleep, yet he still stood.

"Shall I drop him?" the goon Mr. Emmanuel said. "Or shoot you in the head?" He then aimed a pistol at me with his free hand.

"Keep moving; don't hover," Kreios said, and I took his advice, making little dodging movements in the air that would complicate, if nothing else, a pistol shot at that range; about one hundred feet, which I knew thanks to my new precision eyeballs.

The demon spoke up with a deep guttural voice that made me shiver. "I want only one thing, Kreios. And you know what that is."

"I do not," he answered.

"Yes, you do!" the demon prince shouted. He was enraged. "How could you fail to see the most important piece of the puzzle, angel of El? Of course you know!"

Again, Kreios answered him, "I don't know what you want. Whatever it is, demon, I will not give you anything."

Nwaba screamed a vicious tantrum into the clear morning air. "Bring me The Alexander!"

Michael? Why would they want Michael?

"Bring me The Alexander, or I will kill her father!"

Panic started tearing at the edges of my mind.

Then I heard distant shouting, I turned to look. There on the service catwalk of the upper wheelhouse, perched on the precipitous cliff, was Michael. He looked like he was ready for a fight.

"Nwaba!" he shouted down at us. "I am right here! Come and get me!"

Wait. What? How did he get there? And where is Ellie?

CHAPTER XII

THE DEMON PRINCE WASTED not a single passing thread in the web of time; he launched from the wires, flinging himself at Michael Alexander with a single mighty stroke of his great wings.

The cable car was thrust into severe bouncing motions as Nwaba pushed off, bobbing on the wires like a weight on a bungee. It fell, then launched upward and then back down again violently.

The passengers inside were all thrown in different directions.

Mr. Emmanuel fell back, his grip on the bait man John broken by the forces at work. He crashed into the opposite wall of the car. The impact knocked the breath from him.

Kim, the host of the Bloodstone, slid into his feet. Either dead or unconscious, he didn't know and he did not care.

No, what Mr. Emmanuel cared about was the bait man John. He had lost control of him in the swinging motion of the car, being forced to watch in horror as his bargaining chip toppled over the rail and disappeared.

I SAW MY DAD falling and dove after him; there was nothing else to be done. It was horrifying. I managed to catch him, pulling up seconds before we hit the rocks below. He was unconscious, but he was breathing. *What is it with the men in my life needing me to rescue them all the time?!*

I had to find somewhere safe for him. I needed to get Kim. I had to help Michael. The more I thought about it, the more the impossibility of the whole thing became clear to me.

"I can't do everything." I had to do what I could do and trust El to do the rest. "Please, God. Keep them safe. Michael, Kreios and Kim."

I scanned the landscape and spotted a boulder-strewn clearing in the nearby mountains. But there was something there that made me gasp.

"Ellie!"

NWABA THE DEMON PRINCE plucked the boy Michael from the catwalk as easily as an eagle would snatch a trout from a lake, his talons wrapping like prison bars around the boy's midsection. He flew off with his prey, moving swiftly for the business district of Cape Town, for his high tower.

Thoughts raced through his head; options. Perhaps The Alexander could lead him directly to what he desired most after all. Nwaba touched down on the rooftop of the tower by the big elm. He flung Michael to one side as he landed.

He scrambled away, moving toward the great elm tree, which was in full leaf.

Nwaba chuckled at his fear; it was delicious to him. "Now, boy, we can negotiate." He now changed, the chameleon lord, into his favorite suit of clothes. His scaly skin became pure white, his tail thinned to a long wire, his face disturbingly humanoid.

Michael began climbing the tree, communicating fear on his face, in his movements.

Nwaba was amused. "What are you doing, boy? Come down, coward!" he pranced and mocked him, cackling wickedly.

He scampered farther up the tree, grabbing for branches, paying him no heed.

"Come now, boy! I won't hurt you. We must talk, negotiate. I know you are the rightful heir to the Bloodstone. I just want to come to terms with you."

"You know I don't have it," came a voice from within the foliage.

Nwaba was given pause. "So you say," he said, "But that does not matter. Let us find it together." He paused again, pacing, his wire tail whipping around. "I know it calls to you, boy. You are the heir. Surely you have heard its sweet whispers…as I have."

No answer from the tree.

Nwaba crept nearer as he spoke. "Surely, Michael Alexander, you have heard what lies in store. You have seen and heard visions." He was at the base of the tree, the sticky pads of his hands feeling around for a hold, the claws of his feet sinking into the green wood. He began to climb upward. "You are The Alexander."

Silence from above.

"I know what conquests can be made. I can still choose a new host, you know that as well as I; you and I can unite and be truly magnificent!" Nwaba articulated his long wire tail upward into the branches of the tree as he climbed, probing for the boy. "Surely you share my thirst for domination." His voice snapped in contempt for the present situation, for his apparent powerlessness to convince the boy of what he wanted, what he needed.

MR. EMMANUEL REGAINED HIS feet and began firing his pistol, loaded with .45 ACP magnum load hollow points. First he had taken a shot at Airel, but she was too fast, she was there and then gone, diving after the bait man John. He growled in frustration. Then he took aim at the angel Kreios, who was the only one not moving. The first shot went wide.

The angel moved quickly. Before he could fire another shot, Kreios was inside the car, pushing him away from the door, one iron hand grasping his shirt and the other thrusting his pistol skyward.

He thought fast, waving the fingers of his non-firing hand. The hollow point bullet he had just fired began to circle back around.

"COME NOW, BOY! DO not hide! You cannot hide from me. You cannot hide from the Bloodstone."

The tail was now far above. It had threaded its snake-like way through the branches, up and over and through, and was now making its way back downward.

"You are The Alexander, boy." Nwaba saw the boy's foot resting on a branch before his very face. He smiled. He reached up and grabbed hold of it and then shot forward and up, thrusting his face into the face of the boy, spitting, "It has called your name!"

Michael was unperturbed.

This, for a split second, confused the demon prince.

"Yes, I know," the boy said. He showed his hand, in which he grasped Nwaba's tail. It had threaded its way through the tree, up and over a great limb and back down again, and the boy had shrewdly procured it for his own use. "But who are you?"

Very quickly, he looped the wire tail around Nwaba's head, pulled it tight, and leapt from the tree.

KREIOS SQUEEZED POWERFULLY AGAINST the wrist bones of the man's firing hand, first breaking them, then crushing them.

The man cried out in agony but the bullet was now on course; he smiled.

But the angel knew. He turned at the last minute, placing Mr. Emmanuel's head directly into the bullet's new line of trajectory. The last thing Mr. Emmanuel saw was the face of El's most terrible angel, in most terrible aspect: victory.

NWABA WAS HANGED. HE struggled viciously for a few seconds, his eyes shut tight. When the visions that appeared before him became too terrible to bear, he opened them wide and beheld nothing but blackness. The host had expired, he had nowhere to hide.

CHAPTER XIII

KREIOS TOUCHED DOWN ON the rooftop of the tower to find Michael Alexander not only alive, but well.

"Michael," he said, "I should kill you." Kreios did not know what to think about the boy Airel loved. He had harbored so much unbridled hatred toward him since that day on the cliff top that looking at him now…he wondered where it had all gone.

"Would you like to kill me now? Because I also wrecked your truck…"

He was in earnest, which impressed Kreios. He could sense a sea of change within the boy. He responded to him in deadpan, "No. I will not kill you right now. But the truck… perhaps we will talk about that later." He looked up into the tree as the demon Nwaba broke apart into ash and floated away in the breeze. "I will say, however, that I am now an admirer of your work." Words were so much cheaper than actions, Kreios mused. He would see, but perhaps the boy deserved a chance after all.

"Thanks." Michael shifted his feet, looking away. The awkwardness between them thickened.

Kreios looked at him. "You are well. How is this so?"

Michael showed him his chest, which was clear of any sign of the work of the Bloodstone. "Ellie healed me."

"Ellie? Who is Ellie?"

"She's a half breed, an Immortal. We met her while we were trying to catch up with you. You know, along your trail of destruction. But—"

Kreios was grim. "Yes." He thought for a moment. "I suppose I should apologize."

Michael said nothing.

"Michael—"

"—Look, this half-breed girl, Ellie. We don't have time to talk. She needs help. When she healed me...something happened. And I'm afraid the only one who knows what we might be able to do... is you."

"Where is she?"

CHAPTER XIV

KREIOS AND MICHAEL LANDED in the little boulder clearing. He saw John lying in a patch of rough grass off to one side, still heavily drugged. Michael strode quickly over to Airel, who was kneeling before the prostrate form of a girl. *This must be the half-breed Ellie,* Kreios thought as he too approached them.

"Airel!"

Airel leaped to her feet and threw her arms around the boy, embracing him. "Michael, you're... okay?"

"Yeah," he said, looking down at the girl with eyes drenched in outsized responsibility and regret.

Kreios remained off to one side, looking at Michael's expression.

"She saved me," he managed, choking up. "Now she's..."

"We have to do something," Airel said, tears streaming down her face.

Michael pulled her closer to him.

Airel looked from Michael to Kreios with a spark of fear in her eyes. "Where's Kim?"

"She..." Michael began. But he could not finish.

Airel's face became white. She shook her head in disbelief, her eyes wide. She then fell into his arms sobbing. "No!"

Michael held her in his arms like a man would hold his bride of many years, consoling her, comforting her for some great loss; the grief of which he would be there to help her bear for years to come. Kreios was struck by the power of that image then, and the stock of the boy rose in his estimation once more.

So much pain and loss, and Kreios knew the taste of it well. Very well. Today one life had been snuffed. Kim was gone. Perhaps that was for the best, especially given how she had chosen…but it still didn't reduce the sting, especially for Airel, he knew. But he could do something for this Ellie; maybe she could yet be saved.

He gently touched Michael's shoulder. Their eyes met and Michael moved with Airel to one side.

As they moved away, Kreios looked down on the form of the half-breed girl, this Ellie.

He caught his breath, felt his legs go weak. He rushed forward and fell to his knees at her side, choking out his daughter's name: *"Uriel?"*

URIEL

BOOK THREE IN THE *AIREL* SAGA

CHAPTER I

Cape Town, South Africa, present day

KREIOS FELL TO HIS knees in the dirt beside her. His eyes were beyond tender. "Dad," was all she said.

"Eriel," he whispered.

She smiled, weak. "Dad, I've told you a thousand times. It's Uriel." She coughed up blood. "I've missed you."

Kreios broke into heavy wild sobs, weeping bitterly over his daughter. Thousands of years had passed since she had disappeared. He thought she had died! And now…just when he found her again…she was as good as dead. The pain of these thoughts racked him into more despair, and he wept. After a few more moments he recovered enough to ask, "What happened?"

"Easy," she replied, "I took the mark upon myself."

Kreios was stunned, pained, confused. "But that's my fault," was all he could manage. He crouched back on his knees and looked up, squeezing his eyes shut.

"Michael and Airel are…" Uriel began, "…more important. They're crucial, dad."

He looked at her with blazing eyes and said, "But you are crucial to me! I cannot allow this." He stood. Pure love radiated from his countenance; it was unrestrained.

It was dangerous.

He closed his eyes for a long time, remaining motionless.

Finally he broke the silence. "Airel…Airel, take Michael and your father and get off this mountain."

"What?" she said.

He turned to her and said gently, "It will not be safe for you here, child. Not for anyone. You must go."

He turned back to his daughter, to his Eriel—his Uriel. More tears crept up on him and escaped from his eyes. "If we…if what I am about to do makes an end of my daughter, you must go and find what is next for you. I may not be able to continue on." His tone was flat, resigned. He knew what he would do. There was only one choice remaining; there was no sense delaying anything.

"You are ready now, Airel." He turned and looked straight into her. "If I do not continue, you *shall.* Listen carefully for El."

He turned back to Uriel's sick and dying body. "I must now do what I can for her, and I am afraid…I am afraid there is only one way to do that."

"But, Kreios, we just—"

"Please, Airel, do not force me to ask you once again. The pain is too great. You must go; you must take them away from here if you do not wish to die. All of you. It is not safe."

Airel turned to go, reluctance written on her every feature.

Uriel looked into her father's eyes with surprise, having no idea what he was talking about. "Dad?"

"Hush, daughter. And be still."

Cape Town, South Africa, present day

FRANK WISEMAN WATCHED THE sun beginning to burst upon the predawn sky over False Bay from the verandah of his posh villa in Simon's Town. He just hated it, he just hated all of it. His harpy of a wife was scratching and clucking like a yard-bound hen again, nagging him into getting a bit of exercise when it was the last thing he wanted.

"But you'll live longer!" she always said. He hated that too. She only wanted him to live longer so she would have someone to nag. If she didn't have that she wouldn't have a single reason to live, he ventured.

Nevertheless he was up at sunrise. Why? Because he was hopelessly stranded in the rut of his life. The truth was, if he didn't have her around to attempt to make him miserable, he wouldn't have anything either. He had come to enjoy the fight, the constant scrap, after all these years. Sick, but it was endearing.

But he never let that show. It would ruin the game for both of them. They had an unspoken understanding that any kind of truce would be impossible. It would fundamentally change the relationship and then where would they be? *Square one,* he thought.

That made him suffer an incredible split second of anxiety and exhaustion.

"Well, Frank, let's get a move on," she said, her voice strident and grating.

"After you, princess." He used her pet name like an insult.

They walked down the steps together to the beach. She was talking again, and he tuned her out. There was some mention of, "…you've got to get some exercise…" and a little more of, "…at your age, you know…" He rolled his eyes and kept up with her.

The sun was going to peek over the mountains across the bay at any moment. It would be blinding and she would say how magnificent it was and "Oh, Frank, isn't it just lovely to be up and out before the dawn so we can behold all this," but it would be blinding anyway and all it would mean was just the start of another wretched day, with heat, sun, misery, and dear wife Kimberley, in increasing order of irritation.

He kicked at a stone embedded in the sand, but his foot caught on it and he took a tumble, soaking his nice new short pants in the wet sand. "Ow! Dash it all!"

"Frank! Oh, dear! Are you all right?"

"I'm fine. Just help me up, will you?"

She reached to help him. "Are you sure? No broken bones?"

"No, Kimberley, no broken anything. Lucky for you." He tried his best to dust the sand from his bottom, but the wet was still there and it made him uncomfortable, if only just. Yes, it was rather like Kimberley.

He looked down at the offending rock, more than a little bemused at the effect it had taken on his morning exercise.

But it was not a rock.

It was something bright pink.

"Well, now, what is that, do you suppose?" He wasn't asking and she didn't answer. "Princess, will you help me with this?" He kneeled in the sand to dig around the edges of the object.

The more his hands scraped away the wet sand, the more intrigued he became. He did not know where the impulse was coming from, but it seemed…it seemed…it seemed like an adventure.

Frank dug while Kimberley stood with her arms crossed, ticking her tongue in disgust.

Finally, the earth gave up its buried treasure. It had been embedded in the sand by the tides. "Some child's bookbag," Frank exclaimed, beginning to fumble for the zipper.

"Well, don't open it!" she scolded, but he did anyway. "Really. I just don't see how it's any of your business, Frank, I really—"

"Kimberley," Frank said, a different tone in his voice now, "shut up."

She did, though only from shock. Those were not words that were allowed; that was out of bounds.

The zipper fell back to reveal a bright red jewel. As the sun threw open the day, the first rays fell upon the stone and lit it with an unreal light. It reflected off Frank's face, making him appear malevolent, causing Kimberley to shrink back in momentary fear.

But hold, Frank thought, quite unlike himself, *what's this?* The stone was the most beautiful thing he had ever beheld. Still, he wondered what else might be in the knapsack. Perhaps more treasures?

He opened the bag and looked inside it. "It's a book," he said absentmindedly. "A right nice looking one, too." He reached in to pull it out, and as he did so, his fingers brushed against its hidebound cover. Like a shot in the dark, one word rang out in his head:

AIREL.

FAN FICTION

by Kyle Pinkston, writing as *Redstone:*

(American Fork Junior High, American Fork, Utah)

Sawtooth mountains of Idaho, present day

ROARS AND CLASHES RANG out on the mountain as the battle
of angel and demon raged on. Above the fight was Kim. Long red
hair flowed around her as she floated upon the air with her beautiful
Bloodstone in her hand. She stared at it, the demon inside no longer
commanding her. The demon had died, now she was the master.
All the black luscious power of the stone glowing in her hand was
now hers. She contorted her body into a crooked position in the air
and laughed, letting her hair flow out of her face as she subsided to
a chuckle. The redness of her hair grew a deeper blood color when
she committed herself to the stone—it had wanted her to look her
best and she liked it—that way when she killed it wouldn't stain.
After all... blood does take hours to get out of the hair.

She raced to the ground, parting a large boar-like demon from an angel with powerful arms and long black hair. She smiled at the wounded deity and plunged her sword into his heart. He screamed as she wriggled the blade until the hole in his chest became large enough to pull the blade out with ease. She then took her black sword and swung it wildly around her head, feeling the power surge given to her from killing the angel.

Letting the sword release from her grasp, it flew, slicing another angel across the ribs, embedding itself into a demon with four horns coming out of its face. The black robed beast collapsed onto the ground and shriveled into black dust. *Oops,* thought Kim as she sprinted to the sword and cut upward, gashing the maimed angel up the right side of his face. She then took to the air again as a demon Brother and his host fell upon the being.

Kim laughed again.

Now rising up to the height of the trees, she let the Bloodstone's power flow to the demons below. Having them drink it in sent the battle to a new level of frenzy. The demons grew stronger as their human counterparts became crazed with the new invigoration.

They were winning now.

Staying aloft in the trees, Kim convulsed in mid-air, the Bloodstone gripping at her own life force to feed her army of hungry monsters. The strain made the red scars seep and reform on her body, forming her with a display of dark red tattoos, each resembling a time when she had suffered the pain of mortality. But now she was immortal.

Grasping at the stone in agony, she crashed into a nearby tree, sending her to the ground. She stood up and grabbed at the face of a nearby angel, wrenching his neck, snapping it.

I SWUNG MY SWORD with all my might, slicing off the three left arms of a six-armed demon that was grappling with Michael. Shrieking, the beast twisted to the side, a single right arm fighting me off as he continued to choke Michael. Skillfully, I leaped into the air, coming down with a blow that decapitated the demon as it erupted into black smoke.

"Thanks for that one," Michael replied gratefully as I helped him up.

We quickly traded places. I swung my sword and relieved another demon of his head. A yell from behind me caught my attention. I whipped around to see Michael stabbing a large bald man in the side. Head-butting him, Michael sent him tumbling down the hill, hitting two men with bows that were aiming at an angel overhead.

Twenty feet away, Kreios landed with an Earth-shattering boom, arcing his sword largely, slaying three demons and a man in one blow. A demon came up and grabbed at him. Kreios smashed in his face and turned sharply.

"Ariel, Kim is on top of the hill. Get to her before she uses the Bloodstone to summon more demons." Kreios leaped into the air and collided with a large bat-like demon mid-flight, sending out a shower of black dust as he tore through its mid section.

I turned to Michael. He nodded and we started sprinting up the hill. Michael jumped and rolled over the shoulder of a large burly boar demon, plunging the blade of his sword into its lower back. Then, settling on a direct path, we started for the top of the hill.

❧

KREIOS LANDED HARD ON a skinny man with short red hair. Feeling the crack of his ribs, Kreios then worried about the next threat. The two demons fighting nearby angels stopped and turned toward him. *Come to me, you beasts.* They rushed him. Kreios sidestepped and held his sword out. The first demon ran right through the blade, and as he dissolved the mist blocked the view of the other, but Kreios stabbed his face skillfully nevertheless.

"Ho, Kreios!" shouted a nearby angel. When Kreios turned, he saw two angel warriors and noticed one of them was wounded, a large gash on his leg up to his mid torso.

"Get him up to the Shadowers!" Kreios yelled to them. They immediately shot into the air, vanishing.

Kreios had once before used this battle tactic, when he had contended with the Seer for Ke'elei. He trusted this technique from past experience. The wounded would be lifted and new troops would replenish them on the ground. The enemy could not see them, for the shadowers blocked their view.

My warrior brethren, we must exchange ranks. The enemy is receiving energy from the Bloodstone. We need to refresh in order to hold the fight until Ariel is able to destroy the new Seer. Kreios then added to himself, sending his plea to El, *I pray she has the strength to defeat her.*

Kreios was brought immediately back to the battle, parrying a swing from a black sword. He lifted his hilt to the height of his eyes, his blade turned downward so as to block the next horizontal blow. Then he pushed forward and cut upward to slash the man's face. The body then convulsed, black ooze seeping from the man's mouth. Kreios stepped back as the man's demon Brother half clawed its way out of the body.

A mammoth black creature stood before him. Coming to twice his height, it roared ferociously as it spread four huge wings and two enormous arms. *This is more like it!* He cheered to himself as he and the colossal demon took to the sky.

MICHAEL RACED UP THE hill with Ariel. They slashed and jabbed at random as demons started to block their path. Having trouble keeping up with her, Michael started to hurdle the bodies that they had to maneuver around. After cutting down a large black snake from his view, he saw Ariel stopped in awe.

Standing at the peak of the hill before it leveled out stood two enormous beasts. Each was ten feet tall with huge rippling muscles. Their upper bodies were humanoid, but their lower bodies were equine. They were huge demonic centaurs, and they each wielded two long black swords.

"I'll take the big one," Michael joked half-heartedly.

"Not funny," Ariel replied. "I need to get to the top. No way will these guys let us past."

"I'll distract them while you get to Kim. You know as well as I do that the Bloodstone will call to me once I get close. But get to the top once you see an opening."

No other demons were coming anywhere close to the centaur guardians. *That's a good sign,* Michael thought as he ran at them.

The first demon was the only one to move. He raised his sword and met Michael's blade with a fierce clang and a shower of sparks. Falling to the ground, Michael barely rolled to the side in time to dodge the demon thundering his hooves where he'd been just seconds ago. Full speed, he ran and jumped on its back, stabbing its leg. Then he started to try to choke the centaur.

"Go!" he shouted, and Ariel started to run for the gap between the guardians. Then the second demon raised his sword. Michael, in a rush, let go off the crippled demon's throat and seized his sword. He flung it at the other sentinel and watched it sink into his chest.

Ariel had made it past, on to the top of the hill.

A hot shock went through him and he clutched at his chest. The ripping pain was coming from the demon he had impaled. Being half of one he was still connected to them. His father, the previous Seer, had cursed him when he had betrayed him for Ariel. But this pain was new. It felt more real, as if he could hold the sword and remove it from his chest. The other times had been more surreal, mostly in his mind.

This was real.

The colossal being pulled the sword out of his chest and slumped to the ground.

Sighing heavily in relief, Michael looked back at the other one, assuming it had died during the exchange between the other. It had not. It got to its feet and hobbled on its three good legs toward the other one. Crashing together, the beasts merged. A horrible roar came from the heaping black dust as a dark flame burst out of the cloud. Michael ran for his sword and held his position, worried about what was going to come out of the gaseous formation in front of him.

❧

FINALLY I HAD REACHED the top. I had wished that this moment would never come. But it had, and now I had to deal with it.

Kim was floating at the top of the hill. Her red cadaverous eyes turned to me; a huge smile growing on her face, showing that all of her teeth were still sparkly white. "Ariel, sweetie," she chided as I cautiously came nearer, "Why do you look so sad? You were never sad. Only happy, like me!" she laughed, with two voices emanating from her. She came down to meet the ground, swishing her sword on the ground, flinging dirt with every jerky motion.

"Kim, what happened to you?" I pleaded with her. "You don't need to do this. Put the stone down and end this now."

"NO! This is my stone, MINE! And you, Ariel, can come and kill me for it. After all... you gave it to me." I then remembered the time at the cliff, when Michael had killed James, and Kreios had destroyed Tengu. The stone had been discarded there after Kreios had healed Michael with it.

I was dead when this happened, and was brought back in order to kill my friend. This was wrong.

Then Kim rammed into me.

Thrown by the sudden shock, I grasped at the air and straightened myself. Causing the air to ripple into wings around me I shot back at Kim. I pulled up at the last second and swung at her with my sword. A shower of sparks sprayed off the blades as Kim blocked. I punched with my other arm and sent her to the ground. I raced after her. She wheeled around on the ground and kicked with so much force it knocked the wind right out of me. It felt like dodge-ball, when the kid with the strong arm tags you right in the gut, but a bruise was already forming on my chest. Both of us stood and stared at each other.

"Kim, I don't understand!" I yelled at her through the sound of my ears ringing and angels slaying demons. "Tengu can't control you. Throw the Bloodstone away. Remember when everything was normal? Our families, boys, shopping. Don't you want that back?"

Kim chuckled to herself. Straightening up, she roared into a full laugh, "Don't you see? Tengu wasn't ever in charge. *He* was: the great personification of evil. That's who commands me! And I won't let him down. No. No, I'll let him out!" Kim tore the Bloodstone from her neck and hurled it to the ground.

Shattering, the gem released a blast so strong it shook the hillside. A black wave of smoke came rushing out of it. I held up my hands and sword to block it from coming at me. I sank to my knees to try to keep from falling backwards. Then as suddenly as it came out, it rushed back to the stone.

Standing there was my friend, but it wasn't her. An aura of black shadow and flame surrounded her. The shadow formed the image of a man's silhouette.

"Now, Daughter of El. You die."

✦

KREIOS STOOD OVER THE body of the gigantic winged demon. He yelled in victory and raised his blade. *Now, on to the next foe.* He rushed a pair of men. He swung with such great force the two men were sent to either side of him. He then stabbed one as the other stood up. Unable to remove his sword he punched the other, crushing his throat, he fell to the ground soundlessly. The other man on the ground wrapped his hands around Kreios's blade, lodged in his body. Looking down at him, Kreios pulled the blade from his chest.

Warm pain flared in his back, and he turned to meet this next enemy. Another demon stood before him. Stabbing forward and catching the demon in the chest, Kreios felt the wound healing. *There! She's defeating her.*

But his hope was suddenly dashed to pieces as he felt the healing subside, the pain grow. The wound steadily got larger. Dropping to his hands, Kreios reached to his back and felt blood oozing from the wound.

A horde of ten demons came at him, grasping for his sword. It was shattered as they fell upon it. He took hold of the shards and desperately flung them at his enemies, cutting them and impaling them with tiny projectiles. *Well that worked.* Exhausted, he stood, removed a sword from a nearby body, and threw himself again into the fight.

✦

MICHAEL FELL TO THE ground, holding back blood from another wound. The huge black beast before him rumbled deeply with a laugh. The demon had morphed into a dark dragon. It towered over him as it came up onto its hind legs. Its head was crowned with two large spikes jutting backward, black as the night along with the rest of its body. Two small red eyes set into its head glared at him, smelling demon on him but knowing that it was to kill him. Its mouth now stood agape with hundreds of little razor-like teeth.

A burst of red flame spewed from its open jaws and Michael scrambled out of the way just as the grass was scorched into a pile of ash. He ran at the underside of the dragon, slashing upward, covering himself in boiling dragon's blood. Screaming, he ran away from the wound grasping at his shoulders and left arm.

The dragon complimented his yells with a roar of pain, crashing heavily to the ground on all four powerful legs. The dragon took to the sky in a rush, heaving a large gust at Michael. Being tossed onto his feet by the wind, he grasped at the dragon's tail as it slid from the ground.

The weightless experience was cut short as he severed the tail, falling hard to the ground once more. He knew that it could not fly without its counterbalance. He was soon proved right: The dark dragon plunged to the earth with a bone-snapping crunch.

"Well… that was probably the coolest thing I've ever killed."

I STOOD MOTIONLESS, HORRIFIED, not believing what I was seeing. Kim, my best friend until, well—until she became the Seer—stood before me, encompassed by the power of Lucifer, the ultimate evil.

"You can't kill a being sentenced to eternal damnation. I have

waited twenty thousand years to slay you! Once you die and the
Sword of Light is in my hand, I will move onto Kreios... and
Michael... and every other traitorous Son of El that has forsaken
their exaltation to be on this cursed earth!"

Kim then lifted into the air and flew at me. I instinctively flew
to the right, countering her direction and flying above her. She
swerved and gazed up at me, the fire in here eyes tangible and real.
Screaming with a voice not her own, she lunged at me sword first.
"This game will end!" she yelled at me.

"I do not fear you!" I called back at her as I shot into her body
and sent her flying. Both of us yelling, we collided in the air. I could
feel each punch she threw. Each one was unmeasured and wild. I
defended, I could feel her sword clashing with mine.

Finally she kicked me in the chest. I hit the ground but bounced
up. Climbing to my feet after the second impact I braced myself.
Kim smashed the ground twenty feet away.

I found myself in an empty space—nothing but a frameless
door and me. I walked evenly toward it, knowing I must pass
through it to defeat Kim.

The door opened silently and I felt my body grow warm.

I opened my eyes.

Everything was where it had once been. The Sword was now
in my hand, and when I looked at it, the pure intense light was so
strong I had to look away.

The demon was running at me once again, but now all fear left
me.

I was just there with Kim, my friend.

I cut upward, into her heart.

Kim's sword fell out of her hand. She stood shocked before me,
shielding her eyes from the light of the Sword that was now in my
hand. I twisted my blade and remembered Kim—the real Kim. Her

quirky laughter, the stupid jokes, the unrealistic crushes.

Tears ran down my face as I lunged. The hillside around us torn apart amid the battle, the hacked bodies and the hatred, it had ruined such a beautiful place that was once luscious and green.

I plunged Sword deeper into her heart, feeling the evil within her die along with her fragile body.

The evil of the Bloodstone undone, the battle was immediately changed. The demon Brothers lost all their power. The drain I had grown so used to now vanished.

I opened my eyes to see Kim, just herself, the way she was normally.

I looked over the field of battle and saw that the last few demons had been killed.

Michael walked up to the top of the hill half smiling—half out of victory, half out of grief for the loss of my friend.

The cheer from the victorious angels rang out as loud as thunder. We had won. Evil had lost.

Now my life could finally become normal again… maybe…

END

If you want to write Fan Fiction based off the Airel saga, you can find out more information about it at: www.TheWorstBookEver. blogspot.com. With each release we will pick a winner. All sorts of prizes and even a book signing with the author will be given out for each title. If you ever had a dream to be a published author this is your chance! We want to thank Kyle for his rockin story and hope that he enjoys seeing it in this edition of Michael.

Coming Soon from Aaron Patterson...
BREAKING STEELE *(A Sarah Steele Thriller)*

Now available from Aaron Patterson...
SWEET DREAMS *(A Mark Appleton Thriller)*

Look for more titles by Aaron Patterson on Amazon.
SWEET DREAMS
DREAM ON
IN YOUR DREAMS
AIREL
MICHAEL
URIEL: Coming Soon
THE CRAIGSLIST KILLER (Digital Short)
19 (Digital Short)

Coming soon from Chris White:
The Wagner Diary
Book II in the Airel Saga Diary Series (late 2012)

Now available from C.P. White:
Strongbox: a Digital Short
(excerpt)

IT IS SAFE HERE. Warm, cool; cozy. There is light. There is a place for Thea to rest her head. There are walls, clean and sleek, that keep the darkness out. There is routine, normalcy, security. There is a roof, things are orderly inside the strongbox.

There is a door on one side, but a bolt secures it that has never moved in all her memory.

The strongbox is safe. Thea knows this because of the things that are outside it that are dangerous. Interruptions to order and peace always come from outside. First it was noises, she remembers. Strange howls and shrieks. Then a thing from outside slammed into the door, as if the thing knew it was a door and might be broken down—this is how she knows it is safe inside— because it is scary and unsafe outside it.

The things outside want to come in. The things want what Thea has. They want to destroy it from the inside and take it away forever.

Why?

Thea doesn't know why. She knows only her fear.

⁂

THE STRONGBOX IS BULLETPROOF. A vault. Thick panels of glass framed by strong steel. Thea lives inside it in safety; she doesn't need anything.

Occasionally she can see suggestive vistas through the glass, but mostly it's darkness out there. When she looks outside and sees things, she is terrified.

There isn't much to do inside but *be*. She exists, simply, and that is enough. Time blends in an inebriating fog in her mind, a smudgeon that erases desire, hushing the unsettling questions.

Fear gives her quarter and comfort, sates her with limits to knowledge, helps her to feel life inside the box will always be enough. Can it be a wonder that her mind wanders from time to time?

⁂

SHE DREAMS IN FANTASY of a boy, and this boy takes her places and shows her impossible things, speaks to her in a different way and her heart flutters under the intravenous influence of something new and untasted. She gives herself entirely to the fantasy boy, even after he fades and she is pushed up to the surface of awareness, back to the strongbox. She swims downward to dreams and the boy, to the love-feel that he can produce in her chest, in her heart, the flutter.

Is mere existence enough?

❧

AWAKE.

The door is open. The bolt is retracted, and she can *feel* it. It is swung inward and wide on thick hinges, yawning before the black of night outside, and now, for the first time, the darkness charges cold into her world.

Is this a consequence of the boy? She panics.

Thea is pushed out of the box.

She screams; the door closes with authority, and the bolt slams home.

She screams; she wants back inside.

There are things outside.

She fears them.

She fears the unknown.

She feels unprepared.

She feels abandoned.

The lights go out—the beacon the box once was is no more.

With closed fist, she pounds, wails away at it. Though she can no longer see it, she knows it's there, and she wants back inside.

❧

SINCE THE LIGHT IN the box has gone out, it's hard to gauge time.

At first she stood plastered, her back against the box, hyperventilating. At length she sat against it in sorrow. Then she beat against it in rage, cursing it. Then she sat back down again, leaning against it in utter defeat. And now...

She begins to see the wild; the uncivilized and dirty wild.

The fear returns with a vengeance.

There are noises: A flitting sound. A muffled skid. Rustling.

Her eyes adjust to the darkness; there is movement in the shadows.

TIME GOES BY, APPARENTLY. Off to one side, there is light; it is far off. But it increases. It is a bright dull and gray, but it helps Thea to see. It is not the kind of light she knows. Around her are strange and fantastic things that stand upright on the dirt and wave and move in the same breezes that caress her own cheek.

But these green things are not the movement that she heard in the shadows before; these are silent. Mostly; they rustle.

Then she sees what made the flitting sound. It is small, it moves through the air like a dart, but changing directions at will. It is bright in yellow and blue and sometimes red and has spindly legs and can stand on the ground, but Thea notices it seems to prefer to light on the fantastic things that stand on the dirt and wave in the breeze.

She thinks now and marvels at the things, wondering why she understands so little.

But still, these are not what made the noise she heard in the darkness.

Then she hears the noise: there it is again.

It is a voice.

PETRIFIED, SHE WAITS, SITTING on the ground with her back to it, her breathing gagging her, coming in whiffs. Then she sees it:

this is one like her, clothed like she is.

Huddled over in the shadows and mumbling, it rises, approaches her: the one with the voice.

She scrambles upward, trying to get away, increase the distance between them: for this is a thing of which she's not yet dreamt, and it is wholesale horrific to her mind.

But the one thing like her rushes her, closes the distance, and before she can fly in total fear, the one thing has imprisoned her, pressing her against the box bodily, heavy arms to each side of her head, breath hot in her face, hostilely speaking: "Why is it dangerous outside?"

Thea understands the language. But she is too afraid to answer. Even if she does answer, she doesn't know what to say.

"Why are you out of the box?"

Thea's voice, unused, is frail and thin: "I—I was—I was pushed out."

"Why were you pushed out?" The voice of the one thing is deep and resounding, threatening, scary.

It is unlike her own. She can only answer, "It was a consequence of the boy!"

"This—now—is a consequence of the boy."

Thea weeps for this, an enshrouded confirmation of her mistake. She cries deeply within her heart for a revocation of it. For a chance to remove the punishment. "I'll do anything to go back…"

"You can never go back." Then the one thing like her pushes off the wall, away from her, and steps back, regarding her. There is hair on its face that hangs down in matted wisps of gray.

It is strange, like her and yet not like her. "Can I never go back?"

"No."

"Why?"

"You ask the wrong questions."

She looks at the hairy face, confused.

The one thing like her steps away, turns its back to her and begins to walk off.

Suddenly she knows what it will be like to be alone, and for the first time. "Wait!" she calls.

"No. You wait."

ABOUT THE AUTHORS:

AARON PATTERSON:

AARON IS THE FATHER of three kids: Soleil, Kale, and Klayton. He is the author of the bestselling *Mark Appleton* thriller series, *The Airel Saga,* and *The Sarah Steele* thriller series. Aaron worked in the construction field for 11 years and is now a full time writer. Aaron was home schooled and has a bachelors degree in theology. He loves to hike, snowboard, camp, and drink coconut lattes. He is also the founder of StoneHouse Ink and Co-founder of StoneHouse University. He speaks all over the country on the subject of eBooks, writing and the changing publishing world.

Connect with Aaron at his blog: http://theworstbookever.blogspot. com
Friend him on Facebook: www.facebook.com/aaronpatterson
And Twitter: @mstersmith

CHRIS WHITE:

CHRIS WHITE GREW UP living on an old San Francisco city bus that was converted to an RV, living in almost every state of the Union. He spent most of childhood learning how to make fast friends, reading books and doing heroic skids on his coaster-brake bike. He spent most of adolescence playing the trumpet and being a total nerd, building lots and lots of plastic models. He tried college for a couple years, but interrupted that with four years of service as an infantryman in the U.S. Marines. He finished college later, but the Marines taught him far more. He met his wife in Idaho and then spent six months in South Africa with her shortly after they were married. He's tried being a truck driver, bicycle mechanic, executive recruiter, drummer in a rock band and call center robot, but he's always, always been a writer—which he only just realized a few years ago. More recently, Chris took up the trumpet again and is now teaching privately. He has two boys and lives with his family in Idaho.

Look for more eBook titles by Chris White and C.P. White on Amazon.
Connect with Chris at his blog: http://cpwhitemedia.blogspot.com
Friend him on Facebook: www.facebook.com/whatnorthbetrue
And Twitter: @cpwhitemedia
Check out his Great Jammy Adventure series of illustrated books for kids: http://www.jammyadventures.com

CPSIA information can be obtained at www.ICGtesting.com
Printed in the USA
LVOW081225090912

298018LV00002B/2/P